Spoiled Heritage

the Manitobans

JEANNETTE

LEBLEU

RICHTER

 FriesenPress

Suite 300 - 990 Fort St
Victoria, BC, V8V 3K2
Canada

www.friesenpress.com

Copyright © 2020 by Jeannette Lebleu Richter
First Edition — 2020

Cover artwork courtesy of Monique Delisle Schmaltz
Author photo taken by Julie Finck

Photograph courtesy of Archives of Manitoba, Archives, Red River Disturbance 1, Louis Riel & Council [1870] N5396.

All rights reserved. No part of this publication may be reproduced in any form, or by any means, electronic or mechanical, including photocopying, recording, or any information browsing, storage, or retrieval system, without permission in writing from FriesenPress.

ISBN
978-1-5255-4646-4 (Hardcover)
978-1-5255-4647-1 (Paperback)
978-1-5255-4648-8 (eBook)

1. FICTION, HISTORICAL

Distributed to the trade by The Ingram Book Company

In memory of my parents
Edgar Laurent Lebleu and Emma Nault Lebleu

And for my sister
Yvette Lebleu Leuzinger

CHAPTER I

Saint-Cère, April 15, 1882

Votre Grandeur Monseigneur Taché,

I've finished the parish visit. There are 91 families: 500 souls and 285 communicants. Last year I presided over 6 marriages, 36 baptisms, and 7 infant funerals. There were no adult funerals.

In regards to the construction of the convent, I had hoped that the difficulties I was experiencing with *Soeur Supérieur* would not reach you, but as she has found it necessary to discuss them with you, I must defend myself.

La Supérieur underestimates the challenges of building a convent to house nuns, boarders, and day students in a village where a mere 75 years ago, the Cree and Assiniboine massacred one another. The newly arrived *habitants* are poor, and half were against the idea, claiming that they couldn't afford to pay any more taxes. They almost had to be forced to support the new school. In the spirit of obedience, however, I will accept your advice and control my temper when dealing with *la Soeur*.

A government agent has provoked a crisis related to the registering of land titles. He has been travelling throughout the district trying to get farmers to sign over the rights to their property. As he didn't speak a word of French, his visit was uneventful until he arrived at a place where the farmer understood well enough what was wanted. He ran him off by threatening to jam a pitchfork into his rump. He hasn't been seen since.

A hotel with a bar has opened on the main street. I expect that it will bring the usual heartaches.

On a more positive note, I am happy to inform you that I have found a young man in my parish who wishes to enter the priesthood. He's capable though somewhat undisciplined. The training he receives in the *séminaire* should correct this defect. With your generous sponsorship, he can complete his studies at the *Collège* in Saint-Boniface before entering the seminary in Montréal. His family is overjoyed at his vocation. I intend to travel up by train with him, and with your kind indulgence, I will introduce him to you. As you have always said, the Church in Manitoba will best be served by a native son.

Bless me, *Monseigneur*, and believe that I am your most humble and devoted servant,

J.M. Bertrand
Priest of Saint-Cère

CHAPTER 2

Spring 1882

Adrien Larence strode along the streets of the town, accompanied by a new friend, Marcel Lambert. Adrien's younger brother, Xavier, struggled to keep up.

"*Hé!*" gasped Xavier. "Is *Père* making the announcement tonight? About the *séminaire?*"

"*Maudit!*" Adrien exclaimed, glancing back. "Where did you hear that?"

"You were talking to the folks last night in the kitchen. I heard you through the floor grate."

"*Fermes ta maudite gueule!*"

Having been told to shut his damn yap, Xavier's face fell and he dropped back.

With Xavier butted up to the worn saddle, and Adrien holding the reins effortlessly, the bay stallion had taken them the short distance to town. The horse was their family's pride and one extravagance. It was a *Canadien*, a breed developed in Québec for its compact body and sturdy, powerful legs. Its wide hooves were perfect for hauling sledges over ice and snow. They had stabled the stallion in the barn behind Marcel's boarding house and were now headed out on a road pock-marked with patches of dirty, melting snow. It was Easter: joy of the Resurrection and the relief that Lent was over mixed in equal measure.

Adrien walked on, lost in thought and oblivious to the groups of friends and families that crowded the street on their way towards the final party in the log schoolhouse.

He had once dreamed of a different life, had seen himself walking the boulevards in Saint-Boniface like a fat bourgeois, greeting his neighbours and receiving the respect due an educated man. The paucity of money on the farm and his position as the eldest son had killed his dream ... until *Père*. Now his future was bright again, and though the thought of the *soutane*—the long, black, close-fitting tunic that would button up to his neck and reach to his feet—made him a little sick, he was certain he would get used to it. He quickened his pace.

His thoughts turned to his actions from a previous day. He had made his younger cousin fall in love with him. It had been easy, and he had done it callously as a small experiment to prove his power over the opposite sex. Now he regretted it, especially that stupid kiss that had started impulsively and gone further than he had intended. He hoped that his young *cousine* hadn't read too much into it. He hadn't, but his conscience pricked him. 'I'll talk to Justine before *Père* makes his announcement,' he decided.

Summers of clearing brush with horses and winters spent swinging an axe in the far mountains had hardened his body and thickened his hands. His legs bowed slightly, and at 18, he stood six feet tall—a good height for a French-Canadian. With thick, black hair and grey-blue eyes, he was handsome in a messy kind of way—a fact that he took for granted, as all the men in his family were. Earlier, standing before the mirror and running his comb through his hair before setting out, his hand had stopped in midair. 'I'm being vain.' He put down the comb. 'I can change.'

"In the city, we dance at all our parties," Marcel Lambert said, rolling on the balls of his feet. He was one of the men hired to work on the convent-school. "They wanted me to be the head carpenter, but I didn't want all the crap," he had said to Adrien. "I'd rather be the helper. Less shit." He was from Saint-Boniface, the city opposite the provincial capital of

Winnipeg on the Red River. Now that he lived in a small town, he loved to brag about the superior attractions of the city—the *cathédrale* with the single, tall tower, the steamboats loaded with goods from the United States, and the abundance of pretty, stylish girls. It was inevitable that the two young men would meet, and Adrien had found it impossible to ignore Marcel's pushy interest in tonight's party.

They approached the school. The crude building was made of rough-cut logs chinked with plaster. It stood at the front of a large square, cleared of trees. Wagons and carriages were parked everywhere in the yard.

Xavier raced ahead and said, "We haven't had a party since *le Jour de l'An*."

Marcel nodded with a smirk. January and February had been so bleak and killingly cold since the New Year. "In Saint-Boniface, there's no dancing either during Lent. But we manage to go to a few parties in Winnipeg. It's all right as long as the *curés* don't find out."

Across the street, a group of young girls giggled at them.

Marcel pointed towards them. "Are they going to the school?"

"I suppose so," Adrien said with a slight frown. A few bars of music floated from the school. He turned his ear towards it, trying to recognize the style of the playing and who was on the fiddle tonight. The corner of his mouth lifted ruefully as he thought, 'Dancing's another thing I'll have to give up.'

CHAPTER 3

"The best dancer in this village is me," laughed Justine Bélanger, running along the trail beside the river. She hadn't seen Adrien since their kiss in the churchyard, and she was in nervous, happy, high spirits. Turning her head and calling back to be understood, she ran ahead of her friend Louise. Impassable roads, deep snow, and the danger of being caught out in a blizzard had kept the farm and town apart for months, and the gregarious community had grown bored of its own company and the monotonous white. They were ready for the first dance since Christmas.

The river track was still muddy in places where the trees shaded the melting snow, and Justine had to be careful. Her mother had warned her against taking this shortcut, but her eagerness had led her to chance it. Now she had to take care to keep her Sunday boots dry and her long skirt away from the wet branches that grabbed at her hair and slapped against her legs. She deeply inhaled the damp smell of spring that permeated the air. Giddy with its earthy promise, she ran on.

The lights of the small schoolhouse twinkled through the branches of the lightly treed forest. This was the last time she would step across the school's threshold, but she wasn't sorry. With the school benches and tables pushed back, there would be room to dance.

What a treat it was to be walking along the deserted track with her friend. The return trip would be made aboard the family wagon, jostling over the rutted tracks of frozen slush and mud that ridged the road.

Justine jumped lightly over a puddle. Wet branches hung over the path. She let them spring back and sprinkle her friend. *"Asperges me,"* she sang. "Think of it as Holy Water."

"Aie!" Louise yelped, putting her hand up.

Justine laughed and skipped ahead. With ink-stained fingers, she pushed at the stubborn frizz of curls on her forehead. Sleeping with a tuque last night to straighten them out hadn't helped; the wisps sprang up in the damp air. Her dark brown eyes shone with a lively intelligence that she kept guarded, knowing that smart women intimidated men. Compact and strong in body like her peasant ancestors in Québec and Normandy, she exuded health and vigour. However, in the contrary way of human nature, she longed for the poker-straight hair and thin, tall frame of her friend, Louise Lafrenière.

They had met when they were both six and Louise's family, fresh from Québec, had moved onto the river lot next to the Bélanger farm. The Lafrenières had begun with proper intentions of good farming, but thistles and weeds overtook their fields while Étienne Lafrenière tended his trap line. Louise had inherited her tawny skin and straight, black hair from her Algonquin grandmother. The first day at school, one of the boys had pulled her braid and called her *"Sauvagesse,"* and she had put her head down and charged him. She had stumbled painfully when called upon to read. Justine had tried to coach her, but she hadn't improved and said that she hated books. At sixteen, she was already four years out of school. The nuns called her *"une excitée."*

"I hope the men hired to work on the convent will be there tonight," Louise said.

Justine nodded absentmindedly. Her thoughts were on her cousin Adrien. She hadn't seen him since his return on Ash Wednesday, when he had kissed her.

Justine couldn't remember a time when she hadn't loved Adrien. As a child, he had treated her with the indifference and condescension of an older distant cousin—the relationship so distant her mother, Thérèse, had to trace it back several generations. He threw his coat at her when he entered the kitchen, tousled her hair, or ignored her completely when older, prettier girls were around. He had grown older and become so handsome that she was shy with him, losing her natural liveliness and becoming tongue-tied and awkward. '*Mon Dieu!* Why must I be such an idiot around him?' she berated herself after spending an evening in his presence. She acknowledged that he was vain—he went hatless even in the vilest weather—but she forgave his vanity as a negligible venial sin. Then, unexpectedly, he had changed.

"You've grown," he said one day. "You're hardly *ma p'tite cousine* anymore." Then he had sought her out, engaged her in conversation, and seemed to prefer her company to any of the other girls. She had been exhilarated by this, but she remained circumspect, keeping her affection secret to avoid the teasing that would come if Louise or her brothers found out. Several weeks ago, when they found themselves apart from the group spilling out of the church, Adrien had grabbed her hand and pulled her into the woods surrounding the churchyard. Hidden in the trees, he had taken her into his arms. She had closed her eyes, inhaling the scent of pine that came off his jacket. His breath was sweet when his lips touched hers. She pressed against him and opened her mouth.

His eyes opened in surprise. Adrien let her go and stepped back. Hot blood flooded her cheeks.

Later that afternoon, as she punched the bread dough down and prepared the bread pans, she had longed to confide in her mother, but she couldn't force out the words. Thérèse had caught her standing over a round of dough, her floured hands resting on the table as she stared at nothing. "*Justine!*" she scolded. "*T'es dans la lune. T'vas manquer l'pain.*"

Justine had returned to shaping the dough. Her mother was right. If she didn't stop her daydreaming, the dough would be ruined. She had come to an adult woman's decision. Somehow she would escape the watchful eyes of her parents during the dance and make Adrien go with her into the deserted schoolyard.

CHAPTER 4

Justine quickly scanned the assembly as she entered. 'Adrien's not here yet, *merci Seigneur*.' She quickly removed her coat and threw it on the growing pile of buckskin jackets, furs, and woollen coats in the corner that would later make a cozy nest for tired babies and toddlers to sleep on.

A fiddler dragged his bow across the strings of his violin on the teacher's platform. Seated on a chair next to him, a man balanced a button accordion on his knees, fanning it open and squeezing it shut. The fiddle's God-awful screeches slowly transformed into the first poignant notes of "*Un Canadien Errant*." The song about French-Canadians forced into exile after the Lower Canada Rebellion of 1837–38 was wildly popular. Justine hummed it as she made her way towards one of the few remaining empty benches along the wall.

The noise grew as the room filled. Thérèse Bélanger entered with Marie-Ange on her hip, followed by her husband, Joseph, and the rest of the family. She handed the baby to Alexina, her second oldest daughter, and hastened to join her sister, Lucie, who had received a letter from home. Thérèse had left her twin behind in Québec, and she was anxious for news.

Justine's father, Joseph, made his way towards the front of the room, shaking hands and greeting each neighbour as he went. He joined a circle of men conversing animatedly with *Père* Bertrand.

Louise and a gaggle of schoolgirls squeezed Justine to the end of the bench. Louise's boisterousness always attracted a crowd, while Justine's natural reserve grew worse in a gathering such as this. She often wished she could be more like her friend, but tonight she was glad the commotion didn't include her, as it gave her the chance to watch the door.

Adrien entered. Justine glanced around for her parents, saw that they were occupied, and rose and made her way towards him.

Adrien saw her and nodded stiffly. He crossed the space cleared for the dance and joined the men with the priest. Every bench and seat was now taken, and people stood conversing at the edges of the dance floor. Justine threaded her way through the crowd to the front, keeping out of her mother's view. She inched her way to her father's side and elbowed the soft fat on his ribs gently.

Joseph looked at her in surprise. "*Qu'est-ce-que tu veux?*"

The heat rose to her cheeks as the men turned to stare at her. "I … I just want to hear what *Père* has to say."

Joseph frowned but he stepped aside, opening the circle for her.

"As I was saying," the priest said, ignoring her, "the date and place for the Royal Commission's ruling on our land claims has been set. It will be at the end of August. The judges will sit for a week."

As the first priest appointed to their parish and one of the few educated men in the village, *Père* Bertrand commanded their respect. He was an imposing figure with a strong nose, piercing, intelligent eyes, and shoulders that sloped over a barrel chest. He was almost bald; a fringe of remaining hair lay on his collar, and he wore a full, flowing beard that was streaked with grey.

"We followed the law. We surveyed our lots with chains and registered them legally," Albini Préfontaine said.

"The federal government ignores our claims while spending millions of dollars to attract Eastern Europeans," said Denis Péloquin.

"And pays to transport their equipment that's old and broken down," added Victor Gobeil in disgust.

Justine glanced towards the musicians as the first lilting bars of the "Red River Waltz" filled the room.

Joseph stepped back. "I'd better go find my wife."

One by one, the men drifted away, and Justine was left standing alone and exposed. Adrien had his back to her, as he was now engaged in a private conversation with the priest. Dejected, she turned away. At once her hand was taken, and she was led onto the dance floor with a flourish by Rosario Normand, her usual dance partner.

The Normands owned the white, two-storey farmhouse on a prominent hill north of the village. The house looked down on cleared fields and a pasture with a herd of prize black and white dairy cows.

Rosario took her into his arms and held her against a body that was slight but sinewy. A strand of straight, brown hair fell over merry, hazel eyes as he led her expertly around the other dancers. He had lately begun a moustache and was very proud of it. Justine relaxed, gliding mindlessly, but her eyes kept returning to Adrien and the man in the black *soutane*.

Justine grew increasingly vexed as Adrien accompanied *Père* round the room. Instead of partnering him proudly as she had planned, she was forced to partner with her uncles, aunts, brothers, and her sister, Alexina. 'Surely it must almost be time for a break,' she thought, returning to the bench slightly winded after a polka with her mother. For a short, round person, Thérèse was surprisingly light on her feet, and Justine had been danced energetically around the room.

Louise threw herself on the bench. She pointed with her chin towards Adrien. "What's with him tonight? He's being very priestly." She hid her mouth with her hand. "A *soutane* wouldn't hide what's between his legs for long."

Justine stared at the black cloth about the priest's legs. She shut her eyes and shook her head. "That's horrible."

Louise laughed and wiped away the sweat trickling down her temples. "Did you see me with Adrien's new friend, Marcel? He's from Saint-Boniface."

"I did, and I don't think you should spend so much time with him. Remember last year? Aline danced all night with that stranger, and he got beat up after the dance."

Louise snorted. "I don't care. We're just having fun."

The fiddler put his fiddle and bow on the teacher's desk, and his partner slid his accordion off his knees onto the floor. He stood and stretched.

The assembly split into men and women. Thérèse removed the cloth from the box of sandwiches that she had brought. The slices of bread were thick, soft, and still redolent of yeast from the afternoon's baking. She passed the box along and went to help Alexina ladle coffee into chipped ceramic cups from the kettle on the potbellied stove in the corner.

The men took their empty cups outside to the jugs of homebrew that were wrapped in burlap and hidden under blankets in the wagons. Adrien was usually the first to the jugs, but tonight he remained in his orbit around the priest.

Père Bertrand waited for the men to return before stepping to the centre of the room. He raised his hands, and the crowd hushed. "My dear friends, it is with great pleasure that we say goodbye and good riddance to this miserable schoolhouse. Our children have broken their backs studying at rickety desks and freezing under ice-crusted windows long enough. We look forward to the new convent-school that will replace it this fall."

A shout of delight rose to the timbers as the children grabbed one another and danced with joy at the thought of the new schoolhouse. Even those who had grumbled about taxes forgot their grievances and banged their hands together.

Père continued. "For a sum of five hundred dollars a year, the Sisters of the Holy Names of Jesus and Mary have graciously agreed to provide us with five teaching nuns. May they be rewarded with many vocations from this parish."

A murmur of agreement went round the room. Justine searched for Alexina. She sat with their parents, smiling and nodding in agreement.

"I have one more important announcement to make. As you know, it is *Monseigneur Taché's* dearest wish that a native son should minister to the new parishes opening up everywhere in the province. In the past, your priests have come from Québec and France. They do good work, but a local man would know the needs of Manitoba best. I am pleased to announce that I have found such a young man in our parish. Adrien Larence will commence his studies immediately for the priesthood for the Diocese of Saint-Boniface."

The assembly inhaled collectively and waited in stunned silence.

Père began to clap. Others joined and the thin applause grew as the faith of the Roman Catholic community held sway over their doubt.

With a determined smile, Adrien stepped forward to receive their blessing.

Justine's hand rose slowly to her mouth. She escaped into the deserted schoolyard. The newly declared seminarian was the only one to see her go.

CHAPTER 5

'*Un prêtre!* It can't be true. It just can't,' Justine thought, fleeing blindly across the schoolyard to a splintered, unpainted bench on the edge of the ball diamond. "*Mon Dieu, aidez-moi.* Help me," she prayed, collapsing on the bench. So agonized was she that she didn't hear the footsteps approaching and recoiled when a hand gently touched her shoulder.

"Justine, I have to speak to you," Adrien said, dropping down beside her. "I'm sorry that you had to hear it from *Père*. I was going to tell you. I thought he would make the announcement later. There wasn't time."

Shaking with shock, she turned towards him. "You're lying. You had plenty of time. I want only the truth between us." She took a deep breath. "I love you …"

His hands tightened on his knees. "You're my cousin."

Justine continued as if he hadn't interrupted, "… and you love me."

"You don't know what you're saying," he said impatiently. "All you want is marriage and children. I want more than that. I want to escape the drudgery of the farm and this small town. A career in the Church will allow me to study and travel and engage my mind."

'Why,' she realized suddenly, 'he sounds like *Père* in the pulpit.' Her trembling stopped. "We wouldn't have to live here. We could be married and move to Saint-Boniface." The heat rose to her cheeks as she realized what she had proposed, but the words couldn't be taken back even if she had wanted to. She plowed on. "You could find work. There's work in the factories and mills in Winnipeg."

"I don't want to be a slave to the English."

"But a priest? You could be anything … a doctor or a lawyer. I'd wait."

Adrien snorted. "Our farm could never afford to send anyone to the *Collège*. It's impossible. I've got to take what's offered to me. It's my only chance."

'Something's false,' Justine thought. 'It's as if he's trying to convince himself as much as me.'

Clouds that had hidden the moon moved off, and the prairie was washed in a cool, white light. Their shadows fell black and elongated at their feet.

She peered intently at his face. "Do you have a true vocation?"

"Bishop Taché will pay for me to study for the priesthood. My parents are proud of me."

Justine knew the truth now. She stood abruptly.

Startled, Adrien stood too.

She stretched up on tiptoes, threw her arms around his neck, and pressed her mouth against his. He hadn't shaved carefully, and the bristles scraped against the soft skin around her lips.

Adrien tried to pull away, but she clung to him, opening her mouth and knowing instinctively what to do. Pressed against him, Justine felt his response instantly. She dropped her arms and stepped back triumphantly. A small smile played at her mouth.

Adrien looked away.

The door of the school crashed open, and a melee of men tumbled onto the landing and down the step. A woman in a long braid stood illuminated in the door, screaming for them to stop.

Adrien took off at a run towards the fight.

Justine caressed the tender spot where his beard had scraped her lips. The party was ruined, and Thérèse would be anxious to leave. She didn't want her mother to notice that she was missing. She had to hurry back.

On the way home in the wagon, Justine and Alexina sat on the bench behind their parents while Marie-Ange and her brothers lay sandwiched between quilts in the box.

"Were you surprised?" Thérèse asked her husband.

Joseph stared at the reins floating over his team's backs. "About what?"

"About Adrien! The announcement! What else would I be talking about?"

Justine put her arm through her sister's and pulled her close.

"Oh? Wasn't everyone?" Joseph replied.

"That's exactly it. Adrien's never shown any interest in the Church. Quite the opposite." Thérèse turned her head to look at Justine. "What do you think?"

Justine stuck her nose under her scarf. "About what?"

"Am I surrounded by imbeciles tonight? I'm asking you about Adrien."

"I haven't really thought about him." She felt the rush of guilty blood to her cheeks and was glad that it was too dark for her mother to see.

"Well, I won't say anymore except that it seems … doubtful. And that's the kindest word I can use. But we shouldn't question anyone's vocation."

Alexina peeked at her sister, and her mouth lifted in a crooked smile.

The wagon bumped over the icy road, and Justine's thoughts drifted to the sister she held so tight.

A year her junior, Alexina planned to enter the noviciate of the Sisters of the Holy Names of Jesus and Mary immediately after graduation. Even as a little girl, she had been sensitive and spiritual. Justine often woke and saw her kneeling at the foot of their bed and reciting her morning prayers before a makeshift altar that held candles and a crucifix. Thérèse had even sewn a miniature Carmelite habit for her. The chocolate brown tunic and veil with a cream-coloured cape turned her into a miniature version of St. Teresa of Avila, and Alexina had practically worn it out with her prayer-playing. It was a sacrifice, but it was also an honour to have a child enter the Church, and Thérèse and Joseph were humbly proud. Alexina's vocation contrasted so sharply to Adrien's that it was no wonder people questioned his sudden change of heart.

"Lucie told me tonight that Évélyne and Gérard are having second thoughts about leaving Québec," Thérèse said, moving on like a dog on a bone to her favourite topic. "I wish they would come. The children don't know their first cousins."

Justine had never met her aunt and uncle, but she knew them from faded photos and letters that had been read and reread. From her mother's stories of growing up in Québec, she felt as if she had been one of the *habitants* farming the thin strips of land on the *seigneuries* of New France.

Joseph let go of the reins and let the horses have their lead. "There's still good land to be had, and Gérard's used to hard work. They could do it."

"That's not what's holding them back, and you know it. It's all the other things. They're putting in new school regulations to force the French to assimilate in Ontario and *Nouveau Brunswick*. They're afraid the same thing will happen in Manitoba."

The unhurried clip-clop of hooves lulled Joseph, and his head nodded forward.

"I spent some time chatting with Elzéar Goulet's widow tonight," Thérèse said.

His head came up.

"She's here with her children to visit her cousin. She's had a hard time of it since his death. Soldiers recognized Elzéar on the streets of Winnipeg as one of Riel's men after the Uprising. They chased him into the river, and as he tried to swim across to Saint-Boniface, they pelted him with rocks until he went under. The soldiers have never been brought to trial."

The farm appeared around the bend. The horses snorted, a shiver ran down their manes, and their lazy walk turned into a trot as they caught the scent of their barn. Justine sat up, relieved to be home. She'd had enough of sad stories.

CHAPTER 6

The day after the dance, Adrien boarded the train with *Père* Bertrand. As it was his first time on a train, the priest offered him the seat next to the window. Unlike travel on the road where the farms and houses showed their best faces, the rail line sneaked through at the back of properties, and he found that everything seem odd and off-kilter. Madame Rémillard was reaching up to hang diapers on the line and was showing a bare midriff. Manure piles that were normally hidden from sight steamed behind barns, and abandoned plows and implements stood axle-deep in dry, empty grass.

When the whistle blew, announcing the approach of the station, *Père* leaned over him and pointed to the first buildings flashing by on the outskirts of Saint-Boniface. "*Merveilleux*, heh? We've accomplished in a matter of hours what would have taken a day with a wagon."

The city of Saint-Boniface stood on the banks of the deep and fast-flowing Red River. The *Collège*, a large four-storey structure, was located on a side street near the river on acres bestowed to it by the Bishop. Capped by an imposing mansard roof in a style favoured in Québec, a row of symmetrical windows projected out on either side of a centre niche. *Père* had informed him that there were about 130 other males ranging in age from 11 to 22 studying here. Some were boarders like him, and others were day students from the city. Adrien paused on the walk and gazed up at the statue centred in the roof. St. Boniface wore his Bishop's mitre and clasped a book to his chest. Adrien climbed the stairs and entered under the saint's feet.

The dormitory that a young boy led him to on the top floor was high ceilinged and drafty. The boy pointed to a bed with a grey-striped mattress with sheets and blankets folded neatly at the foot. An overhead rod ran round the bed on which hung a thick, unbleached cotton curtain that he could pull for privacy at night. All the curtains were neatly stacked and tied back to the wall by each bed, as it was day, but Adrien could imagine the double rows of white cubicles at night. Adrien smiled. Privacy was a luxury he wasn't used to, as he shared his bedroom with two brothers. Above the metal scrolls at the head of the bed hung a wooden cross with a corpus. A white ceramic bowl and a jug filled with water stood on a white dresser with one drawer by the bed. He stared at his wooden travel trunk that he had placed on the floor. The Larence name, carved by his grandfather, was inlaid elaborately on the honey-coloured, maple lid. It contained his kit: a white shirt for Sunday, an extra pair of woollen trousers, and new, ill-fitting shoes that were his family's parting gift. He had thrown in work clothes at the last minute. He shoved the trunk under the bed. It was no use unpacking; there was nowhere to put his stuff.

Adrien crammed himself into a desk at the back and examined the class. A blackboard took up the front wall next to the door. Letters of the alphabet glowed white at the top of the board with tiny arrows and numbers indicating the direction and sequence of the pen stroke. He saw a name copied in an identical, expert flowing hand at the top right, *Père Tessier*, and under it *Celo! Celas! Celat!* He supposed these were Latin words he was meant to master. Olive-green roller blinds with wooden pulls hanging on strings were drawn at different levels on windows that reached to the ceiling and lined the outside wall. A hubbub of boys of all sizes shuffled in. At the side, a blond boy cranked a sharpener furiously.

A tall, thin priest in a black cassock strode to the teacher's desk. He picked up a brass bell with a black handle and went back to ring the bell vigorously in the hall. When he was done, the priest grasped the lead clapper in the bell to deaden the ring and glanced to the right and the left of the hall one more time. As he was about to shut the door, it was pushed open again by a young man. "*Pardon, Père,*" he said, bowing contritely to the priest and entering. He stepped unhurriedly to the empty desk beside Adrien, slammed his heavy canvas book bag onto the desk, and slid gracefully into his seat.

"Arthur-Joseph Roy!" the priest exclaimed standing under the crucifix above the blackboard. "That's the second time you're late this week."

Adrien guessed that this young man was not a *pensionnaire*, because he saw that he carried a lunch bucket. They were the same age, but the other's clothes were neatly pressed and a linen handkerchief was wound round his neck and tied in a bow in front. His hair was blond, parted sharply, and still wet. He wore a pair of glasses rimmed in gold wire over a long nose. Adrien was just about to write him off as peculiar when Arthur-Joseph turned his head swiftly, looked at him with twinkling eyes, and winked.

"*Excusez-moi* for being late," Arthur-Joseph said pulling himself out of the desk to his feet. He stuck his hand into the canvas bag on his desk and withdrew a thin, folded newspaper. He opened it, and the banner across the front page read in bold black letters: *Le Métis*. "This was just printed off the press at my father's newspaper office. There's news about Riel. The young Métis woman that he met and married while teaching at a Jesuit mission in Montana has just had a baby." He looked down and searched the print with a finger until he found what he was looking for: "Louis Riel and his wife, Marguerite Monet Bellehumeur, gave birth to a boy whom they named Jean." He inhaled deeply after reading the news-clip and looked up with a satisfied smile at the priest.

The priest's scowl lifted, and he smiled back.

Adrien wasn't surprised that Tessier allowed the disruption to his class. The Riels had many cousins in Saint-Boniface and small towns like Saint-Cère, south of the city. Louis' mother was a daughter of Jean-Baptist Lagimodière and Marie Anne Gaboury, the first white couple in the West. Louis' father had been a respected French-Métis leader from the reserve at Île-à-la-Crosse, Saskatchewan. The French and Métis in the province had blood ties to Riel.

The priest's eyes roamed over the class, searching for an innocent, unsuspecting face. "Why is Riel in the States?"

Adrien slid down.

The smaller boys at the front shot their hands up.

Tessier nodded to the boy who had been at the sharpener.

"Because of the execution of Thomas Scott."

The priest's eyes swept the room again until they rested on a big boy with a pimply face in a red shirt at the side. "Was Riel part of the execution squad?"

The huge boy lifted his shoulders slowly. His eyes darted around looking for help.

Tessier shook his head and pointed to the first boy.

"*Non*," the boy said, rising. "But Riel was the head of the provisional government, and he called for Scott's court martial." He paused to search his mind and then added, "Bishop Taché helped Riel take voluntary exile in the States."

"*Correcte*," Tessier said, sliding his hand through the side slit of his *soutane* to his trouser pocket. He fished out a gold *pince-nez*, which he secured to the bridge of his nose. "We'll discuss this further later." His eyes fell on Adrien. "Ah, yes. We have a new student, *Monsieur* Adrien Larence. He's here in preparation for the *séminaire*."

All the heads craned curiously towards the back of the room. Adrien kept staring ahead.

Adrien got used to the school's routine. He attended morning mass and evening prayers in the chapel with the others and kept the copy of *Vie de saints et vies remarquables* that he had been given on his arrival open on his bed-side dresser. It was uncracked but in full view. It wasn't long before the silence permeating the corridors and high-ceilinged rooms got on his nerves, and he began disputing *Père* Tessier in catechism class.

"Why do you say that only baptized Catholics will be saved?" Adrien asked. "What about good Jews and Muslims? Won't they go to heaven?"

"Only those baptized," the priest had answered haughtily.

Arthur-Joseph joined in the discussion. "What about Anglicans? They're baptized."

The priest glared over his glasses at these two students at the back of the room who were too big for their desks. "Only those baptized in the Holy Roman Catholic Church have salvation."

That evening, Tessier retold the incident to his brother priests during dinner in the refectory, and Adrien's reputation as a headstrong student grew.

Ignorant of their increasing scrutiny, Adrien spent his afternoons in the great study hall, his eyes often drawn to the tall windows and dazzling sunlight streaming through the medallion of trees in front of the *Collège*. 'Pa and the boys will be getting the horses and equipment ready for seeding,' he thought, remembering how the fat, lazy horses resisted the doubletree in the spring and how their mouths, grown soft during the winter, gummed the iron bit. Then he caught himself and thought, 'I'm lucky to be here.'

As the Bishop's protégé, for the first time in his life he had no worries about his livelihood or his prospects, but when he drew the curtain round his bed at night, he felt out of sorts. The muscles in his arms and legs twitched with the unaccustomed inactivity. Though it wasn't his habit to ask for permission, he thought it might be best at this time to do so, and he asked for and was given permission to work after classes. He searched for work unsuccessfully in the French community then paid two pennies to cross the new bridge that spanned the river to the warehouse district in Winnipeg.

The shed of Thomas Hill Freight and Ferry Company stood on the western bank, overlooking its fleet of paddlewheel steamboats that plied the river, transporting goods to and from the United States. The quiet was broken by the toot of whistles and the rumbling of trains, loaded with freight, entering and leaving the central yard of the Canadian Pacific Railroad just a few short blocks away.

The dank smell of the swiftly flowing river, swollen with runoff, permeated the air as Adrien stood with his hands in his pockets, contemplating the mountain of square fur bales of muskrat, beaver, and fox on the dock below the sheds. Men bent double carried the fur bales on their backs to the first deck of a paddle wheeler with the name *Selkirk* painted in black letters on the bow. A gruff voice yelled from inside the dark interior of the shed. "Hey, you! Get moving! Help the men with those bales!"

Adrien looked around, wondering what to do. The dock was empty. He shrugged and fell in at the end of the line of men. When it came his turn, he braced his legs when the bale was lifted onto his back. He climbed to the ship's deck, placing his boots firmly on the cross bars nailed across the wooden plank, the muscles on his thighs and back straining with the weight. Several hours later, he returned to the *Collège*, reeking of honest sweat. Coins jingled in his pocket, his body ached, and fresh calluses boiled on his hands, but he was happy and free of tension. From then on, after the dismissal bell, a good, fast walk carried him to the freight sheds where he worked free of the constraints imposed by priests.

One June afternoon, Adrien hoisted a bag of milled flour the size of a small pig to his shoulder from a loaded wagon. He entered the stifling shed, adding his load to a growing wall of stacked bags that climbed to the ceiling. A penetrating wolf whistle cut through the sweltering air in the loading sheds, and he lifted his head curiously. Down the cleared centre aisle, a young woman strode confidently past the stacked crates and staring men, the train of her skirt brushing carelessly over the dust-covered floor. Far from being self-conscious, she seemed to enjoy the leers of the gaping men. Her hair was massed under a veiled hat tied tightly under her chin. She was short with a full-figure that was revealed by a tight-fitting jacket cinched at the waist over round hips. When she came closer, he saw that her face was smooth and unlined. She caught him staring and returned his look with a look of appraisal that was strangely out of keeping with such a young face.

She was followed by her maid, a pretty young woman with a cloud of red hair under a lacy white cap.

"Who's the grand lady?" he asked one of the men near him.

"The boss' daughter. She likes to walk through the sheds."

"Does she have brothers working here?"

"No. She visits her father. They only have one child."

Adrien watched as the women climbed the stairs to the offices above.

Glancing out from the dark interior into the blinding summer light of the open door, he saw the waiting, half-full wagon and returned to work.

CHAPTER 7

Justine left the cool cover of the trees. Since Adrien's departure, she came often to Louise's to be distracted from her thoughts. She glanced around, searching for the cranky gander that patrolled the Lafrenière yard and kept nervously glancing about as she skirted the empty cow barn. She was halfway across the weedy yard when she heard honking and a furious flapping of wings. She grabbed her skirt and raced to the porch, slamming the kitchen door on the beak that reached to pinch her ankle. She leaned against the door, panting.

Louise had seen it all through the window. She laughed, jammed a stained straw hat on her head, and handed Justine another one. "You're in time to help me fetch the cows for milking."

The bird still fretted near the door. Louise gave it a kick in the chest. It squawked indignantly then retreated to its flock. She whistled and two black and white dogs, faintly resembling border collies, ran out of the barn.

The girls made their way to the pasture, stopping now and then to pull at the brome grass that brushed their skirts. They slid the stem out of its sheath to expose the succulent white pulp and then put the stem to their teeth and chewed, releasing its sweet milk.

The air was motionless, almost too hot for mosquitoes. Lazy blue-bellied flies joined the buzz of bees working the clover on either side of the path. The dogs disappeared in the waving grass, showing their whereabouts by the white tips of their upturned tails.

Louise twirled a stem of grass between her fingers, fanning the seed head like a whipping parasol. "Marcel's gone for a few days. His mother lost a baby. He has to go for the funeral."

Justine thought of the homemade crosses with children's names crudely carved in wood in the church cemetery. Two of her brothers lay in the section devoted to children. One was stillborn, and the other had died of rickets, so the doctor said. She remembered her parents' heartbreak and thought, 'Holy Mary, pray for the suffering souls.'

Louise suddenly grimaced and bent over. "My belly is sore."

"This happens every year. It's the rhubarb you're always chewing on."

Louise breathed deeply, waiting for the cramp to leave her. "I can't help it. It perks me up."

The tart fruit unfurled its frond in the garden in early spring and grew wild in the wood. After the bland, white diet of winter, people craved its fresh red nutrients and ate it raw with gobs of sugar on the crimson stalks, puckering at the sweet-sour taste. People ate stewed rhubarb and toast, rhubarb pies, and rhubarb cobbler. They filled their bellies with the dessert-vegetable until their guts cramped and they raced to the outhouse.

Justine heard the light tinkling of bells. The cows were near, hidden from sight, and as yet undisturbed by the dogs. She walked on. Her head was cool under her hat, and the sun warm on her back.

Justine and Louise had seen Marcel at mass the Sunday after the dance. He was kneeling at the back, resting his bum on the pew. Louise had increased the sway of her hips and sashayed down the centre aisle. Marcel was still hanging around when they left the church. The skin under his eye was turning purple and yellow, and the skin on his knuckles was scraped and scabbing over. He had whispered something to Louise that made her laugh, and Justine looked away, embarrassed to be left out of their secret.

Justine had invited Louise for dinner after mass the following Sunday, and Marcel had tagged along. They had gone up to the loft to search for the new kittens that the orange tabby had hidden while Justine stayed in the kitchen to set the table.

Louise interrupted her reverie. "Ma met Wilhémène Larence in the grocery store. Adrien's at the top of his class."

"Well, he's not stupid."

"Madame Larence hasn't had much to brag about. Now that one of her boys is about to be a priest, she's unbearable. Of course everything is discounted by half as soon as the screen door slaps on her fat ass."

Justine made no comment. Sometimes she wondered if gossip wasn't a French-Canadian sport. She hated it and tried not to talk about others.

"Have you heard from the handsome seminarian?" Louise asked.

"Of course not. It wouldn't be appropriate."

"*Sainte Nitouche.*" Louise put her hands together in prayer in front of her chest, mocking her as a goody-goody saint. She sped away with Justine racing after her. The dogs immediately joined the chase, barking and getting in the way. Laughing and gasping for breath, the girls finally halted beside a grove of young willows. Louise pulled out two at the roots and peeled off the bark.

"Did you see the ad in *Le Métis*?" she asked, handing one of the switches to Justine. "The Sisters of Charity—the Grey Nuns—are opening a bilingual Normal School in Saint-Boniface this fall. Any person over the age of fifteen is eligible. You'd get in for sure."

Justine shrugged. "I don't know if my parents could afford it."

"The training and board are free."

Père had often complained about the preparatory classes offered for teachers in Winnipeg. They were entirely in English. "The Normal School will be an improvement. Everyone will have an equal chance," he had said.

They topped a small rise. A dozen black and white cows bent their heads to the grass. Louise whistled and the dogs went to work circling the herd. The cows looked up curiously, lost interest, and continued grazing. Louise and Justine separated, branching out wide. The circle created by the girls and dogs tightened. At Louise's call, a few obedient cows turned towards home, but the other ones kept stubbornly grazing. The dogs darted in, nipping at the tendons above the cows' back hooves. Their bells rang dully as the cows danced away from the teeth. With udders full and swinging, the herd plodded towards the barn and the relief of the evening milking.

"I've been thinking about teaching," Justine said. "Maybe I should apply."

Louise snorted, tearing a handful of grass and whipping it against her thigh as she walked. "I know why you want to go." She added archly, "A priest makes a poor friend for a woman."

Justine lost her temper. "You can mind your own business." She touched her switch to a bony haunch that had plodded to a stop and urged the cows to hurry until the weathered barn came into view.

CHAPTER 8

Saint-Cère, June 30, 1882

Votre Grandeur Monseigneur Taché,

I have excellent news—the dispute over the settlers' original land claims along the *Rivière-au-Rats* has been settled. The Royal Commission studying the situation has absolutely ruled in their favour.

I travelled with men and women of Saint-Cère to the neighbouring village to attend the court, which was held in the station's small waiting room. We were packed tight with a hundred or so in attendance. After examining all the facts and hearing all the petitions, the two judges ruled for the established claims. You can imagine the joy in the cavalcade riding home that evening.

Colonel Dennis was at the bottom of this. He was the surveyor who ran the survey lines without regard to the river-strip holding of the old settlers in Red River, and he was the one who planned the resistance against Riel's provisional government. His failure in that instance has proved no bar to his career in the federal government. Intelligent, tenacious, and filled with hatred for the French Catholic Métis who had checked him then, he has used all the bureaucratic delays in his power to obstruct their land claims. The federal government would have saved itself the absurd cost of this commission had it been more liberal and generous in the treatment of its own citizens.

The Sisters have just arrived and expect to be holding classes in their new convent before winter. They are installed in the rectory until their lodgings are ready. In the meantime, my quarters consist of a small bed behind a screen in the chapel.

Wilhémène Larence told me that her son, Adrien, is making excellent academic progress in the *séminaire*. Thank you once again for accepting his guardianship. He certainly has the intelligence. Whether he possesses the other qualities necessary for the priesthood will be revealed over time.

I have the honour of being your Highness' most humble servant,

J.M. Bertrand
Priest of Saint-Cère

CHAPTER 9

July 1882

Justine gazed at the road unwinding behind the wagon. Beside her, Alexina leaned against dusty burlap bags of wheat filled to bursting for milling into flour in the city.

In the grey light of dawn, Justine had awakened to see her sister praying at the altar near their bed. She had stayed still, luxuriating in the first moments between sleep and wakefulness. "Are you praying that the Holy Names will accept you as a postulant?" she had whispered, turning on her side and resting her head on her arm. Alexina had glanced at her, nodded happily, and closed her eyes to continue her prayers. Her sister had always been sweet and sensitive. She was the peacemaker in the family; her tender heart couldn't stand it when the family quarrelled. She had always known her destiny and was serenely happy. Sometimes Justine had imagined herself in a nun's habit, but since that night in the schoolyard, she knew that she wanted to be Adrien's wife.

Her parents drove the wagon to Saint-Boniface once every summer, and the children took turns going with them. Alexina's interview with the Holy Names had been arranged a long time ago, and Justine had received a letter from the Normal School. She was to present herself to the director, and she was full of apprehension and excitement.

At the halfway point, Joseph stopped the wagon under the shade of a tree. Justine handed the wooden food box and a clay jug of ice water wrapped in burlap to Alexina while Thérèse spread the cloth. The previous morning, her mother had cornered one of the fat chickens in the yard. She knocked it senseless against the chicken coop and slit the dazed bird's throat in one swift move. She had fried the meat to a perfect crispness while the girls prepared the potato salad for their picnic lunch.

They sat on the ground near the wagon. Justine helped herself to a piece of meat and said, "If I don't get the bursary, I won't be going to the Normal School."

"And why wouldn't you?" Thérèse bristled, stopping in the middle of dishing out the potato salad.

"*Excites-toi pas, Maman,*" Alexina said, reminding her mother not to get excited. "Of course, she will get it. Her marks are high."

While the women cleared away the remains of their lunch, Joseph stretched out in the grass and slept. When the wagon got rolling again, gigantic white cumulous clouds mounded at the horizon to the northwest with edges sharply defined against the vault of blue. "Storms tonight," Joseph said. He slapped the reins against the horses' rumps. They threw their heads up, interrupted in their reverie, and picked up their feet. It would be late afternoon before the loaded wagon turned into his brother's yard in Saint-Boniface.

Before the construction of the new bridge, Justine's Uncle Fernand had operated the ferries crossing the Red and Assiniboine Rivers. The flat boats, attached to the shore by cables and manned by oarsmen, ferried wagons and pedestrians from shore to shore. One time when she was a little girl, her uncle had taken her with him. The current and wind had been too strong for the oarsmen, and she and the passengers had been forced to land downriver and climb the steep bank. The construction of the bridge had ended his career. As he was a man of little words, Alice, his wife of 25 years, spoke for him.

Alice's front door opened near the busy corner at the foot of the bridge, leading to the commercial heart of the French capital city. She spent a large part of her day peering out the front window, noting the comings and goings of its citizens. She was in the window when the Bélanger wagon turned in at the gate.

"*La grande visite*," Alice said, flinging open the back door. "The supper is ready to be put on the table."

Stiffly, Justine offered her cheeks for her aunt's kisses. Thérèse had never said so, but Justine could tell that Alice was not her mother's favourite. Thérèse disapproved of impure talk, especially around children, while Alice enjoyed the shock her prurient remarks had whether children were present or not. Justine was wary of this witty aunt with a dirty tongue.

During the night, the clouds that had been building all the previous day unleashed their fury on the city. Justine and Alexina had been startled awake by thunder booming overhead and drawn from their beds to the windows where a magnificent electrical display forked across the sky, turning night into day. "Ooh!" they had gasped in delight when their hair floated in the charged air.

Now the city smelled clean and fresh, and the sky was clear and blue without any trace of the violence of the previous night.

After a smaller breakfast of toast and coffee than she was used to, Justine waited for her parents at the front door. The humid air had frizzed her hair, and she had pinned it up. She had seen the style in an advertisement in *Le Métis*, and she hoped it would make her appear older.

Joseph descended the stairs to the hall, followed by Thérèse and Alexina. He stopped and looked at himself in the grainy hall mirror and pulled at the stiff, high collar of his shirt. "Must you use so much starch?" he complained. The knot holding his black tie slipped, and his tie became undone.

"Now look what you've done," Thérèse scolded, turning him to face her. "Here, let me redo it."

Alice joined them. "Be on your best behaviour, Alexina. *Soeur Supérieur* is very *sévère*. Last week, one of the novices was made to scrub the entire hallway on her hands and knees because she was late for matins."

Spoiled Heritage

Alexina turned a panicked face towards her father.

"Alexina doesn't need to be frightened any more than she already is," Joseph said impatiently, pushing the women out the door before more damage could be done to his daughter's confidence.

The red cinder path crunched underfoot as they walked towards the main street. Justine strolled, enjoying the walk but unaware that the white leather around the soles of her feet was turning a rusty red. "*Sapristi!*" she exclaimed in dismay, looking down. "My new shoes! They're ruined."

"Don't worry," Thérèse assured her. "We can scrub it off at home."

Only slightly reassured, Justine stepped off the cinder walk and continued on the grass verge.

"Look at all the new buildings," Joseph said pointing to the new structures on the boulevard. "There were empty lots here the last time we visited."

At the busy intersection near the bridge, they heard shouts. On the next block, a wagon was mired in mud to the axles. The driver whipped the horses, and they dug in, straining against the cross-iron, but the wheels wouldn't budge. Men ran from every direction to help as an approaching horse-drawn streetcar rang a furious warning bell.

Joseph looked at his wife and raised an eyebrow.

"In your good clothes?" Thérèse asked incredulously.

"*Non, Papa,*" Justine chimed in. "We'll be late for our interviews." She rolled her eyes in exasperation at Alexina.

Elevated boardwalks, rising out of the muck, stretched on either side of the street. Justine stepped onto it and struck her heels loudly against the wooden slats. Mice nested under the wooden sidewalks, and she was terrified that one would run up her long skirts and get trapped in her petticoat.

"I hope that *Tante* Alice is wrong," Alexina expressed aloud to her sister. "Surely *Soeur Supérieur* is not as strict as she says." Ahead, Thérèse and Joseph stopped to greet a storekeeper who was cranking out a cream canvas awning with green stripes.

"She's always negative. There are good people everywhere. These are the Sisters who are coming to the new convent in Saint-Cère. You might teach there one day."

Alexina smiled and nodded.

They turned onto a connecting street. Tall elms grew on the side boulevards, touching their fingers in the middle to form a shady canopy. A plain, one-story building faced with white-washed clapboard was enclosed by a fence of short, white pickets. It was surrounded by the gardens and fruit trees that occupied the block. Joseph unlatched the gate and swung it open for the women to pass through. He lifted a heavy brass knocker in the shape of a lion's head and let it fall heavily against the plate. A rosy-cheeked nun opened the door, nodded at their enquiry, and showed them silently into the adjacent parlour.

Spindly-legged chairs that would hardly bear a man's weight were grouped in threes around the room. Round oak tables on clawed feet clutching opaque marbles separated the groups and held enormous ferns that cascaded to the gleaming floor. The scent of bees' wax permeated the room. A dark brown, overstuffed leather settee sat diagonally across one corner of the room.

'No one would ever lie on that,' Justine thought. Joseph led his wife to it while Justine and Alexina chose chairs nearby.

Joseph gazed around the silent room and observed, "I've never known a houseful of women to be this quiet."

Justine giggled, but she swallowed it and struggled to stay composed for her sister's sake.

Joseph sighed loudly.

This time it was impossible to remain quiet. Caught by an insane, nervous desire to laugh—*le fou rire*—Justine laughed and Thérèse and Joseph joined her.

Alexina's eyes widened with alarm. "*Voyons donc! Arrêtez-vous,*" she scolded.

They were wiping the tears from their eyes when the door glided open and Sister Marie-Eugénie entered. Her habit consisted of a black woollen dress with flat, inverted pleats at the waist. Her hair was hidden under a black veil that fell to the waist, and a white wimple framed her face, restricting the movement of her head. She indicated with an abbreviated nod that they should remain sitting.

Sister Marie-Eugénie addressed Joseph and Thérèse, but she poured her charm and interest on the girl who was a possible candidate. "I'm glad that you are considering joining our order," she said, taking one of the chairs closest to Alexina. "Our work began in Montreal tending to the sick, the poor, and the elderly and has grown to include teaching. It's very rewarding work." She looked over at the parents. "She will take temporary vows."

"*Père* Bertrand has already explained that to us," Joseph said.

Sister Marie-Eugénie continued. "Then if she still wishes to be a nun, she will enter the novitiate, renew her vows of chastity, poverty, and obedience, and begin her training as a novice. Are you prepared for that?"

Alexina nodded shyly.

"*Bien*, it's arranged then." She stood. "I've ordered a *collation*." She opened the door. "We have time for a tour of the convent before it arrives."

They followed her down the empty, polished halls, peeking into the infirmary, then past the nuns' dormitory that was screened from view. At the kitchen, a nun in a grey apron with white stripes stirred a kettle of chicken soup, and Justine was reminded of her meagre breakfast. In the small candlelit chapel, they dipped their fingers into a copper font of holy water, made the sign of the cross, and entered. The Superior led them to the front and pointed at an enormous painting above the altar.

"The four nuns stepping onto the shore in Saint-Boniface arrived in 1874. They travelled by train from Montreal, across the Great Lakes by steamer, and lastly by barge to Winnipeg. The panel was painted by one of our sisters." Alexina, Thérèse, and Joseph were impressed by the depiction and complimented it warmly, making Sister Marie-Eugénie smile. Justine didn't join in. She could see that the painting was crudely executed. The nuns were unnaturally and stiffly posed, and the boat in the background seemed oddly out of perspective.

A *collation* of tea and small sugar cookies dotted with raspberry jam waited for them in the parlour.

"I believe that you're just fifteen," Sister Marie-Eugénie said, passing a china cup to Alexina. "Fifteen is too young to enter our community,"

Alexina looked at her mother imploringly. Thérèse shook her head and kept quietly sipping her tea.

"Alexina has to complete her studies." She offered the plate of delicate cookies to Joseph, who helped himself to two. They ate, sipped their tea, and waited for her to continue. Sister carefully placed her cup on its saucer and turned to Alexina. In a solemn voice, as if bestowing a blessing, she said, "In a year's time, if you freely desire to enter the order, the Holy Names will receive you as a postulant and guide your vocation."

Alexina's smile spread up her cheeks to her eyes. Her face radiated happiness. They bowed and left.

On the sidewalk, Alexina clapped her hands. "I'm so happy. I almost died, when she said I was too young."

Thérèse smiled. "You don't know how oblique nuns can be. I wasn't worried for a minute."

They walked past a large building made of white oak logs. Five dormer windows poked out from the attic on the two-storeyed building. Eight double windows, flanked by green shutters and arranged symmetrically on each floor, made an imposing facade. "This is the Grey Nuns' convent where you'll be boarding," Thérèse said, pointing it out to Justine.

"*Oui, oui, Maman,*" Justine said impatiently, trying to hurry her mother who seemed intent on sightseeing. "We don't have time for that now. I'll be late for my appointment."

The foyer in the brick building housing the *École Normale Bilingue* smelled of new lumber and fresh paint. The director, M. Bernier, was waiting in his office.

"We have a family of Berniers in Saint-Cère," Joseph said. "Would you be related to them?"

"He's my uncle," replied the director and enquired in turn whether the Bélangers that he knew in the city were relatives of theirs. When the genealogy was satisfactorily established, he turned to Justine. "I see that your grades are very good."

Justine looked down in embarrassment.

The director picked up a letter. It was covered in spiky script. "As requested, *Père* Bertrand has sent this letter of morality. He says that you are a young woman of character and polite, pleasant, and hard working." He paused to smile. "Based on his recommendation, I believe that I can accept you as a *normalienne*."

Joseph and Thérèse smiled proudly at Justine.

"The course lasts two years, during which time you'll board at the convent. The government will give you a bursary of $200 for your expenses. Present yourself for commencement in September."

Alexina hugged her sister on the cinder walk outside the school. She took her sister's arm, and they fell into line behind their parents on the walk back to their aunt and uncle's house. A young priest in a black *soutane* approached, and they all squeezed to one side to allow him to pass. He lifted the biretta off his head in greeting and then turned into the gravel driveway leading to the *Collège*.

CHAPTER 10

Adrien hurried down the wide central staircase, wondering who could be asking for him. Since he had started at the *Collège*, he had never had a visitor. The train fare from Saint-Cère cost too much for his family, and besides, they would be busy haying at this time of year. The long corridor extending to the right and left at the bottom of the stairs gleamed with highly polished linoleum. He crossed to the foyer. A young woman stood silhouetted in the side window of the front door, chatting to the brother porter who had answered her ring. She seemed familiar. Where had he seen her before?

"Larence, this young woman wishes to ask you something," said the brother porter responsible for answering the door. He bent his elbows, retracted his hands into the wide sleeves of his tunic at his belly, and planted his feet.

The girl introduced herself. "I'm Esther Hill. My father, Thomas, owns the freight and ferry company across the river."

Adrien flushed. He remembered her knowing look in the shed. The brother's eyes gleamed with interest, but he remained silent, suspicious of her motives.

"I expressed an interest in improving my French to my father's secretary, and he told me there was a young man working for us and studying at the College," she said. "He gave me Monsieur Larence's name as a possible tutor."

"You are aware that this young man is preparing for the *séminaire*," the brother said.

"Oh? I didn't know. But would it matter?"

Her perfume scented the enclosed foyer. Adrien looked her over appreciatively. Her summer dress was green with small yellow flowers, and the bodice was tight. A Catholic woman would have felt out of place in this house of boys and men, but she didn't seem to notice.

"I'll do it," Adrien blurted.

The brother's mouth tightened. "The Superior must give his permission first."

Adrien had turned his head so that he was facing her and gave her a teasing, conspiratorial smile. He nodded absentmindedly.

She opened the drawstring of the reticule overlaid with gold-net that swung on her wrist and pulled out a calling card. "Our telephone number is at the bottom. It's 52." She offered it to Adrien then drew it back. "… but perhaps you don't have a telephone here."

The brother's nose went up. "The Bishop has one that we can use."

"Good. After you've spoken to the Superior, call and we'll arrange the time."

They watched her descend to the circle drive. The brother turned on his heel while shaking his head. "She's rouged her lips. I detest artifice in women."

Adrien's mouth twitched. What did a grey-haired monk in sandals know?

The Superior was at his desk in the office. As soon as they entered, the brother began. "A young woman by the name of Hill has requested Larence as a French tutor. Her father owns the steamship company across the river."

The Superior laid his fountain pen down on the blotter so as not to stain the page he was writing on and leaned back. "Thomas Hill? I've heard of him. His name is often in the newspaper."

The brother snorted. "Larence is still in the early days of his formation. I don't think it would be wise."

The Superior glanced at Adrien. "You'll remember your place?"

"Of course, *Père*."

"Then you have my permission." He glanced at his robed brother cleric. "The *Collège* is always in need of influential friends."

Adrien could hear them arguing as he went down the hall, but he didn't care. He raced up the stairs, taking the steps two at a time.

Adrien crossed the bridge with his briefcase, turning north away from the sheds towards a fashionable residential district created by a loop in the river called Point Douglas. He kept checking the card until he found the matching iron numbers on a brick pillar at the entrance of a long drive. A house the colour of faded paper roses and elaborately decorated with wooden gingerbread stood in a square of green so lush it looked like velvet. A screened veranda ran around the front and side to an asymmetrical corner tower under an array of multiple steep roofs. '*Crisse! Ça dû couter une fortune*,' he thought, climbing the stairs to the entrance. It must have cost a fortune. Glass medallions graced a set of double doors leading into the house. He twisted the brass turnkey and heard a clear, crisp ring. A black and white wavy figure hurried towards him.

It was the maid with the red hair that he had seen following Esther that hot day in the shed. "*Allô*," he said when she let him in.

Her waist was so small that she had the strings of her white apron wrapped twice around her middle. A profusion of flaming red hair was tucked under her cap.

She dimpled under his scrutiny.

He caught sight of himself reflected in the pieces of leaded glass and preened to his full height, glad to be wearing civilian clothing and not the black cassock that would be required in the seminary.

Panels of honey-coloured wood extended to the lofty ceiling and covered the wide, ornate staircase on the right. The foyer was a room in itself, and several doors opened off it.

"I'm Adrien, the French tutor of Miss Hill," he said, following her across the room to closed double doors.

"And I'm Adele," she said, giggling at his French accent. She knocked on the set of doors, moved aside to let him enter, and then quietly closed the door.

A green carpet with trailing vines and flowers ran to the edge of the room. His feet sank into it. He had never felt anything so soft. On the mantel over the glazed tile fireplace leaned a framed wedding photograph in rich, brown sepia. The proud groom sat in a chair with one of his legs resting on the other over highly polished boots. The bride in creamy lace under a crown of wax flowers stood behind him. Her hand lay woodenly on his shoulder.

Esther closed the catalogue she had been looking through, tossed it on the settee, and stood. The painted women in party dresses on the cover seemed too thin to be real. "Do you mind if I call you Adrien?" she asked leading him to a bay window where two chairs were arranged before a leather-topped desk.

His name sounded foreign and different when she said it. "*Bien sûr,*" Adrien said suddenly uneasy and missing the competence of his native language. He unbuckled the scuffed, brown case that Tessier had loaned him and pulled out a faded orange copy of Corneille's *Le Cid*. Esther looked up with a frown after she turned it over in her hand. "It's a story set in the 1600s in Spain," he explained. "It's about two lovers, Chimène and Rodrigue. He kills her father in a duel of honour. You can read her part, and I'll be Rodrigue." He pulled out her chair. "We shall begin?"

When he heard the grandfather clock's deep chime in the hall, he looked up in surprise.

Several weeks later, with grey clouds touching the treetops and the air so sweltering that even the mosquitoes refused to fly, Esther asked him to stay and have iced tea on the veranda. Far away thunder growled, and he talked about the farmers back home and how they needed rain. Another clap of thunder boomed, closer this time.

Droplets of condensation sweated the crystal tumbler in his hand and ice tinkled as he sipped the cold tea in silence. He preferred sweet tea, but he said nothing. She seemed to want to ask him something.

"Why do you want to become a priest?"

He put the glass down and sat back, surprised at her directness.

Esther continued, "Mother says it's barbaric to sacrifice handsome young men to the altar. Men in our Church marry. Isn't it squandering God's gift?"

Adrien swallowed. How could he explain to this pretty, Protestant girl about the requirement of chastity and the priesthood? Especially in English! He remembered that St. Paul had a lot to say on the subject. He recited, "A man with a wife is solicitous for the things of the world, and he is divided."

Esther's shoulders sagged and her mouth came down in a pout.

'Christ! I sound like Tessier,' he thought staring unhappily at the approaching storm.

CHAPTER II

Late August 1882

Mad barking erupted in the back yard. "What are those fools barking at?" Justine wondered, going to the kitchen window. Louise had exited the trees behind the barn and was walking towards the house, following the split-rail fence that bordered the garden. Justine was bursting with news and ran out to meet her friend.

The dogs kept up their mindless barking. "*Taisez-vous!*" Justine ordered. Crestfallen, having been told to shut up, they flattened their ears and slunk away with their tails tucked in.

"Where have you been?" Justine asked, grabbing Louise and kissing her cheeks. "I've hardly seen you all summer."

Stiffly, Louise accepted the kisses. "Marcel's been keeping me occupied."

"I'm going to become jealous," Justine teased. "I have news to tell you. But first come in and have some water."

A black pump was bolted to the kitchen sink under a window that faced the farmyard. Thérèse was one of the few lucky women to have running water in the house. It smelt of rotten eggs and could tarnish silver pots and trays but that was of little consequence, as Thérèse only had a few silver spoons to worry about. Mercifully the water didn't have to be hauled from the river in buckets. It came in by pipe from an artesian well in the barn that ran day and night through two rough cement baths to cool the cans of milk and cream.

Justine pumped the handle vigorously, and ice-cold water gushed into a white enamel pitcher with a red ring on the lip. She poured some into a glass.

Louise gulped it down. She wiped the wet from her lips with the back of her hand, took a breath, and asked, "So what's your news?"

"Let's sit outside where it's cooler," Justine suggested.

While excavating for the foundation of the house, Joseph had unearthed a huge, flat fieldstone. Too heavy to move, they left it where they found it for a step to the front door that was never used. Tall elms shaded it, and the cold stone was always a refreshing place to sit on a hot, summer afternoon. Justine was superstitious about good luck and thought you could jinx your chances with pride, so though she had to tuck her hands under her legs to keep still, she said calmly, "I'm going to the Normal School. I got the bursary. I have to promise to teach for two years in the province. I suppose it's a way to repay the government." She expected Louise to congratulate her, but she just sat, silently picking lint off her skirt. Justine leaned forward and bent her head to better see Louise's face. "*As-tu donné ta langue au chat?* Has the cat got your tongue? It was you who first gave me the idea."

Louise took a deep breath as if to begin, but then let it go. She continued to pick at her skirt.

Alarmed, Justine sat up. "What's wrong? Has something happened to your family?"

Louise turned her head towards her friend. "I'm pregnant."

"Oh!" Justine breathed. This was the worst thing that could happen to a young girl in the strict Catholic society. The misstep was unforgiveable and would not be forgotten either. She placed her hand on Louise's to stay her picking. "What are you going to do?"

Louise's top lip trembled, but then she folded the lip between her teeth and lifted her chin. "You'll have to treat me with more respect. I'm going to be *Madame* Lambert soon."

There was no other way out. But to marry such a man …

Louise regained her composure. "Pa and Marcel are making the arrangements with *Père* Bertrand right now. I'm glad it's him and not me to get the lecture."

Justine wondered how Louise could be so blind to the disgrace or how she could even think of marrying a man like that.

Joseph's team appeared on the dirt road. Dust curled up from their hooves, and he sat on the iron seat with his feet braced against the mower. The horses needed no urging when returning from their day's work, and the reins lay slack on their backs as they trotted home to the barn.

"I'd better get back," Louise said rising and brushing dirt from the back of her skirt. "You'll be my bridesmaid."

"Of course," Justine said rising and hugging her friend. Louise crossed the yard and disappeared after a final wave into the trees. Tears that she had been fighting rolled down her cheeks, and she started to shake uncontrollably. 'That could be me … if Adrien had wanted me.'

The reading of the marriage banns at three consecutive Sunday masses threw the villagers into a tizzy. The news ran from house to house as they correctly guessed the reason. While they disapproved self-righteously, it never crossed their minds to miss the wedding.

Justine and Louise had spent hours when they were young playing with their paper-dolls, folding the paper tabs to change the dresses on the figures. One of the cut-outs was a bride in a black taffeta dress with a row of creamy lace at the collar, cuffs, and hem. "We could sew some lace on the dress I wore to the dance," Justine suggested. "With the lace ruffles at the hem, it'll be the right length for you, and no one will know that it's mine."

Though the threshing had begun and farmers were racing to bring the crop in, the ceremony was set for Sunday when everyone, including farmers, rested and went to mass.

On the day of the wedding, Justine paced outside the packed church, waiting for Louise. She held a bouquet of white daisies and yellow black-eyed Susans. In the other hand, she held a white prayer book to give to Louise as a wedding gift.

The wagon rolled up loaded with Lafrenières, and she hurried towards it. "Hurry! You're late," she called.

Louise was already on the ground. Her morning sickness was over, and her dusky skin glowed. A light feathering of rose powder accentuated her high cheekbones. Her straight black hair swung loosely down her back, pinned at the temples with airy, white baby's breath. Justine handed her the bouquet of wild flowers and the prayer book. At the doors of the church, Louise positioned the gifts over the slight bulge of her belly, and took her father's arm.

At Louise's nod, the music began. Justine stepped forward with a smile pasted on her face and stared ahead, daring anyone to injure her friend.

Marcel stood before the communion rail in a borrowed brown suit that turned his sallow skin yellow. He grinned foolishly at the young men crowded into the back pew before kneeling with Louise at the *prie-Dieu* reserved for the bride and groom. *Père* began the prayers of the marriage sacrament, and Justine's hand rose automatically to her forehead for the sign of the cross.

Louise took Marcel's arm when it was all over, walked up the aisle, and smiled at the young, envious girls in the pews. She refused to acknowledge the disapproval on the faces of the older parishioners as they passed. At the back, Marcel tried to stop and talk to the men in the last pew, but Louise dragged at his arm. "C'mon. Let's go. Lunch is waiting."

Père's carriage led the parade of wagons to the Lafrenière farm while young riders whooped and raced ahead. Marcel drove the next wagon with Louise beside him. At the gate, he stood up and slapped the reins on the backs of the plodding team. Startled out of their reverie, they tossed their heads and galloped off towards the barn. Marcel fell back onto the seat. "Whoa," he yelled and pulled back on the reins with all his might to no avail. The horses raced past the tables and chairs set up in the front yard and rattled to a stop where they always did—at the barn. "*Imbécile*," Louise said when he helped her down. She picked her way back to the house, holding up the lace on her black skirt, mindful of the manure piles dotting the yard. Marcel followed to the catcalls of his friends and the laughter of the guests getting out of their wagons near the front yard.

Tables made up of raw planks and covered by white sheets that fluttered in the breeze stood in the shady front yard. Justine, Thérèse, and Alexina had spent the day before in the Lafrenière kitchen with other neighbour women making egg and ham sandwiches. They had wrapped the sandwiches in wax paper and packed them into large boxes for today's midday meal. In order to take communion, the wedding guests had abstained from food and drink since midnight the previous night. They were starved, and this lunch would break their fast. Sliced cucumbers and tomatoes so fresh you could taste the sun waited under towels with the platters of sandwiches on the tables. *Père* took his place at the head table. He raised his hand to bless the food. Marcel grinned and Louise giggled as they bowed their heads and joined everyone in saying, "*Bénissez-nous Seigneur …*"

After the lunch, Rosario rolled up his sleeves and asked Joseph to be his partner at the horseshoe pit. Other teams formed. Someone called to *Père* and dragged over a chair for him near the pit. Others joined him until there were several rows of spectators. They chose their favourites, cheering when the horseshoe ringed the iron stake and jeering when the horseshoe thudded into the hard-packed dirt too far away to score.

Louise insisted that Marcel stay at her side while she opened the few gifts. She handed him pillow cases and tea towels embroidered in yellow, pink, and green silk and trimmed with cotton lace. She pointed out the small stitches. He glanced without interest and looked longingly towards the game of horseshoes. Justine hid a smile. Louise detested handwork. Her stitches were uneven, and the knots that should have been invisible were big and showing.

The afternoon passed. Children screamed and chased one another across the yard or played hide-and-seek in the hayloft or trees. Women chatted at the tables over coffee and sweet tea while their babies napped in baskets at their feet. The light waned, shadows lengthened, and *Père* was called once again to bless the meal that Louise's aunts had been preparing all afternoon. Tables groaned under the plates of turkey and spicy *tourtières*, bowls of fluffy, mashed potatoes, and carrots sweetened with brown sugar and butter.

As was the custom, the children were the last to eat. Thérèse went to the kitchen to help wash their plates. As she walked by, Louise's grandmother said, "Don't bother. They can eat off the dirty plates." Thérèse ignored her and rolled up her sleeves as she walked to the house. They toasted the bride and groom with sweet chokecherry wine, and then Marcel and Louise walked through the guests with a basket, handing out a finger of wedding cake rich with a dozen eggs, dates and nuts, and redolent of brandy.

Père called for his carriage.

"Finally," Louise said out of the corner of her mouth to Marcel and Justine as they waved goodbye to his carriage. "Now the dancing can begin."

Marcel pulled a silver flask out of his jacket and unscrewed the cap. "Want some?" he asked after he took a swig. Justine scrunched up her nose, but Louise put it to her lips and tipped back her head.

By the light of lanterns hanging on the trees, the groom led the bride in their first dance as man and wife on the parched grass of late summer. One time around and Marcel waved for everyone to join in. Rosario claimed Justine. They waltzed to a familiar love song and then continued as the fiddle picked up the tempo with a livelier tune. The children paired up and danced wildly. Rosario guided Justine deftly away from the careening youngsters. The night stayed warm, the stars twinkled in the clear, black sky, and every man came in turn to dance with Louise.

During a lull when the musicians took a break, Louise plopped down on the bench next to Justine. She slipped out of her shoes and wriggled her toes. "Oh, that feels good. Have you seen Marcel?"

Justine pointed to a group of young men in the circle of light thrown from the kitchen window.

Louise toed into her shoes. "I'd better go see what he's doing."

The men stopped talking as she approached.

Justine heard her scolding Marcel across the yard. The men shifted in embarrassment around the young groom.

Louise led Marcel back to the dancers. The groom took her hand and crushed her against him, stumbling clumsily during the waltz. The tune suddenly became livelier, and he bent her backward until she was inches above the dirt dance floor. Marcel suddenly released her, and Louise fell on her back.

Justine's hand came up over her mouth in consternation.

Instead of helping his wife up, Marcel crouched down and kicked out his heels like a Russian Cossack dancer that he had seen once in Winnipeg. A circle formed around him, clapping the time as the fiddler goaded him on by going ever faster. Louise struggled up. She entered the circle with her hands on her hips, and then she grabbed a handful of her skirt, hiked it to her knees, and matched Marcel step for step, kicking out too.

Later that night, Venus glowed like a diamond in the blue-grey east as Justine and Louise shouldered Marcel up the stairs to the bedroom in the Lafrenière house. A nightgown with pink ribbons lay nicely folded on the wooden chair under the window. They rolled him onto the bed and stood looking at the unconscious man. His tie was loose, brown spots dribbled down the front of his white shirt, and his pants were covered with dry grass and dirt from where he had fallen.

Justine finally turned and whispered. "Let me help you take off your wedding dress."

Louise lifted her hair and bent her head allowing Justine to get at the buttons on the back of her dress. Through the window, a line of crimson flamed at the eastern horizon. Louise sighed. "I never thought *you'd* be undressing me on my wedding night." She was still laughing when Justine tiptoed out.

CHAPTER 12

Without the wedding to distract her, Justine could now devote her time to worrying about moving to the city and her studies at the Normal School. "The city girls are always so smartly dressed, and I hardly have anything to wear," she complained to Thérèse as she entered her bedroom one rainy day with a pile of freshly ironed clothes. Several black and grey skirts, white blouses, and sets of undergarments lay on her bed. "And they wear such pretty shoes," she said, staring regretfully at the black sturdy ones on her feet.

"Those shoes will take you where you want to go faster than a fancy pair," Thérèse said, laying the clothes on the dresser near the bed.

"But *Maman*, couldn't I have at least one pair of black patent shoes? I saw a pair in the window in the village. We could take the buggy. Papa doesn't need the team; it's too wet to work in the fields today."

Thérèse put her hands on the back of her hips and stretched. She had spent the morning ironing clothes with two heavy flat-irons, pressing with one while the other reheated on the hot kitchen stove. She had had to be attentive; the iron handle could burn if you forgot to wrap it with a pad. She complained about it every week yet insisted on ironing every piece of the family's apparel down to their underclothes. And Justine knew that her gregarious mother could always be persuaded to interrupt her work for a trip to town.

Joseph refused at first. "The horses need to rest."

"Justine can't go to the city *pauvre comme Job*," Thérèse insisted. "She needs a few things. Why don't you come too? You can visit with Armand in the livery shop."

Justine and Alexina pulled the buggy out of its shelter, swept it clean of cobwebs and dirt, and backed a horse into the shafts.

Wilhémène Larence was leaving as Thérèse, Alexina, and Justine entered the General Store. '*Ah, non!*' thought Justine. '*Sapré malchance.* We'll be here forever listening to her brag.'

The decent formalities were hardly over when Madame Larence said, "Adrien's doing extremely well at his studies and surpasses all the Bishop's expectations. He …"

"*Merveilleux,*" Thérèse said, cutting her off smoothly. "Have you heard about Justine's good news? She's leaving for the Normal School in Saint-Boniface on Saturday. We're shopping for some new things for her. She can't go in old clothes."

"*Ah, oui,*" Wilhémène said, blinking in surprise at the sudden change of topic. She turned to Justine. "*Félicitations.*"

"Do you have anything to send to Adrien?" Justine asked politely. "I could deliver it for you. The convent is just down the street."

Thérèse raised an eyebrow and looked at her questioningly.

Wilhémène Larence's eyes narrowed. Having a son as a priest raised the family status for French Catholics. There would be many occasions of reflected glory when Adrien lifted the gold chalice on the altar. Wilhémène had too much to lose to mince her words. "Adrien is studying for the priesthood. He mustn't be distracted by young women. I trust your mother has explained that to you."

"Of course," Thérèse flared. "Justine's a well-brought-up girl. She was just trying to be helpful."

Wilhémène let out a puff of indignant air. "Then I leave it to you. Good day."

"That woman!" Thérèse exclaimed, turning away. "Insinuating that my girls are not well brought-up."

Alexina whispered to her sister. "*Maman*'s fierce when she's defending her chicks, heh?" But she was talking to the air. Justine had moved away and was bent over the glass cabinet near the register, studiously examining the display of hand mirrors and brushes

That night, Xavier rode over and handed her a small parcel wrapped in brown paper.

Her family accompanied Justine to the train station. She was the first to leave, and it was an occasion that no one could miss, especially if it included the train.

"You're the first Bélanger to ride the train," Joseph said, searching the horizon for a plume of smoke. Since he had heard the plaintive call of the whistle and felt the earth tremble with the approach of the first train, Joseph had been in love with trains. His oldest sons, Ti-Jos and Hilaire, shared his passion and knew each engine and engineer by name.

"Oh, *Pa*," Justine said when they heard the chug of the engine as a black dot appeared on the horizon. "You're the one who wants to ride the train. I wish you could come."

"Worry yourself not," he said. "I'll get my turn."

A whirlwind of cinders and dirt blew up, snatching their breath away as the train slowed and stopped with an ear-splitting screech.

"I'll pray for you ... every night," Alexina whispered kissing her cheek.

Terrified by the hiss of steam and the rumble of the black engine, Marie-Ange hid her face in her mother's neck and refused to look up. Justine threw her arms around them and squeezed them both. With a quick wave, she boarded the train.

Tante Alice insisted on going with Justine to the convent the next morning. "*Ma chère*, you must have family support. The Sisters won't take advantage when they see who accompanies you."

Justine's stomach had been cramping all morning. "*Merci*," she said, grateful for once for the company of her bossy aunt.

They were asked to wait for *Soeur Supérieur* in the parlour. "Feel free to visit if you get homesick," Alice said, staring around and taking one of the chairs grouped around the table and fern. "*Oncle* is always happy to have you. You're his favourite, you know."

Justine was too excited to sit. She peeked in the hall. A nun approached, moving quickly on silent feet. Justine retreated to the chair beside her aunt, planted her feet together, and folded her hands in her lap.

Soeur Supérieur entered with the swish of a multi-layered black skirt. An oversized cross dangled from a cord at her neck. She knit her fingers together, and her hands disappeared in the deep folds of her sleeves. She nodded slightly and said, "*Bonjour*."

Alice spoke first. "I'm Justine's aunt, *Madame* Fernand Bélanger."

The wimple surrounding her face impeded the nun's view, so she swivelled her head to face Alice. "I know. I've seen you many times in the window when I had occasion to take the ferry." Alice and her coterie of gossipy friends were well known. The religious communities disapproved of them.

"I could help Justine put her things away in the dormitory," Alice said.

"*Vous êtes gentille*, but that won't be necessary," the nun said sweetly, leading the way to the door. "Thank you for assisting your niece."

Justine hid her smile. Before Alice could gather her wits, she had been ushered out, and the door closed firmly in her face.

"*Le dortoir* is on the top floor," the nun said, as they climbed a wide set of stairs. She explained the order of the day. "First bell at seven. Then chapel at seven-thirty. Breakfast at eight." Justine's head whirled with times and bells, but when they reached the dormitory, she was too intimidated to ask the nun to repeat the information. Two rows of beds, neatly made up with white sheets and blankets, were lined up on the sides of the long room. One bed at the end was unmade. It had a grey mattress with linen folded at the foot. "That's your bed. I'll show you how to fold the corners properly." The nun floated the sheet on the mattress, lifted the foot, and tucked the sheet under. She straightened the sheet, let it drop over the edge of the bed, made a sharp diagonal fold at the foot, and slipped it under. She pulled it apart. "You try now."

Justine thought of her mother as she struggled with the sheets and blankets. The beds in their house were made without too much care; sheets were bunched and shoved under mattresses. This was a much better way. After several tries, the nun nodded. "I'll leave you now to unpack," she said. "You're free for the afternoon. Chapel is at four."

Justine's bed now looked exactly like all the others in the room. She waited until the sound of the nun's retreating footsteps thinned to silence before she sat on the bed, bouncing a bit to test the springs. She reached out and touched the curtain of her sleeping cubicle, fingering the coarse cotton. She brought her fingers to her nose and sniffed. The clean smell of bleach reminded her of her mother's steaming kitchen on wash day. She sniffed it again, feeling less lonely. 'I'll unpack later,' she thought. 'I better hurry.' She held her new hand mirror before her face. Stubborn curls escaped the pins. She freed her hair and tied it back with a red satin ribbon. She pinched her cheeks and picked up Adrien's parcel from the bed.

The drive split in two, forming an island of trees in front of the *Collège's* grand facade. The school was near the centre of the metropolis in a large parterre of flowers, gardens, and neat rows of fruit-bearing trees. Deer followed the river valley, piercing to the city's heart for the tender vegetables, sweet plums, and Saskatoon and gooseberries carefully tended by the brothers and boarders.

Justine ran up the long flight of stairs and rang the bell.

A brother in a brown tunic and sandals answered her ring.

"*Bonjour*, Frère," she said, holding out the parcel wrapped in brown paper. "I have something for my cousin Adrien Larence from his mother."

"*Certainement, Mademoiselle,*" the brother said formally. His fingers touched hers as he made to take it from her. "I'll deliver it to him."

Justine clutched the package. "*Excusez-moi, Frère,* but I prefer to speak to him personally. I have private family messages."

His hands recoiled as if her fingers were hot. He turned away stiffly. "*Bien!* You may wait in the parlour while I get him."

Except for sturdier chairs and the lingering smell of pipe and cigar smoke, the room was furnished in the same unembellished style as the convent.

"Justine! What are you doing here?" Adrien exclaimed when he entered the room.

Instead of smiling, his eyebrows pulled together in a frown. The rehearsed speech flew out of her head. "I hoped that you would be glad to see someone from home," she said haughtily, offering him the wrapped package. "Your mother sent you this."

He ignored it, glanced over his shoulder into the hall, and closed the door. Chairs were arranged in a neat row. He slouched onto the nearest one and left her standing.

Justine was surprised at his bad manners. "Don't you like it here?"

He straightened. "Yes, I do. I do like it here."

"Could I sit?" she asked awkwardly.

"Oh, of course. *Pardon,*" he said as if remembering to be polite.

She chose a chair near him.

He sat forward, resting his arms on his knees, letting his hands hang loosely while he stared at the floor. They were no longer thick and callused and burned by the sun. They were white and soft; the hands of a priest. 'It's different for him,' Justine thought, remembering the serenity of Alexina's vocation. "I'm attending the Normal School and boarding with the Grey Nuns. We'll be neighbours." She handed him the parcel. "Here, it's from your mother."

"*Merci,*" he said, dropping it to the floor.

"Aren't you happy for me? Have you forgotten your friends?"

He stood. "You don't understand. You're so innocent."

"Since when is innocence a crime? Why are you making me feel guilty when I've done nothing wrong?"

"My destiny lays elsewhere. We're cousins. Nothing more." He thought of something. "What about Rosario? What would he say if he knew you came here to see me?"

"What?" she exclaimed, blinking in surprise. "He's a friend. That's all."

"He's always liked you. Don't lie about it."

"You're calling me a liar? This place hasn't improved your character."

Red climbed out of his neck and over his cheeks.

"At least you still have the decency to blush."

A bell tinkled from somewhere. With a relieved look, he said, "Chapel." He pulled open the door for her. Brother porter walked to and fro in the hall silently reading his breviary.

Justine lifted her chin, nodded politely, and marched out.

Arthur-Joseph was at the printing press setting the last of the print when Adrien entered the newspaper shop. Adrien had begun stopping in at the newspaper whenever he saw the lights on in the evening. He and Arthur-Joseph Roy had found they had many things in common since that day in class when they had baited *Père* Tessier about Muslims and Anglicans. Arthur-Joseph's father, Alain Roy, had founded the weekly *Le Métis* shortly after the Riel Uprising in the early 1870s to voice concerns over Indian and Métis land rights and to fight for the promised amnesty of those who had participated in the Uprising.

Arthur-Joseph dropped the last metal letter in place and wiped the greasy metal shavings that clung to his fingers on a dirty rag. "There's a new chief of police in the city." He counted off on his fingers. "Armed robbery, loose horses, vehicles on the sidewalks, and prostitutes on Annabella Street. Three thousand crimes committed last year." Arthur-Joseph liked spouting off lists—bits of unlikely information clung to his mind like lint.

Adrien slid the metal letters back and forth with his finger.

Arthur-Joseph stopped Adrien from playing with the letters by pulling the ink-stained canvas cover over the huge press for the night. He glanced at Adrien. "Why the long face?"

"Oh, my *cousine* visited me today. She's studying at the Normal School. We disagreed about something."

"A fight! With a woman. Always interesting." Arthur-Joseph's eyes glinted with interest, and he raised an inquisitive eyebrow.

Adrien picked up the fresh newspaper and began to read.

Arthur-Joseph, seeing that there was no more to be learned, changed the subject. "There's a card party at *Tante* Alice's tonight, and we're going." The French were passionate about cards, and on any night of the week you could find a game to drop into in most houses. Justine's aunt had invited them to make up a table because she liked handsome young people at her parties. She said they made her feel young.

The endless hours of light that graced the long summer days were slowly coming to an end, and the two young men walked home in the dark after the card party. Harvest dust from the fields surrounding the city floated in the still air and scented the night with sweetness.

"The farmers are having a good run," Adrien commented. "They'll be happy."

"Oh?" Arthur-Joseph sniffed. "Yeah, I guess so." An orb of dust circled the street lights.

Justine had been at the party. She had avoided Adrien and answered his polite enquiries in clipped sentences.

"That *cousine* of yours is sure pretty," Arthur-Joseph said.

"True, but don't get her mad."

"She was very sweet towards me."

Arthur-Joseph's blue eyes and blond hair stood out in the dark haired, brown-eyed French community, and his habit of intense listening made him attractive to both men and women. Adrien felt compelled to protect his cousin. "The convent girls are all in love with you. Isn't that enough?"

Arthur-Joseph laughed. "What if she's the one?"

"She's from the country. Leave her alone."

"Is this concern appropriate for a seminarian?"

"I just don't want her to get hurt. That's all."

CHAPTER 13

Mid-September, 1882

Her disappointment over Adrien had the predictable result, and Justine spent the next three weeks miserably homesick. She wrote letters to Alexina and walked to the high bank overlooking the river, watching the sluggish water move north. Sometimes she stepped into the cool, dim interior of the *cathédrale*, finding comfort in the prayers that were so ingrained she couldn't remember not knowing them. When the *Collègiens* walked two by two to services, she caught herself searching for Adrien's dark head and tall body at the end of the line.

'What was wrong with him?' she wondered. She found to her surprise that the intellectual and physical discipline imposed by the nuns and the simple efficiency of the convent suited her. The leaves had turned orange and red, but summer refused to cede and the days continued long and hot for this first autumn away from home. She discovered an artificial grotto of fieldstone and grey cement in the church grounds and went there to read in the sun.

One hot afternoon after classes, Justine carried a book to the grotto. She followed a beaten path through the cemetery surrounding the *cathédrale*, detouring around the dark-green colourations of disturbed soil that marked the graves. She passed under the shade of the *cathédrale*'s belltower rising above the steeply pitched roof over the front entrance. A tall, elongated cone topped the tower, and a gold cross gleamed at its slender tip. Justine sat on a stone bench, spotted with orange lichens, that had been placed before a statue of the Blessed Virgin. She opened Pierre Chauveau's *Charles Guérin*, thumbing past the stamped *Nihil Obstat* on the first page to the break where the second section began. In the dirt under the surrounding lilac hedge, sparrows chirped and dusted their wings.

The hot sun touched her arms and back luxuriously as she sank into the story. 'Can't he see that Marichette loves him?' she thought, angry at Charles for abandoning his childhood sweetheart. A whinny made her look up. Two riders rode by. One was Adrien and the other was a young woman. His head was bent attentively towards the woman, and he didn't see her. 'She rich,' Justine thought. There was something proud in the way she held her back so straight, and her tan jacket and matching riding skirt looked expensive.

The woman reined in her horse and pointed towards the church steps. Adrien shook his head, but his brown horse with a white patch on the forehead wheeled around, dancing expectantly on the loose gravel. The woman insisted. Adrien hoisted his shoulders in a shrug, swung his leg smoothly over the saddle, and dismounted with a hop. Her gloved hands let go the reins, and she leaned towards him. He put his hands on her waist and lifted her down. They climbed the steps and entered the *cathédrale*. The horses didn't move. They were ground-trained and would stand on the spot where the reins had fallen.

The door to the sacristy swung open without a sound, and Justine slipped in. She moved up the side aisle beneath the Stations of the Cross, her ears straining and her feet barely touching the painted brown boards. She stopped near the last pew and pressed herself into the shadows near the wall.

The opaque glass of the windows bathed the foyer in milky light. Adrien stood near an oak table, flipping through a black leather-bound book with pages edged in gold while the woman walked around curiously. A confessional box divided in three booths was to the right of the entrance. The centre compartment had a door with a trellised top panel. The two side booths were draped in a heavy green cloth. She lifted the curtain and peeked in.

"What's this?"

"It's for confessions. The priest sits behind the door, and we kneel behind the curtains to confess our sins."

"Can a seminarian hear confessions? Would you like to hear mine?"

"*Non*. Not today. And perhaps never."

His voice had dropped so low that Justine leaned forward. Had she heard him correctly?

He leaned his hip against the table and self-consciously turned the pages.

Rows of votive candles flickered in small red, blue, and green glasses on a brass stand. In the centre was a slotted metal box. She went over to it. "What are these for?"

"People put coins in the box then light a candle. They ask for the intercession of saints in their problems."

Thin wooden reeds with blackened tips were stuck helter-skelter in a tin of sand by the offering box. She took one, touched it to a flame, and lit a new candle. "You can pay for this … next time you come to mass." She walked to the table and looked over his shoulder at his book. "Is that Italian?"

He laughed. "It's Latin. The mass is in Latin, but everything else is French."

She moved in front of him, rose up on tiptoes, and kissed him lightly on the lips.

Justine stopped breathing. '*L'éffrontée!*' she thought in disgust. That girl was an insolent, spoiled brat. He should slap her face.

Instead Adrien's arm dropped to the woman's waist, and he pulled her closer.

Justine let out a strangled cry like a fox with its leg caught in a trap.

Adrien looked up and saw her. He stepped quickly away from the woman.

Justine turned and fled.

All the boarders except Justine slept in their curtained compartments of white. She heard the rustle of sheets when they turned in their sleep, and at the far end, a young girl cried out in a dream. She finally fell asleep after beating her pillow flat and woke with a groan and a pounding headache at the sound of the bell ringing for chapel.

CHAPTER 14

The sun was just showing itself when Adrien stepped on the landing at the convent. 'God,' he prayed. 'I hope she hasn't betrayed me.' An elderly nun with a surprisingly unlined face answered his urgent knocking. When he asked for Justine, her eyes narrowed, and she asked, "*T'es pas le protégé de Taché?*"

"Taché is my patron," Adrien said working to keep his expression blank. "*Justine est ma cousine.*"

"Everyone's at morning mass."

"It'll only take a minute."

Her mouth twisted. She didn't seem to believe him, but she inclined her head and went to fetch Justine.

While he waited, he relived the scene in the church after Justine had fled. He had told Esther that they must leave right away. Surprised, she had resisted, and he had almost dragged her out of the church. He had helped her mount, and then he had slapped her mare's rump. The horse tore off. Jumping on his own horse, he had raced after her, catching Esther at the bridge. Their horses' hooves rang as they galloped across to Winnipeg.

He heard rapid footsteps and saw Justine round the corner. She was dressed like the teacher she wanted to be in a grey skirt and white blouse with a small green and blue striped tie. Her eyes sparked with anger.

"You've got the effrontery to come here after what I saw?"

Out of breath, the nun appeared. A narrow oak table had been placed to one side under a painting of the community's foundress, Mother d'Youville. She put her hand on the table, panting to catch her breath. A vase of giant orange and yellow marigolds was centred under the painting. After glancing in their direction, the nun began removing the spent flowers from the vase.

"I need to speak to you privately," Adrien whispered, pushing Justine out onto the landing.

The early morning air was cool. Justine shivered and hugged her arms into her body.

"Yesterday was a mistake," Adrien said in a rush. "We were out for a ride. She had seen the spire of the *cathédrale* from Winnipeg, but she had never been inside, so she asked me to show it to her. I didn't expect her to kiss me. Nothing else happened. We left the church right after you saw us."

"She was flirting with you. *Will you hear my confession?*" Justine said mimicking Esther's flirtatious voice. "Then she kissed you. You didn't mind, did you *Monsieur le Séminarien?*"

Adrien gritted his teeth.

"Who was she … that woman? What's her name?"

"Esther Hill. Her father owns the freight sheds and paddle-wheelers on the other side of the river."

"I could see by her fine clothes that she was rich. Well, she's too fine for the likes of you."

Hurt pride flitted across Adrien's face. "She wanted to improve her French. I've been tutoring her all summer. I'm sorry for what you saw in the church. I want to continue with my studies."

Justine's shivering increased. "You're sorry that you got caught."

"*Calmes-toi,*" he said, putting his hand on her arm to calm her. "Nothing more happened, I swear. If you tell anyone about this, I'll get in trouble. They'll kick me out."

Her hand rose to her chest, and she said incredulously. "*I cause you* trouble?"

"Promise you won't tell anyone," he pleaded, taking her trembling hands. "You know how important this is for me. I can't go anywhere without my studies. You know how it is in my family."

"You're still going to be a priest?"

He looked down and slowly shook his head. "When I finish college, I'll study something else."

"What about *Père* and Bishop Taché? What about all the money they're investing in you?"

"The Church can afford it. You have to help me, Justine," he said squeezing her fingers. "I swear that nothing more happened in the church. I'll make it right. I just need time, that's all. Please, don't tell."

"Let go," she said tugging to free herself.

He wouldn't let go her hands.

She stopped struggling and looked out towards the east. The sun was rising in a crystal blue sky without a cloud. The harvesters would be happy. She exhaled with a long sigh.

Adrien lifted her hands to his mouth and kissed them. "You won't be sorry. I swear. *Merci, merci mille fois.*"

CHAPTER 15

September 30, 1882

Votre Grandeur Monseigneur Taché,

I read that the Lieutenant-Governor has refused to sign the bill abolishing the printing of official documents in French. Bravo! Such a bill would not have been possible in the past. It is the result of the gerrymander that redistributed electoral boundaries and reduced French representation in the legislature. We hear so much about the British ideal of "fair play"! I give thanks daily that the language and religious rights of French Catholics are so clearly defined in the Manitoba Act. Catholics attend Catholic schools; Protestants attend the Protestant schools. Each goes to their school as they go to their church; each supports their school as they support their church. Let us pray that this harmony between race and faith continues.

I have the honour of being your humble servant,
J.M. Bertrand

CHAPTER 16

Late November 1882

Adrien dipped his fingers into the font of holy water, crossed himself, and slipped out of the *cathédrale* before the last of the Friday night Stations of the Cross. The memory of a long, lazy autumn lay blanketed by snow and gripped by a cold that went to the bone. Adrien lit a cigarette and inhaled deeply. As he stood there shivering, his eyes glanced over the rows of grey tombstones surrounding the church. A movement behind the largest monument stopped him. There was something black crouching at the base.

The image of a bear flashed to his mind; they often climbed out of the wooded river valley and entered the city in search of berries. He shook his head and snorted. 'Fool! They're deep in hibernation by now.' He narrowed his eyes and looked harder. The thing stood. Arms and legs unfolded. It was a man in a chequered black-and-red jacket motioning wildly for him to come. Adrien chuckled and ran down the steps with his cigarette pinched between his fingers.

"*Tabernacle.* I thought you'd never come out. It's freezing out here," Marcel said, dancing to keep warm.

"Where's Louise?"

"At home with her folks. She can't travel. C'mon. Let's go for a drink."

Parishioners were leaving the church; their voices floated out clear to them in the frigid air. Adrien flicked his cigarette away and began walking away fast. "Only one. They do a final bed check at ten."

The innkeeper dumped crushed cigarettes and cigars into a rusty can and began listlessly dragging a grey cloth over the sticky counter where Adrien and Marcel sat.

Marcel lifted his glass, saluted the empty room, and not for the first time sang *"Prendre un p'tit coup c'est agréable."* He chuckled. "Taking a small drink is agreeable," the popular French-Canadian drinking song stated. He had been singing it all night. At the last verse, he tipped the glass up, drained it, and then licked the last drops of beer from the rim.

Adrien pushed away from the bar. "Let's go." His forehead wrinkled as he swayed and concentrated on the process of buttoning his jacket.

Marcel draped an arm over his shoulder. "The *Collège* doors will be locked by now. You can sleep at my parents' house." Linked hip to hip, they bumped against the doorframe before finally making it out. A high and distant moon etched their shadows on the trampled snow of the deserted street. They approached the Bishop's palace. On a clothesline at the back of the yard, the Bishop's combination underwear were frozen stiff into boards and sparkled with frost in the moonlight. On the next block, bloomers and long stringed cotton camisoles swung white on the convent's clothesline.

Marcel pointed to the Bishop's back yard. "I've got an idea."

Snow filled their boots, chilling their ankles, as they took giant steps across the yard to the first line. The combinations dangled high above their heads. Marcel jumped up clumsily. His arm swept beneath the cuffs, and his hand grabbed nothing. He went down with a grunt on his hands and knees in the snow.

"Sans dessein," Adrien said, calling his friend a "witless idiot." He leapt and caught the cuffs. The wooden pegs pinning the underwear to the line held for a split second and then broke. Pieces flew through the air and were lost in the snow. Adrien fell backward under the stars with the

frozen combinations clutched to his chest. He heaved himself up. "Take the shoulders," he said. "I'll take the legs." With the underwear between them like a stretcher, they marched to the convent. The nuns had the bloomers grouped together on the line. "There," Adrien said, nodding with his head towards them. Panties flew in the air to make room for the combination underwear. "*Un p'tit detail,*" Adrien said, returning to the line. He stuffed the arms of the Bishop's combinations into the crotches of the neighbouring bloomers. Marcel tilted back his head and yipped like a coyote. Adrien threw his arms up and yelled, "*Celo! Celas! Celat!*"

A light appeared in one of the dormitory windows down the street.

A discrete knock interrupted *Père* Tessier's class the next morning. He opened the door a crack and listened to a whispered message, glancing towards the back of the room where Adrien sat. "Larence, you're wanted at the *palais. Dépêches-toi.*"

Nobody had ever been summoned to the Bishop's palace before. A buzz grew and heads turned to stare as Adrien gathered his things.

Adrien had met the Bishop only once, but like all Catholics, he knew all about him. At 22 and not yet ordained, Taché had stepped ashore from a *canot allège*. The express canoe manned by elite voyageurs, who worked 18 hours a day, had sped him across the Great Lakes to the Red River settlement. He had been ordained later that fall in the Diocese of Saint-Boniface, a vast area that stretched west to the lush Pacific shore and north to the frozen Arctic. The diocese was still pitiably poor with wooden shacks and few workers when Taché eventually inherited it. Now after 40 years, convents, boarding schools, hospices, hospitals, and orphanages dotted his domain. The stone *cathédrale* was one of the best edifices of its kind in the North-West. The long struggle had suited him; he had the look of a much younger man.

Adrien glanced at the recently installed telephone booth beneath the hall stairs in the palace. The bi-fold doors were partially open, and the light was still on over the telephone box. Someone had forgotten to click it off.

A young vicar led Adrien to Taché's office. The prelate sat at his desk, reading his breviary—a book of prescribed prayers to be said daily by Catholic clergy. Gold that had once gilded the pages of the black leather-bound book had long ago worn off. Taché closed the book and indicated one of the oak chairs before his desk. He lifted the thin gold wires from around his ears, peeled the frame carefully from his face, and laid the glasses on the desk.

"*Mon fils*, you've been my guest for a number of months. Yes?"

"Since spring, *Excellence*," Adrien said relieved to see the Bishop's composed manner, but he sat rigidly forward, not touching the back of the chair.

A beige report card with his name on it lay folded on the right of the Bishop's desk. Taché reached for it and opened it. Fine writing and numbers flowed on black lines. The prelate nodded. "I see that you have achieved ... as expected. Did we treat you well?"

"Certainly, Excellency," Adrien said smiling respectfully.

Years of authority made the Bishop blunt. "Then why have you disgraced us?"

Guilt inspired by monthly confessions swept over Adrien. His eyes went to the bookcase behind the Bishop. Dark red, green, and black parish registers, like the one in the rectory at home, filled the shelves. He had seen *Père* record the date and time and particulars of the funerals, baptisms, and marriages in the same Saint-Cère registers.

The Bishop folded his hands on the report card. "I've been informed that you were missing last night, and when you returned, it was obvious that you had been drinking."

"I was with a friend," Adrien rushed to explain. "It got too late to return. I didn't want to disturb anyone so I spent the night with him at his parents' house."

Taché's lips turned slightly down. "There were 'irregularities' on the clothesline at the convent that night."

Adrien hoped he looked innocent. "Oh?"

The Bishop's shoulders drooped tiredly. "My son, we can no longer support you for the priesthood." He pushed back from the desk, and his hands dropped on his lap. The wool *soutane* covering his knees was shiny from wear. "It's not only this transgression. You challenge Tessier and the teachings of the Church. Do you disagree with this assessment?"

Adrien sagged. "*Non, Monseigneur.*"

Taché sat back, forming a teepee over his substantial belly with the tips of his fingers. A long moment passed before he spoke again. "I am reluctant to abandon you completely. There's a carpenter shop nearby that is in need of an apprentice. I have arranged a place for you with the owner, *Monsieur* Petit. Here's the address." He handed a sheet of paper to Adrien. "His wife is part of the women's temperance movement. They believe in the total abstention from liquor. You would do well to listen to their advice."

"Yes, Excellence," Adrien said, folding the paper. "And thank you."

With the authority of the Church, Taché waved his hand and Adrien was dismissed.

Not bothering with the buttons of his coat, he rushed up the street to *Le Métis*.

CHAPTER 17

Christmas 1882

Justine had twisted her curls into a tight roll at the back of her head, and now the punishing pins had brought on a headache. She rested her forehead on the train's frosted window and looked out on an expanse of white flitting by. At the far horizon, a dark line of leafless aspen stood against the encroaching axes and spreading farm fields like doomed soldiers. She closed her eyes and pressed her fingers against her temples.

Alice had informed her of the news of Adrien's dismissal at one of her card parties. Justine had spent the rest of the evening misplaying her cards and watching the clock. In the days that followed, she resolutely avoided the gossip flying about the convent regarding him and devoted herself to her studies. She was so successful that when she crossed the entrance hall to the library with an armful of books, she was surprised to see red and green paper chains crisscrossing at the ceiling.

Now unbelievably, she was already home for the holidays. Her train ride home had been uneventful, but it had tired her out, and she had gone to bed early. It was still dark when Justine entered the kitchen the next morning. Thérèse was cutting lard into a bowl of flour at the table, and a cauldron of ground venison, pork, and beef spiced with cloves simmered on the stove. "*Bonjour, Maman*," she said, lifting the heavy lid and dipping a spoon for a taste. "Umm … it's good to be home." She unhooked her apron from the nail above the wood-box, pulled the bib over her head, and tied the long strings behind her back.

Thérèse's forehead pleated with worry. "You've lost weight. The food at the convent mustn't be very good."

"*Maman*, don't fuss," Justine said impatiently.

Hurt flashed across her mother's face.

"I'm sorry," Justine said, instantly contrite. "I've been studying hard, that's all. The food's all right. I'll pick up again during the holidays with your good cooking."

Thérèse's face cleared. She divided the soft, elastic dough evenly into six parts, shaping them into balls. She floured a rolling pin and began flattening and stretching the dough until she could see through it. Then, careful not to let it tear, she peeled the sticky, translucent circle off the table and plopped it onto a metal pie plate.

Justine filled the pie with the meat from the stove. Her mother placed the top crust, and then Justine used a fork to prick six swirls fanning out from the centre air-vent.

Thérèse started on the next pie. "Adrien's no longer at the *Collège*."

Justine dusted off her hands silently.

Her mother continued. "There's talk in the village. Wilhémène Larence gets all prickly and won't talk about her son. Suddenly she's a saint and against gossip." Thérèse opened the oven door and put the first pie on the centre rack. "Have you seen him? Do you know why he was sent away?"

"*Maman*, you know what convents are like—hardly the place to meet men."

"You haven't talked to him at all then?"

"I've seen him at card parties, but we were never at the same table, and he was always with the newspaper man's son, Arthur-Joseph Roy."

Thérèse's eyebrows met as she thought. "It must be something serious."

Alexina descended the stairs with Marie-Ange on her hip and crossed to the living room where the Christmas tree was. She sang "*Mon beau sapin*," the French version of the German hymn "*O Tannenbaum*," and pointed to the delicately intricate paper snowflakes she had cut.

Thérèse fanned another handful of flour over the table. "Just as well. He wasn't suited for the priesthood." She looked up over her glasses at her daughter. "Or for you, my girl."

Justine threw the fork she was holding onto the floured table. "I'm grown up, *Maman*. You needn't lecture me anymore." She stormed out of the kitchen and joined her sisters at the Christmas tree.

It was the shortest day of the year. The sun rose late, gave short hours of weak light, and left long evenings of lamplight and cold. As Justine cleared the breakfast dishes, she heard a horse approaching at a slow gallop. It stopped near the house. Leather creaked as the rider dismounted. Footsteps rang across the porch, and then knuckles rapped sharply on the door. It opened and a visitor stepped in, enveloped in cloud as the frigid air vaporized in the warm kitchen. Rosario appeared out of the vapour. He undid the blue muffler he had wrapped round his face and smiled at Justine. Her youngest brothers, Zéphirin and David, having seen him from the living room, rushed at him. Marie-Ange toddled over too, but she lost her nerve and ran instead to hide behind her mother.

"Let me take off these cold clothes first," he said, holding the boys off with one hand. He stepped out of his felt-lined boots. A ribbon of yellow diamonds painted on black ran around the edges of the room. This decoration was popular in Québec, and Thérèse and Joseph had taken great pains to reproduce it in their farm kitchen. Rosario placed his boots on one of the yellow diamonds and dropped his leather coat and mittens lined in creamy lamb's wool on top.

He stepped over to Justine, and she offered her cheek for the usual feathered kiss, but he turned his head at the last moment and kissed her mouth. The corners of her mouth went down, and she turned away.

Joseph had heard the horse and entered the kitchen, carrying a homemade checkerboard covered in alternating black and mustard squares. A winter visitor always meant a game of checkers in the Bélanger home. He was a champion player who rarely lost, and he especially enjoyed trouncing young men. David ran back to the dining-room, reached for a battered tobacco tin on the sideboard, and emptied the red and black roundels onto the board on the dining-room table. "Red or black. Your choice," Joseph said, leading the way out of the kitchen. "You can go first," he added magnanimously. The children arranged themselves behind their father, forming a family phalanx of support.

Rosario ran his hand over his moustache, and the game began with the children pointing out to their father areas of weakness and strategies of attack against him.

Shouts were heard from the road, and Justine went to the window. Marcel and Louise's sleigh entered the yard. It negotiated a wide arc, narrowly missing a fence post half-hidden in the snow. The horse slid to a stop at the house, looking wild-eyed and with its sides heaving. Louise slowly climbed down from the sleigh. Her belly strained against the polished horn buttons of her red coat. Keeping her hand on the rail, she made her way slowly up the snow-covered steps. She went straight to Justine, unmindful of the trail of melting snow she left behind. Justine folded at the hips to reach over Louise's belly and kissed her friend's cold, rosy cheeks. She helped her out of her coat and pulled up a chair at the table. "How are you feeling?"

Marcel stood behind Rosario observing the game. Louise ordered him to help her remove her boots. While he unbuckled her overshoes, she added, "I'm very well … considering this baby."

The young Bélanger children stared curiously at Louise, and Thérèse shot a warning look at Justine. In their chaste, Catholic society, pregnancy was never discussed. A brother or sister's arrival coincided with the visit of a neighbour lady in a voluminous white apron. She took over the kitchen and bossed everyone. Birth and the role of their parents in it was a mystery.

Louise sat back unmindful of the stir she had created.

Joseph killed Rosario's red king, and the children returned their attention to the game. Justine poured two cups of steaming coffee and placed sugar and a small jug of fresh cream on the table. "I saw the new school and convent when we drove through the village. It's much bigger than I imagined."

"The nuns moved out of the rectory and into the convent. School started late, but the kids are attending now," Louise said licking the thick cream from her spoon. "It means that Marcel's out of work. He picks up odd jobs here and there and helps Pa with chores. He'll be going to the woods to lumberjack after Christmas. We need the money."

The time the two friends had spent apart was as nothing as Louise confided in Justine as she always had. "I just wish he wouldn't stop at the hotel so often. He's promised to stop drinking when the baby arrives." She blew on the coffee before taking a sip. "Have you heard about Adrien?"

Justine folded her hands primly on her lap. "I haven't seen him since September."

Louise's eyes crinkled. "You're very irritating when you're being holy."

"*Mais enfin*," Justine said impatiently. "I really know less than you about it."

Louise raised the cup to her mouth and looked at her slyly. "You might have another try at him, eh?"

"It's over between us." Justine's nose went up. "I've made up my mind."

Loud moans came from the dining-room as Rosario double-jumped Joseph's blacks.

"That's good, because Marcel says Adrien's coming home for the holidays." Rosario threw up his fists in triumph at his move.

Louise pointed with her chin towards the dining room. "And he isn't here just for the checkers."

Justine grabbed their cups. "Leave this alone. It's over. I've made up my mind."

Louise patted her belly. "Yeah, yeah. But it's a long way from the head to the heart."

With the fasting and prayer of Advent behind them and the miracle of the Baby King sung and wondered over, it was time to step out. Having eaten their fill of rich Christmas cake and satiated on maple fudge, Saint-Cère was ready to dance.

The sweet scent of new lumber permeated the dance hall for the *soirée* above the new dry-goods store in town. Rosario had arrived uninvited in the Normand sleigh just as the Bélangers prepared to climb into their large family one. "Anyone need a ride?" he asked, directing his question to Justine. His warm breath on the cold air had combined to coat his moustache white, giving him a grizzled old look. Justine exchanged a smile with her sister Alexina, gave Rosario her hand, and stepped up. Zéphirin and David pleaded to be allowed to go with their sister. At a nod from their mother, they clambered up and squeezed between them. A heavy buffalo robe covered their knees, and the hot rocks that he had provided on the floor heated their feet. Rosario touched the whip lightly to the horse's flank, and the sleigh slid off smoothly with a jingle of bells in lightly falling snow and the voices of the boys urging their father's heavier sleigh to hurry.

Rosario helped her out of her coat, placed his hand at the small of her back, and steered her forward. "Louise is sitting by the windows. I'll take care of these coats."

Louise caught sight of her and waved. "*Allô!* Sit," she said, patting the space beside her. The cachet of the married state had distinguished her, and a group of schoolgirls had formed around her. "Are the girls carrying muffs in the city?" someone asked Justine. "Have you met any of the *Collégiens?*" asked another.

The ladies of Saint-Boniface were famous for their fashion. Justine was pleased to comply. "Well, the women are wearing their hair swept up with a frizzled bang on the forehead. For once my hair is in style." She laughed as her fingers touched her own curls. "The dresses have small floral prints …" Justine's voice trailed off. The girls no longer listened; their eyes had slid away to the door when Adrien and his brothers entered. Wet snow covered Adrien's black hair. He bent his head, shook off the snow, and pushed it back into place with his fingers.

Justine turned away and searched for Rosario. He, feeling her eyes on him, came to join her.

In the corner, the leader of the band began to tap a slow three-quarter rhythm.

"I'll get you a drink," Rosario offered.

"But the music is beginning," she argued.

"I'll be right back," he said, leaving her and pushing his way through the crowd to the tables at the side with refreshments.

The bow touched the fiddle, and the accordion joined in for the first grand notes of the "Waves of the Danube" waltz.

Justine watched Adrien from behind the girls. He had shed his coat and been circulating round the edge of the room across from her. He stopped when he saw her, crossed the floor, and advanced deliberately towards her.

'Oh no,' Justine thought, looking around desperately. 'He can't be coming for the first dance. The dance floor is empty. Everyone will see.'

Adrien acknowledged her with a stiff bow then offered her his hand. "Can I have this dance?"

She put her hand in his and allowed him to lead her onto the dance floor. She had no choice; to do otherwise would make things worse.

Adrien kept his smile fixed as he swept her silently round the room under the curious eyes of the villagers. 'He loves this,' she thought. 'He loves being the centre of attention. He doesn't care that they'll start gossiping about me.' She wondered what Rosario would think and only relaxed when other couples joined them.

Finally, when there was no one else near, he bent his head and whispered, "Forgive me."

She stiffened.

"It would be too hard to lose your friendship. I can't live with you thinking badly of me."

He wasn't as good a dancer as Rosario. His steps were somewhat heavy to the lilting beat, but he kept his back straight, and the arms that held her were confident and strong as they waltzed slowly round the room. Against her good reason and because she wanted to believe he was good, she forgave him. As she did, she let his arms support more of her weight.

He knew at once that she had forgiven him. He looked down at her. "Thank you for keeping my secret. I suppose you know I'm not at the *Collège* anymore. My plans for the priesthood lasted six months. You were right."

She wondered about the pretty, expensively dressed woman she had seen him kissing in the church.

As if reading her mind, he said, "She's gone away."

Justine lifted her head. Despair and pain darkened his face. She looked away as pity for him washed over her.

After the waltz, he walked her back to Louise.

Marcel had joined his wife. "You've returned!" he said to Adrien, saluting his friend with a glass of lemonade with a smell that reminded Justine of the rubbing alcohol Thérèse kept in her medicine chest. "The pleasures of a wife are not to be underestimated," Marcel continued, next saluting his wife's belly. Louise joined the men's laughter, but Justine stood by mute and embarrassed. Marcel continued, "So you got kicked out. You're better off. I used to work at Petit's shop. When I go to Saint-Boniface, I'll look you up."

On New Year's morning, Joseph held his hand self-consciously over the heads of his family as they kneeled around him in the kitchen for the paternal blessing. The night before, his children had hung their clean, everyday woollen stockings at the foot of their beds and had awakened early to find a mandarin orange swelling the toe. A handful of hazelnuts, a couple of black Brazil nuts, and a ribbon of hard peppermint candy topped it. Only at Christmas did the compact mandarin oranges appear, wrapped in thin paper and shipped in wooden crates a foot square. Zéphirin, David, and Marie-Ange gobbled theirs up, but Justine hid hers in her drawer, saving it to savour each succulent, sweet section later.

Presents wrapped in red and green paper lay on the dining-room table, and the children kept peeking at them during Joseph's prayer. At his last word, they rushed the door.

Justine picked up Marie-Ange to save her from being trampled and followed the family through the dining room into the living room at the front of the house. A red velvet sofa that was only for visitors or special occasions occupied the corner across from the tree. Thérèse and Joseph were seated there, and the girls joined them while Alexina handed out gifts. A cloth doll with satin lips the colour of strawberries and black button eyes leaned against the trunk of the tree, hidden from sight. Alexina had spent hours in the lamplight over it, each stitch tiny, meticulous, and perfect. She knelt, retrieved it from where she had hidden it, and handed it to Marie-Ange. The little girl squealed and jumped up. Her hands squeezed the dolly's body in a paroxysm of delight as she threw herself at her sister. Alexina beamed as she caught her and accepted the little girl's kisses of thanks.

David, Zéphirin, and Hilaire received the pocketknives they had seen and coveted in the glass display case at the general store. David quickly pried his open and slid his thumb along the shining blade. He stared stupidly as a thin, red line appeared.

Thérèse glared at her husband. "I warned you." She got to her feet and scooped the six-year-old away for a bandage. "He's too young for a knife."

As was the custom in French-Catholic society, their first-born son had been baptised Joseph like his father and grandfather before him, but he had always been Ti-Jos. His gift was woollen underwear with long arms and legs and a flap at the back. He thanked his parents and then put the long johns aside by his feet.

"They'll keep you warm," Joseph commented.

"Yours were getting too small," Thérèse added, returning with David, who held up his thumb with the thick cotton bandage and returned to his knife.

Thérèse assumed the responsibility of handing out presents to her older daughters. She placed a heavy parcel in Justine's lap.

Justine tore at the paper. "Oh! A book!" she exclaimed. "Garneau's *Histoire du Canada*. I've always wanted this. How did you know?" She sniffed the pages, ran her fingers over the leather binding, and finally opened it. The stiff spine cracked open.

"*Père* suggested it," Joseph explained. "He thought you could use it when you're teaching."

Alexina was the last, and when she opened her gift, she found a black, leather pouch that fit in the palm of her hand. She opened the flap and drew out a rosary. The wooden beads were arranged in a circle of five groups of ten, each group separated by a single bead. A short strand of five beads culminating with a wooden cross hung from a medal at the first decade. "Thank you," she said going over to kiss her parents. "I'll ask *Père* to bless it next Sunday."

A delicious smell of savoury filled the house. Thérèse led the way back to the kitchen. "The *tourtières* are ready."

A long object wrapped in flour bags lay in the wood-box by the stove. Joseph waited for everyone to be seated before he went to the box, cleared off a few logs, and pulled it out. Resting the long body wrapped in white on his open, upturned palms, Joseph crossed over to Ti-Jos. He placed it on the table in front of his oldest boy. "It's time you had one of these for your own, *mon gars*."

Ti-Jos grew quiet and sat up. He ran his hands over the object. He looked at his parents. He lifted up the cloth-hidden present and tested its weight. He looked again at his parents in wonder and then whooped and stood up to tear off the flour sacks. His hands fixed around the stock and barrel as tears ran down his face. His first gun.

Since he had been old enough to hold a gun, Ti-Jos had supplied partridges, squirrels, and rabbits for the family board. The angry blackbirds with white eyes that attacked the farm cats as they walked lazily across the yard and the thieving black and white magpies gathered round the dog dishes didn't stand a chance when Ti-Jos had them in his sight. This Winchester rifle was meant for bigger prey like deer, elk, and bear. It had a new lever action. Under the barrel, a full-length tube held rifle shells—seven in the magazine and one in the firing chamber. It would be the meat-getter for the family.

That night, Justine searched for the new Winchester among the others leaning on the wall by the back door. "Papa, do you know where Ti-Jos' new gun is? I'd like to look at it." She knew how to shoot. She shot the skunks that wanted to live under the sheds and the foxes that killed her mother's hens.

Joseph looked up from the paper. "They say that the North West Mounted Police has ordered over 750 of these guns." He continued reading. "He must have it in the bedroom."

When Justine entered the boys' bedroom, they were asleep. She lifted the lamp and looked around. She couldn't see the rifle anywhere. She tiptoed over to Ti-Jos' bed. The brown, blue, and black coverlet that Thérèse had quilted from old coats and suits had partially slipped to the floor. Justine lifted a corner and passed the lamp under the bed. Nothing. Where would he have put that gun? Out of the corner of her eye she spotted something dark and black on her brother's pillow. 'A mouse!' she thought hurriedly stepping back. The black thing remained on the pillow. She looked closer. The muzzle of the Winchester lay near Ti-Jos' head. His arms were wrapped around the barrel. She backed quietly out of the room.

It was bitterly cold, but thankfully the Christmas season passed without a blizzard. However, the train that took Justine back to the city travelled through heavy snow and a strong wind from the north. Justine was thoroughly chilled by the time she reached the convent. As she closed the door against the weather and dropped her bag with relief, she inhaled the stuffy but peaceful air of the convent.

It was always colder at the river, where strong Arctic winds swept along the ice unencumbered from the north. As every room in the convent was cold, Justine went to the dining hall where there was a chance of warmth and to catch up with her friends.

In fact, that was what she was doing just a week later, when a student rushed in and ran over to them. Something terrible had been found in the river last night. A man had been drawing water from a hole in the ice when a small wooden box floated up. He pried it open and found the bodies of newborn twins. The details were gruesome, but Justine could not turn away. "The bodies were perfectly preserved in the icy water and bore red marks on their throats," the girl said.

Justine put her hands to her throat. "*Mon Dieu*! How horrible."

"Who would do such a thing?" another asked.

"A man must have built the box," someone said. "Only a man could carry the box to the river."

"It must have been one of the immigrants. Maybe they already had too many children and couldn't feed more," a stout girl said.

Justine wondered how the mother felt. The crime appalled her, but the thoughts she turned on the woman were not of blame but of pity.

The next day, the nuns cancelled classes. The students attended the funeral, and then under a grey sky, the girls followed the priest to the graveyard. Two policemen carried the light wooden casket to the periphery of the cemetery. A grave had been dug in the section of unconsecrated ground reserved for those who had died without baptism.

There was little hope of finding the murderers.

CHAPTER 18

Winter 1883

The red and green paper chains had long since been fed to the kitchen fire. Out the frosted windows, the white continued to gleam monotonous and still. "Too cold to snow," the old ones said in sweaters buttoned to the neck. They moved their card games to the kitchen and played Barouche while rotating out of the chair nearest to the stove. Books were dusted off and reread and passed from hand to hand. Finally, when they thought they couldn't stand the boredom for one more day, an article appeared in the newspaper about the sex trade on the English side of the river that cured their *ennui*.

For as long as anyone could remember, the whorehouses on Douglas Point, not far from the Hill residence, had been operating without police interference. Reverend Frederic Wilcox, a newly arrived Congregationalist minister, wanted to change that. He was determined to drive the prostitutes out of the city.

Arthur-Joseph was alone in the paper-strewn office of *Le Métis* when Adrien dropped in. "Listen to this," he said, reading from the newspaper in his hand. "'In these abodes of vice are the depths of immorality, debauchery, and death. In their swinish precincts, the youth of our land are beguiled and ruined, body and soul.' English preachers have a grandiose way with words. It makes everything seem wonderfully bad. I wish we had priests who talked like that."

Adrien came and stood behind him. "The sermon on Sunday would be more interesting."

Arthur-Joseph lifted his chin towards the last paragraph. "Look, it says here that Thomas Hill supports Wilcox's campaign. He says the houses corrupt the children passing on their way to school, and he objects to the *bagarres* late at night."

Adrien hadn't heard or seen any brawls near the Hill mansion when he went there to tutor Esther. He leaned closer to read for himself.

Adrien rented a room on the top floor of a store adjacent to the new railroad tracks not far from the main boulevard in Saint-Boniface. The cold penetrated the flimsy wooden walls, but it was cheap and close to Petit's workshop and the job Taché had arranged for him.

He arrived early the first day of work and looked around the empty office. Above the dusty desk hung a framed picture of St. Joseph and Jesus at work in their wood shop in Nazareth. Joseph guided the plane in his young son's hands as the tool sliced curls of wood from a creamy plank. Saint Joseph's hands were slender and white—remarkably free of the scars of a carpenter's trade.

Pépère Larence, Adrien's grandfather, had been a carpenter. While they worked together, his grandfather had told him about the tradition of woodcraft in Canada. Laval, the first Bishop of New France, had established a trade school on the outskirts of the city of Québec. Ornate wooden altars, statues, and furniture for public buildings were crafted there. The *habitants* acquired a taste for quality and filled their homes with armoires, chests, tables, and chairs that were plain, simple, and beautiful.

The gossip was true about the Petits—they were dead against drinking. The women's temperance movement was sweeping North America, and Petit's wife had persuaded him to join. Sobriety and the total abstention from liquor was their goal. The Roman Catholic Church had always been prohibitionist. Bishop Laval noting the ravages inflicted by alcohol on the Natives and colonists of New France had campaigned for prohibition during his 50-year career. However, the governor, *le Comte de Frontenac*, was a worldly man who enjoyed wine at his *soirées* and theatricals, and he opposed the Bishop outright.

Adrien was surprised that Monsieur Petit would ascribe to such a Puritan view about liquor. That view fit the style of the English on the other side of the river, and he had confidence that his compatriots on the French side would be more sensible. In spite of the gossip, Adrien felt immediately at home in the sawdust-covered shop.

One evening when he was bored and couldn't stand the sound of the cold wind whistling through the cracks in his room, Adrien went to *Tante* Alice's. Justine was there, and he took the chair opposite to partner with her. While he dealt the cards, he teased her about her studies. "I expect you're the star of the class."

Several tables with groups of players had been set up in the living room. *Tante* was seated at the one in the middle of the room that was convenient to every conversation. She answered for Justine. "She's the smartest girl in her class. *Soeur Supérieur* told me so."

"*Ma tante*, you exaggerate," Justine protested.

Alice glanced knowingly at the married couple at her table. "I would've had success in school too had your uncle not been in such a hurry to marry."

Justine inspected her cards.

Alice continued. "I read a book last year. It was quite interesting, though I can't say exactly what it was about now."

Adrien cleared his throat for Justine to look at him. He winked. She hid her smile behind a fan of cards.

"What's trump again?" Adrien asked, leading out with an ace.

CHAPTER 19

1883

Justine saw Adrien infrequently that winter. He worked long days in the carpentry shop, and a cycle of heavy snow followed by bitter cold kept citizens indoors. To help pass the time, Arthur-Joseph smuggled a copy of Jean-Jacques Rousseau's *Émile* to her.

"Don't let the nuns catch you reading it. It's on the Index or *Librorum Prohibitorum*, as Père would say. It has very interesting things to say that a teacher should know."

Justine knew that the Index was a list of books forbidden to Catholics. Rousseau believed that children should be taught with sympathy and according to their interests. However, in *Émile*, he also attacked traditional Christian beliefs. She covered her copy in brown paper and read it with interest under the eyes of the supervising nun during study hall. She asked Arthur-Joseph if he had other Rousseau books and was given *The Social Contract*. She read it and wondered why the Church objected to the idea that man was inherently good.

The days lengthened, the snow receded slowly under the strengthening sun, and with a happy heart she saw her first orange-breasted robin hop busily in the convent yard.

Justine went home to Saint-Cère and an exceptional summer. The immense valley spreading away from the Red River became a Camelot of sunny days and refreshing evening rain. In the fertile valley soil, Joseph's cows grew fat on lush green grass, and the fields of wheat, oats, and barley grew tall with heavy heads that bent and swayed in the gentle winds. Joseph scanned the sky for thunderheads a dozen times a day, trying not to be hopeful about the harvest—it was bad luck to talk about the promising crop before it was in the bin. Under no circumstances was the garden ever allowed to fail, and Justine grew brown while weeding and watering the rows of cucumbers, tomatoes, peas, beans, and watermelons. Louise came by often with her new baby strapped to her back on a papoose board. Aurore was a solemn child with black hair that stuck straight up like the bristles on a hairbrush. She refused to smile, even at Justine's gentle coaxing. Rosario worked away in the lumber camps, and she was at peace in the carefree summer.

The race to harvest the grain began early in August under blue skies and hot, dry winds. Finally, when the last bushel of grain had been thrashed and granaries were so full that grain leaked through the cracks, Joseph took a deep breath and allowed that it had been a good year. When classes resumed in the fall, a tanned and content Justine returned to the city.

The Red River had long since glazed with ice and lay under a blanket of crusted snow. Adrien, Arthur-Joseph, and Justine made up the small group of young people hurrying across the bridge to Winnipeg. A fierce wind from the north ran along the ice, pinched their cheeks, and tore at their hats and thick winter coats. The recently opened Princess Opera House was performing Verdi's *La Traviata* for the first time, and they had purchased tickets. When they reached the shelter of buildings and were finally away from the tearing wind, the group split into couples. Arthur-Joseph walked ahead of Adrien and Justine with a friend. He turned and, walking backward a few steps, said to his friends, "I've received a letter from Sara Riel. She's very ill."

Sara was Louis Riel's sister and a nun. Immediately after taking her final vows with the Sisters of Charity as a young woman of 23, she had travelled a thousand miles by Red River cart to Ile-à-la-Crosse in northern Saskatchewan. There, she assisted Bishop Vital Grandin with the mission on the reserve where her father, Louis Riel Sr., had been raised. Tuberculosis was endemic on the reserves, and she had contracted the disease.

"Will she be able to make the trip back?" Justine asked.

Arthur-Joseph grimaced and shook his head. The girl he accompanied was a pretty *normalienne* who attended classes with Justine. He tucked her hand into the crook of his arm and pulled her in closer on the pretext of keeping her warm.

Adrien took Justine's hand and tucked it into his arm too. She let herself be drawn into him, but he didn't shorten his stride, and she had to take quick, short steps to keep up.

Arthur-Joseph glanced back and said, *"Attention aux loups, ma belle."*

Justine pulled her arm away. "You needn't warn me about wolves. I'm well aware of his defects."

Adrien stopped and brought his hand to his head in a military salute. "I know when I'm not wanted." He dropped back to attend to another girl, a blonde in a velvet hat of blue that exactly matched her eyes.

Justine lifted her chin—he would soon find out how dim she was. Besides, she felt pretty tonight. The dress that she wore was new and by far the most beautiful she had ever owned. She had discovered the pale-violet dress on a mannequin in one of the store windows on Provencher Boulevard ridiculously marked down. At her enquiry, the clerk had removed it from the window and pointed out a small tear in the skirt's semi-transparent fabric. It was hardly noticeable, and Justine had bought it on the spot. Sister Aline de Jésus was an expert with the needle, and her fingers had worked their magic on the fine crepe.

As she'd finished dressing for the opera that night, Justine had attached borrowed pearl drops to her earlobes. After inspecting her reflection in her hand mirror and turning her head from side to side to admire the translucent, milky pearls dangling above the ruffle on her dress, she had smiled approvingly. For once, the halo that was her hair was behaving.

With a shake of her head, Justine ran to Arthur-Joseph and took his free arm. Sleighs and carriages were filling the street before the Princess Opera House. The theatre in the new three-storey building could hold over 1000 people. The citizens of Winnipeg were justly proud of their new opera house. The previous theatre had a stable attached at the rear, and the odour of manure often wafted over the audience during the performances. Justine, Adrien, and Arthur-Joseph went in through the entrance cut into the corner of the building and joined the rest of their group huddled around a wood stove, one of several scattered round. Voices rose as the excitement grew in the cavernous, chilly entrance hall until finally the bell rang, calling them in. Justine followed her friends as they climbed to the cheap seats in the last row of the first balcony.

The orchestra sent up the first discordant notes of warm-up, and Justine slipped down to the balcony's polished brass rail. Far below, men in black tuxedos and women in evening gowns crowded the aisles, searching for the red velvet seats that matched their tickets.

"I'm going to sit down there someday—in the best seats," Adrien said, joining her.

Justine frowned, looking down. "Why do you always want to be like them?"

"Because they're the ones with money. Do you see any *habitants* down there?"

The hum of voices from the main floor increased as people stepped on toes and slid over folded knees to get to their seats.

"The doors of business are closed to us."

"Not for me."

Justine cocked her ear towards the orchestra pit. Snippets of music began to sound familiar.

Adrien gazed down. Suddenly he pointed to a box on the right of the auditorium with curtains that were pulled half-across, shielding the occupants from the audience. "Look! I bet that's where the prostitutes are."

"Really? How do you know?"

"I read it in the paper. Prostitutes have been buying the best seats, and it's not good for business. The theatre has been trying to discourage them from coming by segregating them in a special curtained section. Let's take a look."

Justine shook her head nervously. "I don't want to get in trouble. What if we get caught?"

He took her hand. "So what if we do?"

The gaslights had been dimmed in the lobby, and it was empty. The loges that they had seen from the balcony opened onto a separate passage. They walked down the hall to the furthest one. Adrien drew the heavy, green velvet curtain aside, and they slipped in at the opening bars of the opera. A Parisian salon appeared on the stage, and two women at the front of the box sat engrossed. Adrien pushed Justine deeper into the shadows at the back of the box, and they stood behind the two unknowing women. Desperately trying to control their breathing, they waited as Alfredo declared his love to Violetta.

The prostitutes were women in their mid-thirties and in the prime of their beauty. Their long hair was piled high on their heads, and curls fringed their foreheads over a mask of thick makeup. White shoulders glowed in the stage light over dresses that exposed the plump globs of their breasts. Justine glanced at Adrien uncomfortably. His eyes too had found the front of their dresses. She dug her elbow into his ribs and pushed him back through the curtain into the passage.

A small, smoky cafe operated around the corner from the opera house. It was full of opera-goers, but Arthur-Joseph spotted an open table at the back and pulled up chairs for everyone.

"You know the box with the closed curtains?" Adrien asked his friend.

As a reporter, Arthur-Joseph prided himself in knowing all the business of both cities on either side of the bridge. "If you mean the one for the prostitutes, I know all about it."

Adrien's eyes twinkled. "Justine and I went there during the performance. We saw them."

"Why didn't you ask me?" Arthur-Joseph demanded.

Adrien winked at Justine. "Because three's a crowd."

The women's eyes opened in surprise as they turned to Justine. The corners of her mouth lifted. They all began at once.

"What were they wearing?"

"Were they pretty?"

It was late when Justine and the blonde girl stole up the long flight of stairs to the dormitory. In their hurry, they forgot about the creaky step that grated like an ungreased hinge. They cringed and froze, hoping that the dormitory sister hadn't heard. All remained quiet. They breathed a sigh of relief, and choking back laughter, they crept into the dormitory. The curtains around the beds were closed around the sleepers and formed an aisle of white down the centre of the long room. Justine dropped her coat and twirled down the aisle past the beds, the soft crepe skirt flaring up like a pansy about her legs.

"*T'es folle!*" the blonde whispered with a giggle. "Stop or you'll get us in trouble."

Justine pirouetted one more time, grabbed her coat, and swished the curtain closed around her bed. She carefully removed the borrowed pearls and set them on the nightstand. She unbuttoned her dress and hung it carefully over the scrolls on the iron footboard. She stepped out of her underclothes quickly, retrieved her flannel nightgown from under her pillow, and pulled it swiftly over her head. A skim of ice floated on her washbasin, so she shot into bed, promising to wash her face twice as clean in the morning. She drew her legs up and scrunched her feet in the folds of flannelette.

"*Notre Père* ..." she began. But she was too excited to pray, too thrilled to have stood near Adrien in the dark loge with the scent of the women's perfume heavy in the air. How instantly furious she had become when she saw his eyes linger on their exposed skin. She burrowed further into the flannelette. She began the "Our Father" again, reciting it over and over until she slipped into sleep.

Advent was again upon them and preparations for the Christmas services began. Both good singers and bad joined the choir, much as both saints and sinners went to church. Justine joined, as she had a pretty voice and loved to sing, and Adrien dropped in because he had nothing better to do.

The choir was invited to the house of Adrien's boss one night after practice. On the way home, under a black velvet vault alive with a million twinkling diamonds, Justine began in a pure, high voice: "*Venez, divin Messie, nous rendre espoir et nous sauver! Vous êtes notre vie!*" She paused for the tenors to join her in singing the ancient, "O come, divine Messiah!" They came in, shouting to the stars: "*Venez, venez, venez!*"

Petit poured coffee from a blue enamelled pot as they were gathered in the kitchen. "See, you've just spent an evening singing and enjoying yourselves without liquor. You can have fun without it. *La ruine de la société* ..."

Adrien stood with Justine in the arch separating the kitchen from the dining room. He began whistling the drinking song under his breath that he and Marcel had sung, "*Prendre un p'tit coup, c'est agréable* ..."

Justine's brow wrinkled at his insolence, and she wondered why he would openly goad his boss.

Petit reddened and turned to face Adrien. "Now that you've found work in the city, you think you're smart. We'll see how fast you get ahead in the English world."

"The pay's better," Adrien shot back.

Questioning faces turned towards him.

"I'm starting work at Sommers. It's a new store on Main Street."

Exploding pops mixed with the smell of burning butter filled the room. Madame Petit pushed and pulled a wire basket with yellow kernels over an open ring on the kitchen stove. The crowd turned their attention to her.

"Why are you leaving?" Justine demanded.

"I want to be rich and successful, and I can't in Saint-Boniface."

"But we'll lose you."

"C'est pas la Chine."

Justine bit her lip. The English sector across the river was a world away.

CHAPTER 20

Christmas 1883

Justine stared out of the train's frosted window, lulled by the rhythm of the wheels striking the steel joins on her way home. Her frizzy curls had been unmanageable today. She had finally thrown her hairpins down in frustration on the dresser, gathered her thick hair with her hand, and tied it back with a ribbon. The fields and farms speeding past began to look familiar. Ahead, several cows browsed quietly near the track. The engineer pulled a string, and the quiet was blasted away by an ear-splitting shriek from the engine's air whistle. The cows looked up, threw their shoulders away from the track, and stampeded over the hill.

A sign with white letters on black announcing Saint-Cère whizzed by, and then the station came into view. Justine stood to retrieve her valise from the overhead rack. The hinge had caught in the brown mesh, and she struggled to get it down, pulling and tugging in the swaying train. A man reached up and lifted it down.

Cinders peppered the track and crunched under Justine's boots as she stepped down. Other than the agent who was busy loading cans of milk into the freight car, the station was deserted. "*Sapristi!*" she cursed, using the corrupted word for sacristy. "The family's not here ... they mustn't have received my letter." She looked down at her fashionable black boots trimmed in black rabbit fur that ran over the arch and around the ankle. They fit neatly over her shoes, but her toes were always cold. 'I'll have to ask the agent for help.'

She heard the sound of drumming hooves and looked up. At the top of the street, a sleigh appeared with a driver urging his horse. It wasn't her father. He'd never drive the sleigh that fast through town. The bright sun on the snow blinded her. She raised her hand to shield her eyes and heard Rosario call hello.

"Sorry I'm late," he said, leaping down. "It took longer than I thought to pick up supplies." He grabbed her valise from her hand.

"I was surprised that no one was here to meet me. I was just about to ask for help."

Rosario put her valise with the feed sacks in the back. "I was coming for supplies and thought I'd meet the train. No use two sleighs making the trip."

Rosario had come around to where Justine stood and held out his hand to help her up. She put her foot on the step and was halfway up when he gave her bum a push so that she landed with a thud on the seat. Chuckling, he hopped across her and took the reins. With a practiced snap of the wrist, the reins slapped the fat rump of the horse, and the sleigh slid off. "It's good to see you. I missed you last summer."

Justine turned her head and stared at the dark evergreens that bordered the road, still piqued at being treated so unceremoniously.

Rosario kept right on talking. "*Père*'s been acting like a detective. Money was going missing from the alms box at the church, and *Père* set a trap to catch the thief. He sprinkled ash over the coins in the box. When one of the Fredette boys showed up with dirty hands to serve mass, *Père* confronted him, and he admitted that he was the culprit."

Try as she might, Justine was not one to remain mad for long. She turned towards Rosario. "What did *Père* do?"

"He told the Fredettes, and their boy got a licking he won't forget."

The green roof and white siding of the Bélanger house was just visible through the trees when Rosario pulled back on the reins. The horse flared its nostrils, snuffled noisily, and stopped.

"Why are we stopping?" she asked, inching away from him.

"I've got something for you." From inside his sheepskin jacket, he pulled out a slender, brown leather box with a gold catch and held it out to her.

Justine shook her head rapidly and jammed her hands between her knees.

He put the box on her lap and sat back. "We're not moving until you open it."

A hawk circled high above in the blue sky. Justine glanced at the house. It wasn't that far; she could walk. She removed her gloves and took the box. The leather felt soft and buttery to the touch. She ran her fingers along the edges to the catch and released it with her thumbnail. The lid sprang open. A gold cross and chain lay on a bed of white satin.

Rosario lifted the chain out of the box and held it up. The cross twisted and turned, gleaming in the sun.

"Oh," Justine breathed, struck by its beauty.

"I thought of you when I saw it," he said with a smile and dropped the chain and cross into her hand. "Think of it as a mark of our friendship. If our friendship ever breaks, you can give it back."

"Don't say such things. We'll always be friends."

She fingered the chased filigree of the cross. It was so beautiful, but she hesitated, weighing the propriety of accepting such a gift. Then she bent her head and fumbled under her hair to insert the clasp into the ring.

"Let me help," Rosario said. He caught her hair and lifted it off her neck.

"Thank you," she said quietly, dropping the chain and cross under the collar of her dress.

Justine greeted her family and quickly unpacked. She donned Joseph's chores jacket with the scent of sour milk and notes of cow urine and pulled on an old tuque.

"You're going out?" Joseph protested. "But you've only just arrived."

"I want to see Louise and Aurore. I'll be back before dark."

Justine checked the sky before entering the woods. The sky was blue and the sun brilliant in the cold. It would be safe to take the shortcut along the river. The brushy woods that lined the banks were silent as she passed. Here and there, circles pockmarked the ice where her brothers had fished for trout. Prairie-chicken tracks meandered over the fresh snow until disappearing into the woods. A fox's cat-like prints crossed the ice until they veered suddenly off to the right and were lost in the woods. The cold bit her cheeks and numbed her forehead, and she began to run. With relief, she detected the clean scent of a kitchen fire.

Louise sat with Aurore at the table, playing with yellow, green, red, and blue wooden blocks with letters of the alphabet stamped on their sides. She smiled when Justine entered, set the baby on the floor, and lumbered towards the door.

"I just got home this morning," Justine explained as she offered Louise her cold cheeks. "Let me hold Aurore, but let me warm my hands first." She rubbed her hands briskly and blew on her fingers before taking the baby. Aurore smiled apprehensively then her delicate mouth quivered, and she held out her arms imploringly to her mother.

Justine's mouth went down, and she handed her back. "I was hoping she would remember me."

"*Elle fait sauvage.* Making strange," Marcel said from the rocking chair by the stove. His foot was wrapped in a white bandage and propped on a crutch of willow branches. An old copy of *Le Métis* lay open on his knees.

"What on earth happened to you?" Justine asked him.

Marcel glanced sheepishly at Louise. "Just a little accident chopping wood."

Louise shot him a withering look. She put a bowl of sugar and a pitcher of sweet cream on the table beside a chipped cup filled with upturned spoons. "Could you get the coffee?" she asked Justine. She lowered herself onto a chair and settled Aurore on the diminishing space between her belly and knees. After the cups had been filled and sweetened with sugar and cream, she absentmindedly touched a fingertip to the sugar in the bowl and offered the sweet to the baby. "So what's your news?"

Before Justine could begin, Marcel snapped the paper smartly against his knees and said, "The revenue from the new Provencher Bridge is $100 a day. At two cents a crossing that's …." His brow creased as he attempted to calculate the sum in his head.

Justine surveyed the table. Breakfast crumbs and dried-on food littered the yellow-chequered oilcloth. "Five thousand," she said quietly.

"Just what I was about to say," he said, tapping the newspaper with his index finger. "*Crisse*! That's a lot of people crossing that bridge every day."

Louise added more sugar to her coffee. "So what's new in the city?"

"There's a new opera house," Justine offered.

Marcel sat up. "Did you see the prostitutes?"

Justine hesitated. "Only from the back."

The interruptions continued until Louise, losing her patience, put Aurore down with her blocks and went to a basket near the wall filled with raw wool the colour of cream. She carried an apron-full to Justine. They pulled the soft fibre apart, picking out grass seeds, bits of straw, and dried manure. When every bit of debris had been picked out and their hands oiled with the sweet lanolin in the wool, they stretched the gauzy wool over the wire faces of two carding paddles and began combing the wool into soft batts. Justine glanced at Marcel. His eyes were half-closed. The next time she looked, his chin lay on his chest.

"It's too bad about his accident," she whispered.

"He almost chopped his foot off. He didn't get home until dark. I needed wood for the kitchen, and I wouldn't let him off because I could smell liquor on his breath. He went out into the yard, I heard a yell, and he was back in the house gushing blood. Damn fool."

Justine chewed her lip uncomfortably. Two freshly killed rabbits lay on top of iron traps on the floor near the door. Several rifles leaned in the corner nearby. "Don't speak so about your husband."

Louise and Marcel had moved into an empty log cabin on the Lafrenière farm. As Louise had promised at her wedding, she supplemented the family's income by taking in laundry. She had bragged how the first pains of labour hit when she was bending over the washtub.

Justine checked to see if Marcel was indeed asleep then said quietly, "Rosario gave me something."

Louise caressed her belly. "Hope it isn't one of these."

Justine inhaled sharply. "If you're going to talk like that, I won't show you!"

"C'mon, you know I was only teasing."

Mollified, Justine pulled the chain from under her dress. The cross twirled as it swung from her fingers.

Louise touched the delicate filigree. "Is it an engagement gift?"

"Don't be silly," Justine said, dropping it back under her dress. "It's just a gift between friends."

"Why are you hiding it then?"

"I am not! I'm … I'm still getting used to it."

"Puh!" Louise said in disbelief. "You liked it, and you accepted it. Rosario will assume something."

"That's not how it was at all," Justine insisted, gathering up the cups.

"*Pas si vite*—not so fast," Louise said catching her friend's wrist. "Marcel says that Adrien's crossed over to the city. He's in Winnipeg. That's why you're accepting Rosario's gift."

"What has Adrien to do with this?" Justine exclaimed. "Honestly, I don't know why we remain friends."

Louise smiled smugly.

The sky was greying in the early December dusk as Justine laid the dirty cups in the sink. "I have to go. I don't want to get caught out in the dark."

Adrien stayed in the city that year and joined his friends on Christmas Eve in the crowded choir loft for midnight mass. After the Bishop had departed, his shoulders sagging under a heavily embroidered gold chasuble that covered him to his ankles, the vicar who led the choir clipped off the last note with a flourish and palmed a bravo to the choir. The singers banged the kneelers up and crowded down the winding stairs, eager for the midnight feast of *réveillon*.

Instead of leaving, Adrien descended to the railing above the main floor. He knelt and with his hands hanging over the railing, observed the milling crowd below. Mothers in fur coats and matching fur hats hurried their sleepy children forward. They had *réveillon* to serve at home. Their men, with the youngest child asleep on their shoulders, tarried heedlessly and exchanged "*Joyeux Noël*" in the crowded aisles.

Except for a few faithful who knelt here and there in the great *cathédrale*, the church was now empty. Adrien remained in the flickering candlelight.

A solitary priest accompanied by a young seminarian began the Mass of the Dawn. This mass, without hymns or sermons and truncated motions, was soon sped through, and the priest began the prayers for the third and final Mass of the Day. Now only nuns, widows, and the truly devout answered the rushed prayers.

A carpet of diamonds spread before him when Adrien left the church. He couldn't explain the impulse that had made him stay for the three masses. He thought of Tessier and wondered what he would think of this display of devotion. His stomach growled, and he hurried away to the *réveillon* party at the home of *Tante* Alice.

CHAPTER 21

January 1884

Adrien shifted the heavy canvas bag of tools and clothes to his other hand and fished a piece of paper out of his pocket. He rechecked the address and then entered an area of the city that was a grid of short streets stretching away from the river. The railroad to bind the nation had brought an influx of single men, and the tall, narrow houses with skimpy front yards had rooms for rent. Makeshift canvas tents hastily set up on empty lots also provided accommodation.

On a corner, Adrien stopped in front of a house with an annex that had been recently added at the back. Undisturbed snow lay several feet deep on the front steps. He followed a hard-packed path around to the annex. Timbers and wooden boards poked out of the drifts in the back yard. Another path led to the double outhouse in the back. He knocked, waited, and raised his hand to knock again when he heard a heavy tread and the door opened to a powerful smell of fried cabbage. A stout woman with a flat, round, expressionless face filled the doorway. He had thought to use his charm on her, but instead he showed her the piece of paper and asked, "You have a room to rent?"

She opened the door and stepped aside. Adrien squeezed around her. A narrow entrance hall led to the back with stairs on the left. She motioned with her head for him to follow her up. He followed slowly, keeping well behind and glancing no further up her legs than the rolled stockings at her ankles. At the top, Adrien glanced expectantly around the landing at several closed doors, but the woman turned and opened a door that was narrower than the others. An even steeper stair led to the space under the roof. She grabbed hold of the handrail and began hauling herself up. A hall down the middle divided the cavernous attic with two rooms opening on each side. A small square window at the far end let in some light that was insufficient to cut the winter's gloom. Trying to catch her breath, the woman gestured to the first room.

Adrien pushed open the door and frowned. The partitions dividing the rooms were flimsy, and the ceiling was open to the roof. A thin mattress barely covered the metal spring of the narrow iron bed. A flat pillow lay on a grey blanket with a black stripe on the ends that reminded him of the ones he had seen in railroad sleeper cars. He turned towards her. "Do you have a heavier blanket for this bed?"

She lifted her shoulders and shook her head.

He thought she understood him well enough, but he pulled an imaginary blanket around his shoulders and repeated, "Another blanket?"

Her eyes narrowed. She held up two fingers.

Adrien had folded the bills for the first week's rent and had them in his pocket. He counted them into her hand.

She poked the bills with the two fingers of her other hand.

"All right, all right," he said, peeling off two more dollars.

She slipped them into her apron pocket, and turning, put her hand on the rail to descend.

Adrien dropped his bag with a thud on the rough, unpainted floorboards and sat on the bed. Straw poked from a tear in the mattress fabric. '*Une paillasse!* And probably not fresh either,' he thought, stretching out. His breath plumed before his face as he looked up. Pinpricks of light poked through yellowed newspapers tacked to the roof. He'd get his mother to send him up one of her quilts on the train. He rolled over, pulled the collar of his fleece jacket up to his neck, and hugged his arms tight.

The wooden buildings with false-fronts extending above the roof to create a more impressive façade were a staple of the boomtown architecture of the West, but now substantial brick buildings were slowly replacing them in the prosperous city core. The manufacture where Adrien was about to begin work took up an entire block just off the main avenues of Portage and Main. Tall white letters painted on red brick under the flat roof boldly announced: Sommers Manufacturing Company.

The company boasted that a woman could stroll along the store's spacious aisles while her grocery list was being filled by an obliging clerk in the grocery department. She could then visit with her neighbours in the fabric department and finish off by admiring the display of fine armchairs, tables, beds, and wardrobes in the furnishings department. Sommers believed that good furniture that was locally produced in his shop without the costly freight rates from the East would sell well at fair prices. After store closing on Saturday evening, he slid the massive doors that separated the selling floor from the attached wood shop and personally supervised the placement of furniture in the showroom. Before dust had a chance to settle on the lacquered wood, the pieces were sold and delivered to the blocks of new houses springing up around the city.

Adrien arrived early on his first day of work. The shop was quiet and empty, and the floor swept clean of sawdust. As he sat and waited at the office, other men entered from the alley. Doors banged open, lunch pails clattered, and the low voices of men at the start of the workday filled the room. On the furthest outside wall, an immense woodcutting saw sputtered and trembled as it tightened large canvas straps and belts around pulleys and wheels. One of the operators, a man from Petit's shop, recognized Adrien and waved. When more men he knew from Saint-Boniface appeared, he relaxed and the tension that he felt in this new environment left his body.

A big man with his pants hitched high over a substantial belly and held up by suspenders walked around slowly, inspecting the shop. He walked stiffly; his feet seemed like they were made of wooden blocks, and he had the look of a man preoccupied with pain. Adrien approached him at one of the lathes in the centre aisle.

"*Monsieur* McMurtry …" he began and then stopped; he had promised himself not to use his native tongue in the shop. "Sir," he began again, "you told me to report for work today."

The foreman's brow wrinkled as he worked to remember him. "Ah, yes. Well, let's see what you can do." Four slender, curved chair legs were lying on the floor close by. He pointed to them. "Make one of those on that lathe."

A length of cherry wood lay in the cradle of the lathe. Adrien slid onto the stool, silently thanking his grandfather for teaching him how to carve with a lathe. His foot found the pedal and pumped forward and back, forward and back. The lathe turned slowly. His foot pumped faster. When the wood was spinning blindly, he leaned forward and touched the wood with his chisel. Fragments flew with a screech that increased with the pressure of the tool. The top curve of the leg appeared sleek like a horse's muscled shoulder. The chisel moved down, forming a slender leg that ended in a clawed foot curled over a ball. Adrien lifted his foot off the pedal. Sawdust whitened his black hair.

McMurtry nodded. He pointed to a vacant station. "That's yours. See if you can make three more of those."

Adrien was almost finished the next cabriole when he heard someone shouting at him from behind.

"Frenchy! Give a hand."

The pedal's rhythm kept steady.

The voice was now on top of him. "Hey, Frenchy! Didn't you hear me?"

Adrien didn't look up; the piece would be ruined if he stopped now. When he was finished carving the ball, his foot stopped, and he turned his head.

A small man in oversize grey coveralls stood behind him.

"My name's Adrien. Adrien Larence."

"And I'm Dennis, the assistant shop boss." He pointed at himself with his thumb. "Get out on the dock. They need help unloading."

Adrien shrugged and stood.

Dray wagons piled with skinned logs and pulled by teams of heavy horses waited in a line in the alley. He climbed onto the first one and helped slide the logs onto the loading dock. He didn't mind hard labour; it just didn't make sense to stop skilled work for it.

Adrien had just returned to his station and was placing the third piece of cherry wood into the cradle when the boss and his assistant walked by.

"Aren't you done those yet?" McMurtry asked.

Behind the foreman, Dennis smirked as if pleased with himself.

Adrien clamped his mouth shut, bent his head, and increased the speed of his lathe.

Adrien contributed more than his share to the stock of fine furniture sold on the other side of the wall. McMurtry was a master carpenter who demanded the best craftsmanship from his men, but he was always fair and had earned their respect. Adrien learned everything he could from him, but Dennis took pleasure in interrupting his work.

"*J'vais lui battre la merde,*" he said one day, sliding onto the bench for lunch with the other French-Canadians. He unwrapped the lunch that he had paid his landlady to make for him. The sandwiches were thick slices of pork with runs of fat topped with thinly sliced onion and heavily sprinkled with salt and pepper. The combination had repelled him at first, but he had grown fond of the taste.

The men laughed at the thought of Adrien beating the shit out of the assistant boss. "Better you get picked on than us."

Light lingered in the evening, and the brothels near the Hill mansion grew rowdy once again. Arthur-Joseph met Adrien sometimes for dinner after work in the long evenings. They strolled along the streets of ill repute, laughing when the women on the porches signalled them to come in. One time they encountered a parade of Salvation Army members marching down the street with placards decrying the social conditions in Winnipeg as the worst in North America. Arthur-Joseph pointed out two women passing by in the crowd. They were sisters and physicians who had recently opened a practice together for the treatment of women and children exclusively.

"Why only them?" Adrien wondered.

"It would be improper for them to treat men."

Adrien read what the crusading doctors had to say in the newspapers with relish, but he had no desire to frequent the houses.

CHAPTER 22

Spring 1884

Few people were out on the street as Adrien walked to work in the early hour, and the few that were walked quickly and kept their heads down, passing without seeing. Pools of melted snow dotted the street, pink glass that mirrored the morning sky. At the corner, milk bottles rattled as a horse-drawn delivery wagon plodded across the steel streetcar lines imbedded in the road. Adrien turned into the dark alley leading to the shop. Several men stood on the loading dock staring at a sheet of paper freshly nailed to the shop door. They wondered what it meant and stepped aside to make room for him.

Adrien's finger followed the print, stopping after every sentence to explain in French. "McMurtry's retiring … Trained persons can apply … Applications must be in English." The men looked at one another anxiously.

"It's his gout."

"I knew this was coming. He can hardly walk."

A young boy who ran errands in the shop piped up, "Will Dennis be the boss now?"

Someone grumbled, "With our luck. He's the next Anglo in line." They turned and entered the shop.

Adrien reread the notice. He could apply. The job should go to the best man. He looked around. The alley was deserted. He tore the paper notice from the nail and stuffed it inside his jacket.

Adrien chewed the stub of his pencil, crossed out, corrected, and redrafted the letter of application until his hand was numb. At last he was ready to write the final copy. He dipped his pen into the inkbottle. When he was done, he laid a blotting paper over the finished page to absorb any excess ink. When he was sure it was perfectly dry, he folded the page in three, ran his finger over the folds to sharpen them neatly, and dropped it into an envelope. Sommers would be impressed with this letter, he was certain.

Later that afternoon, Dennis threw his lunch-pail with a bang on the foreman's desk and glanced proprietarily over the workshop. He strutted from station to station down the centre aisle. At Adrien's lathe, he stopped and whispered in his ear. "Too bad about your application."

Adrien kept his head down, the pedal steady. "*Manges la marde,*" he said under his breath. He could imagine what had happened in Sommers' office that morning—Sommers opening the letter, glancing at the signature, and letting it flutter unread into the wastebasket by his desk.

CHAPTER 23

May 1884

Adrien opened his eyes to the pinpricks of light poking through the attic roof and smiled—the day stretched before him with nothing to do. He threw off the quilt, dressed quickly, and left without encountering his landlady. It was going to be a good day. He crossed the bridge to the boardwalk along the French boulevard. The wooden boards sprang comfortably under his step, the azure sky soared high and clear, a warm wind ruffled his dark hair, and the street was crowded with people strolling and luxuriating in the first truly warm day of spring. He heard snippets of conversations in French and stopped to listen, feeling the comfort of home. Arthur-Joseph hurried on the other side of the street with his heavy canvas book-bag on his shoulder. Adrien hopped off the boardwalk, dodged a horse and wagon in the street, and caught up with his friend. "Where are you going in such a hurry?"

"I'm going to the newspaper office. Julie Riel's going to visit her son in Montana, and I've offered to accompany her." Arthur-Joseph hoisted the bag higher on his shoulder and kept on walking. "Louis has been ill. He's forbidden her from taking the long journey, but she's going just the same. You know how mothers are."

Julie Riel was the youngest daughter of the first white woman in the West, Marie-Anne Gaboury, and her husband, Jean-Baptiste. Many of the old settlers were descendants of Marie-Anne and thus related in some way. The Larences weren't kin to the Riels, but Adrien considered Louis a hero who defended minority rights. When Macdonald had forced Riel into exile in the States instead of giving him his promised amnesty, Adrien had been outraged. "What's the news about Louis?"

"He's still teaching at St. Peter's mission. He and Marguerite had a girl last fall, Angélique, a sister to Jean. Louis became an American citizen last year."

Adrien stopped dead. "Why would he do that?"

"A cousin of his, André Nault, was attacked in North Dakota by Canadian soldiers who had illegally crossed the border. They beat him with their rifle butts until he was almost dead. To secure his own safety, Louis sought for and secured U.S. citizenship."

Adrien hurried to catch up with his friend.

"The Indians at the mission are poor, and Madame Riel is taking a wagon of food and clothing along to distribute to them." They turned left onto the street where *Le Métis* had its office. "Louis is returning to Canada. The federal government is surveying land into square lots along the South Saskatchewan, and the Métis fear losing their river lots like they did in Manitoba. The Métis have asked Louis to be their leader. He'll be going to Saskatchewan with his family at the end of the school term, and Julie's anxious to get on the road before Louis heads back north."

Walking into the newspaper office, Adrien saw that paper littered the floor and covered every flat space. He shook his head and wondered as he always did how the newspaper made it out to the street every week.

The monstrous printing press at the back completely filled the room, leaving just enough space to walk around it. Arthur-Joseph's father, his bum perched against a high stool, stood at the front of his press, setting metal letters on a narrow, silver tray. Metal shavings and ink gum covered the floor under his feet.

Arthur-Joseph threw his bag in the corner and went to stand by the stool. "*Pa*, Madame Riel's going to visit Louis in Montana. She's asked me to accompany her."

The father looked at his son out of the corner of his eye and stated flatly, "You've been pushing yourself on Madame Riel."

The son stepped closer. "*Non, Pa*," he insisted, his eyes wide with innocence. "She's glad to have me accompany her."

Adrien had approached too and stood on the other side of the stool. He bit his lips not to laugh at the earnestness of his friend.

The printer kept setting the tray; words were separated by metal spacers.

Arthur-Joseph insisted, "You'd go if you were me."

The printer sighed. "*Vas t'en*. And try not to be a nuisance."

Arthur-Joseph stepped away. Behind his father's back, he winked at Adrien and raised his arms like he had seen a triumphant boxer do after a successful match.

As they were about to leave the office, his father called from the press room, "Take some money out of the cash box in my desk. And make yourself useful while you're down there. Write something for the paper about Riel."

CHAPTER 24

June 1884

Justine looked out from her place on the stage beside four other young women. It was graduation day at last, and tomorrow Alexina would enter the convent. She smiled at her family in the third row. Hilaire and Zéphirin peered curiously at the crowd milling in the large hall while David kicked his feet waiting for the ceremony to start. Their faces had been scrubbed shiny, and their hair slicked down on either side of a sharp part. Alexina had Marie-Ange on her knee and was amusing the toddler with a length of thick string for a cat's cradle on her chubby fingers. Ti-Jos sat beside his parents near the centre of the aisle. At the far back in the last row, Justine saw her *Tante* Alice and *Oncle* Fernand.

The latecomers lined the side aisles when Monsieur Bernier, the superintendent in charge of Manitoba's French Catholic schools, walked to the podium. He congratulated the successful first graduates and made a point of welcoming the parents of the American girl beside Justine; students were coming up from the States to attend French schools in Saint-Boniface, which were known for their high standards and rigour.

Other dignitaries followed. Justine fanned her face with her program. Hot, humid air had lain oppressively on the city for weeks and though the tall windows on either side of the hall stood open, the packed room had become stiflingly hot. Bishop Taché had yet to speak, and Justine glanced nervously at Marie-Ange. Her neat ringlets had loosened from being passed from lap to lap, and her cheeks glowed alarmingly red.

Justine looked at the list on her program. The Bishop was next, thank God. She liked his speeches. He filled them with stories and characters from the early settlement. A pragmatic man, he was full of sound advice on living a holy life. However, he was notoriously long-winded, and it was getting hotter.

Bishop Taché rose. Joseph signalled to his oldest son, and Ti-Jos scooped the baby up. Marie-Ange's startled face looked back over her brother's shoulder as she was carried out.

Justine looked heavenward and mouthed, "Thank you, Lord."

Bishop Taché gripped the podium and looked out over the audience. "The Red River colony had 2000 souls when I came as a young priest 40 years ago. Half of them belonged to my parish. The population is ten times that now …"

After more than an hour, the graduates had practically melted on the stage, but Bishop Taché's brow showed no trace of sweat as he returned to his chair.

Justine's heart raced as *la Soeur Directrice* walked on stage with a box of rolled parchment tied with blue ribbon. When her name was called, she rose and went forward proudly for the certificate stamped with the official seal of Manitoba. She glanced at the audience. A wide smile stretched across Thérèse's face while Joseph wiped something from his cheeks.

Justine paused at the door and glanced one last time at the empty dormitory. The beds had been stripped, and thin, grey mattresses lay on the bare springs. Freshly washed and ironed white sheets lay at the foot of each bed, ready for September and the new class of *normaliennes*. How insecure and lonely she had been that first day, but also full of hope about Adrien. She shook her head and went downstairs.

The door to the principal's office was partially opened as she passed by. *Soeur Supérieur* was at her desk, her head bent over her work. All

Justine could see was the top of her veil. She stepped in, clearing her throat, "*Merci, ma soeur.*"

The nun put her pen down and looked up. A large crucifix dangled from a black cord around her neck. When she came to her feet, she grabbed the foot of the heavy cross to stop it hitting the desk. "*Félicitations,*" she said, coming around the desk to give Justine an abbreviated hug that didn't include much touching. "I'm told that you've secured the teaching position in Saint-Cère."

"Yes, it's the new rural school. I have all the grades to teach."

"Many are in the same situation in country schools. And as your sister, Alexina, is entering the convent down the street," the nun said, returning to her desk and picking up her pen, "we'll have the pleasure of meeting again."

Justine had been dismissed. "*Oui, ma soeur,*" she said, backing out.

As usual, the Bélangers stayed with Alice and Fernand. The small house overflowed with children when the two families gathered but, by laying the youngest crosswise four to a bed in the children's bedroom, eight could sleep there. The bigger boys had their own room, and Alexina and Justine joined their older cousins Yvonne and Irène in the other bedroom.

The date of Alexina's entrance into the convent had been chosen to coincide with Justine's graduation, and in everyone's opinion, it was an excellent reason to have a party. To get ready for it, they carried the dining-room table out and pushed the flocked red velvet chesterfield and chair set under the windows for the dance; neighbours could be relied upon for extra chairs. The large brown piano by the stairs belonged to Alice. She had learned to play while at the convent, and she played with gusto.

In the small room that the cousins shared, shoes littered the floor, half-open drawers revealed jumbled contents, and stockings and chemises lay on the bed. With her mouth full of pins, Justine stood before the dresser's oval mirror fixing her hair. When she was satisfied that the roll on the back of her head was smooth and securely pinned, she carefully lifted her purple Georgette dress from her valise and shook it out.

"*Ah, qu'elle est belle,*" Alexina exclaimed at the pretty party dress. "Let me help you put it on."

Justine raised her arms, and the ruffled dress slipped over her shoulders. The soft, full skirt swung round her legs, and she twirled, exhilarated by the playful luxury of the skirt.

Yvonne was brushing powdered rouge over her cheeks at the mirror. She finished off by touching the tip of her baby finger to the powder and dabbing it on her lips. "Here," she said, handing the rouge pot to Justine. "Try some. Do it lightly and no one will ever guess."

Justine followed her cousin's directions, and when she was done, cocked her head at the smiling reflection. The cheeks above the ruffle glowed, and the rouged lips suited the purple dress perfectly. "Alexina," she said, turning. "Try some."

Alexina shook her head vigorously.

She held the pot closer and teased. "Last chance before entering the convent."

Alexina wore her favourite blue dress with a white collar and matching buttons closed to the neck. The corners of her lips lifted. "I've no need of that."

Justine's heart constricted. Her sister's unblemished, rosy face glowed, and her thick brown hair glistened with health. So young. So pretty. Justine didn't resent her sister's vocation, but she feared that once inside the convent, Alexina would be lost to her forever.

Alexina squeezed her sister's arm. "When I get up in the morning, all I have to do is scrub my face and put on my veil and habit. I won't be bothered by makeup or what to wear to attract beaus."

Laughing voices drifted up the stairs, and the moment of sadness passed. Alexina turned. "I'll go down and welcome the guests while you finish dressing."

After a final look in the mirror, Justine followed her cousins down the steep stairs. She was glad to be with her pretty cousins and wasn't unaffected by the admiring glances that the trio attracted from the men assembled in the living room.

Adrien stood with Arthur-Joseph and a group of young men near the front door. He held a glass of yellowish liquid close to his friend's face to punctuate the points he was making. Alexina was paging through sheets of music at the piano as Alice twirled the round seat on the oak piano stool to adjust it to her own height when Justine joined them.

Alexina placed the sheets on the piano before her aunt. "Play this waltz by Johann Strauss, please."

Alice glanced at the music and pushed the sheets away. "I will, but later. If I play that now, they'll think they're at a concert and sit down." She pulled at her fingers and then spread them wide over the black and white keys and banged the first chord of a *galop*, a version of the polka that mimicked the gait of a horse.

Something brushed against her skirt, and Justine turned to find Adrien beside her. His eyes danced, and his full lips stretched into a broad smile.

She caught a whiff of something sour and fanned the air in front of her face. "Phew!' she said wrinkling her nose. "You've started early."

"Nothing wrong with that," he said. He leaned in. "Before you scold me more, I want to tell you how pretty you look in that dress."

Delight flashed through her, and she turned her head away to hide her blush.

He stumbled against her, and her hand went out to the piano to steady herself and him. She shook him off, and without a backward glance, she walked over and asked her brother Ti-Jos, who was sitting on the stairs with some other young men, to dance.

Every chair in the house was in use. Elderly couples sat at the edges, watching the dancers and tapping their feet to the music, while others stood to visit and laugh. Justine was not allowed to sit down; as one of the guests of honour, a constant line of men wanted to dance with her. Just when she thought the music couldn't be finer, and she couldn't be happier, a Michif, a Métis neighbour, slipped in through the kitchen with a fiddle and bow. A big-shouldered man with a hairless face, he wore a wool vest open over a white shirt without a collar. Metal armbands circled around thick upper arms held his shirtsleeves in place. Justine clapped her hands when she saw him, and an expectant hush fell over the party as the dancers moved out of the way to let him get to the piano. He nodded at Alice, and then cocking his head to her piano, tightened and loosened the tuners until his notes matched hers.

Spoiled Heritage

One last nod, then his bow touched his strings confidently, and the notes to "The Red River Jig" filled the room. An old man with a full beard rose out of his chair and wobbled to the centre of the room. His feet tapped the floor, and the sound of flying hooves filled the room with each toe-tap. The Michif knew him. He smiled and challenged the dancer with a slight increase of tempo. The *gigueur* breathed harder and sweat beaded his forehead. When he stumbled and fell out of step, a younger dancer jumped in with more intricate steps. The bow went faster. The jigger danced alone until another dancer faced him, challenging him with more foot patterns. The second man fell out. One man, dripping in sweat and stepping wildly, tapped alone now against the fiddler's flying bow. Justine's hands grew red and hot from clapping the time. The fiddler gave one final flourish and bowed to the dancer. A tie! Arms flew up as the crowd laughed and cheered their agreement.

Alice stood up. "*J'ai besoin d'un coup,*" she said, joining the men outside on the veranda for a drink.

The heat of the day continued oppressively as the evening wore on, and the house became unbearably hot—a situation worsened by cigarette smoke. Alexina and Justine joined Arthur-Joseph and Adrien and other young people on the sidewalk by a lilac hedge that perfumed the night with the sweet scent of its purple flowers. The deep, full-throated croak of frogs on the muddy banks of the river could be heard a block away.

"Let's go down to the river," Arthur-Joseph suggested.

The sisters set off, arm in arm and stepping in unison. Adrien followed with his friend.

They all stopped on the ridge and stared down at the steep bank that fell to the water.

"There's an easy path down," Arthur-Joseph said. "We use it all the time to go swimming." He pointed to the right. A barely discernable path opened in a break of the underbrush. He disappeared down into the brush, calling to his friends to follow.

Alexina pulled her arm away from Justine. "I'd better not."

"But this is your last chance to have fun," Justine protested.

"*Ma'an* might need my help." Alexina shook her head firmly. "I'm going back."

The moon had bathed the escarpment in white light. It laid a swath of silver on the dark, slow-moving water. Justine sighed and turned to go with her sister.

"I'll walk you to the house," Adrien offered.

"Don't be silly," Alexina said to her sister. "I'll be all right. You go on without me. I don't want to ruin your evening."

Justine and Adrien exchanged glances, and then they turned together towards the river. At the top of the bank, he took her hand to help her down the clay path that was greasy from a late afternoon rain.

The escarpment split in two where the path turned left to form a small clearing, and they stopped to look across the slow-moving water at the city. Most of the streets on the English side of the river were dark, but a faint light reflected in the sky from the newly installed gaslights on Main Street.

Adrien broke the silence. "I deserved to get that promotion. I was cheated, but next time it'll be different. My work is being noticed at Sommers."

"For your sake, I hope you're right. But I don't think that'll ever happen. Not with the English."

The moon patterned Justine's face with shadows of light and turned her dress to cream. A frizz of hair had escaped from the tight chignon as she danced and curled at her neck and forehead.

He turned her suddenly, caught her by the arms, and pulled her to him. Bending his head, he crushed her mouth with his lips. The faint, sour smell and cruelty of the kiss disgusted Justine. When he released her, her arm went back, her hand went up, and she slapped his face.

He blinked in surprise, and then he grabbed her and kissed her again, only harder.

Justine struggled to free her face, but then realized that her struggles were only enflaming him, and she went still in his arms. The moment she stopped struggling, he let her go. The soft skin around her mouth burned from his beard. The ruffle on her dress was torn.

He shook his head as if coming to his senses. "Forgive me. I'm not myself."

Tears filled Justine's eyes. She turned and ran back up the escarpment.

Cigarettes glowed in the dark of the veranda as people cooled off outside. Justine skirted the house. Through the dining room and living room windows, dancers spun and twirled. In the kitchen, Alexina and Thérèse piled sandwiches on trays. She put her finger to her lips and motioned to her sister to follow her, and they crept up the back stairs to their cousins' bedroom.

When the door was firmly closed, Alexina exclaimed at her sister's tear-stained and swollen face. "What on earth? What happened?" She pointed to the torn ruffle. "Did Adrien do that?"

Justine fingers went to her throat. The torn ruffle trailed down the front of her dress. "He … he must have. I never noticed."

Alexina whirled around and put her hand on the doorknob. "I'm going to tell *Pa* and Ti-Jos. They won't stand for this."

Justine put her hands up. "*Non!* I don't want hard feelings."

"Did he do anything else?"

"No!"

"What happened?"

Justine's eyes filled with tears. Her throat closed, and she was unable to describe the scene above the river.

Alexina searched her face. "Are you sure nothing happened?"

Justine willed herself to breathe slowly. She didn't want to burden her sister on the eve of entering the convent. "Maybe I overreacted."

Alexina's eyebrow lifted sceptically, but she turned from the door. "Let me get you out of this dress."

Justine let her sister undo the buttons on the back of the dress and slide it gently off her shoulders.

"Step out of it," Alexina said. She kicked the dress away from Justine's feet. "I'll get undressed too."

Alexina's rosary lay in its velvet pouch on the dresser. When they were both ready for bed, she pulled out the beads. "We'll say the rosary together," she said climbing into bed and pushing over to the wall. "I'll lead," she said putting her finger and thumb of the right hand on the first bead. "You answer." They were on the last decade when the floor squeaked outside their door. They fell silent and still.

Yvonne tiptoed into the room. "Sh!" she whispered to Irène. "They're asleep."

There was the sound of undressing, and the bed on the opposite wall creaked. Alexina relaxed beside her, and quiet, regular breathing filled the room as Justine stared into the night.

Justine woke to find her cousins gone and her sister dressed and brushing her hair at the dresser. "I must have slept in. Is everybody up?"

Alexina nodded and kept running the brush through the long strands of silky hair. From below came the smell of charred toast and coffee.

"Do you have everything?" Justine asked, swinging her feet to the floor.

A small case lay open on the floor by Alexina's feet. On the top lay a framed black and white photo of the family staring stiffly at the camera, and beside it, was the white first-communion prayer book that her godparents had given her. On its pearlescent cover, a little girl in a white veil gazed adoringly at a chalice and host. Alexina handed the hairbrush to her sister. "Here, I give this to you. It's my parting gift."

Justine accepted it sadly. Alexina's hair would be cut short today. Long hair was a nuisance under a veil.

Alexina snapped the case shut. "If you're coming, you'd better hurry."

Justine sprang to her feet.

Everyone was on the street for the final goodbye. Alexina received the hugs and well wishes of Alice and Fernand's family first, reserving the hard leave-taking from her younger brothers and sisters for the last. She kissed Hilaire, Zéphirin, and David in turn. "Be good and remember to say your prayers," she admonished teasingly. Ti-Jos had Marie-Ange on his hip. She kissed his cheek and warned, "Take care when you're out hunting." Marie-Ange's big, brown eyes watched the proceeding curiously as she sucked her thumb. Alexina took her up into her arms, hid her face in the baby's neck, and inhaled her baby scent for a long moment.

Spoiled Heritage

Joseph cleared his throat. "We'd better be going."

He opened the gate and let his wife and daughters into the yard with the white picket fence. At the door, he lifted the heavy knocker and let it fall loudly against the plate. A spider appeared from under the whitewashed clapboards and traipsed delicately across on long legs. A red-faced nun in a tight wimple opened the door and greeted them. She nodded politely and led them to the parlour. Nothing had changed since Alexina's interview two years ago. The chairs were in the exact same groupings of three and four, and the brown unaccommodating and overstuffed settee still occupied one corner. The delicious aroma of chicken soup wafted from the kitchen at the back.

Alexina gripped her mother's hands as they sat together on the settee while Justine and Joseph sat on chairs flanking it on either side.

The occasion was mixed with joy and sorrow for the Bélangers. The Church exhorted parents to encourage vocations in their children. Thérèse and Joseph had prayed for the honour of giving a child to the Church, but today they were relinquishing their precious daughter. Alexina would spend her first month as a postulant in a silent retreat—a trench of time that would mark her separation from the world and entrance into the spiritual life. Thereafter, she would only visit her parents accompanied by another nun and would only communicate with them with her superior's permission.

Alexina kept smiling reassuringly at her parents as they breathed in the silence of the convent. A glow of serenity suffused her face. Thérèse and Joseph smiled back tentatively. This was their destiny.

Justine sat lost in her own thoughts. She couldn't stop reliving the scene on the escarpment above the river. 'That was the last straw,' she thought. 'It was frightening what he did.'

CHAPTER 25

Early October 1884

"The new convent school in town is too far for the farm children," *Père* had said during his homily one Sunday after Christmas. "They need a rural school that they can walk to all year. There will be a meeting of all taxpayers following today's mass."

His idea was not universally accepted.

"The taxes will rise."

"Why should we pay for a school? We don't have children."

"I can't read or write, and I live all the same. My children will do no worse than me."

Père reminded them that since the taxes were divided equitably between French Catholics and English Protestants, the salary of the teacher and the operation of the school would be paid by the government. When he reminded them that ignorance was the agent of Satan, Rosario's father offered to donate the land, and a show of hands carried the motion. The school would be built in the middle of a catchment area of five miles—a distance deemed reasonable for children to walk or ride.

With a confidence bred by youthful ignorance, Justine became the teacher, principal, and janitor of the small one-room school. The day began with the *Notre Père*, followed by a half-hour of catechism. The texts and her manuals came from Québec, and the two shelves of library books held French classics. The last half-hour of the day was devoted to the teaching of English.

The Normands had offered Justine a room, but she thought she'd better not. It would be awkward with Rosario. Besides, she had always felt uncomfortable in that house. Rose Normand enjoyed her reputation as a spotless housekeeper, and Justine was used to a house that was clean but tossed. She felt ill at ease without books, papers, and toys lying about. Rosario had coaxed and argued, but she could not be persuaded. She made living arrangements with a farm family by the name of Poirier and walked to school with their children.

Every subject in grades one to nine was hers to teach. She taught one grade while the others worked on their assignments, and by combining classes wherever possible, she made it through her hectic days. The large desks at the back of the room for the older boys would remain empty until after they finished helping with the harvest. They would return when the snow fell. She hoped they would like her and not make trouble.

Late one evening, Justine prepared for bed and realized that she hadn't thought of the scene with Adrien once during the day. She leapt into bed and fell immediately into an exhausted, peaceful sleep.

One afternoon in late fall, long after the children had been sent home, Justine sat at her desk before a pile of open scribblers. A movement in the window on her right made her turn her head. A horse and rider cantered down the hill towards the school. It was Rosario in his usual stained, broad-brimmed, brown hat riding over to make sure that the stove had a supply of chopped wood and the crock was full of water.

She bent her head and scribbled faster. The canter of hooves ceased, followed by the creaking of leather. Boot heels struck against the wooden steps of the school.

Rosario marched between the rows of double desks. Justine was still correcting when he slid her chair away from her desk with her in it. "Come on! You've worked long enough for one day. Let's walk to the river. It might be the last warm day, and I have something to show you."

The sun was low on the west horizon as they crossed the deserted schoolyard, which was silent now that the summer birds had gone and the insects had died off. Justine told him she had finally got the little boys to stop peeing in the bushes and use the outhouse. Rosario chuckled. All farm boys did that. They walked through dead and dusty summer grass that sent seed umbrellas floating in the still air. Seed hitchhikers hooked their sharp spines to her skirt and caught a ride. At the end of the yard, clusters of orange rose hips drooped from spent rose bushes. Rosario grabbed a handful and offered her some.

Justine scrunched up her nose. "They're too sour. They're better in tea."

"They're not that bad," he said, biting one of the bottle-shaped pods. He spit it out.

"I warned you."

It was cooler when they entered the woods. They followed a meandering trail used by wild animals to the little river that flowed behind the Normand farm. A tree had fallen across their path. Rosario scrambled over it and held out his hand to her. "Here, let me help you."

Justine shook her head and struggled over it on her own. "I can do it."

"*Tête de caboche!*" he laughed, calling her a stubborn cabbage head.

They came out of the shady trees into an open space that had been recently cleared. The glistening river, shrunken in the summer heat, flowed quietly on one side while tall oaks and silver larch marked the boundary of the clearing. The autumn light cast the whole in orange and gold, and the sweet smell of freshly logged trees scented the air.

"*Ma foi! Que c'est beau,*" Justine exclaimed at the beauty.

Rosario flung out his arms. "I'm going to build my house here this winter. Come, and I'll tell you all about it."

He led her to a stripped log and made her sit. Taking giant steps, he paced out a large square, and then he faced the southeast and stretched as wide as he could. "Here will be the kitchen with windows to catch the morning sun." He turned to face her then whipped off his hat and sent it flying at her feet. His eyes twinkled and an eyebrow rose mischievously, as if he waited for her approbation.

Justine sat in a shaft of light. The sun burned the cross where it touched the skin under her blouse. Without thinking, she pulled it out and let it dangle from her collar. She looked up.

The sun touched the gold in his brown hair. He was as tall as Adrien but more slender in the hips. Any woman would be lucky to be his wife ... blessed. His roots were imbedded in Manitoba's soil, intertwined with the culture of French in Saint-Cère and the faith of their parish. So different from a life of an ambitious dreamer. Rosario's wife would be secure—and loved.

Decency showed in his eyes and humour in the deeply tanned laugh lines around Rosario's eyes as he approached. He pulled gently on the fragile chain and dragged Justine with it. She closed her eyes and inhaled. His shirt smelled of the sun. The hands that held her face were calloused and rough as he kissed her. Then he lifted Justine off her feet and twirled her round and round until she closed her eyes against the whirling trees. A startled squirrel chirruped angrily at them and raced away, leaping from branch to branch until it was lost in the trees.

CHAPTER 26

Mid October 1884

Justine luxuriated in the last touch of autumn as she went in and out of the shadows cast by the trees that lined the road to the village. Specks floated in the sunbeams scented with the sweet remnants of summer grasses and harvested grain. At her *Oncle* Armand's blacksmith shop, she visited with her *Tante* Lucie until Joseph's wagon appeared to take her the rest of the way home for the weekend.

Thérèse and Lucie's children visited freely, and the Bélanger wagon often returned with Justine's sixteen-year-old cousin, Rosalie, as it did this time. Justine remembered Rosalie's large eyes, fringed with thick eyelashes, peeking shyly over the top of the table. With white skin and black curls, Rosalie had grown to be as pretty as her mother and aunt.

Ti-Jos was Rosalie's favourite. She especially liked how he looked after animals. In the spring, he bottle-fed orphan calves until they could stand splay-legged over a pail and slurp the creamy milk. At lambing time when sudden spring storms dumped heavy snow, he rescued the cold, wet lambs and brought them to the kitchen. There he would dry them with towels before laying them on the open oven door to get warm. He even took on the runt of the pig litter, even though Joseph warned that it wouldn't work and wouldn't pay. The piglet lived, but it never thrived and was more work than what it was worth. In the barn, he took care not to step on the kittens that mewled and got tangled under his feet while milking. And when he hunted, he was careful to kill with one shot.

Rosalie was stepping into her boots, and Thérèse was ladling steaming porridge into Marie-Ange's bowl when Justine came into the kitchen the next morning. The Bélangers had been successful in their family planning, and no other babies had followed Marie-Ange. The iron crib had been dismantled and put away in the hay shed, and the tray removed on the high chair. The chair fit under the table so that Marie-Ange could eat with the grown ups.

As soon as Thérèse turned away, Marie-Ange dipped her spoon into the sugar bowl and dumped a heaping spoonful of brown over her porridge. She was going for more when her mother saw her. "*Arrêtes donc!*" Thérèse exclaimed, catching Marie-Ange's hand in mid-air and forcing her to dump the sugar back into the bowl.

"Are you going to the barn, Rosalie?" Justine asked. "I'll go with you." She slipped on her mother's brown chore jacket and her rubber boots.

A lantern dangled on a cross-beam halfway up the centre alley of the barn, casting a circle of light in the gloomy dark. Black and white cows hung their heads over mangers, munching contentedly on fresh hay. Justine followed Rosalie down the middle of the alley, careful to keep away from the tails and the sudden eruptions to which cows are prone.

Ti-Jos was with the first cow in the furthest stall. Rosalie poured a thimble of bleach into a pail of water nearby, took a cloth off a hook, and dipped it. She wrung it out and handed it to him. He stooped and ran the cloth over the cow's bag and down each teat. When the udder was clean, Ti-Jos feigned throwing the cloth at his sister.

Justine jumped back. He chuckled, and the rag splashed into the pail of disinfectant instead. A milking stool with a slot big enough for a hand cut out of the seat stood at the side of the stall. He toed it closer, placed a clean pail under the cow's bag, and sat. He pressed his head against the cow. White jets pinged into the bottom of the pail. The barn cats moved in, rubbing wantonly against his legs. Ti-Jos whistled through his teeth. The cats looked up expectantly and a spray of hot milk splashed against their faces and on their paws.

Justine stepped closer to watch them lick milk off their whiskers and fur. A jet of white landed on her boot. *"Tannant,"* she said and retreated. Her brother always teased. Laughter followed her as she left to feed the chickens for her mother.

That evening, Ti-Jos and Rosalie sat side by side on the bench behind the kitchen table, staring at their plates. Thickly sliced fresh bread sat on a plate beside a bowl of pale butter and a tall pitcher of milk. Justine and Thérèse carried the fried potatoes and buttered carrots to the table and then set a platter filled with pork chops in front of Joseph.

Justine tried to tie a bib around Marie-Ange's neck, but the toddler screamed and tore it off. *"Ma p'tite têtue,"* she said, tussling her hair—her little sister could be so pigheaded.

Joseph helped himself to the meat. All the plates passed first to him in an orderly manner, and then the boys dove to help themselves.

Thérèse checked the table. "Is there anything else before I sit down?"

The plates before the young couple remained empty.

"Qu'est-ce-qu'il y a? Why aren't you eating? Is something wrong?"

Rosalie's cheeks flamed against her white porcelain skin. Her brown eyes fringed with thick eyelashes grew enormous.

Ti-Jos' back came off the wall. "We want to get married."

Thérèse slowly sank down. A piece of potato caught in the tines of Joseph's fork hovered before his mouth. Zéphirin and David sensed that something was wrong and giggled nervously while Hilaire watched, silent and curious.

"Taisez-vous," Thérèse scolded.

A note in their mother's voice warned them. They shushed.

Thérèse looked at Joseph. *"Mère de Dieu!* Tell them it's impossible."

Joseph lowered his fork gently to his plate. His eyebrows moved together as he searched for the right words. "You know why brothers and sisters are kept apart in the herd. Blood relations must not breed. The offspring could be deformed."

The blood drained from Ti-Jos' face, but he repeated stubbornly, "We want to get married."

Justine's heart ached—her brother hated confrontation.

Thérèse's shoulders slumped. "It's forbidden by the Church."

Ti-Jos legs shook uncontrollably, vibrating the table.

Justine stuck her cold hands under her legs. Why hadn't they seen this coming?

Joseph nodded at Hilaire. "Take the mare and fetch your *tante* and *oncle*. Get them to bring *Père* Bertrand. And don't say a word to anyone. The people in town don't need to know our *affaires*."

Thérèse and Justine were shovelling the cold food from the ruined meal into the slop pail for the pigs when Lucie and Armand entered the kitchen with *Père*. Thérèse glanced at the boys, "Take Marie-Ange upstairs."

Ti-Jos and Rosalie hadn't moved off the bench.

"*Bonsoir, Père*," Joseph said rising hurriedly to pull out a chair.

The presence of a priest in a Catholic home was usually a grand occasion. *Père's* parish visit in the spring called for the dusting of pictures, mantles, clocks, and vases and the washing of walls and every dish in the house. Today was different. Thérèse forgot the stained apron round her waist, and Joseph was in his work socks with a red knit row at the top.

Lucie raised a questioning eyebrow towards her sister as she and Armand found chairs, but Thérèse just shook her head helplessly and came to sit by Justine.

Joseph began bluntly without his usual charm. "*Père*, Ti-Jos and Rosalie want to get married. Tell them what the Church says about marriage between first cousins."

Hilaire's knock had interrupted the dinner at the rectory, and crumbs still lodged between the buttons of the priest's *soutane*. He brushed at them before beginning. "Your mothers are sisters, I understand. Do you know what that means?"

Ti-Jos' heels tapped the floor under the table, but he met the priest's gaze. "Yes."

"Consanguinity is forbidden in marriage. The offspring of such unions can be deformed or mentally arrested. Do you want that for your children?"

Ti-Jos chin went up. "We won't have children."

"Birth control is a mortal sin."

Thérèse and Joseph exchanged a glance.

'Birth control?' Justine wondered. Was there such a thing? How was it done?

Rosalie's cheeks flamed hotter, and she slid down a little on the bench.

"The marriage of first cousins is expressly banned by the Church. You would be excommunicated."

Justine stopped breathing. Excommunication meant more than simple exclusion from the sacraments—it meant damnation and hell.

Rosalie began to weep softly.

Ti-Jos turned his head and looked at her for a long moment. He let go her hand and went to stand in the middle of the kitchen.

Justine yearned to comfort him; he looked so defeated—so broken. She didn't move. The Church was right. First cousins couldn't marry.

"*Voyons, mes enfants*," the priest said raising his hands in a conciliatory way. "No more of this foolishness. You're young; there will be other loves. Ask for God's help in this. Now let me bless you."

Armand and Lucie stood and Justine went to stand with her parents by Ti-Jos. Rosalie hung her head and remained on the bench, silently weeping. *Père* raised his right hand and extended his two fingers. It was the signal to kneel and everyone did except for the big boy in the centre of the kitchen. Ti-Jos kept standing until Joseph tugged at his arm and pulled him to his knees.

CHAPTER 27

Late October 1884

The sun had strength at midday, but it set earlier and like a miser dragged the heat of the day with it. The cycle of insects was thankfully over except for a few drowsy flies that crawled out of the cracks. Overhead, the harsh, throaty honks of geese broke the quiet as they formed and reformed their Vs, taking their turn at the front as leader. On the congested street in the city, Adrien heard their call, gazed up at the long uneven strings, and longed to be home.

Justine stretched and sat for a moment enjoying the few minutes at the end of the day when her classroom was clean, orderly, and empty. The littlest girls helped her keep the classroom clean. They loved their teacher, were eager to help, and ignored the sneers of the older girls for whom the appeal of cleaning the classroom had long gone. The four rows of desks sat on iron bases that were screwed onto long wooden boards beneath. Her two little helpers had raced around lifting the hinged seats out of the way before running the mop beneath. They erased the blackboard and then went outside to bang the chalk out of the brushes. Justine warned them not to get their clothes dirty, but they returned covered in white chalk dust and looking like ghosts. She had brushed them off and sent them home.

Justine worked at her desk until her gnawing stomach told her that it was getting late. She glanced at the clock next to the school's new map of Canada. The vast area east of Manitoba called the North West Territories was an empty grey blot until it met the blue of the Arctic Ocean and the green of British Columbia. She secured the buckles on her book satchel and slipped into her new coat, pausing to run her fingers over the luxuriously soft woollen fabric. The first thing she had bought with her initial pay was a bag of hard candy for her brothers and sister. The rest she had spent on this dark green coat that fastened with large bone buttons. It was more than she could sensibly afford, but the green was the green of junipers colouring the British Columbia forest on the map, and she couldn't resist.

The day had been miserably wet and cold. The rain had finally stopped, but heavy, grey clouds hung overhead, pressing against the earth. Justine listened for the click of the latch before descending the wet, slippery steps. She was halfway across the field when she heard the explosion of guns in the woods. A frantic doe burst from the brush and raced across the schoolyard. With a graceful leap, it bounded into the trees on the other side and disappeared. From where the deer had fled, another volley of gunfire exploded. The deer had been chased towards rifles that waited for her in the brush. Justine had no doubt that the deer was dead—the men were all good shots and the hunt was absolutely necessary—but Justine's heart ached for the graceful, terrified animal.

Four horses with riders trotted out of the brush. They caught sight of her and lowered their rifles. The man in the lead slid his gun into its sheath on the saddle and trotted towards her. "*Allez!*" he yelled back at the others. "*On s'verra à la cabane.*" They would meet at the shack.

Justine recognized the stallion. The reddish-brown coat, the wide hooves, and short, powerful legs were unmistakable. "*Bien non!*" she muttered, marching on.

Adrien had pulled his slouch hat well down over his ears, and the brim drooped wetly as he rode towards her. His buckskin jacket was the colour of wet leaves and had a leather fringe on the sleeves and shoulders that streamed behind as he rode. He kicked his heels into his horse's belly, urging him on, and then he stood in the stirrups before dismounting on the run. He laughed and landed on his boots in front of her.

The cold had reddened the skin under his beard, and his light blue eyes had turned as grey as the sky. Justine thought of the dress with the torn ruffle at the back of her closet at home. "Always the show off," she said and stepped around him.

He reached for her satchel. "I'll walk you home."

Her fingers tightened on the handle. Then she remembered that she was a teacher and this was the yard where her students played. She was too old to play tug-of-war. She let go of the satchel and began walking.

Adrien grinned and fell in beside her companionably. "*Ma'an* told me you were teaching at the new country school and boarding at the Poiriers. What will you do when it snows?"

The stallion's head went down, and he plodded behind.

"When the weather's good, I walk with the children. *Monsieur* Poirier says I can take the horse and buggy when it turns cold."

They left the yard and took a path skirting a pasture fenced with rough-cut poles. Red cows with white faces and almost grown calves raised their heads to stare at them. All at once, they took a notion to be frightened and turned and stampeded away.

Adrien laughed, "Crazy animals."

Justine nodded with a smile.

Several dogs barked but didn't come closer as they passed the hill dominated by the Normand farm.

"I've been promoted," Adrien said. "I'm a carver now. I'll be foreman soon."

Justine thought he was too young, but she didn't want to argue. "That's good."

Poiriers' hip-roofed barn appeared through the trees, followed by wooden sheds and granaries that were unpainted. A yellow, two-storey house with a veranda around it stood beyond. A barbwire fence that deterred the cows while allowing the chickens to peck and grub around the house squared the yard.

They stopped at the crooked gate of willow poles that held the wire for the fence. The white Normand house could be seen through the leafless trees. Adrien nodded to it with his head. "That's a pretty farm." His eyes twinkled as he added, "And close to the school too."

Justine thought of Rosario and his kiss in the clearing. It was the happiest she had been in months. She took her satchel out his hands and pushed open the gate. "I'll thank you to mind your own business. You have no right to tell me what to do." The chickens that had been pecking the ground quietly near the gate flew up hysterically when she wrenched it open, but then calmly returned to pecking around her feet. "Get away," she said crossly, giving them a kick. She climbed resolutely to the house.

He watched until the door closed and then mounted. A few white flakes popped like corn in the frigid air. He lifted his collar and turned the stallion towards the trees.

Adrien's promotion to wood carver had an unexpected and pleasant outcome. When Dennis saw tiny birds appearing around the swirling eyes of Birdseye Maple in Adrien's hands, he stopped interrupting his work. But the taunts continued.

One day, Adrien saw Dennis talking to a new man at a station. The bib of the foreman's baggy, loose coverall dangled near the spinning wheel.

Dennis caught him watching. "What are you looking at, Frenchy?"

Adrien dropped his eyes. The meadowlark in his hand was almost done.

At the back of the workshop, the steam engine puffed and trembled as it powered the saw to a high whine as it sliced into the wood. The men in the shop were accustomed to the whining crescendo followed by a moment of quiet before the whine took up again; they had learned to shut their ears to it. Adrien was intent on etching the black stripe on the bird when he detected a hesitation in the steam engine's rhythmic chuffing. A shriek was followed by a heart-stopping scream and then a screech as the saw shuddered and stopped. Every head went up. Every hand froze. The shop grew eerily silent. Then came horrified shouting.

Adrien ran to the back. Dennis lay partially under the saw in the sawdust. His eyes were closed in a face that was slowly turning grey. Tendons hung like strips of white rubber and torn muscle showed at the gaping hole where his shoulder used to be. Adrien tore his eyes away and looked up. Flesh mixed with grease on the overhanging chains, and here and there, strips of blue denim fluttered like flags. The belts and chains had caught Dennis' coverall, whipped it into a twisted rope, and pulled his arm into the whirling belts and pulleys. The saw operator's quick reaction had saved Dennis' life. He had thrown a timber between the whirling belts and chains to stop his machine. The blood was spreading, slowly turning the sawdust red. Adrien tore off his shirt, bunched it into a ball, and stuffed it into the pulsing wound.

Adrien walked past the saw on his way to meet Sommers two days later. The sawdust was gone, and the saw lay in pieces on the floor. Except for the stain that could have been anything on the canvas belt, there were no remnants of the accident.

Sommers sat at Dennis' desk holding a flat, scarred, yellow pencil that had been crudely sharpened with a knife.

"You asked for me, *monsieur*?"

"That was a terrible accident. Terrible."

"Yes."

Sommers dug his nail into the pencil's soft wood then looked up. "How old are you?"

"Thirty," Adrien lied.

"Dennis has to be replaced. Do you think you could handle running the shop for a month?"

Adrien's heart beat wildly, but he forced his face to remain calm. "You won't regret this, *patron*."

Sommers threw the pencil down and stood. "You may as well clean the stuff out of this desk. Dennis won't be back."

When the last man left the shop, Adrien hauled a cardboard box to Dennis' desk. Under old receipts, crumbs, and sawdust, he found a small wood level. A bubble floated in a tube of yellow liquid. He played with it, sliding the bubble to the right and left until, holding it perfectly horizontal, it floated in place between two vertical black lines at the middle. He put it on the desk and emptied the remaining stuff into the box.

A month later, Adrien climbed to the office mezzanine overlooking the store with a sheet of paper covered with columns and figures. The shop had been profitable during his time as foreman, and he had the numbers to prove it.

Sommers sat at his desk, speaking to a man in a dark waistcoat, who had his back to the open door when Adrien knocked. "*Excusez-moi, patron*, but you asked for this."

"Put the report on my desk. I'll deal with it later."

The man in the waistcoat turned, and Adrien recognized him. "Good day, Mr. Hill."

Hill nodded, staring silently as Adrien went across the room to hand in his report.

The rain had turned to sleet overnight. Muck clung to his boots on his walk to work the next day, and the first flakes of winter melted on his face as he turned into the dark alley behind the shop. Ahead, men milled about on the loading dock. Adrien began to run. He rushed up the stairs and pushed his way through. A heavy, iron padlock had appeared overnight, locking the door. An announcement with a list of names had been nailed to the wood beside. "*Qu'est-ce-que ça dit?*" his men wanted to know. "Why are we locked out?"

Adrien read aloud. "It says there's no work. The men listed are being let go."

"Lumber is stacked to the ceiling."

"The carpenters can't keep up with the orders. There's plenty of work …"

"It doesn't make sense!"

Adrien's finger followed the list. "Bethelette … Larence … Massicotte … It's the French who are being sacked."

The men roared. They rushed forward, attacking the padlock and door with their hands and feet. Spent, they left the alley in twos and threes under the falling snow and crossed the bridge to Saint-Boniface.

A hotel with rooms to rent above the tavern occupied the southeast corner of the street near the bridge. The sign had been turned to "Closed" and the curtains drawn as they passed by. "Tourond will let us in," Adrien said, leading the men round to the back where the hotelkeeper lived. "He never refuses a paying customer."

They banged on the scuffed door. "Open up."

A window with a curtain on a string occupied the top-half of the door. A hairy wrist pulled the curtain aside. The door opened a crack, and the innkeeper appeared. A long flap of hair that he combed over his bald head from ear to ear stood up at the back of his head. Long slender fingers patted it back in place, and he let them in. Stale beer and tobacco smoke hit Adrien as he followed the innkeeper through to the bar. Scrawny ankles flashed white above sloppy shoes as the innkeeper lifted the hinged counter and slipped behind the bar. At the front of the tavern, light made its way weakly through top windowpanes that hadn't been washed in years.

The men sat at a counter dotted with sticky rings of liquor. A thumbed copy of the *Winnipeg Free Press* lay in a disordered pile under the mirror at the corner of the bar. Letters blazed in black on the front page announcing the arrival of workers from Britain and Ontario. Adrien pointed to it and saluted with his glass.

Glass crunched under Adrien's boots in the alley the next day when he returned to pick up his pay. Every window in the shop had been smashed during the night.

CHAPTER 28

Early November 1884

As winter took hold, Justine's visits home became less frequent, and Ti-Jos' melancholy over the situation with Rosalie deepened.

He's quit school and spends all his time alone in the woods, Thérèse wrote to Justine. *I'm so worried.* After receiving this letter, Justine vowed to return home soon.

In late November, Justine prepared an afternoon of candy making in the school for the *fête de la Sainte-Catherine*. In ancient times, Paris churches displayed Saint Catherine's statue on the feast of old maids—single women who were older than twenty. They wore paper bonnets and placed a wreath on the statue's head. In New France, the foundress of the first religious order in Canada, Marguerite Bourgeoys, made molasses toffee on the saint's feast day to attract First Nations girls to her schools, and the tradition continued. Justine buttered her hands and pulled the toffee until it changed from gold to white. Then her students cut the rope into pieces that were wrapped in small squares of wax paper and were twisted shut at both ends.

Toffee was Ti-Jos' favourite, and Justine brought some home on her next visit the following weekend. "Have some," she coaxed when he returned from the barn. He shook his head and shrugged. His jacket hung loosely from his shoulders. It had stretched the seams across his back in the summer. Instead, he took his gun from the corner by the door. "There are deer tracks in the yard. I'll see if I can get one."

Justine had watched him from the kitchen window. He walked slowly towards the trees at the back of the yard with his head down. He entered the woods and was lost from sight. Justine had mentioned it to her mother. "He seems so unhappy."

"He'll feel better in the spring," Thérèse replied firmly.

By late Sunday afternoon, Ti-Jos hadn't returned, and Justine was forced to leave without saying goodbye to him. Her parents didn't seem overly concerned. It was the way of hunters to absent themselves for a while. They reappeared with fresh meat and skins when they needed clean clothes and some society. There was no need for worry.

Justine couldn't get her brother out of her mind. She thought of him when she woke and at the few quiet times during the school day. He seemed to be at her side when she walked home. 'Is he thinking about me too?' she wondered. Two weeks passed. One day after school, she found a letter addressed to her on the table in the Poirier kitchen. She tore open the envelope.

> *Ti-Jos is still not back. Something is terribly wrong. Your father and Hilaire went out looking for him this morning. I'm so worried. Please come as soon as you can. Oncle Armand can drive you home in his carriage.*

Except for a light in the kitchen windows, the house was dark when Justine drove into the yard. Patches of snow dotted the lawn and garden, and the stems of blackened rhubarb lay rubbery and limp in the flowerbed beside the house. She had decided to drive the carriage herself. "We might need it tomorrow," she had told her *oncle*, taking the reins.

Worry had creased Armand's forehead. "Should I tell Rosalie?" Justine had nodded numbly.

Thérèse opened the door as soon as Justine set foot on the steps. Her eyes were red and her face swollen.

"Oh, *maman*," Justine said taking her in her arms.

Thérèse wiped the end of her nose with the back of her hand. "I didn't cry all day," she sniffed. "I didn't want to upset the children. But now I can't seem to stop."

"Let me make you some tea. We'll all feel better."

They were on the second pot when they heard the dogs. They ran to the window. Two riders and horses disengaged from the woods.

Thérèse squinted against the dark. "It's Papa and Hilaire, but where's Ti-Jos?"

A third horse finally appeared out of the gloom. Its head drooped as it plodded under a shapeless bundle lashed to its back. Thérèse screamed and Justine caught her as she fell.

Joseph and Justine entered the sacristy. *Père* pulled the purple chasuble—the sleeveless vestment made of two panels that covered him front and back during mass—over his head. He handed it to the altar boy to hang in the armoire designated for mass vestments.

A stubble of grey whiskers showed on Joseph's cheeks. The once taut skin was soft and flabby. "There's been an accident."

Père slipped the matching stole over his head. "An accident?"

Joseph stared at him. "It's Ti-Jos."

Père handed the strip of purple silk to the server. The altar boy took the stole and cocked his head curiously while draping it over the chasuble on the hanger.

Justine gave a sharp nod towards the door.

The altar boy's face fell, and he went out.

Joseph swallowed. "He's dead. We found him in the hunting shack." His mouth opened again but no sound came out.

Justine spoke. "He must have been cleaning his rifle and it went off."

"When did this happen?" *Père* asked.

"He's been gone from the house two weeks."

"Was he still upset about Rosalie?"

Joseph lifted his shoulders. "He's been unhappy."

The sound of parishioners leaving the church came to them. Their voices echoed hollowly from the back, and then the church grew silent.

The alb, the white vestment worn under the chasuble, reached to *Père*'s feet. "A person committing suicide can't have a Catholic funeral or be buried in sacred ground."

"It was an accident, I'm telling you," Joseph said pulling himself straight. "The gun went off."

"Have you gone to the police?"

"The police don't need to be involved."

"What do you want of me?"

Her father seemed so tired. Justine said angrily, "My brother needs a Christian burial."

Père took a deep breath. "There are too many suspicious circumstances surrounding his death."

Joseph's voice rose. "It's you who says so."

"The laws of the Church are clear on this point."

Justine insisted. "You could make an exception."

"The laws are clear."

They rode swiftly and silently to the neighbouring village of St. Malo to the priest known to be a fighter. *Père* Ritchot was one of the three emissaries sent by Bishop Taché to Ottawa to plead the Métis' cause after the 1870 Uprising. He had been thrown into prison in Ontario for his efforts but continued to fight for their rights.

Justine sagged in her chair in Father Ritchot's office, folding and unfolding the pleats on her skirt. The trip would have been challenging for even an experienced rider, but the journey had restored Joseph. He explained the circumstances calmly and requested the last rights and burial for his son.

The Church of Rome had a chain of authority that was set in cement. The priest eyed them coldly. "You aren't of this parish. Why don't you ask *Père* Bertrand?"

Joseph and Justine exchanged glances. "We have. He refuses."

A thick, wiry grey beard ran part way down the priest's chest. He brushed its long hairs. "Why?"

"*Père* doubts the circumstances around the death."

"Is there reason to question?"

Joseph cleared his throat. "Ti-Jos asked for permission to marry my wife's niece, his first cousin. It was denied of course. He was despondent over this."

"And you? How do you think your son died?" Ritchot asked.

Joseph stared at the priest without flinching. "It was a hunting accident."

Ritchot sprinkled holy water over the casket as Ti-Jos was slowly lowered into his grave in the St. Malo cemetery.

Rosario had appeared out of nowhere and took the place next to Justine. She had forgotten her gloves and clasped her cold hands in front, caressing over and over the amethyst ring set in curlicues of silver that Ti-Jos had given her. Rosario reached and took her hand to stay it.

Lucie and Armand and their family stood behind the first row of mourners. Rosalie was not among them. They had searched the house, but she could not be found.

CHAPTER 29

Late November 1884

Adrien stood by the attic window in the grey morning light, thumbing the *Free Press*. He had searched for work, but with immigrants flooding the city, there wasn't much hope. Now his rent was overdue, and he had been avoiding his landlady for a week. Every morning, he waited and watched for her to trudge across the yard to the outhouse. When the narrow door closed behind her, he escaped to the street and returned late at night when the house was dark. Adrien flipped to the last page of the paper. An artist had drawn an advertisement announcing a new hotel in the city. Pencil-thin women under immense hats stood on the steps and descended from carriages under the hotel's portico. Rich, portly men on tiny feet escorted them. What would it be like to work in such a place? Just then a wedge of light from the kitchen illuminated the yard below. He folded the paper tightly and stuck it inside his coat. He needn't hurry; his landlady would be occupied for a while.

The Grand Hotel where he found work as a bellman proved to be appropriately named. The palatial entrance had a ceiling that soared, the carpets were thick, and the marble staircase that was the colour of old bone and veined in black was wide and substantial. A moose head with a soft muzzle hanging drolly over its chin observed the comings and goings of Winnipeg's elite at the immense reception desk. The bellman's stand was advantageously placed near the door. Adrien smiled as he said *Madame* and *Mademoiselle* and took charge of the female clientele. By the surreptitious glances they cast back at him when he left, he also knew that the hotel's maroon jacket and black pants fit him very well.

One evening, he delivered a tray of drinks to an upper floor. The empty tray hung at his fingertips as he sauntered down the hall past a string of brown doors with iron numbers. He rounded the far corner. The tray rattled to the floor as he collided with a girl running down an adjoining hall. He stumbled and grabbed her arms to prevent her from falling. *"Pardon, mam'selle,"* he said, staring at a cloud of red hair. He knew this woman. She was Esther's maid.

Adele's green eyes widened in fear. Adrien recognized that look. He had seen it on animals caught in trap-lines at Saint-Cère. Before he could say another word, her head rolled back and she fainted, slipping through his fingers like water. From somewhere, he heard the click of a tumbler as it fell into a lock. He glanced up, but the long hall was empty. This had to be bad. He slid an arm under her knees and around her shoulders and carried her to the servant stairs. On the top iron step, he crouched beside her. "Adele, Adele," he called softly.

Adele opened her eyes slowly and blinked. Her forehead wrinkled as she gazed around disoriented. When her eyes found his face, she started to cry.

"What's wrong?" he asked, bending over her awkwardly.

"I'm in terrible trouble."

Adrien folded his knees and sat. "What kind of trouble?"

Tears dripped off her cheeks, slid over her jaw, and down her throat to the collar of her dress.

"What could be so bad?"

"I don't know what to do. I'll lose my job. I've nowhere to go."

Adrien hung his hands between his knees and gazed down the long flight of iron stairs and finally understood. "What about the father? If he's in this hotel, he's rich. Is he from out of town? Won't he marry you?"

"He lives in Winnipeg. He won't have anything more to do with me. He's offering money, that's all."

The iron step under them vibrated with Adele's trembling. Adrien slipped out of his maroon jacket and laid it around her shoulders. "There must be someone who'll help. Do you have a sister or an aunt who could take the baby?"

Adele shook her head. "I'm alone."

"What about Miss Hill? She might help."

"No respectable household would want me as a maid."

"I've heard that nuns at the convent take in orphans in Saint-Boniface. You could give it up."

Adele shook her head vehemently. "It's impossible. I'd be ruined."

Their voices echoed hollowly against the iron stairs alternating to the right and left up to the roof and down to the basement. Adrien pulled her into his shoulder. A door opened at the bottom of the stairwell. They heard a match strike and then smoke from a cigarette drifted up. "Someone's sneaking a smoke," he whispered. By the time the door opened and closed, and they were alone once again, her trembling had stopped. She stood shakily and handed him back his jacket. "I'm sorry to have bothered you with this."

"There must be something I can do. Let me ask around."

Her lips thinned to a line. She turned, and with her hand on the rail, she descended the stairs.

Adrien leaned on his stand and stared unhappily out the window at the falling rain. The streets would be a quagmire of muck in the morning. The empty lobby echoed as the night clerk closed the hotel register and sauntered over with a deck of cards. "Want a game?"

Adrien shook his head.

The clerk shuffled the cards. "It's going to be a quiet night. No one's going out on a night like this." He divided the deck in two and fanned the two halves together. The edge of every card fell into place in the opposite stack. He jogged them into a single deck. "Why so glum?"

One side of Adrien's mouth turned up. "I have a friend who's in trouble."

"Woman friend or man friend?" the clerk asked, shuffling again. "If it's a man friend, it's the law. If it's a woman friend, then that's a whole different kind of trouble."

"She's a woman."

"She pregnant?"

Adrien nodded.

The clerk cut the deck. "You the father?"

"*Merde!* I hardly know her."

The cards fanned again. "She want the baby?"

"I suppose so, but it's difficult. She has no one to help her."

The clerk glanced around and then lowered his voice. "Has she thought about an abortion?"

"An abortion!" Adrien exclaimed. "That's dangerous. I read some place that a woman died last year after having an abortion."

"This will be safer. There's a doctor that does it. One of the maids had one last year."

"But it's against the law."

The clerk snorted. "Do you want his name or not?"

Adele arrived at the hotel in tears and begged him to come with her to her appointment with the doctor that morning. The manager looked over from his place under the moose head and glared at the commotion. Adrien had no choice.

The smell of medicine and disinfectant hit them when they entered the doctor's full waiting room. Curious eyes bored into his back as Adrien led Adele to some empty chairs next to a woman with a small boy on her lap. His face was grey, and his head lay limply on his mother's shoulder. Adrien sat silently and willed himself invisible until the nurse called Adele and led them into one of several connecting examination rooms.

A white, enamelled cabinet with rows of instruments glistening behind the glass doors stood in the corner. Brown medicine bottles with labels and cork stoppers were lined on the top shelf. Beneath it was a shelf of surgical instruments. The array of shiny forceps, scalpels, and picks fascinated Adrien, and though he knew it was morbid under the circumstances, he couldn't stop staring. Several saws at the bottom of the cabinet—some with thick blades and some with thin—were arranged in a row. With a sickening start, he realized what they were for and turned away.

The door connecting to another room opened, and Dr. Mitchell entered the room carrying a file. He was a tall man with white hair and gold-rimmed glasses. He frowned at Adrien, went round his desk briskly, and laid the file down. He addressed Adele while nodding his head towards Adrien. "I hope this young man will make good and marry you."

Adrien held up his hands firmly, palms outward. "This has nothing to do with me. The baby's not mine. I'm just a friend."

The doctor returned to Adele. "Is that true? You're about three months pregnant."

Adele shook her head. "He's not the father."

"Will the father marry you?"

Adele's eyes wandered to the cabinet. "There's no possibility of that, sir."

Dr. Mitchell lowered his head and stared over the thin, gold wire of his glasses. "Perhaps an aunt or a sister could help you. Have you thought of that?"

"She's no family," Adrien interrupted. "She's an *immigrante*. She came alone from Ireland."

"Let her speak," Dr. Mitchell said impatiently. "You could give the baby up."

Adele wrung her hands. "I can't continue with this pregnancy. I'll lose my job, and I have no place to go. You're the only one to help me now."

Dr. Mitchell's eyes narrowed. "Who told you I could help? What you're suggesting is a serious crime in Canada." He glanced at Adrien. "Did he put you up to this? Who told you I would do this?"

Adele pulled her shoulders up. "I've been praying for God's help."

Dr. Mitchell snorted. "Then you know that what you're asking is condemned by your God."

Adele began to cry softly. "I've no choice. You're my only hope."

Dr. Mitchell sat back, joined his fingers into a steeple, and brought them to his mouth. In the other room, his nurse murmured and the observation table creaked as someone climbed onto it. He rose slowly. "Ask the nurse to arrange for an appointment in two days' time. I'll perform curettage on your womb, which, for your information, is the scraping of the lining of the uterus. Tell anyone who asks it was for excessive menstrual bleeding." At the door, he added, "Now compose yourself. And don't leave together … the waiting room is full of gossips."

Adrien didn't think it was possible to improve the Grand Hotel, but it did indeed become grander in the evening. Under dimmed lights, the day-time business clientele transformed into showy men and women dining at tables draped in white before a confusing array of crystal glasses, English china, and silver-plate. One night, Adrien noticed a woman dining alone in full view and coldly ignoring those around her. Adrien's eyebrow lifted. She was one of the prostitutes who had been in the segregated booth at the opera.

"What's she doing here?" he asked the headwaiter during a lull in his shift.

"Advertising," the headwaiter said lifting his nose. "That's Belle Fontaine. She owns Winnipeg's largest whorehouse—it's not far from here on Annabella Street." As a family man who attended church on Sunday, the headwaiter disapproved of such activity. He shook his head. "There are three times as many brothels as churches in the city." A hand waved from across the room, and he picked up a decanter of red wine and left to attend to the guest.

Adrien spent the evening staring at her from behind the date palm at the door to the dining room. A tight corset lifted a bosom of soft, white flesh falling out of a dangerously low-cut dress. Her curls were piled high on her head as before, and a single long, blonde ringlet dangled before

Spoiled Heritage

each ear. Her cat-shaped eyes were heavily outlined in black accentuating large grey eyes. Adrien couldn't rightly say if she would be pretty or plain under the makeup, but with it she was frighteningly beautiful.

Two days later, the sky beyond the blood red curtains of the hotel windows showed grey and dark as Adrien chatted with the clerk at the counter. A group of businessmen entered, and as they stopped to scrape the muck from their boots, a small figure scurried in behind them.

Adele hurried across the lobby. She had lost her hat, and red tendrils hung damply on her head. Her wide eyes glistened over tear-washed cheeks.

The door behind Adrien's stand opened to a small storage room. He grabbed Adele's hand, walked her quickly, and pushed her inside. Steamer trunks and suitcases covered in red and yellow stickers were stacked against the wall. Umbrellas leaned in the far corner, and a snow shovel hid behind the door. He made her sit on a silver trunk with brass straps by the wall and sat silently next to her. He didn't know what to say. What do you say to a woman who's just had an abortion? "Do you want to tell me about it?"

He felt her weight as she leaned against him. Such a small body—like a girl's really. "It's done now. The worst is behind you. Think of the future."

Adele shook her head.

"It's for the best."

She whispered something so low he didn't hear. He bent his head. "What?"

"I couldn't do it."

Adrien thought of his sisters. How disgraced they would be. How devastated. For one crazy moment, he almost offered himself as Adele's husband. Instead he asked, "Do the Hills know?"

"No," she said softly.

He brushed away the tendrils of red hair clinging to her wet face. "What about the father? You said he was willing to give you money."

"I think he meant to pay the doctor when the baby was born."

Adrien harrumphed. "It's not my business, but who is the father?"

"Angus McQuaid. His father is Mr. Hill's friend."

Adrien chewed the skin around his thumbnail. "Maybe he'll pay for more. Maybe we can get some cash too … for your future."

Adele's chin went up. "He's never given me money."

"We could insist. We could make him." Even to his own ears, it sounded like bravado and false courage. "I don't think he'd like the story of an illegitimate child getting around."

Adele took his hand and held it to her face.

Adele stood at the window, silhouetted in black against the day's bright light, and gazed down at the street in front of the Grand Hotel.

A key jabbed several times at the lock. "Shit," a man's voice said through the door. A click, then a rattle, and the door swung open.

Adele didn't move.

Angus McQuaid entered and without pausing, skirted round the bed. "What do you mean by summoning me in the middle of a work day?" He had almost reached her when a movement in the narrow mirror above the dresser across the room caught his eye. He whipped around.

Adrien pushed up the arms of his maroon jacket and moved away from the corner.

"What's going on?" McQuaid demanded.

Adele rested her hands on her belly. "I said I would have an abortion. I changed my mind."

The young man with the large blond moustache lifted his shoulders nonchalantly. "That's your business."

Adele's jaw clenched. "I'm going to have the baby."

McQuaid turned to Adrien with his palms up. "I don't even know if the child is mine."

Adrien's fists clenched. "Adele's word is good enough for me."

Adele let her arms fall. "You were going to pay for the doctor. I need that money now."

McQuaid chewed the long hairs of his moustache. A long breath escaped him, and then he opened his jacket and pulled out his wallet.

Adrien inhaled. He had never seen so many bills.

"I can give you a hundred," McQuaid said. "That should be enough."

Adele shook her head. "No, it isn't."

McQuaid frowned. "Well? How much then?"

Adele looked at Adrien. They had agreed that the price of a new house—$500—would be fair. "One thousand."

Angus' mouth dropped open. "You're insane. I don't have that kind of money."

"Your family does. Get it from them. If I don't get every penny, I'll denounce you to the public."

Adele shivered. Adrien moved closer and put his arm around her. The hotel turned off its hot water registers in unoccupied rooms, and it was cold.

Sweat glistened on McQuaid's forehead. "How do I know that you won't keep coming after me?"

"I'm giving the baby up for adoption as soon as it's born," Adele said. "Once the baby is safely placed, you'll never hear from me again." She looked up at Adrien. "We're people of our word."

Adrien smiled. She looked like the strong avenging angel on one of the prayer cards that *mémère*, his grandmother, kept in her prayer book to mark the place.

CHAPTER 30

Early December 1884

Belle Fontaine sat at her usual place the evening of Adele's failed abortion appointment. Adrien pulled his jacket down over his hips, picked up the potted palm by the door, and carried it to the window alcove near her table. He put the palm on the empty plant pedestal, and turned the pot several times, making a show of finding the plant's best presentation to the room. He stole a glance at Belle. She silently sipped her soup. He slid a white envelope from under the sleeve of his jacket, sidestepped to the table, and placed the letter near her coffee cup. Flint-grey eyes looked up at him. She lifted an eyebrow and returned to sipping her soup.

The bellman stand had an unobstructed view of the dining room, and when Belle appeared, Adrien hurried forward to open the door for her. He stepped aside to let her pass, and she gave him a hard, appraising look that lingered over him until he felt hot blood rush to his face. She laughed and went out.

Adrien whistled for a taxi carriage waiting down the street and helped her in. As it began to pull away, she pulled back the curtain and said, "Tomorrow, after midnight."

The hotel page had carried a message to Adele the next morning. Now in the moonlight, Adrien walked along the thick, leafless hedge that bordered the far side of the drive up to the Hill mansion. The summer verandas where he had sat with Esther sipping cold tea seemed forlorn and abandoned to the oncoming winter. A feeble light shone from a kitchen window at the back, but the windows in the corner tower and under the gingerbread stared blindly into the night. Gravel crunched under Adrien's feet, and he stepped off the drive to wait in the shadows under the hedge. The light flicked off, and a woman in a cinched coat appeared from the back of the house, pulling on gloves as she hurried down the drive. Adrien stepped into the moonlight and waved. "C'mon," he whispered, taking Adele's arm. "It's not far."

They hurried silently on empty streets, passing homes where people slept. Finally, they came to the neighbourhood created by a loop of the river—the seven blocks that were the object of the crusade against vice that Adrien had read about.

The tinny, mechanical music of a player piano and then a woman's unnatural, hysterical laughter greeted them as they approached.

Adele's steps faltered

"We're almost there," Adrien told her.

Belle's house occupied the largest lot at the end of the street with a back yard that overlooked the river. Several sturdy wooden chairs and benches sprinkled the bank. Clients lazed there in the summer to flee the city's sweltering heat and catch the breeze. Brightly lit windows were decorated with red curtains trimmed with dancing, black pompoms.

Adrien and Adele followed a beaten path to the back. The back door opened to the ground without a step and lay in darkness. Adrien rapped sharply. The wind racing down the river blew down their necks, and they turned their backs against it. He rapped again, louder this time.

Someone struggled with the lock. The door cracked open and a dishevelled boy peered out sleepily.

Adrien pushed the door open. "We have an appointment with Belle."

The boy flattened himself against the wall to let them pass.

A kerosene lantern with the wick turned down cast a circle of weak light in the chilly kitchen. The boy looked longingly at a leather settee with a crumpled, grey blanket laying on it, but then he took the light and led them up an enclosed staircase to the second floor.

Gold gaslights dangled from the ceiling and lit the long corridor with muted orange. On the right, several closed doors marched down one side of the hall. On the opposite wall was a double door that was also shut. Adrien looked back to ask the boy, but the stairs were empty and dark. He placed his hand on the small of Adele's back, opened one of the double doors, and propelled her into a darkened room.

Adele swung around. "Wait." She faced him in the slice of light from the hall. "We can't come in here."

"We can't knock on those bedroom doors either," Adrien said. When he stepped round the door to shut it, he saw her.

Belle sat at a desk before a large leather-bound ledger and watched them coldly. Beyond her, through glass doors, stood a large bed with a pink satin coverlet and covered with pink pillows.

"*Pardon*," Adrien rushed to explain. "Your boy left us in the hall. I didn't want to knock on the bedrooms."

Belle wore another tightly corseted gown that was cut low. The same blonde curls dangled stiffly at her ears. Though it was long past midnight, like all creatures of the night, she was fresh and alert. She slammed the ledger shut, moved it to one side, and pointed to two cream-coloured chairs before her desk. "What's this all about?"

Adrien had never seen such fancy chairs. Carved leaves and garland ran around the oval back above a seat upholstered in stripes of varying pink silk. He pulled a chair back for Adele, and then lowered himself carefully onto the delicate seat. He pointed at Adele with his thumb. "My friend here is in trouble. As soon as her employers find out, she'll be fired."

Belle stared coldly. "What kind of trouble?"

Adrien shifted, waving his hand in the general direction of Adele waist. "She's *en famille* …" He couldn't find the English word for it and settled on making a rolling motion with his hands at his belly.

Adele's green eyes darkened as she lifted her chin. "I'm pregnant."

"Do what's right and marry her," Belle said to Adrien.

Adele clenched her hands on her lap, and she leaned forward. "No! It's not what you think. Adrien's just a friend. He's helping me out."

Belle sat back in her chair. "So what's this got to do with me?"

Adrien glanced at Adele. At her nod, he said, "Perhaps she could work for you ... until the baby is born."

Belle turned to Adele. "Are you able to work?"

"I'll do anything you want."

A corner of Belle's brightly painted mouth turned up. "Well not *anything* ... not in your condition."

Adele sat straighter. "The Hills say that I'm a good maid."

At the Hill name, Belle's eyes narrowed slightly, but she said nothing. "And then what? What happens after? What will you do after the baby comes?"

Adrien's hand moved to cover the clenched fists in his friend's lap. "The Sisters of the Holy Names take orphans for adoption. We'll leave it at their convent."

Heavy boots scraped the hallway, and a body lurched against the wall followed by giggles. The three fell silent. When it was quiet again, Belle laid her hands on the desk. Meaty flesh enclosed a ring with a blood red stone on the ring finger of her right hand and another ring with a deep blue stone on her left hand. "When it's time. Call at the back. I'll let them know. They'll be waiting for you." She pulled the ledger closer and resumed her work without looking up.

At the door, Adele turned and said, "I'll pay you back some day. I promise."

Belle lifted her eyes from the ledger. "How could you ever help me?"

CHAPTER 31

Mid December 1884

Just before Christmas, Adrien received a letter from Adele. Her room was next to the kitchen so that she could respond to calls during the night. It was small but warmer than her room at the Hills. On her first day while mopping the bedrooms, Adele had found a metal plate about as big as a teacup, flush to the floor under the bed. She lifted the hinged plate and discovered a hole with a brass tube leading down. She later learned that the tube emptied in a box on the bar. The client threw his coins down the tube when he had finished, so the bartender knew the girl above had been duly paid. As expected, Belle wasn't friendly with anyone except the men clients. Adele thanked him again for not taking his share of the extortion money and told him that she had hidden the bills in the box of mouse and rat traps beneath the kitchen sink. She was as content as she could be and would send for him when the time came.

Adrien finished rereading her letter when a stir at the doors made him look up. Premier John Norquay entered the hotel and greeted everyone with a *bonhomie* typical of politicians before an election. Norquay boasted about his Native grandmother and had won the province's first election as the leader of the English Metis. At six feet tall and weighing 300 pounds, the Premier was a big man—a cartoon of him crushing the dainty chairs in the Governor General's salon had entertained Winnipeggers for weeks. The hotel was hosting his campaign fund-raiser tonight. Norquay swept up the stairs with his entourage to the banquet rooms on the first floor.

Adrien spent the evening watching the clock and hearing bursts of laughter and applause from overhead. When the long hand had gone round twice, a crowd descended in waves to the lobby. The Premier was the last to appear, continuing to shake hands and chat with unflagging energy as he went down the stairs. Adrien stepped forward with the Premier's coat and hat and then went outside to open his carriage door. When he returned, he noticed that the velvet curtains to the small anteroom located off the lobby were closed. He asked the desk clerk about it and was told the room had been reserved for a private party of government supporters and members of the legislature.

Adrien carried a bucket and a slotted hand-shovel nonchalantly to the standing ashtray beside the anteroom. He drove the shovel into the sand and dragged it through. Out came mashed cigar butts and broken cigarettes. He was refilling the sand when he heard a voice he thought he recognized.

"French-Catholics in Manitoba should be forced to assimilate into the public schools," Thomas Hill said. "The dual system that we have costs too much money."

"But there's a dual system in Québec," someone argued. "It was put in place to protect the minority. In Québec's case, it's the English."

"And see what that has brought," Hill responded. "It's been over a hundred years since France was driven off the continent, and Québec still isn't English."

"When Manitoba joined Confederation, most of the schools were French and run by the Church. They simply continued as before," the first man answered stubbornly.

"That was then. Now the English are the majority."

Adrien inched closer to the curtains. He clasped his hands at his back and stood as if he were serving the anteroom.

Hill continued, "Lord Durham was right. He said in his report that French-Canadians were without history and culture and should be assimilated. I agree."

Adrien remembered the heated discussion he had had about democracy with Arthur-Joseph at the Collège. When a majority of an electorate placed its own interests first at the expense of those in a minority, it was like that of a tyrant or despot using his power on the weak and marginalized. He waited for someone in the anteroom to have the guts to say something. After an interval, chairs scraped back, and the men began to say their goodbyes.

Adrien returned to his station.

Hill crossed the lobby in the company of a young, blond man who held the door for him and allowed him to pass.

Adrien sat at a table near the window of the café. People hurried along the sidewalk and dodged horses and wagons as they crossed the snow-covered street. He was about to dip his spoon into a bowl of steaming vegetable soup when Adele appeared in the reversed letters of the cafe window. A bundle of brown, paper-wrapped parcels rested on a slight bulge at her middle. He rapped on the glass and waved her in.

"How is it at Belle's?" he asked pulling out a chair opposite him. "Would you like a coffee?"

"I prefer tea."

He called out to the woman behind the counter, and the tea arrived in a large brown pot. Adele gave it time to steep to a dark brown, then wrapped her hands around the steaming cup and waited as he mopped up the last of his soup with a piece of bread.

Adrien wiped his mouth with the back of his hand and sat back. "You look well…" His eyes dropped to her waist. "Uh, I mean … healthy."

Adele forced a small smile. "I'm fine. It's not so bad at Belle's. The place needs cleaning like any other house. Just more interesting." Her voice trailed off, and she looked down at her chapped, rough hands. "I'm glad we met. I have an idea that I want to talk to you about. I'd like to start a business, but I can't do it on my own—a woman can't alone. The money's in a safe place, but it's not doing me any good. It's not growing."

Adrien's eyes rounded. "Pardon me for reminding you, but you're about to have a baby and you're not married."

Adele held her hands up palm outwards. "Listen. There's an unfinished house on the west side of the city in one of the new neighbourhoods. I walk by it all the time. At first there was hammering day and night, but now it's quiet. The owner must have run out of money. We could buy it, finish it, and make a profit when we sell. You could do the work."

Adrien shook his head. "That's too much for one man. I'd need someone to help me."

"You must know other carpenters."

Adrien chewed his lip. "There's a friend in Saint-Cère. He's always looking for work."

The red frizz around Adele's face began to vibrate. "We could do it. You won't be sorry. This could be the beginning of a profitable partnership."

Adrien stood up and fumbled in his pocket for change. Bronze, nickel, and silver coins rattled to the tabletop. "I hope you're right."

Adele met Adrien later that day in the café with $500 arranged neatly in an envelope. "This should be enough for the house, but try to get it for less when you make the deal."

She was on her second pot of tea when he returned with the bill of ownership scribbled on a crinkled piece of paper. She examined it, then looked up under an arched eyebrow.

Adrien shrugged.

Adele's voice rose. "Did you have to give him all the money? I told you to get it for less."

Adrien snatched the paper back. "The man broke his leg, and he's out of work. He has a family. What kind of a *sans coeur* do you take me for?"

A couple at the counter stopped eating and turned their heads to look at him.

Adele exhaled with a sigh. "You're not hard-hearted. I didn't mean that." She put her hand on his arm and pulled him down to the chair beside her.

Adele complained to Adrien that the men stopped talking and stared when she entered the hardware stores and lumberyards to buy materials for their house. They demanded she pay cash though she knew very well that everyone else got credit. "You're in need of a wedding band aren't you, missy?" one storeowner had said to her. Adrien began accompanying her when she shopped.

Justine went home as often as the snow stayed away in the months following Ti-Jos' death, but the house was so quiet and Thérèse and Joseph so unhappy, she escaped to her friend's as often as she could. She followed the frozen river under a blue, cold sky and found Louise in the washhouse attached to the kitchen. Aurore played with a rag doll beside a straw basket that held her new baby brother, Étienne. The lean-to had a wood stove and served as a summer kitchen. In August, when the plains sweltered and it was too hot in the house, it served as a kitchen for canning vegetables and fruits. It now doubled as Louise's laundry. Layers of hard, orangey-brown bars of soap separated by sheets of thick wax paper lay in a wooden box under a slated laundry bench. Old *mémère* Lafrenière had made the soap in the summer by cooking pig fat in a kettle over an open fire in the yard. Once the fat had melted to a liquid, she added lye from wood ash. The rendered fat set up as soap.

Louise poured hot water into the washtub, grabbed a bar, and tossed it in. She dumped in a pile of shirts, rolled up her sleeves, and then submerged her arms to her elbows searching for the bar. She rubbed the soap vigorously into the collar of a red and black flannel shirt and began scrubbing it against the aluminum ripples of the scrub board. "Marcel's going to the city," she puffed above the steam. "Adrien's got work for him."

Étienne was swaddled tightly and cocooned against the sides of the basket. He stretched and squirmed against his bindings and mewled feebly like a kitten. Justine picked him up, and cradling his head in her hand, she laid him on her shoulder. Planting her feet apart, she began swaying from side to side.

"We could use the money," Louise continued, pulling the dripping shirt out of the water. "At least I won't get pregnant while he's away." Two heavy rollers were attached to the washtub. She tucked the collar in between the rollers while her other hand turned the wheel. The shirt passed through, and the water squeezed out. "Two babies in two years and him without a job. He walks by, and I get pregnant." The wet shirt went over a wooden rack beside the stove to dry.

The mewling had turned insistent. Justine patted Étienne's back and switched from swaying to bouncing gently up and down, but the baby would not be consoled. He began the terrifying breathless scream of a newborn. Justine gave up. "Here, take him. I'll trade places with you."

Louise smiled gratefully and dried her reddened hands. Dirty laundry was piled on the bench. She moved it aside and unbuttoned her dress. The baby latched on hungrily.

A basket of men's dirty combinations and underwear stood under the tub. Justine tried to stop smelling. She swirled her hands through the water and searched for the bar of lye soap.

Adrien saw Marcel arrive through the stud walls dividing the first floor and waved him in. They greeted one another, and then Marcel tied his leather tool belt around his waist and knelt down beside Adrien to work. They were almost finished tacking laths to the studs in the hall when Adele arrived.

"This is my partner, Adele Fitzgerald."

Marcel stared at the straining buttons on her blue coat. "*Hostie de calice*," he exclaimed—the host and the chalice—one of his favourite sacramental swears.

Adele turned a furious face at Adrien, but he only grinned. She couldn't understand a word, but she knew that they were laughing about her. She turned on her heel, grabbed the broom, and began sweeping sawdust and pieces of wood angrily into a pile.

Adrien took the broom from her and put his arm around her shoulders. "I'm sorry. I was just teasing. Let's begin again."

The work on the house progressed nicely; Marcel could work hard if he worked side by side with another. Whenever Adele could get away, she came to the site. Sometimes when she went early, she detected a sour smell on them. She covered her nose and said from under her hand. "You're wasting your money."

Adrien dismissed her. "Don't worry."

But Adele did worry about their drinking. She often scolded them and repeated the story she had heard at the Hills. A farmwoman had been married to a drinking man who wasted his wages on liquor and came home drunk to terrorize her and the children. She was out hanging her wash on the line when the new owners of the farm drove into the yard. Her husband had sold the farm without informing her, and he had every right because women couldn't own property. The children were also his by law. Adrien and Marcel shook their heads at that injustice and kept on.

Lights glowed faintly through the falling snow as Adrien walked towards the office of *Le Métis* in Saint-Boniface. As promised, Arthur-Joseph had written about his journey to Montana with Louis Riel's mother during the summer. The article had been circulated widely throughout the West and was read with great interest in Québec.

Adrien remembered almost every word.

> *On November 2, 1869, Riel and a group of 400 men recruited from the fur-brigades took peaceful possession of*

Upper Fort Garry. On the same day, a group of Métis led by Lépine prevented the newly appointed Lieutenant Governor, William McDougall, from entering the colony at the United States border. McDougall was under orders to proclaim Manitoba a colony after the transfer of lands from the Hudson's Bay Company to Canada. However, he entered Manitoba and made his proclamation before the transfer of land from the Hudson's Bay Company had officially occurred and before being sworn in as governor.

The people of Red River, used to local representation on a roughly equal French and English basis since 1855, had not been consulted about the annexation, and they objected to Canada's high-handed measures. A provisional government was established and declared the colony independent until given full status as a province with a list of constitutional rights that included the protection of the French language, separate Catholic schools, and recognition of Métis land claims.

Riel fled to the United States after the Uprising in 1870 and the execution of Thomas Scott. Scott, a violent and boisterous racist, had been captured several times and held prisoner in Fort Garry for repeatedly defying Riel's provisional government. While in prison, Scott had assaulted Riel and provoked and insulted his Métis guards with racist slurs. When Scott continued to incite insubordination against the guards amongst the other prisoners, Riel finally ordered a court martial—a special tribunal often employed on the prairie. Urged on by the nervous guards, he thought it necessary to intimidate the Canadian conspirators that Scott was a part of and show Canada that the Métis government must be taken seriously.

Scott was found guilty by the court and shot the following day by a Métis firing squad. The execution created *an uproar of protest in English Canada, and a warrant for Riel's arrest was issued in Ontario with a reward of $5,000. At the urging of Bishop Taché, and the repeated assurances from Prime Minister Macdonald that amnesty would be given to all the insurgents involved in the Uprising, Riel accepted $1,000 from the federal government for his needs in the United States and the support of his family in Red River and sought voluntary exile.*

With the exception of Riel and Lépine, Bishop Taché finally procured the promised amnesty for all the Métis involved in the Uprising. The Catholic Church stood for law and order and basically abandoned Riel in the ensuing years. The Church in the West urged obedience to civil authority though a few independent priests and the province of Québec stood solidly with Riel and the French Métis. Louis was acclaimed into office for the riding of Provencher three times but had been unable to take his seat due to the warrant for his arrest. He finally managed to sign the parliamentary register in Ottawa then fled from the capital's police to the United States. He found the separation from his family and people difficult, and he moved back and forth between the two countries before accepting a teaching post at the Jesuit mission in Montana, where he married the young French Métis woman, Marguerite Monet Bellehumeur, and had two children. To secure his safety, he had to become an American citizen.

This past spring, men from the east had begun surveying the river lots at Batoche into American squares again, and the Métis in Saskatchewan feared losing their farms as they had in Manitoba. Four Métis from Batoche—Gabriel Dumont, Moise Ouellet, James Isbister, and Michel Dumas—rode 800 miles from Saskatchewan to Montana to ask Riel to be their leader. Riel promised to join them with his family in July.

Adrien wondered if the lighted windows meant that his friend had returned from Ottawa. The Métis had been pleading for federal intervention over their land rights for years, and at Riel's request, Arthur-Joseph had delivered the last of the petitions in support of them to the Prime Minister.

Adrien caught sight of his friend through the watery glass. Arthur-Joseph sat at his desk, lost in thought and chewing the callous on his writing finger. Adrien entered, swept off his gloves, and sent them sailing through the air to land on a page of freshly inked writing.

"Hey," Arthur-Joseph yelled, grabbing the sheet away. "I'm working on something about Riel."

A chair with wires intersecting underneath to support its rickety legs and dappled with specks of bygone paint sat near the window. Adrien dragged it closer and sat. He stretched out and crossed one ankle over the other. "How are the Riels?"

"They're destitute. The priests have been giving them aide. Louis wants compensation for the land he owned by the river in Saint-Boniface and the hardship he's endured during exile. The English press says he's a mercenary, but he is owed the money." Arthur-Joseph opened the bottom drawer of his desk and pulled out a bottle of Chivas and two glasses. "There's a lot of unrest in Saskatchewan."

Adrien examined the label on the bottle. "Scotch? Your palate has improved since your trip to the capital."

Arthur-Joseph nodded and handed him a glass with a generous portion of brown liquid. "I acquired a taste for it." He swirled the scotch in his glass. "The white settlers around Prince Albert are angry because the Canadian Pacific Railway's main line has been rerouted south, and the value of their land has collapsed. The Indians have agreed to settle on reserves, but the federal government hasn't signed the treaties or paid for their rights. Therefore, their land claims are still valid; the Métis river strips are on their unextinguished land claims—areas where historic land treaties weren't signed. The buffalo herds are gone, and the Indians are being fed by the Métis. It's a mess."

Adrien sniffed his drink. "How was Riel this summer?"

"His speeches were moderate and calm. The old settlers like him because he asks for a peaceful presentation of grievances. The Métis like him because in his manners and appearance he looks like one of them yet he talks and acts like one of their respected priests."

"Will the Indians support him?"

"Riel secretly met with Big Bear, the Plains Cree chief this summer. But their grievances have little in common. I don't believe the two movements will join."

The liquor flowed down Adrien's throat smooth and warm. "It's the Métis and Indians and old settlers. Like in Manitoba in 1870."

Arthur-Joseph looked down at the letter he had rescued. "The difference is there's a federal police force of 1000 men at the ready."

CHAPTER 32

March 1885

Adrien checked the newspaper for weeks and then months, but the federal government didn't respond to the petition that Arthur-Joseph had delivered. He rode the horse-drawn streetcar to work every day.

The conductor clicked to his team, the big hooves lifted, and the streetcar creaked forward. Adrien made his way to the bench at the far back, put his lunch kit on the floor between his feet, and looked out the window with half-closed eyes. Hard-packed and dirty snow buried the city still, but the March sun had strength during the day. Water dripped from roofs, and rivulets ran at the edge of yards to the ways and roads, turning everything to muck. The conversation of two men sharing the bench disturbed his reverie.

"Those damn Métis," one said. "They're rebelling again. This time it's Saskatchewan. They set up a provisional government."

"Always whining about their land claims and rights and responsible government," the other added.

"They elected Riel as their president. The damn murderer."

Adrien pushed his spine up against the seat. "Manitoba has full provincial rights because of Riel."

They stared. "Yeah? And what about Scott? He has to be punished for Scott's death."

Blood rushed to Adrien's face, his breathing quickened, and as always when he was upset, he slipped into his native tongue. "Scott was an *agitateur*. He had lots of chances, but he kept making trouble for Riel and the Métis."

"You French are always bellyaching. The last time I looked, the British won the war, not you. If you don't like it here, go back to France."

"You go back. We've been here longer than you."

The man by the window half-stood, and reaching across his friend, punched Adrien in the face.

Adrien shook his head as if to clear it. He put his hand up to his eye. Blood smeared his fingers. Another fist came at him, and he pulled his arm back to defend himself, but his collar was caught by the second man. He wrestled free, landed a punch to the gut of his assailant, and whirled, but his assailants jumped on him and they all crashed to the floor.

Adele was ministering to him when Arthur-Joseph visited the building site later. Adrien's eye had puffed shut, and deep purple stained the eyesocket. She had oiled the cut before pressing a thin, white bandage onto it. Brown blotches stained the scrapes and cuts on his knuckles where she had applied disinfectant.

Arthur-Joseph whistled. "Hope the other guy looks worse than you."

"There were two of them," Adele explained. "This is what happens now in Winnipeg if you defend Riel and the Métis."

Adrien shrugged.

Arthur-Joseph crossed his left arm over his chest and then rested his other arm on it and rubbed his chin. "I'm going to Saskatchewan. Come with me."

Adele's eyes grew big, and she gripped her hands together over an apron that poorly camouflaged her belly. "You can't. You have to keep working on the house."

Adrien's jaw clenched as he stared stubbornly at her.

A week later, a bent figure in a pith helmet sat on a valise at the end of the platform. He had a stubby pencil in his hand and was scribbling in a small handbook. Arthur-Joseph looked up when he heard Adrien approaching, folded his notebook, and put it away in one of his flat breast pockets with flaps. Two more flat pockets below the belt completed his adventurer's jacket. The beige pith helmet, the size of a melon, had a short brim at the front and back. Adrien laughed, "You look like a detective." He himself wore jodhpurs—breeches made for horseback that were full above the knees and closely fitted under his tightly laced, knee-high work boots. A full backpack hung loosely from leather straps and bobbed on his back.

In Regina, they rented horses and joined a group of North-West Mounted Police on the 200-mile journey to Fort Carleton near Duck Lake. At the fort, Arthur-Joseph asked for an interview with the commander, Major Crozier, and the policeman invited them into his crowded office.

Arthur-Joseph took out his pad and pencil and explained. "We're going to Batoche. The people back home are eager for news about the Rebellion."

A large moustache with tails camouflaged Crozier's weak chin. "It's a dangerous situation. There's great discontent among the Indians and half-breeds. I've sent another telegram regarding the settlement of land claims to the Prime Minister, urging immediate action." He moved the hand-written papers on his desk until he found a typed sheet and handed it to Arthur-Joseph. "The situation is of course acerbated by the disappearance of the large buffalo herds."

Arthur-Joseph scribbled as fast as he could. "If the Métis can't hunt, how can they live?"

"They're mainly engaged in trading, raising cattle, and freighting along the South Saskatchewan River." Crozier twisted the long hairs on the tail of his moustache. "The priests are urging them to keep peaceful and farm, but I haven't seen much of that."

Adrien snorted, then embarrassed, looked away at the Major's grey greatcoat hanging by the door. The priests would preach that. They always preached obedience to authority.

Arthur-Joseph slumped in the saddle. The ride to the Métis settlement of Batoche high above the South Saskatchewan had taken two days.

A general store, an inn, and a few houses with stables behind made up the main street, and a handful of connecting streets sloped to the river where a ferry was tied. Higher up the slope, a silver steeple shone in the sunlight above a substantial white church. Horses and wagons crowded around the entrance.

Arthur-Joseph flicked a rein and pointed. "Everyone's at the church. Riel and Dumont might be there. Come on."

They tied up their horses and entered the church. People crowded every pew from the altar to the back doors and up into the small choir loft over the entrance. Adrien and Arthur-Joseph joined the row of men leaning against the walls in the side aisle at the right. A black iron stove encumbered the middle of the centre aisle. A stovepipe rose several feet to an elbow that veered left to an exhaust hole in the exterior wall. On a shelf over the altar stood a small statue of a woman with her arms open imploringly. Adrien recognized her as Mary of Grace; her left knee was slightly bent, and her bare foot crushed the head of a serpent coiled beneath her long, trailing green skirt edged in gold. He whispered to the man nearest him to find out what was going on. "*Qu'est-ce qui ce passe?*"

"It's the last day of the novena. We're asking for Mary's help. We've been praying for nine days."

Arthur-Joseph nudged him in the ribs and nodded to the front pew. "Gabriel Dumont."

Adrien stretched to look.

Dumont wore a long buckskin jacket over a shirt that he wore loosely belted over his plaid pants. He had cinched two wide beaded bands beneath each knee lifting the pant leg to reveal soft brown moccasins.

His hair was untrimmed and bore the permanent notch of a man accustomed to a hat.

Adrien searched every pew and then craned to peer up at the loft. Riel wasn't anywhere in the church. "Where's Louis?" Adrien whispered again to the man beside him.

"The priest says he will deny the sacraments to anyone taking up arms, so Louis refuses to attend."

After the service, Adrien and Arthur-Joseph rode with Dumont to his command camp near Duck Lake to meet Riel. After throwing their bedrolls in one of the dozen canvas tents, a young Métis showed them around the camp. The three stopped on the ridge and gazed down at grazing animals. Horses pawed the crusted snow and nibbled at dried, spent grass.

"What a thin, sorry lot," Adrien remarked.

Their guide shrugged. "We sold the best horses to the soldiers at the Fort last winter. Had to … our families were starving."

Adrien pulled out a pouch of tobacco and walked with Arthur-Joseph towards a group of men seated on skins and smoking pipes around a large central fire. Adrien was filling his second pipe when a young hunter galloped up. Standing in the stirrups, he raced round the circle whooping and waving a rifle. Fire glinted off the barrel and shiny stock. The rider reined hard, and the horse threw its head up, rolling its eyes wildly as it stiffened its knees and dug its hooves in. The hunter snugged the rifle into his shoulder, took a deep breath, squinted, and took aim. A slender willow 400 feet away split in two.

Stunned silence gripped the men around the fire and then exploded as men rushed the rider.

A man jumped at the horse, trying to grab the rifle. "Where'd you get such a gun?"

The rider held it out of reach above his head, laughing. "I borrowed it from a drunk soldier at the fort. He won't notice it gone until tomorrow." He lowered his arm and let them take the rifle.

When the gun came round to Adrien, he noticed the Enfield-Snider stamp on the smooth wooden stock. The slender barrel was topped by a sheathed bayonet. He passed it on to another.

Rough hands examined the gun carefully and caressed it for its beauty. "Our rifles are only good for half that distance, and we're low on ammunition," one of the men said. "If there's a battle, we'll have to loot the downed men on the field for guns and ammunition," added another.

Riel stepped out of the shadows to warm his hands at the fire.

Adrien sat cross-legged on the opposite side and gazed at him through the flames. He was surprised by his appearance. The fastidious leader wore his hair long, and his usually trimmed beard was unkempt.

The rider strode to Riel with the Snider-Enfield. Riel balanced the rifle in his hands, approving the weight and then pulled the scabbard off the bayonet. The knife flashed white in the firelight. In a calm but strong voice that everyone could hear, Riel said, "Don't worry, my brothers. A few warning shots that can be heard in Ottawa and they'll negotiate. We won't need rifles like this."

Arthur-Joseph approached Riel in the flickering firelight. Riel recognized him immediately when he bowed and took Arthur-Joseph's hand warmly in his own.

Adrien tapped his empty pipe on his boot and stood. In the west, a tipped, silver sickle leaked moonlight over the waiting prairie.

Later that night, the sound of regular, pounding hooves and shouting woke him. He shook Arthur-Joseph awake, and they ran to join Dumont and Riel and the others on the ridge. A lone rider, the advance scout, urged his horse up the hill in the grey light. "Major Crozier's patrol has been sighted on the road near Duck Lake."

Dumont turned and yelled to his men. "Saddle the horses."

Riel caught his arm. "Do not be the first to open fire."

Dumont nodded.

Crozier's force of about 100 police and volunteers hid behind sleighs on the road to Duck Lake. Adrien counted Dumont's men as they rode with Riel. As Dumont did during the buffalo hunt, he signalled his men and 25 rode into the trees and shrubs bordering the road.

Dumont turned to his brother Isidore Dumont. "Take the young Cree chief, Assiwyn, and ask for a meeting. I don't want to start killing them. I want to take prisoners. If they try to kill us, then we will them."

Adrien and Arthur-Joseph galloped to a hiding place apart from the men and watched helplessly from the trees.

Isidore rode forward. Assiwyn, who was unarmed and carrying a white flag, followed. They slowly approached the force. Major Crozier and his interpreter, who held his rifle across his lap, detached themselves from the troupe and rode towards the two men. As they met, Assiwyn leaned forward and grabbed the barrel of the interpreter's gun to point the rifle away. The rifle exploded, and Assiwyn sagged. Before Isidore could fire his rifle, the interpreter drew his revolver and shot Dumont's brother through the head. The two men slid to the ground, and Crozier and McKay galloped back to the patrol.

Dumont's marksmen opened fire from the cover of the trees. Riel rode fearlessly, exposed to the gunfire in the middle of the hollow, with no other weapon than the crucifix that he held high.

Crozier signalled for his men to retreat. Three policemen and nine volunteers lay dead in the snow.

Dumont's men broke from the trees in pursuit. "After them!" someone yelled. "Exterminate them!"

Riel replied quietly, the cross in his hand, "We have had enough of that. Let them go."

When Adrien and Arthur-Joseph rode up, several Métis were searching the bodies. They rose tiredly and, shaking their heads, said, "Crozier's men must have removed the guns and ammunition from the dead before retreating."

Blood covered Dumont's face as he rode towards Riel. A bullet had grazed his head. Arthur-Joseph and Adrien joined them.

"It's hard," Dumont said, "to leave exposed to the dogs the bodies of our enemies. There's an empty house in the town where they could be safely held."

Riel nodded. "Send a messenger to Fort Carlton offering safe conduct to collect their dead."

Arthur-Joseph and Adrien helped load the casualties onto wagons. As they left the battlefield, they rode past the abandoned cannon. Bodies of downed horses lay in the dry, finished grass of winter.

The young Métis who had shown them the camp found them later that night. He had come for their horses. They were to catch a ride with the wagons carrying the dead to Fort Carlton and home.

CHAPTER 33

April 1885

Worshippers flowed round them as Adrien and Marcel exited the *cathédrale*. Easter mass was over, the fast of Lent done. The long winter was at its end, and the faithful rejoiced. Adrien lifted his face, luxuriating in the warmth of the spring sunshine. He felt a tug.

"I'm hosting a card party tomorrow night," *Tante* Alice said. "Be sure to come." Adrien stared down at the gloved hand on his arm. Green velvet. Adele's favourite. She was close to her time.

Adrien slid the newspaper that Arthur-Joseph had given him inside his coat as he crossed the bridge. Big Bear's band of Cree had massacred two Catholic missionaries, an Indian Agent, and some whites at Frog Lake. The resistance that he had witnessed at Duck Lake had escalated into the North-West Rebellion in Saskatchewan.

Tante Alice had set her tables up in the living room, and Adrien joined her and Marcel at a middle one.

"It's terrible about the priests," a woman said, taking the chair across from Adrien. "They do so much for the missions."

A man in a slender moustache said, "The Indians forced the surrender of Fort Pitt last week."

Marcel flicked the ashes from his cigarette into the ashtray by his elbow. "Did Riel have anything to do with it?"

Tante Alice dealt the cards briskly. "Arthur-Joseph says that the Indians are acting alone. Louis had nothing to do with it."

The players fell silent, arranging their cards in suits, colours, and diminishing numbers.

Marcel was Alice's partner. He led out with a black joker. She glared at him and tried to shove his card back. But it was too late—their opponent had jumped on his card. The trick was won, but the power of the joker was lost. The tricks accumulated against Alice and Marcel. When it was over, Alice gave Marcel a disgusted look and called for a change of tables.

Adrien slid into Marcel's chair. "Mind if I am your partner?" he asked Alice.

She nodded distractedly and pushed the deck towards him. He shuffled the cards, split the deck in two, and fanned them back together. He started to shuffle again while asking casually, "Have you heard anything of Alexina? It's been almost a year since she entered the convent?"

"*Soeur Supérieur* tells me that she's doing exceptionally well. I always said Alexina would be a nun one day." She cranked her head over her shoulder and looked at her husband for corroboration. "Didn't I, Fernand?" He ignored her and continued playing.

Adrien dealt the cards. "What does a young postulant do besides study?"

Alice kept her eyes on her cards. "The Holy Names have an orphanage, and the postulants take care of the infants and young children. Alexina works in the nursery most of the day."

The player on his right played a high club. With a yelp, Alice trumped it and swept up the trick.

Adrien smiled. The Holy Names. He would remember that.

A week passed without word from Adele, and Adrien sent a messenger to Belle's asking about her.

"She had the baby. It's a boy," he read aloud to Marcel on the return letter. "I have to go tonight."

A man in work clothes staggered down the steps of the veranda. Light from the curtained windows glowed red, and music spilled from the open door that he had left ajar. Adrien waited across the street until a girl with loose blonde hair flowing down her back shut it, and the street was quiet. He hurried to the back of the house.

Belle opened the door and led him to the kitchen.

Adele sat on the leather settee with a baby wrapped in a grey, woollen blanket. The boy they had met before sat on the stairs and looked longingly at his blanket. She looked up dully. "Do you want to see him?" She lifted the cloth triangle away from the baby's face. Delicate gold eyelashes fringed the translucent eyelids, and silky red hair covered a perfectly shaped head.

Adele's fingers trembled as they passed over the thin skin at the baby's temples. Tenderly, she touched her lips to his head as if willing the one kiss to last a lifetime.

"How do you plan to carry him?" Belle asked.

"In my arms, I suppose."

Belle snorted. A folded cotton sheet lay on the table. She snapped it open and then let it billow to the floor. Taking hold of the sheet in the middle, she ripped it in two. Then she ripped it in half again. She folded the square several times and prepared a sturdy sling. Knotting the ends over his shoulder, she said, "That'll do."

Adele inhaled the baby's damp sweetness. Tears ran down her cheeks as she offered him to Adrien.

Adrien had held babies before but the frail vulnerability of a newborn always filled him with fear. He offered first one arm then the other to receive him.

Belle stepped forward. "Good grief," she scolded, taking the baby from Adele and settling him inside the sling. "Get going while the streets are still empty."

Adrien crouched in the bushes surrounding the darkened convent and stared at the black, night windows. *Maudit!* Why weren't they opening the damn door? He had tried the knob before setting the baby down and had found it securely locked—not surprising for a house full of women. Bending his neck, he had slipped the sling over his head and carefully laid the baby on the landing. His fingers had groped the door until high up in the middle they found the iron plate with a knocker. He lifted the heavy knocker and let it fall several times before he stepped over the bundle and ran to the bushes. If they didn't open soon, he'd have to chance knocking again. He shivered and pulled the collar of his jacket up. The baby squirmed in its cocoon, and the cloth triangle created by a corner of the blanket moved above his face. He couldn't be left on the landing in this cold much longer. The breath pluming above Adrien's face came faster. He had to chance knocking again; it was dangerously cold for a baby. He sprinted across the yard and up the step. His fist was raised to knock when the door opened. A young nun in a white night gown buttoned to the throat stared out. A cap with complicated lacings hid her hair. She lifted the lantern she carried, and the pale-yellow light illuminated his face.

Alexina recoiled. "Adrien! But what are you doing here? Are you in trouble?"

Adrien spun and leapt off the step. As he ran, he called over his shoulder, "Don't tell anyone."

"Wait," Alexina called, but he kept running.

Adrien watched from his hiding place in the hedge as Alexina put the lantern down and picked the baby up. She cradled him in her arms, snuggling his face with hers. A light flickered in a window followed by others. More nuns, dressed similarly in white, joined her. They peered at the dark yard trying to see what the night concealed and then went back into the convent.

Adrien stood. They'd be opening the blanket now. They'd find a leather pouch filled with gold coins and the unsigned note that Adele had written. The money was for the baby's immediate care; she promised to send more to the family that adopted him. Alexina would assume that it was his baby. He hoped that she would keep his secret, but he didn't much care. He had ruined his reputation when he crossed to the English side of the river.

CHAPTER 34

April 1885

Justine trudged along the road to town. Though the days were warmer and the light lasted beyond supper, here and there patches of dirty, crusted snow gleamed white in the woods lining the road. She had forgotten her gloves, and the hand gripping the handle of her valise was exposed. She switched hands, stuffing her cold hand in her warm pocket, and enjoyed the immediate relief. A crow flew to the top branches of a tree and balanced there with the few remaining battered, leathery leaves. His hard, glassy eyes followed her.

Crows were the earliest birds of spring, often returning before the blizzards had ceased. "*L'hiver des corneilles,*" Joseph called those spring storms—winter of the crows. The crows may have been harbingers of spring, but Justine hated their harsh cawing and their brazen nerve in the farmyard. If Ti-Jos were here, he'd take care of that sassy bird. She caught herself and pushed the thought away. She shouted, and the bird flew off with an unhurried, insolent flapping of glossy, black wings.

It had been a hard, lonely winter since Ti-Jos' death, filled with grief and regret and bitter recriminations against the Church and against him. Justine went home often, and every time she went, she was struck by the silence and emptiness of the house and the guilty clipping off of laughter when Marie-Ange and her brothers forgot their grief.

"You know," Thérèse had confided to her one day over coffee, "ever since I saw his body strapped to that horse, I have the impression that the sun has dimmed." Her mother's face had slowly cracked into a grimace of grief and dry tears.

"Oh, *Maman*! Try not to think about it," Justine had cried helplessly.

Justine had cast about for a way to distract her parents. She thought that a change of scene might help and suggested a trip to Saint-Boniface. Her father had yet to ride a train. It would be her treat. Thérèse immediately refused, but Justine saw a glimmer of interest in Joseph's eyes. Before he could change his mind, the ticket was bought and on a cloudy day in March, Joseph had boarded the train. The last thing to go in his brown carpet bag was a chunk of fruit cake wrapped in brown paper and cotton cloth for Alexina.

Her father was returning today. They were to meet at the station, and Justine would accompany him home on the farm wagon, but first she had to stop at the post office. It had been two weeks since she had heard from Alexina. Perhaps there would be a letter from her sister.

Justine had read that Jane Austen, the great English author of *Pride and Prejudice*, wrote in the margins or between the lines of the original letter in different colour ink when answering her sister, Cassandra. The original went back and forth until the page was covered in black, blue, or red ink. Alexina declared it a marvellous idea and suggested they do the same. Not only would it be a novel thing to do, it would save on expensive writing paper.

Justine stepped away from the wicket and tore open her sister's letter. She found a fresh, new sheet. There had been plenty of free space on the letter she had last posted. It was Alexina's writing, but it was hardly recognizable. Words had been scratched out and black ink splotched near the signature. She had written hurriedly and in a high state of agitation. "*Ma chère soeur*," the letter began. "*You won't believe what I just found* on the convent step ..." Justine's eyes raced over the lines, devouring the details, hardly registering what Alexina wrote. "Knowing your feelings in the past for this person, I feel that it is my duty as a loving sister to reveal the name of the father to you." Justine stared. "I caught Adrien Larence on the landing as he was abandoning the baby. He fled without saying anything."

Justine read on. "I ask you in the name of Jesus, Mary, and Joseph not to reveal this to anyone. For the baby's sake, this must be kept a secret. I know that this news must be disheartening for you considering your friendship with Adrien in the past. I too feel deceived. I always thought that Adrien was basically good.

"I must close, the baby is crying. He's always hungry.

"Remember that you are always in my prayers. Your loving sister, Alexina."

Justine gazed out the post office window. Saint-Cère's main street was empty. The villagers were gone to their supper, and the storeowners were pulling down the blinds and locking up. She remembered the scene in the *cathédrale* when she had surprised Adrien with that woman in the rich clothes. She thought of the strangled twins found in the river and shuddered.

"Closing time, *Mademoiselle* Bélanger," the postmaster reminded her. He released the catches holding up the metal curtain. It slid down smoothly along the rails, and the wicket closed.

"*Oh, pardonnez-moi,*" Justine said, startled out of her reverie. The lonely train whistle blew from the north. She fixed a smile on her face and picked up her valise. She must appear unchanged when she met Joseph and the family.

The team and wagon waited under the white station sign that proclaimed Saint-Cère. Hilaire, Zéphirin, and David stood on the platform, excitedly peering down the track while Marie-Ange squatted near the rails playing with cinders. Thérèse pulled her up, dusted the brown off her hands, and led her up the station stairs. The whistle shrieked another warning, the brakes screamed as they grabbed the rail, and the train screeched to a stop in a blast of dirt and dust that took their breath away. Justine hurried up just as her father stepped to the platform. He laid his carpetbag down carefully on the wood planks.

Thérèse offered him her cheek. "Everyone wanted to come to meet your train. There wasn't enough room in the carriage, so we took the wagon."

Marie-Ange's long legs dangled from her perch on her mother's hip—she was too big to be carried like a baby. Thérèse handed her to her husband. Joseph took her, rubbing his whiskers over her soft cheeks. Marie-Ange squirmed and begged to be let down.

The boys watched awkwardly, not knowing if they should kiss their father like they wanted to, as they had when they were little, or shake his hand like grown-ups. Joseph grabbed the three of them and gave them a hug. Before letting them go, he rubbed his knuckles against their heads.

They broke away, rubbing their scalps.

"You had a good trip, *Papa?*" Justine enquired as she kissed his cheeks.

Joseph nodded, watching the boys as they jostled one another near his brown bag. "Careful! Stay away from my bag."

The station agent carried out a bag of mail and swung it to the conductor in the open door of the mail car.

The engine trembled as it powered up, forcing the wheels to turn and drag the cars away from the station.

Hilaire bent over the carpetbag. "I'll put this on the wagon for you."

Joseph grabbed the handles. "*Non!* I can do it myself."

Thérèse frowned. "If you want to carry your bag, we'll let you. No need to get into a huff about it."

The boys raced to the wagon. Marie-Ange scrambled after them, calling them to wait for her. Instead of tossing his bag on the back of the wagon where it usually went, Joseph laid it gently on the boards at the front and stood gripping the handles.

Thérèse walked by impatiently. "Well, let's go. We have to get home for chores before the light goes."

Joseph undid the latch of the carpetbag, and the metal frame snapped open. "I have something to show you."

Something moved in the dark interior.

David stretched on tiptoes for a better look. "It's a puppy. You've brought us another of *Oncle* Fernand's pups from the city."

Justine craned to see over her brother's head.

Joseph eyed his wife nervously. "It's something better." He pulled the opening wide. A baby in a grey blanket stared unseeingly up.

Her children moved away to let her see. "*Mon Dieu!* What have you done?"

"I couldn't leave him, Thérèse. Someone abandoned him on the steps of the convent. The poor little soul. I just couldn't."

Blood drained from Justine's face. She peeked again at the baby. Relief flooded over her at the gleaming reddish-gold hair—at least he didn't have the black hair that Adrien's family was so proud of.

"You shouldn't have done this without consulting me," Thérèse said.

"It broke my heart to see him abandoned."

Justine watched her father. His sad and grief-stricken face seemed lighter.

"There's room in our family for him," Joseph continued.

Thérèse climbed on the wagon and took the reins. "Let's get going."

The children's eyes grew wide. Their mother never drove when their father was around. They scrambled into the box.

Joseph helped Justine up then placed the bag on her lap. He had barely got on when Thérèse slapped the reins. The horses jumped ahead, and the wagon rolled forward.

"What's his name?" David finally asked when the village was behind them.

"Benjamin," Joseph said firmly, keeping his eyes on the road ahead.

CHAPTER 35

May 1885

Adrien looked up from his paintbrush as Adele entered. She was as slender as the girl he had first seen at Hill's. No one would ever suspect that she'd had a baby.

Adele ran her hand over the smooth walls near the door and gazed at the light-filled rooms. "You'll never guess who I just met."

Adrien dipped his brush into the can of dark ochre.

"Hill's son-in-law. The one who married Esther last year. He was driving by in his carriage and called out to me as I turned into the yard." She raised her hand and patted her hair. The corners of her mouth lifted. "He recognized me."

Adrien wiped up a drop of deep orange-brown that had splattered on the floor.

"He wants to buy a house. He'd like to look at ours."

Adrien nodded and dragged his brush along the baseboard.

Adrien knelt in the grass hammering together the board sidewalk when Adele pushed open the new gate and entered the yard. "I have some news," she said, hoisting a bag that was big enough to hold groceries higher on her shoulder. "I sold the house."

Adrien sat on his heels. "Without consulting me?"

"I got more than we were asking. Here, look." She opened her bag. Packages of new bills tied with string lay at the bottom.

Adrien reached in for a stack, fanning the bills with the cracked fingernail on his thumb. "Can I guess who?"

Adele nodded.

Adrien threw the stack back into the bag. "The Hills can afford to spend some of their money."

Adele groped beneath the stacks, pulled out a bottle of red wine, and waggled it in front of his face. "Belle won't miss this."

They leaned against the dry sink and drank the wine in chipped cups.

Adele stared at the crimson liquid. "I have another plan. I want to start a bigger project."

Adrien sipped his wine. "Oh?"

"I want to build a hotel."

He laughed. "*Un hôtel?* Are you crazy?"

"We've got enough money. You could help me, and I'll run it."

He shook his head. "This is more than a house. Who'll help me build it?"

"The men who were fired at Sommers. They're still looking for work."

Children's playful screams came from the street, and a woman called to a dog. Adrien wiped his mouth with the back of his hand and picked up the bottle. "I suppose you have the location picked out."

"Oh, yes! It's further west ... on Colony Street. It's an empty field, but the city is expanding in that direction, and the lots are practically free."

Adrien kept shaking his head while he refilled their cups. At least with the house sold, Marcel could take the first available train home. He had been claiming he was needed at the farm, but his comments had become so bawdy, Adele and Adrien both knew that what was needed was the conjugal bed.

CHAPTER 36

June 1885

The astonishing news of Joseph's return with an orphan had stunned the villagers and created a babble of gossip that divided into two groups—those who thought it noble and others who thought it crazy.

Her brothers, Hilaire, Zéphirin, and David, had whispered to Justine about the situation at their house the week following the baby's arrival. "*Ma'an's* been furious with everyone," Hilaire said. "She didn't help clean the cobwebs or wash off the fly specks on the iron crib when we fetched it from the barn."

Zéphirin added, "We had to find the bedding and help *Pa* make Benjamin's bed." David nodded, "*Papa* has to feed the baby the bottle and …" His eyes grew enormous. "Change its diapers!" Then one morning when they entered the kitchen, they had found Thérèse in her rocker with the baby on her shoulder. Both were asleep.

"It's better at home now?" Justine asked.

The three boys nodded as one.

Justine's coins jangled into the tin alms box beneath tiers of red, blue, and yellow glasses under the wooden statue of the Virgin. She touched the fire to the wick, and the blue glass flickered to life. She pressed her fingers to her forehead, chest, and shoulders then knelt. At the main altar, a young man who had assisted the priest busied himself with clearing away the vestiges of Sunday mass. He refolded the purificator, the white square embroidered with crosses, and laid it over the empty water and wine cruets on the glass tray. He hurried away, and she bowed her head over her hands.

Still unsettled and filled with wretched disappointment since reading Alexina's letter, Justine hid her face with her hands. She remembered how charmed she had been by Adrien and his handsome looks and fit body. His touch had thrilled her. How could she have been so naïve, she wondered, filled with disgust. He had abandoned his own child, and now she bore the burden of his secret. By keeping quiet, wasn't she culpable and part of the sin? He was despicable and immoral! She was truly finished with him. She touched her fingers to her forehead and rose.

She stood for a moment at the entrance, blinking at the bright light and luxuriating in the heat after the dark, cool interior of the church. She heard a whinny from the trees lining the churchyard and looked up. Rosario waited in the shade with his palomino, Jack. He had rolled up his sleeves, and the sun-kissed skin on his arms and face glowed with health. The sun had touched his face accentuating the deep laugh lines radiating from his eyes, giving him a merry air. The hips in the saddle were narrow, the legs hugging the horse sinewy and strong.

He trotted Jack to the church. "Want to go for a ride?"

The golden horse gently snuffled her hand, and she turned her fingers to let it sniff. Its white mane and tail had been recently brushed and fell like silk over its shoulders and haunches. Rippled muscles twitched away flies from its thick, glistening coat. Jack was fit, well-fed, and cared-for like the Normand cattle she saw browsing and fattening in pastures next to their well-tended fields. This was Rosario's home; he would never wish to leave it.

She slipped her hand into Rosario's, and he helped her onto the saddle then got on behind her. He handed her the reins, resting his free hands at her waist. His tongue clicked and Jack turned into a field lush with fingerlings of green.

"That's quite the story. Your father and the baby," Rosario began. "Do they know who left the baby?"

"The police are looking into it. So far there's nothing." Justine was glad that he couldn't see her face. "I don't think they'll ever find out."

Jack's hooves drummed the earth.

To defend her family, Justine added, "Benjamin is the best-natured baby. It's the best thing that could have happened—under the circumstances."

"I was thinking that too," Rosario said quietly.

At the far edge of the field, a piece of fence had been removed and a path cleared through the trees to the river. They followed the traces of wagon wheels in the beaten grass to the clearing that she had seen last autumn. The spring melt had swollen the quiet, shallow river at the bottom of the clearing, and it gurgled as it ran over the shallow rocks. A square log house, bathed in sunshine, occupied the centre of the clearing.

"*Ah, qu'elle est jolie,*" Justine exclaimed, craning her head back to compliment the man behind her.

Rosario grinned. He pressed his knees into Jack's flanks, and the horse began to circle the house. "I've put two windows on every side. I like a house that has a lot of light." The wavy panes of glass caught their reflection—two riders astride a golden horse. Rosario rode with relaxed confidence. The hair that fell straight over his forehead gleamed with health. 'He's handsome,' she thought with surprise.

Jack stopped at the front door. Rosario helped Justine slide to the ground, and then he swung his leg over the saddle horn and hopped down.

He let her pass through into the empty house. The living room opened on the left with a window facing south. He pointed to the east-facing window in the kitchen on the right. "It's sunny in here first thing in the morning." He led her past the stairs to a door at the back of the kitchen. A small hall opened to two bedrooms. Justine entered the first bedroom and walked to the windows. Trees stood on three sides of the clearing. "I'll clear the trees eventually, and fields will take their place."

They returned to the stairs and sat together on the bottom step, looking out into the sun. The yard fell to the river, and beyond, the prairie opened to a field of oats with a fenced pasture where black and white cows and a few horses grazed.

The cross that Justine always wore dangled from the chain above her collar. He caught it with his fingers and gently dragged Justine towards him.

The corners of Justine's mouth lifted. He smelled of fresh air. She closed her eyes and leaned forward.

She looked around again. A trap door with an iron ring that led to the cellar had been cut into the kitchen floor by the stairs. She would have to cover that with one of Thérèse's colourful rag-rugs.

Justine sat in her pew and blushed red while *Père* Bertrand read the marriage banns declaring that she, Justine Bélanger, and Rosario Normand would marry. She stole a glance at Rosario across the aisle. He winked. A smile crept to her lips and spread to her eyes as she raised her head.

CHAPTER 37

December 12, 1885

In the early dark, Adrien walked past stores in the city centre, unmindful of the evergreen boughs, red velvet ribbons, and pink glass ornaments displayed so pleasingly in the windows. A dreaded hush lay over the city. The streets were empty and strangely deserted. Adrien pulled up his collar and quickened his pace. A few blocks ahead, several men straggled into the street and were joined by others until the street filled with angry men. One of the leaders carried a pole with a straw effigy that dangled from a rope. The face of Louis Riel was painted on the broken head.

Adrien moved into the shadows by the buildings. A thickset man with short legs grabbed his arm and pulled him towards the wave of men. "Come on! We're goin' to the river," he yelled. "It's a good night for a bonfire. Gonna give the bastard the send-off he deserves." Adrien struggled to tear his arm free, but the surge of bodies carried him, insisting that he be with them. He fought against the press of arms, shoulders, and bodies until suddenly he was through and free. He glanced with relief at their backs and groped inside the breast pocket of his coat. Arthur-Joseph's letter was still there tucked inside a thin copy of *Le Métis*. The bridge loomed ahead in the dark. He began to run.

During the spring and summer, the events unfolding in Saskatchewan and the North-West Rebellion had transfixed the nation. Reports of Indian outrages and the killing of several civilians and priests blazed across national newspapers. Alarmed citizens clamoured for action. The federal government quickly called for troops. The departing militiamen in Ontario were hailed as heroes while Québec, gripped by a wave of patriotism, supplied a full third of the troops heading west. The French in Manitoba recalled the hatred and hostility directed towards them after the Uprising and were filled with a deep foreboding and fear for Louis Riel and their Métis kinsmen in Saskatchewan.

Canadians avidly followed the movement of the militia riding north in coaches and open flatcars around the Great Lakes. Parts of the railroad were unfinished, and the men either marched or were transported in sleighs over the incomplete sections. The Métis and Indian success against the police and military at Duck Lake, Fish Creek, and Cut Knife Hill caused increasing concern.

"General Middleton's army has to cross 200 miles of wilderness after it leaves the railroad at Fort Qu'Appelle to reinforce the troops in the north," they said, tracing the dotted line of the railroad over the map. They shook their heads hopelessly; it couldn't be done. The army marched north, completing the forced trek in five days. Then the superior forces of infantry, artillery, and cavalry overcame the badly outnumbered Métis in a short, sharp battle at Batoche. The threatened Indian uprising dissolved, and Riel surrendered a few days later.

Adrien and Arthur-Joseph had followed the escort of soldiers guarding Louis south towards the railroad. The spring sun warmed their shoulders and beat down on their heads, but as soon as the sun set, a chill from the north froze them in their bedrolls. Riel was kept under guard in a tent next to Major Middleton's. He appeared careworn and haggard and was dressed poorer than the other Métis prisoners.

Arthur-Joseph wrote daily reports, sending them ahead with the military mail to the next telegraph station.

Incessant coughing disturbed Adrien on the third night. He turned his back and pulled his blanket closer. When he woke, Riel walked by with his guards. The prisoner wore a grey, military greatcoat like the one that Adrien had seen in Major Crozier's office.

Adrien shook his friend awake—two spots of fever reddened Arthur-Joseph's cheeks.

It took the cavalcade escorting Riel seven days to ride to Moose Jaw. A waiting train filled with jubilant, returning soldiers waited for them. As soon as they found out who the prisoner was, the men in uniform rushed to the windows and doors to shout insults at the man boarding under guard.

Arthur-Joseph and Adrien walked through the cars, stepping over gear and equipment that had spilt in the aisles. They were stopped by a locked door at the mail car. They dropped their bags on the sooty floor and sat with their backs against the connecting door for the long ride to Winnipeg.

Arthur-Joseph spoke in Adrien's ear. "It's good that we're going home. Riel will get a fair trial in Winnipeg. *Un prisonnier* in Manitoba has bilingual rights. The twelve-man jury will be men of Louis' peers, and the judge will be from the superior court where the independence of a judge is guaranteed by law." Suddenly, Arthur-Joseph doubled over caught by a fit of coughing.

"Get some sleep. You won't be any help to Riel if you're dead." Adrien rested his head against the swaying coach and closed his eyes. A change in the rhythmic clack, clack, clackety, clack of the wheels woke him. A black sign with Regina painted in white letters flashed by. The train slowed and then rocked gently as it left the main track and entered a siding. The conductor opened the door connecting to the mail car, and a blast of cold air rushed in.

Arthur-Joseph leaned out of the way. "Why are we stopping here?"

"We've just received orders to stop the train and deliver the prisoner to the police in Regina."

"You can't do that."

"You can if you're the Prime Minister," the conductor said, continuing down the train.

Arthur-Joseph coughed into his hand. When he was able to breathe, the look he shared with Adrien was full of concern. "None of Riel's rights apply in the Territories."

Riel and his two guards appeared in the gap connecting the cars at their backs. They stepped off the train, and Riel was led to some waiting wagons.

Adrien and Arthur-Joseph scrambled after them. They stood on the gravel and looked up the track. The conductor swung down from the end car with a small wooden step that he placed on the ground. He reached up to help a woman with a child on her hip, and then he lifted a small boy down and set him beside her.

"*Mon Dieu!*" Arthur-Joseph exclaimed. "It's Marguerite Riel! And Jean! And Angélique! I didn't know she was on the train." He began to run but stopped and folded over with coughing.

Adrien searched the track. Marguerite and the children were being helped onto one of the wagons. "You aren't any help like this. I'll go with her. You carry on to Winnipeg."

Arthur-Joseph wheezed and shook his head weakly. "I have to stay. Who'll post my reports?"

Adrien shoved him up the stairs of the moving train with his bag. "I'll do it."

He ran after Marguerite's wagon, tossed his bag on the box, and leaped on.

Marguerite looked back startled. One arm tightened instinctively around the baby on her lap, and the other arm pulled Jean close.

"*N'ayez pas peur, Madame Riel,*" Adrien said creeping up to kneel behind her. "I'm Arthur-Joseph's friend. You remember—he visited you in Montana last year."

Her face was ashen with fatigue. She nodded silently and returned to staring at her husband's stooped back in the lead wagon.

At the North-West Mounted Police barracks, when the guards shackled Riel to a ball and chain, Jean began to cry. The crying ceased when Marguerite bent and said quietly, "A white policeman is watching."

A hush fell over the packed courtroom when Adrien led Marguerite to the front row close to the prisoner's dock in the centre of the room. As they took their seats, a woman in the row behind whispered loudly to the lady next to her. "She and the children hid in a cave at Batoche. She had a miscarriage …" Adrien turned and shot her a warning look. She lifted her chin but fell silent. He stole a glance at Marguerite, but she simply stared ahead stiffly and seemed not to notice.

The trial was over before Arthur-Joseph could return. It took five days for six white Anglo-Saxon Protestant settlers to find a French-speaking Catholic Métis of American citizenship guilty of high treason. An English stipendiary judge, dependent on the federal government for his wages, sentenced Riel to the gallows.

Adrien had to go home, and Arthur-Joseph returned to Regina to his place by Marguerite. They waited throughout the fall as, one by one, Riel's appeals were dismissed. Marguerite asked him to attend her at the execution.

Adrien read the article that Arthur-Joseph wrote about the events on November 15 in *Le Métis*.

> *In the morning, after bidding his wife goodbye, Riel climbed the long stair without fear to the scaffold in the company of his confessor, Father André. His clothing was well brushed and his hair well combed. Seeing that the priest was overcome, Riel said, 'Courage, bon courage, Père.'*

Then after a short prayer, recommending his soul to God, the trap door opened. Death was instantaneous, quiet, and peaceful. His features remained calm and the body was not contorted. His body was in a plain pine box and released at midnight on the third day after his death.

A funeral mass was conducted in a Catholic church. The sealed box was conveyed by freight train to Winnipeg, where the body was transferred to an ornate coffin paid for by friends and relatives. A wagon transported him to his mother's house, where he reposed for several days while hundreds came to pray and pay their last respects.

Bishop Taché put aside his condemnation of the Rebellion and permitted them to bury Riel next to his father's grave at the *cathédrale*. Prominent Métis would carry Louis' coffin the six miles to the *cathédrale* from Julie Riel's house. Arthur-Joseph would be one of the ten men on the first shift under the coffin. He wrote Adrien to come.

Adrien caught sight of the wooden cross nailed to the peak of the roof. Through the trees, the Riel house glowed red in the light of a huge bonfire blazing in the snow-covered garden. Men and women in fur coats with children subdued and quiet at their side warmed themselves at the fire. Adrien searched for his friend among the prominent Métis at the front door of the house. Red sashes were wound around their waist then tied in a knot on the right side. The two, long ends of the sash fell from the knot. Riel's coffin reposed near a row of caragana on two long wooden poles. Several people knelt before it with their heads bowed and softly weeping. A man in a deer-stalker hat of heavy wool tweed with the ear flaps pulled down waited with other men near the hedge.

"It's about to begin," Arthur-Joseph said as Adrien approached. "You can take my place when I get tired."

Adrien nodded and stepped aside when the lead Métis raised an arm wrapped in a red sash. Arthur-Joseph took his place along with the other five men on either side of the coffin. The Métis with the sash around his arm shouted, *"En l'air!"* and the men bent to the poles, lifting the coffin with a mighty effort. They staggered at first, distributing the weight of the box evenly on their shoulders. Then their spines straightened, and they stood solid. The leader's voice rang in the clear, cold air: *"En avance!"* The crowd parted and an avenue appeared.

Riel's family moved up. Riel's brothers supported Marguerite and her tiny mother-in-law, Julie. A hand pulled the curtain back from the front window on the house, and Riel's children appeared in the arms of two older women dressed in black. Angélique's head lay on a shoulder—she was almost asleep—while Jean looked on curiously.

The coffin entered the street, and a monotone voice of a woman began to recite the Hail Mary. *"Sainte Marie, Mère de Dieu, Priez pour nous, pêcheurs, maintenant et à l'heure do notre mort."*

Adrien followed at the side, keeping Arthur-Joseph in sight. At the second mile, he was certain that he would be called upon soon. He was the stronger one. But mile two passed, and still Arthur-Joseph would not cede his place. Other men bigger than him called for replacements, but Arthur-Joseph kept moving forward doggedly. Only at the fifth mile when the leader ordered a rest did he signal Adrien to take his place. The coffin rose again high on Adrien's shoulders while Arthur-Joseph walked beside him in a second line of Métis with red sashes.

Candle light from the tall windows flickered on dark shapes crouched under the bushes at the periphery of the *cathédrale*. Adrien pointed with his chin to Arthur-Joseph. "Someone's there. I think they have guns."

"C'est des tireurs Métis," Arthur-Joseph said, glancing at the riflemen. "There's been talk that Orangemen will disrupt the service. They might desecrate the body."

A large crowd waited in the churchyard. They closed around the coffin and accompanied Riel into the church.

CHAPTER 38

January 1886

Snow mounded on the Riel grave, and the frost that formed at the corners of the windowpanes crept steadily upwards over the thin, wavy glass. Christmas passed quietly, as no one had the heart for festivities. In Québec, public opinion turned against the Prime Minister for his role in Riel's death. Crowds massed on the Champs de Mars in Montreal, condemning the government. In Manitoba, the newspapers reported on the decline of the French population—immigration out of Québec had almost ceased while English-Protestants from Ontario flooded the province. Arthur-Joseph wondered in his editorials if the rights that Riel had enshrined for the French in the Manitoba Act would hold.

Marcel and Louise visited his parents in Saint-Boniface after Christmas, and Adrien joined them for fruitcake and coffee.

Louise wore the same dress that she had worn on her wedding day. It had faded and frayed seams strained at her thickening waist. A slender strip of leather worn at the forehead and beaded with red and blue beads secured the black, luminous hair that she wore loose.

Louise put her hand on Marcel's knee and tossed her hair back. "We're not the only ones having a baby—Justine's expecting too. We'll both have babies in the spring."

Adrien glanced at Marcel. Louise had wanted him to rise to the bait. "A natural consequence of marriage. I wish her and Rosario well."

Louise sagged. Her hand left Marcel's knee and lifted to pat the beads on her forehead.

Adrien followed Adele into the Congregational church. A new minister, Reverend Sharp from the United States, was preaching. He came with a reputation as a fiery orator, and she wanted Adrien to come with her and hear him preach. Adrien finally gave in, as he was curious to see the inside of a Protestant church. As was his habit when entering a church, his hand searched for the small font of holy water on the wall beside the entrance doors. He found none and, instead, he touched his dry fingers to his forehead and made a quick, abbreviated sign of the cross, looking around self-consciously to see if anyone had noticed. They entered the third pew from the back.

A bare wooden cross—empty without the body of Christ—centred enormously on the front wall. A plain, dark brown pulpit stood on the left with the choir stalls and organ on the right. Accustomed to statues, the sweet scent of incense, and the glint of silver and gold accessories, Adrien found this altar stark and coldly uninviting. He was equally shocked that the faithful greeted one another happily as they entered and conversed loudly and cheerfully in the pews. The absence of reverent silence struck him as quite remarkable. *Père* had shot him thunderous looks when he dared to whisper to Xavier when they served as altar boys together. "My parish priest wouldn't approve," he whispered to Adele.

"Approve of what?" she asked, removing her gloves.

"The talking!" Several heads turned and looked at him curiously. He sank down to the bench.

Fixed to the back of each pew was a rail with holes, the size of a quarter, bored at regular intervals. He pointed with his chin. "Are those for umbrellas or canes?"

Adele giggled. "No. They're for the communion glasses for the wine."

Adrien drew his chin back in shock. "People have communion wine?"

"Yes. When they take communion on Communion Sunday."

Adrien's mouth twitched. He had tasted the wine while filling the cruets in the sacristy before mass—all altar boys did— even though it was forbidden.

The pews had filled and the congregation settled when the back doors opened and a tall, beefy man in a dark blue uniform entered. He removed the flat, fur cap that was part of his uniform, tucked it under his arm, and walked down the centre aisle to the front pew. He entered it, forcing the people to push over and make room.

Adrien raised an eyebrow at Adele.

She whispered behind her hand, "It's the Chief of Police. Sam Sherwood. I saw him at Belle's during the last raid."

A clock with black Roman numerals on a white face ticked on the wall behind the pulpit. The tip of the minute hand had just touched the hour when a small man in a suit and black shirt with a white reversed collar entered from a side room. He took his place beneath the cross while the choir stood to sing "Onward Christian Soldiers."

Adrien shifted from one foot to the other. He was used to music drifting down from the high loft above. By the fifth verse, the melody that an army could march to was firmly fixed in his head, but he kept his mouth shut stubbornly and prayed that the interminable hymn would end.

When it finally did, Reverend Sharp ascended the pulpit and opened a large, black Bible to a page marked with a purple ribbon. With the patience of a practiced orator, he looked out at the congregation until all the shuffling and rearranging had ended and all eyes were fixed on him before announcing in a clear, ringing voice, "Book of Genesis, chapter 19, 'The Sinfulness of Sodom.'"

Adrien knew the story; he had heard it many times, but this man did more than just read the sacred scripture. His face grew grim at Sodom and Gomorrah's sinful intent against God's two angels. His voice swelled with righteous anger when burning sulphur rained down on the whole valley, the two cities, and the people there. When Reverend Sharp finished, Adrien and the whole assembly sat caught in a hypnotic trance.

The minister closed his eyes and bowed his head. Every head copied him; Adrien inclined his head slightly and closed his eyes too, but after a full minute, his eyes opened and he peeked at those around him.

Reverend Sharp's fist pounded the pulpit, and Adele jumped. "On the outskirts of Ephesus in the infamous Groves of Daphne, crowds of licentious votaries held a perpetual festival of vice. So on the banks of the Red River in Winnipeg, stand in unblushing impudence the same monstrous iniquity."

Adrien frowned at Adele.

Reverend Sharp pointed an accusing finger at his congregation. "In these abodes of vice are the depths of immorality, debauchery, and death. In their swinish precincts, the youth of our land are beguiled and ruined, body and soul."

"He's talking about Belle," Adrien whispered.

Adele's nostrils flared. "That's not true about the kids. Belle chased a bunch of them away last weekend."

The minister continued. "We are proud members of the Anglo-Saxon race, rulers of the world. Only by recapturing the respect for womanly virtues that prevailed when knighthood was in power will the present generation rise above and overcome the social evil of common bawdy houses found on Douglas Pointe."

Adrien bit his lips. He wasn't of the Anglo-Saxon race and was free to sin as much as he wanted.

The pew grew harder as the minute hand began its second journey round the clock. Adrien shifted position, uncomfortable and annoyed by the small man at the pulpit—Sharp seemed to be excited by the vices he enumerated.

Reverend Sharp finally paused for so long that Adrien looked around nervously. "Let us drive out these libertines who out-Judas Judas!" the minister yelled. "I invite the male members of this congregation to stay after the service for a special meeting." He stepped down from the pulpit and returned to his chair beneath the cross.

Adrien stood, wrapped his red scarf around his neck, and was about to follow the women and children out when Adele pushed him back down on the pew. "You have to stay. It sounds like the new minister wants to shut Belle down. She'll want to know."

"What's this got to do with me?" he spluttered. "I'm not Anglo-Saxon."

"You have to. Come by after."

Sam Sherwood relaxed in the front pew. He crossed his legs and draped one arm over the back of the bench.

Reverend Sharp came to stand in the centre aisle. "The heart of this young city beats on the side of purity and right. Brothels operate in broad daylight, around the clock, seven days a week in Winnipeg." He wagged his finger at the Chief. "The police have done nothing to drive these women out of the city."

The Chief dropped his arm. "The prostitutes in this city are regulated. They are in a segregated area. Would you rather see them in the hotels or the train station? Or on the street?"

"Segregation does not segregate and regulation does not regulate," Reverend Sharp thundered. "Your police do not enforce the law."

"My men fine the keepers of bawdy houses and the girls regularly."

"Your small fines are a license of sorts. After your scheduled raids…" The minister fingered parentheses around *scheduled*. "… the houses reopen, and it's business as usual."

A man rose on the far side of the church. With a start, Adrien recognized Thomas Hill.

"I own property near the houses," Hill said. "The neighbourhood used to be a quiet place, but now there's constant traffic and noise at all hours. It's disturbing the peace and the value of my property. This has to stop."

Men nodded in agreement.

The Chief continued to sit comfortably, but he raised his voice to be heard throughout the church. "Prostitution began with the human race and will end with the human race."

Reverend Sharp's face reddened over the white turned collar as he stared accusingly at the Chief. "Your half-hearted methods of policing allow vice to run rampant in the city. There is no city in Canada where the law is as defied as in Winnipeg." His fiery eyes turned on the men in the pews. "This city has become as sinful as Sodom and Gomorrah. The bawdy houses must be closed at Douglas Pointe. Stand if you agree with me."

Feeling like a hypocrite, Adrien rose with the other men.

The Chief remained seated.

The minister stepped closer. "Every man in this church agrees with me. What will you do now?"

The Chief rose slowly. He opened his fur hat and placed it on his head with the point facing forward like the prow of a ship. "I'll see what I can do."

Belle wore a kimono of cream silk belted at the waist and embroidered with blue, green, and yellow-headed *perroquets*. Though it was early, her eyes were heavily made up with black that accentuated the flecks of dark in her grey eyes. Adrien stared, awed as always by her terrible beauty and the sexuality that the kimono barely hid. He wiped his hand on his pants before offering her his hand.

Belle shook his hand and turned to Adele. "What's going on?"

Adele explained breathlessly. "The new minister preached at the Congregation church this morning. His name's Reverend Sharp. He's a fiery speaker, so I invited Adrien."

Belle sighed. "Get on with it."

"He went on and on about debauchery and the houses of sin. He asked the men to remain after the service. I made Adrien stay."

Belle looked at Adrien. "So?"

"He says the bordellos are a blight on the city and wants them cleared from Douglas Pointe."

Belle's foot twitched. "I pay my fines."

"Sam Sherwood was there and said the same thing, but he couldn't convince the minister. Thomas Hill was there too. He said the value of his house was declining since the whorehouses moved into his neighbourhood."

Belle's head came up. "Thomas Hill said that?"

"*Oui*, and every man stood with the minister. The Chief had no other choice but to agree to clean out this neighbourhood."

Belle sighed. She moved to the kitchen table and sat down wearily on a kitchen chair. "Where am I supposed to get another place?"

Adele looked nervously at Adrien then she took a deep breath. "We have a place, Adrien and me. We've been building a hotel on the outskirts of town. It's almost finished."

Adrien's mouth dropped.

Belle hands fell on her lap. "Where did you get the money? Have you been stealing from me?"

"No! It's the money from the baby's father."

Belle's right hand rose. The ruby on her finger flared red as she gnawed the skin of her thumbnail. "Where is it, the hotel?"

"It's away from Main Street at the end of the trolley line. There aren't any neighbours yet."

Adele slipped her cold hand into Adrien's.

CHAPTER 39

May 1886

Arthur-Joseph passed through the open doors of the hotel and entered the sunny lobby. Adele stood by an open window while Adrien struggled with a maroon, over-stuffed chair to a spot she was pointing at.

"Marguerite Riel is dead," Arthur-Joseph said. "We just got word. She died a few days ago."

The chair thumped down. "What? How?"

"No one knows. Malnutrition or tuberculosis. It's bad on the reserves."

"She seemed weak at the trial, but I thought it was all the stress and the miscarriage."

Adele's hands rose to her throat. "Oh! How horrible. I'm so sorry. What about the children?"

"Angélique is staying with her grandmother at the Riel homestead, and there are plans to send Jean to Montreal."

Adele tucked her hand under Arthur-Joseph's arm. "Come. Let's have a drink." She led the way into the dining room. A bar with a row of bottles that reflected double in the mirror took up the long side of the room. She called for champagne and three glasses to a man lazily polishing glassware.

"We were just about to celebrate the opening of the hotel. You can join us."

"This is fancy," Arthur-Joseph said, resting his foot on the shiny brass rail. He patted the pad in his pocket. "I'll write it up in our newspaper."

Adrien lit a cigarette and inhaled.

The smoke drifted to Adele's face, and she pushed the ashtray away. "We don't want to advertise."

"That's ridiculous. Every new business has to advertise. If it's the money, I'll do it for free this time. No need to thank me." Arthur-Joseph's eyes rose to a huge, framed painting above the mirror. A young, corpulent woman reposed on her side on a bed of ferns. Long brown tresses caressed her shoulder and small breasts. One hand rested on a white thigh above a thatch of tight black curls. The soft smile on her lips invited examination, and her black eyes stared brazenly. Arthur-Joseph blinked and looked away.

Adrien chuckled.

Arthur-Joseph sucked in his cheeks. "*C'est risqué!* I'd expect to find it in a house of … of ill-repute, not your hotel."

Adele poured champagne into their glasses. "Well, actually…" Bubbles rose to the top and foamed down the sides. "Belle Fontaine's moving her business here."

"Belle Fontaine! The one in the paper?" Arthur-Joseph swivelled around, taking in the blood-coloured wallpaper, the red drapes, and the pianola in the corner. His glance fell on the spittoon by his feet. He looked closer. Men ringed the bowl. "*Diable!*" He wagged his finger at Adrien. "You're a sly one."

Adrien stubbed out his cigarette. "I'm out of it. *J'ai pas l'gout.*"

"What do you mean? You don't have the taste for it?"

"Belle helped Adele out once, and she's returning the favour." Adrien reached for a glass, raised it, and saluted Adele.

Pink-orange flooded the eastern sky as Justine smiled at the baby nestled in the crook of her arm. She felt strangely empty without the baby in her womb. Rosario stretched out beside her with his arm draped on the pillow above her head.

Justine ran her fingers over the crown of light brown hair. "He looks like you." The baby turned his head and nuzzled his mother, searching for her breast. The modesty that she had shown on her wedding night had fled during the hours of darkness and labour. Justine opened her nightgown and teased the baby's mouth with her nipple. She laughed. "He really is like you."

CHAPTER 40

Late May 1886

Justine rushed around the kitchen. A late spring, impassable roads, then calving and lambing had kept the families apart, and the Bélangers had yet to meet the baby, Jules-Joseph. A spell of hot, dry days had finally dried the roads, and the family was coming for noon dinner after Sunday mass. A starched and pristine white cloth covered the table, and she had set the cutlery according to the etiquette the nuns had taught her—the knife blades faced in towards the plate to prove the host meant no harm. Jules-Joseph slept swaddled and tucked against the side of a large straw basket by the stove. Pale-blue and daffodil-yellow thread honeycombed the neck of his flannelette gown.

Justine looked at the clock. *Père* would be finishing his sermon now. Fresh buns cooled on trays on the counter. She brushed the tops with butter, piled them in a basket, and put it on the table under a white tea cloth. She looked again at the clock. The mass was over; they would be on the road. She had to hurry. Her fingers were fumbling with the last buttons of her good Sunday dress when she heard the wagon. She ran her hand over her hair. It had frizzed during her exertions in the kitchen. There was nothing she could do about that now, so she hurriedly tied it back with a string.

She opened the front door and ran down the steps. The wagon had hardly rolled to a stop when Hilaire, Zéphirin, and David jumped down in a whorl of arms and legs to be the first to reach her. Marie-Ange's chubby, short legs were the last to touch the ground. She shoved and pushed her way through the forest of pants to tug on her sister's skirt and demanded immediate attention. Justine opened her arms and gathered them all in.

Rosario rounded the corner of the barn, leading a knobby kneed, wobbly black and white calf. He tied it to an iron ring near the barn door and crossed the yard to greet them.

Joseph climbed down carefully. Before he was firmly on the ground, Justine threw herself against him. *"Attention, ma fille,"* he said with a grimace, sidestepping to regain his balance. He gripped Justine firmly by the forearms and stood her away from him. With a great show, he examined her from head to toe. A wide grin spread across his face. "You look like a young mother should. Round in all the right places—like your mother."

"Who's round?" Rosario asked, draping his arm around his wife.

The boys' eyes glided over their older sister then, embarrassed, they quickly looked away.

Rosario laughed and squeezed his wife.

Justine shook her head with a smile. She looked up at her mother who sat in the wagon with a squirming Benjamin on her lap. "Aren't you coming down, *Maman?*"

"In a moment," Thérèse said.

Benjamin fought to get free, until he slipped out of her hands and fell heavily onto a brown blanket piled loosely on the wagon floor.

"Aie!" A head with a short black veil popped up.

"Alexina!" Justine exclaimed. "What's this? When did you arrive?"

Alexina threw off the blanket and stood. Though she took care to keep the skirt of her habit modestly close to her legs and went slowly down the long step, the ankles that peeked out in black hose looked slender and young. "The Superior of Novices gave me permission to visit."

"You didn't come alone? A nun can never go anywhere unaccompanied."

"Do you remember Irène Joubert? She entered the novitiate last fall. She's visiting her parents in the village. We travelled together."

Benjamin cried to get down and reached out to Justine. She raised her arms, and he let himself fall into them. She staggered under his weight and let him slip to the ground. *"Mon Dieu! Quel tunnne."* She ruffled his hair. In contrast to the dark hair and dark-brown eyes of the Bélanger family, Benjamin had blond hair with a hint of red like a cherub, and his eyes were blue and crystal-clear.

Justine led her mother and sister straight to the basket in the kitchen. Jules-Joseph scrunched his face and stretched his back when she unwrapped his swaddling blanket. The family gathered around searching for a resemblance until they finally agreed he looked like Justine. But the week before, the Normands had declared him the image of his father.

Marie-Ange had had enough of the usurper. *"J'ai faim."*

Justine laughed. "Of course you are. Dinner is almost ready."

The nasty, bad-tempered rooster had torn a hole in her hose and bit her ankle for the last time yesterday. It rested golden and steaming in her roasting pan.

Justine put the plate of meat respectfully before her father and waited for him to say the grace. A bowl of fluffy potatoes mashed to perfection with fresh cream and butter was passed next, followed by bowls of corn, carrots, and peas brought up from the cellar under the trap-door covered with the colourful rag-rug. The pitcher of gravy went round last. David poured it over his food until it dripped off his plate.

"Quel cochon!" Thérèse said, chiding him for his piggishness.

He wiped it up sheepishly then licked it off his fingers with relish.

They finished with raisin pies.

Rosario pushed back his chair and stood. He looked at the boys. "I have to introduce that black and white calf to its adoptive mother. Who's going to help?"

The mother cow had rejected the calf tied to the ring at the barn and refused to let it suck. Another cow had given birth to a stillborn calf in the far corner of the pasture. Rosario had ridden out to check the pasture and found the dead calf. He brought the carcass home and skinned it in the barn. He would tie the hide around the orphan and fool the second cow into thinking it was her calf. Sometimes it worked.

Joseph and the boys went with him. Benjamin slipped into his boots too, but Thérèse whisked him up for his nap instead. They could hear him singing in the back bedroom while they did the dishes.

Jules-Joseph mewled and squirmed in his basket. In the tufts of grass at the edge of the yard, the purple heads of wild peas swayed on the tips of their stems, and Justine suggested that they have their tea in the sun while she nursed him. They dragged their chairs to the trampled dirt in front of the cabin. A grey cat with black stripes and nipples swinging loosely under her belly left the barn and crept across the yard. An orange kitten dangled from her mouth. "Look, Marie-Ange," Justine said pointing with her head. "She's hiding her babies in the haystack. See if you can find them."

Marie-Ange raced after the cat.

Justine laid Jules on her shoulder and patted his back. Soundly asleep on his cheek, he slept on. An early fly buzzed by in the quiet. Benjamin's singing had trailed off.

"Benjamin has a lot of spirit," Justine said.

Thérèse's lips drew in. "Your father spoils him. He'll ruin the child yet with all his favours."

Over at the haystack near the ground, Marie-Ange frantically pulled handfuls of straw out. She reached into the hole and pulled out the orange kitten. She pressed it to her heart and nuzzled its head. The striped mother jumped down from the top of the stack where she had been anxiously watching. She wound and rubbed herself against the little girl's legs.

"We've been receiving gifts of money for Benjamin," Thérèse continued. "*Père* gives us an envelope of dollars every month. He won't tell who sends it. He claims he doesn't know, but I'm sure he does. He knows everything. I've been spending it on the entire family." She looked at her daughters. "Do you think it's wrong not to save it for Benjamin?"

Alexina's eyes widened. "The baby was given to the entire family. I'm positive that the benefactor would want the family to enjoy the money. After all, Benjamin benefits too."

Thérèse sighed, "I wish I knew who his mother was."

"We don't need to know everything, *Maman*. Where is your faith? We must trust in the wisdom of God in this matter."

Alexina didn't wear the full habit of the Holy Names. She was a novice, and that would happen at her final vows. But the veil that she wore, the black woollen dress that was buttoned close at the collar, and the black crucifix encased in silver that hung round her neck imbued her with the authority of the Church, and Joseph and Thérèse sought her advice first in all things now. Justine felt no sting in being displaced by her younger sister—Alexina had always wanted to do good and be good, and she could never be jealous of that.

The lines on Thérèse's forehead smoothed. "Yes, of course. It's all in God's hands."

Shouts erupted from the barn as an excited cow ran out of the dark interior. At its heels followed the black and white calf draped with an extra skin. Zéphirin ran to open the gate to the pasture, and David and Hilaire chased them out.

Marie-Ange walked slowly across the yard with the kitten clawing its way up her sweater. She came forward to show her treasure to her mother.

Thérèse wrapped her fingers around the kitten's soft body and gently detached its claws from the wool of the sweater. She held it tight against her breast and stroked the soft orange fur. The lids on the blue eyes closed, its body relaxed, and purring started in its throat. The soft *ronron* completed the silence.

CHAPTER 41

June 1886

Adrien rode through the city, controlling the prancing, black mare under him with a relaxed hand. He had spotted her at an auction at the train barns and saw in the thick, crimpy mane, the full broad breast, and round, muscular rump that were the same traits of his family's grey stallion. He would have her bred in Saint-Cère and hoped that the strong characteristics would show in her foal. Also, she might win a few races, as the Canadian horse was a reputedly good trotter and pacer. The name printed on the auction tag said Élisa, and he kept it. The pretty name suited her.

Aspen, white birch, chokecherry, and Saskatoon trees covered the fork of land where the swollen Assiniboine joined the rushing Red River. He turned the mare's head onto a trail that meandered westward along the smaller river. Since forgotten time, the small river had served as the boundary between the northern Cree and members of the Sioux Nation, the Dakotas, and Assiniboines in the south. As he rode, he wondered if the Métis had followed this track on similar horses and what the First Nations people thought of the streets spreading out from the river and obliterating their hunting grounds.

Fire had destroyed the first legislature on Main Street, and its square, brick replacement stood in an empty expanse sloping gently to the river. The red, white, and blue Union Jack with the indiscernible badge of the province in the centre fluttered atop the rooftop platform ornamented with an iron rail. The wind snapped the flag as they rode by, and Élisa's wide-set ears flattened. "*Calmes-toi. Calmes-toi,*" he said, bending to her head and caressing the thick mane. Beyond the legislature to the north, a tall structure rose out of the prairie tabletop. Adele's hotel was the sole occupant in the immediate grid of blocks, but houses had begun to creep nearer from the city.

Adrien backed Élisa out of the stall and walked her around in the alley. Arthur-Joseph whistled, running his hand along her rump. "She must have cost a fortune."

The mare nipped at Adrien's shirt for a treat. "Adele bought me out of the hotel, remember?" He retrieved two sugar cubes from his breast pocket. On an open flat palm, he held them up to her nose. Soft lips folded over the cubes, and she lapped them up, sniffing his hand for more. He rubbed her muzzle proudly. "*Gloutonne.*"

Adrien wore fawn-coloured riding breeches and tall boots laced to the knee like his friend, but there the similarity ended—while Arthur-Joseph's brown boots shone, Adrien's were scuffed with a wad of muck and hay stuck between the heel and the sole.

Adrien backed a reddish-brown gelding out of the next stall—the castrated male wouldn't bother his mare and was calm enough for Arthur-Joseph to ride. "I have something else to show you."

"What?"

Adrien's eyes twinkled. "You'll see."

They rode out of the stable into the bright, hot sun and away from the blocks in the city core.

Arthur-Joseph bounced stiffly in the saddle. "Bishop Taché asked me to fetch the old Indian Kapeyakwaskonam from Stony Mountain gaol last week. You remember—we met him as *Une Flèche* at Batoche.

The soldiers took him prisoner with Riel. When he left the prison, he was wrapped in one of those cheap Hudson Bay blankets with the narrow stripes, and he could hardly walk. He just shuffled away towards the wagon."

A white and brown terrier suddenly dashed out of an alley, yapping at the heels of the horses. The gelding shied, crashing its rump against Élisa. She danced aside, almost unseating Adrien. "*Va-t'en Maudit!*" he yelled, steadying his horse. The dog tucked in its tail and slunk away with an ill-tempered backward glance.

Arthur-Joseph continued. "The old man was sentenced to three years for being with the rebels. It would have been better if he had been sentenced to hang. His health was so broken, I had to lift him onto the back of the wagon. He lay back there, too weak to move. I took *Une Flèche* to the *palais*. The Bishop had a small room fixed up for him upstairs in his residence."

They entered a quiet, residential neighbourhood with wide streets and newly planted elms. At the second corner, Adrien dug his heels into Élisa's flanks and raced down the street. At a square brick house, he reined her in and leapt off. Three dormers with round tops projected from the hip roof. A small portico supported by columns shielded the front door. Adrien unlatched the gate to the white picket and swung it wide.

Arthur-Joseph rode up. "*P'tit Crisse!* Don't tell me this is yours?"

Adrien grinned. "C'mon, I'll show you around."

Adrien ran his fingers along the lintel above the door and found the long, grey key. He stuck the hollow shaft into the keyhole and wiggled it, searching for the sweet spot. He twisted and the bolts slid open. "I got a job at a telegraph office," he said, stepping in. "It won't take long for me to get ahead."

Arthur-Joseph hesitated and looked at the trees lining the river not far from the house. The *cathédrale's* bell-tower shone silver through the canopy of leaves.

"But … it's on the wrong side of the river."

Furious knocking brought Adrien to his front door a few days later. He swung the door open and found Arthur-Joseph's young brother gasping for breath. "Léon! What are you doing here?"

"You have to come quick," the boy said, gulping for air. "To the Bishop's house. *Une Flèche* is dying. My brother wants you to come."

Élisa, still saddled from a ride to Adele's, grazed the tall grass near the picket fence. Adrien whistled. "We'll ride back together." The mare's head went up, her ears twitched, and she trotted towards them. He pulled Léon up to sit behind him. "Hang on," he said, digging his heels into her sides. Élisa's hooves rang and sparked against the metal as they galloped across the bridge towards the *cathédrale* spire.

Adrien entered the dying man's room and quietly closed the door. Arthur-Joseph sat across from a white-haired priest in a black cassock beside the bed. *Une Flèche's* withered body lay under white sheets tucked severely under the mattress. 'The nuns must be looking after him.' Adrien stood at Arthur-Joseph's shoulder. The dying man's shallow breath hesitated for a while after each exhalation, as if the body was deciding to live or die in each long moment. The priest looked up from the open prayer book on his lap and nodded, but then his lips resumed the age-old Latin prayers for the dying.

"*Une Flèche* asked to be baptized yesterday," Arthur-Joseph whispered. On the bedside table was a crystal plate with a vial of sacred chrism for the anointing of the sick and a cruet of holy water. In front of it, in a brass bowl, a braid of smoking sweet grass twined around chunks of burning incense. Tendrils of the double-perfumed smoke rose up as an oblation to *Une Flèche's* ancestors and the purification of his sins. "He heard that you were with Louis at his trial. He wanted you here. He wants Louis' strong medicine."

Une Flèche slowly opened his eyes. With a great effort, he opened his cracked lips and spoke.

Adrien raised an eyebrow enquiringly, but Arthur-Joseph shook his head. The words were neither English nor French.

The priest's long career had been in the missions. He bent over the dying man and waved for Adrien to approach. *Une Flèche* spoke again.

"Louis rode in front of the Métis trenches that day at Batoche," the priest interpreted. "His hand held the cross high. They were kept safe that day from the soldiers' bullets. *Une Flèche* wishes the same strong medicine for the journey to his ancestors."

Adrien took the wasted hand. He heard a soft rustling of leaves as the last breath was expelled, then silence. The priest began the final prayers of commendation.

CHAPTER 42

July 1886

Adrien rode Élisa six days a week to his new job in the telegraph office that was part of the complex of shops, roundhouses, tracks, railcars, engines, and stables in the centre of Winnipeg. Telegrams within one mile of the office were run by 12- to 14-year-old boys, while Adrien and Élisa delivered the others further out.

The telegraph office had three telegraph stations. An office made of half-walls and windows that didn't reach the ceiling occupied a corner at the back. An oak banister ran the width of the room, separating the stations from the public. A sloped writing desk, equipped with forms, pens, and a bottle of ink was fixed to the middle of the railing for customers to write telegrams. A framed picture of Queen Victoria with a small, silver and diamond crown over the white mourning veil that she had worn since the death of her beloved Albert hung on the wall high over the first station. Beneath it, a railway schedule hung crookedly from a nail. Beside it, a large map showed the railroad lines radiating across Western Canada.

During lulls in his ten-hour shift, Adrien spent time at the station with a young man working the telegraph key. A manual with the Morse code lay on top of his desk, and Adrien studied it. Thus began a game of exchanging messages using dots and dashes. It wasn't long before Adrien could decipher an incoming message simply by listening to the sounder without referring to the paper tape.

He returned to the office one night to find Hughes, the office manager, waiting for him beside a newly installed station. Hughes waved him over and pointed to a shiny telegraph key with a flat-topped knob on a narrow, curved bar. When Adrien depressed the knob against the spring tension, it formed a circuit for electricity to flow and signals could be sent. "It's yours. See what you can do."

The key began emitting *dits* and *dahs*. Adrien leaned on the station, listened intently, and scribbled down the incoming message. At closing, he sat at his station, chewing his pencil. Deeply satisfied, he surveyed his new workplace. The railing ought to be moved out—there'd be more room for the operators to work.

The telegraph office served both sides of the river, and French customers always asked for Adrien. One day, a priest with a linen clerical collar and a black, silk neckerchief tied in a bow under his chin entered the office. A well-proportioned head balanced on the slender shoulders of the middle-aged, handsome man. He had parted his grey hair smartly on the right, slicked it back, and combed it away from his face. Gold-rimmed wire glasses were tucked around well-formed ears. Intelligent eyes quickly scanned the room.

Adrien approached the balustrade. "*Bonjour, Père.* Can I be of assistance?"

"*Bonjour, mon fils.*" The priest spoke softly, turning away from the other operators. "I was told you could be trusted."

Adrien straightened. "*Bien sûr, Père.*"

"The little boy, Jean Riel, has to be safeguarded."

Adrien bent his head closer. "Is he in danger?"

The priest nodded. "Jean is going to Montreal under an assumed name. Family friends will take care of him there, and he can attend school."

Adrien gestured towards the forms and pencils. "Write your message. I'll send it immediately."

The priest caught Adrien's sleeve. Long slender fingers pressed a small folded paper against his palm. "Wire that to Montreal. I'll write another telegram for your records."

Adrien tapped out the news that a small boy named Louis Monet would arrive at the Montreal station on next Tuesday's train from the west. It was signed Henri Drummond.

Adrien let himself in at the Roy family home. He had his hand on the worn ball topping the newel to the stairs at the right of the hall and was about to climb to Arthur-Joseph's bedroom when he glanced at the kitchen in the back. A small boy in a dark suit sat at the table. His thick hair had been parted low on his head. The tops of his boots folded down stylishly over the foot. Madame Roy hovered over him with a plate of cookies, and one of her daughters placed a tall glass of milk in front of him. The little boy's dark eyes stared blankly, and his hands didn't move from his lap.

Adrien ran up the stairs two at a time and into Arthur-Joseph's bedroom. "What's going on? Jean Riel's in the kitchen."

Several white shirts and black trousers with shaving gear and brushes lay on the bed beside an empty valise. Arthur-Joseph pushed aside the clothes and sat dejectedly on the bed. "I'm accompanying Jean on the train to Montreal."

"Is it really so dangerous for the little boy?"

Arthur-Joseph picked up a shoehorn made of bone and tapped it against his knee. He looked up. "How did you find out? No one's supposed to know."

"A priest came in and sent a telegram."

Arthur-Joseph nodded. "Henri Drummond. Taché has invited him to teach at the *Collège*."

The front door banged open. They heard shouts and ran to the top of the stairs.

Louis' brother, Alexandre Riel, stood behind his mother with his arms crossed and blocking the door. Julie wore mourning black. A black apron overlay her skirt, and a black scarf covered the thick plaits of hair on her neck. Her arms wrapped around a little boy in a suit that was too hot for the day.

Drummond hurried into the telegraph office the next day with a telegram from Taché to his archbishop in Québec. Julie Riel refused to let her grandson go.

Adrien arrived at work several weeks later to find that he shared his station with another operator. A young man faced him, painstakingly tapping out a message. When he was done, he reached across the desk and offered his hand.

"Hi. I'm Allan Hughes." Reams of ticker tape, papers, and manuals cluttered his side of the desk. Gold flashed from the ring on his right hand. "Sorry about this. With the office so busy, my uncle asked me to help out."

Adrien glanced surreptitiously at the ring. Diamond chips flanked a blood-red stone. No man in Saint-Cère wore rings—a ring could cost a man his finger if it caught on a nail when he jumped off a wagon.

A tan woollen jacket hung on the back of Hughes' chair across from him. The pale-yellow lining with thin green stripes made of silk looked rich and soft. The shine on Adrien's black trousers reflected in the windows of the corner office. The office manager rifled through files in his filing cabinet. The gold in his hair had faded, his shoulders were slightly rounded, and a belly pushed against his belt, but he was an older version of his nephew.

Each morning when he came to work, long strands of ticker tape from night telegrams piled like spaghetti under the stations. Adrien suggested a night shift, and the manager hired two young men on a trial basis. The telegraph keys got quiet in the dark hours of early morning, and one foggy night, the two men dared one another to jump from the roof of the telegraph office to their neighbour's roof. The roofs were slick in the fog, and one of them slipped to the alley and broke his ankle.

Hughes fired them and hired two women for the night shift. The women proved perfect for the work, and Hughes hired two others for the day shift. The women's presence restored civility to the exclusively male environment. Adrien went back to swearing in his mother tongue, though the French *sacres* referred to sacred church objects and weren't nearly as satisfying as the English curses aimed at parts of the body and sexual functions.

CHAPTER 43

December 1886

The smell of roasting turkey and the sound of laughter woke Adrien, and he stretched his cramped muscles. He had spent the night on the cold floor in Arthur-Joseph's bedroom, sleeping off the excess of the midnight *réveillon*. He threw off the quilt that he had wrapped himself in and saw that he was still dressed. He splashed cold water from the basin on the stand beside the door, ran the comb through his hair, and went down.

A Christmas tree in the corner of the living room filled the house with a forest scent of pine. Stiffly starched white stars and angels that Arthur-Joseph's grandmother had crocheted decorated the tree, and fragile pink glass ornaments in the shape of teardrops dangled at the tips of its branches. Monsieur Roy looked up from pouring a yellow, milky liquid into glasses. He was proud of his dandelion wine. He used only the yellow petals and claimed that it was better when aged for a year. But he hadn't been able to corroborate that, as he and his brothers could never wait. He looked disapprovingly at the bristles on Adrien's cheeks and his wrinkled clothes. He signalled the stairs with his head, and Adrien turned on his heel and went back up.

After Adrien had shaved and put on a clean white shirt, he went to the kitchen for a glass of tomato juice. The thick, red liquid that was full of seeds tasted sweet and smelled of summer. Madame Roy prepared the juice in her summer kitchen behind the house, and jars of it brightened her pantry shelves during the winter.

Excited men's voices grew loud from the living room. Adrien wandered down the hall and squeezed by one of the Roy cousins blocking the doorway. "What's going on?"

"Arthur-Joseph just announced that he's running for a seat in the legislature."

Adrien laughed and joined his friend by the fake fireplace. "Is this a joke? You don't know anything about politics."

Arthur-Joseph raised his chin. "I can learn."

"But why?"

"Someone has to stand up for our rights. Haven't you noticed that the streets are filled with immigrants? We're a minority now."

Madame Roy's nephew in the black cassock and the dry look of an intellectual sat across the room, with one leg resting lazily on the other. He addressed him from where he sat loud enough to be heard by everyone. "I fear that you've become cynical, cousin. *Les Anglais*—the English are our friends."

Arthur-Joseph squared his hips and planted his feet firmly. "The provincial government tried to abolish the publication of official documents in French last month."

The seminarian bristled. "The Lieutenant Governor never signed that bill into law."

"If he hadn't flatly refused, we would now not be able to read our own laws."

Adrien exchanged his glass for a glass of dandelion wine. He gazed at the murky liquid. "How can we help?"

Arthur-Joseph's eyes twinkled as he spun around. He turned out his empty pockets. A piece of lint floated to the floor.

The tension in the room lifted, and the men dug into their pockets. The hat going round filled. The uncle with the droopy, white moustache asked, "Who's the candidate for Winnipeg? Who's running for the English party?"

Monsieur Roy answered for his son. "It's Thomas Hill. The man who owns the Freight and Ferry Company across the river."

Several months later, Adrien found himself returning from the telegraph office beneath a sky filled with stars twinkling in the early winter night. The cold made his house seem emptier, and he went to the kitchen to light the fire in the stove. When the fire was well and truly burning, he pulled a long splinter from one of the logs beside the stove and put it to the fire. Sheltering the flame carefully with his hand, he carried it to the kerosene lamp, lifted the glass chimney, and touched the burning tip to the wick. A stink of coal and paraffin filled the room.

He was carrying the lamp up to bed when he heard scrunching and tramping on the front steps.

The door swung open, and Arthur-Joseph hurried in with a gust of wind and snow. "*Carême!*" he said, putting his shoulder to the door against the pushing wind until he heard the latch click and hold. He kicked off his rubber galoshes. "I'm staying with you tonight. The legislature sat 'til the trolley quit running. I'll freeze walking across the bridge."

Adrien backed down the stairs. "You'll have to be happy with the chesterfield." He lifted the lamp to light the living room. An over-stuffed, velvet sofa, the deep purple of chokecherries in August, sat on squashed, round legs in an otherwise empty room.

Arthur-Joseph unwound his blue cashmere scarf and threw his hat and coat on the sofa. "It'll do."

Adrien threw more wood on the kitchen fire. "How are the big shots at the legislature?"

Blotches of burgundy, indigo, and ochre paint splattered the kitchen table. Two rickety chairs with matching blotches stood half-pulled out. The glue had let go of the rungs under the seat, and heavy wire crisscrossed beneath, securing the opposite legs. Arthur-Joseph took the nearest one. "I made my inaugural speech today." A smile expanded across his face. "It went very well."

Adrien went to a cupboard and groped around the top shelf. "I think I have some wine around here." He pulled out a green bottle, dusted off his hands, and found two cups with the handles broken off. He put the cups on the table.

Arthur-Joseph pulled folded pages from inside his jacket. He opened the pages and flattened the creases with his hand. Spidery, penciled notes dotted everything. "Thomas Hill gave his first speech today too. I scribbled as much as I could down in the margin. I can't believe he had the nerve to say what he did in the legislature." His finger rapidly scrolled down the lines until it came to a part underlined in thick, black strokes. He read, "*Every consideration argues the desirability of abolishing this useless and troublesome excrescence at the earliest possible date.*"

"Excrescence?" Was that the same as *excrément?* "What's he talking about?"

Arthur-Joseph threw the papers across the table. "Our Catholic schools! They're going after French-Catholics." He waggled a finger in front of Adrien's face. "It doesn't matter how hard you work or how smart you are. None of us will be allowed to make it—not on our side of the river."

Adrien looked down. Excrescence? *Merde!* It sounded better in English.

CHAPTER 44

October 1887

The late rising sun flooded Justine's kitchen in orange. André lay on his blue quilt on the floor, folding his shoulder under in order to roll from his back to his stomach. She was tired from breast-feeding, and she called him *mon p'tit loup*—her little wolf—but the creases and rolls of fat on his arms and legs filled her with pride. Jules played nearby with pieces of boards and blocks of wood. Rosario returned from the barn as she toasted bread over the open round on the stove. She put the toast down next to a plate of eggs, fried potatoes, and several rashers of bacon, and then slipped into Rosario's old sweater with half the buttons missing and went out for her turn with the chores.

As she stepped away from the protection of the house, a warm wind lifted her skirt and threw tendrils of hair across her face. She looked up. The tops of the evergreens trembled and swayed in the quickening wind. As he had promised, Rosario had enlarged the clearing by cutting down trees and then used the logs for a barn. The land that rolled away across the river to the east offered a vista of flat, rolling prairie with fences to pasture their cattle and horses. However, a wall of trees still surrounded their cabin on three sides.

Rain hadn't interrupted the harvest, and they had rejoiced over that, but that had been a month ago, and there still had not been any rain. The woods were dry, and the dead grass scratched bare feet. She looked at the high, empty, blue sky and began to pray for rain.

Dry leaves pushed by the wind rolled by as Justine crossed the yard. She entered the lean-to on the barn that served as her chicken coop, picked up a bucket of feed, and came out into the page-wire enclosure where her chickens spent the day. "*Poules, poules, poules,*" she called out to her hens, sweeping handfuls of grain in a graceful arc. The hens followed her as she progressed through the enclosure. Their cackling deepened to a contented murmur as they pecked for grain. This quiet time with her birds had become Justine's favourite—and the egg-money was hers.

She refilled her pail and walked down to the pond where she kept her geese. A small dam of rocks and soil diverted the flow of the river into a deep pond. The birds expected her—they left the water and waddled up the slope. She threw out the first handful of feed and then stopped. She wrinkled her nose. There was something bitter, acrid in the wind. She sniffed again and looked up. The treetops in the north had faded to grey. Smoke! Smoke in the trees and coming to them on the wind. Her pail clattered to the ground setting the geese squawking. She hitched her skirt up to her knees and ran to the house.

"There's fire to the north. I can smell it," she gasped, rushing into the kitchen.

She hurried outside with Rosario. Ash floated in the air, carried by the rising wind. The sky had turned brown, and the air was thick with smoke.

The hill with the Normand house commanded a view of the surrounding prairie. "I'm going over to Pa's. I'll see what he wants to do."

Jack and the other horses paced nervously back and forth along the fence in the pasture. Rosario whistled shrilly, and his Palomino flung up his head and trotted to him. He grabbed a fistful of golden mane and galloped bareback without a glance up the hill.

The farm's black and white dog, Pitou, whined and paced back and forth on the veranda. "Be quiet," Justine scolded sternly. He usually crawled towards her and begged for forgiveness when she used such a tone. Today his ears folded down, his tail tucked in, and he crept away. Justine's alarm increased. To calm herself, she returned to her daily routine of clearing away breakfast and dressing the boys. But she left the kitchen door open, and her eyes returned constantly to the house on the hill. 'Why is he taking so long?' she had asked for the tenth time when he finally appeared. Riding fast, he rode into the barn, ducking his head just in time to miss the top of the door. He led Jack out fully saddled and tied him to the ring by the door. A whirling dervish of wind danced across the yard and caught Rosario in a whorl of dust, dirt, and leaves before spinning on to the open field. The wind had not abated.

"The men have decided to wait and see," Rosario said. "If we see flames, we'll head out to set our own fire. We'll try to stop it that way."

Justine knew what had to be done. She had been in the Lafrenière kitchen while Louise's father told of fighting the great prairie fires. A strip of fire would be lit in front of the advancing flames. Then they would walk behind the strip over the charred, blackened soil, hoping to starve the advancing fire and thus extinguish it. This was the way First Nations people had stopped prairie grass fires for thousands of years and how the Blackfoot got their name.

An opaque disk high in the sky and rimmed in red bathed the earth in a yellowish-brown light. Jules cried that the smoke burned his throat, and André fussed and wouldn't be consoled, but still the flames did not appear. Justine and Rosario finally gave up the pretext of work and sat on the veranda with the boys before an amazing exodus of animals fleeing through their farmyard. Partridges and foxes—accustomed enemies—ran together united in flight. Deer skirted the edges of the trees, turning to glance with frightened eyes at the pursuing menace. Justine's geese and chickens flew up, squawking fearfully as a wolf braved the open yard to the pasture. The setting sky was an amphitheatre of angry red in the west when at last they caught sight of the flames.

Rosario drew on a pair of thick boots. "I'm going to light a firebreak in the field beyond the trees. It'll keep it from the house."

Justine squeezed her hands in front of her chest. "What if it doesn't?"

"The wind is shifting away from us. You'll be safe."

Justine hugged her ribs.

"If the fire's not stopped by the firebreak, go down to the pond with the boys. The water will protect you."

Jules stared at them. Two frown lines puckered the skin between his eyebrows. Justine swung him onto her hip.

Rosario ran for Jack. Instead of taking the road, they galloped down to the river, splashed across, and disappeared beyond the trees.

The air had grown as breathlessly hot as an August night when the wind shifted again. Justine couldn't wait any longer. She led Jules to the crib where André slept. "You be a good boy," she whispered, lifting him into the crib with his brother. "*Maman* will be right back." At the door, she looked around. Jules' brown eyes observed her through the widely spaced iron bars of the crib as he quietly sucked his thumb.

Justine opened the gates and chased the horses out of the pasture. She ran to the barn. She threw open the doors, letting in orange light that was as bright as day. She untied the halters and backed the cows out of their stalls into the alley. She slapped their rumps yelling at them to go out. She opened the pigpen and chased the pigs into the alley. The square of orange light at the end of the alley beyond the doors glowed unnaturally red and hot. The animals balked and refused. Crying in fear and frustration, she pushed and shoved helplessly. She left them. Tears mixed with sweat coursed down her face as she walked past the quiet coop where her hens had settled for the night. There was nothing she could do.

From over the treetops, flames licked and the fire sounded like a dragon roaring to life. Justine raced to her desk, dumped out the leather satchel she had used for school, and ran to the crib. She woke André and sandwiched him inside the satchel. He squirmed and resisted, but she pushed him down. "*Oui, il faut. Sois un bon garçon et écoutes à Maman.*" He had to. He had to be a good boy and listen to his mother. She drew the straps over her shoulders and buckled the satchel tightly to her chest. She snatched the woollen blanket from their bed and, clutching Jules by the hand, they went down to the river.

She threw the blanket out over the water in the pond. It floated for a moment then, heavy and wet, it started to sink. She glanced at the woods behind the cabin to the west. Fire leapt from tree to tree. Fur brushed her hand. Her heart stopped. An animal leaned into her skirt. "Oh, Pitou," she cried, looking down and grabbing his ruff. "Come. Come with us into the water." The fire roared again. Pitou trembled. Justine could not hold him. He bolted.

They descended into the icy water as noise grew and fire flamed above them. With Jules on her hip and André whimpering on her back, she sank down. "*Courage,*" she repeated. "*Bon courage.*" She pulled the wet, heavy blanket over their heads like a canopy. The current pulled at her heavy skirt. Her arms ached from holding Jules and André out of the water under the heavy wet blanket. The water slowly turned to liquid gold and warmed as the fire roared towards them. "*Notre Père qui êtes aux cieux …*"

It grew quiet. The light faded under the canopy. Jules shivered, and she lifted the edge of the blanket. Like the night the angels had passed through Egypt and spared the children of Israel, the flames had passed over them. She let go of the blanket. It floated away to catch on the dam. In the burned and ravaged wood, tendrils of smoke spiralled with an occasional hiss and pop. She staggered up the incline, weighed down by her wet skirt and petticoat with the baby on her back and Jules still in her arms. Where was Rosario?

The singed bodies of hens and ducks dotted the yard as she walked to the barn. Pots of flames licked at the burned timbers of the barn. In a corner piled high lay their dead cows and pigs, their faces twisted grotesquely in pain and fear. Their legs stuck out stiffly, and a stench of burned hair and skin filled the air. Justine pushed Jules' face into her shoulder and turned away.

She fell to her knees before the charred timbers of the cabin. The roof and rafters were gone, and blackened timbers showed where the rooms had been. Only the stone kitchen chimney and floor remained. She heard a whine that was almost a cry. She cocked her head. There it was again. From the house. She slipped the straps off her shoulders and laid André on the ground and told Jules to stay. She entered the house, stepping gingerly, toeing the boards to see if they were sound. The whining grew louder. She inched forward to the square on the floor where the trap door to the cellar had once been and gazed down into the blackness. A body the size of a wolf stood alert with its head up. She crouched down and peered closer. Pitou!

Pink glistened between patches of singed fur, and the thin, fragile skin on the tips of his ears had burned to blackened stubs. "Oh, you poor thing," she said, flattening her body on the floor. "Come. Jump! Jump to me." The dog tried but missed and fell backward into the cellar. She called again and this time when Pitou leapt, she grabbed his ruff and hauled him up. He leaned against her, trembling and begging for help. "You're safe. You're safe," Justine said, wrapping her arms around its neck.

Soon afterwards, Rosario found them huddled around the dog in the burned yard and ran to them. "The fire suddenly veered towards the cabin. There was nothing we could do. I thought I had lost you." He looked around at the burned fences, barn, and cabin and the blackened trees. "*C'est un miracle!* I can't believe that you escaped." He circled Justine with his arms.

The enormity of her ordeal washed over Justine, and she sagged against him. "Your parents' house? Is it gone too?"

"The wind came around at the last minute, and the fire turned on itself. It burned halfway up the hill to Pa's, but then it stopped. Their place was spared."

The winter spent at Rosario's parents after the fire was long, and the view from the white house on the hill was heartbreaking. Blackened trees leaned at awkward angles, the forest at their feet lay in black ruin, and the air reeked of soot and charred wood. Fires smoldered underground and sometimes flared up under the snow. One night, Justine woke in a panic at the smell of fresh smoke and rushed to the windows.

"It's just another ground fire in the forest," Rosario said, joining her to look out on the ruins of their cabin and burned forest. "There's nothing left to burn. Come back to bed."

The tears that Justine had held back all day glistened on her cheeks. "Will we ever be able to rebuild?"

"*Bien sûr*," he said hugging her shoulders. "I'm ordering the timbers tomorrow."

"But the forest …"

"Mother-Nature is extremely strong. God wants her to survive."

"Yes," Justine said wiping the tears away with her fingers. "She does. I believe that."

"Come back to bed."

During the days, Justine did her best to keep Jules and André quiet and their sticky hands off her in-laws' furniture and walls. Her boys grew nervous at being shushed so often. Rose Normand insisted on doing all the cooking, so Justine did the laundry and the cleaning. She did her best, although nothing she did ever seemed right. "Cleanliness trumps kindness in Rose Normand's house," Thérèse told Justine during one of her rare visits home.

Rose was an outspoken woman, not afraid to speak her mind. Justine had once overheard her mother-in-law tell *Père* Bertrand that the snakes in Québec were so long, they could wrap around a house. The priest had blinked and walked away without a word. Justine had bit her lips to keep from laughing, glad she had a baby in her arms to turn her attention to.

One day, shortly after Christmas, Justine was preparing the table for dinner, laying out plates and cutlery while Rose peeled potatoes at the sink. Without warning, her mother-in-law said, "There haven't been any bloody rags in the wash for some time." Justine's hand stopped in midair over a plate. She counted back. Heat flamed from her neck to her cheeks.

Rose Normand set the pot of potatoes to boil, and then she went to the table and straightened one of the knives. "I hope your cabin will be rebuilt by the time of your delivery."

Justine's jaw ached with the effort, but she held back her reply. Later that night, she repeated every word to Rosario.

Melting snow dripped and echoed loudly from the eavestroughs outside the kitchen windows while Justine swept the floor. A crow landing awkwardly in a poplar tree caught her eye. Another followed it. They argued then flew off. Justine looked around. The house was quiet. Rose was upstairs. Quickly, she swept the toast crumbs, dirt, and dried peas from last night's supper behind the door with a promise for later. She called to André and Jules, who were playing while washing up in the bowl on the vanity near the back door, "*Venez, venez! Le printemps est arrivé.*" Spring had arrived. They stepped out, leaving behind the black and brown striped mittens, tuques, and scarves that she had knit for them. Giddy with freedom, with the sun warming their heads and a warm wind on their cheeks, they made their way down the hill. Halfway across the pasture, Justine looked up at the ruined forest. A tinge of green! She was sure of it! She crouched beside the boys, and pointed. "Look! The woods are turning green. *Ah, que le Dieu est bon!*"

    Rosario looked up from the log he was skinning by the foundation of the house. With André on her hip and Jules in hand, Justine hurried towards him.

CHAPTER 45

August 1888

Mother Nature had kept her promise. Prairie grasses lived beneath the burned, blackened soil, kept alive by a thick network of roots. By June, an abundance of pink onion, white anemone, yellow primrose, and red and yellow columbine covered the black stubble.

The fields falling away to the east of the cabin were a patchwork of vibrant yellow-green when Rosario and the neighbours hoisted the last great log into place. They had worked all day, setting the ridge pole, and then the rafters, and at last laying the logs for the walls. When Justine slipped under Rosario's arm to wave thanks to the departing wagons, the fresh logs of the cabin behind them glowed tangerine in the setting sun. With a fixed smile, she said, "We're moving back next week."

Rosario looked down at her in dismay. "But the interior walls aren't up. You can see through the partitions to the back."

Justine's chin went up. "We'll stay in a tent. There's a level spot where the coop used to be. I can't live with your mother any longer."

Rosario shook his head with a tired sigh.

The sky stayed high and blue and the air hot and fair. By August, the surrounding fields turned from green to gold and whispered at night in the dry wind.

"You've got more muscles than I have," Rosario teased as she hammered the windowsill above the dry sink in the kitchen.

He took the hammer from her hand and finished nailing the sill.

Justine pushed the wet tendrils off her forehead and lowered herself into a nearby chair. She examined her hands—they were a mess of calluses and broken fingernails. "Look!" she said holding them up for Rosario to see. "*C'est des vraies cicatrices.*"

"Yes, they do look like the stigmata that Jesus had on his hands … and who's to blame for that?"

Justine flipped her hands over and hid them on her lap. "The house is almost finished, and there's still a month before the baby arrives."

He pulled her up and folded forward over her belly to kiss her. "Will you be all right here alone tonight?"

"Of course," she said resting her forehead on him. "There's plenty of time."

André had been playing with leftover pieces of wood by the chair. He dragged himself up and stood hanging on Justine's skirt. Rosario picked him up with one arm and settled him on his hip. He grabbed Jules around the waist with his other arm. "Help *Papa* pack."

Justine followed them into their bedroom.

Rosario dragged his duffle bag from under the bed and loosened the strings. He had set the baby down on the floor, and André was crawling dangerously close to the ceramic chamber pot ringed with yellow flowers that they used in the winter. Justine pushed it further under the bed with her foot and lifted him onto the bed. "Jules," she said. "Ask *Papa* to tell you about the new horse that he's going to buy to replace the one that foundered after getting into a feed bin." The horse had been reluctant to walk and unable to get up after that, and Rosario had had to shoot it.

Jules crawled up on his mother's lap. "*Oui, Papa.* Tell about the Diablo horse."

Rosario threw his shaving kit, socks, and underwear in the bottom of the bag. "He's a descendant of Blanco Diablo, a famous horse from Mexico."

Jules' eyes rounded. "Are you going to Mexico?"

Rosario laughed. "No, it's too far. Our horse comes from a reserve west of Winnipeg on the White Horse Plains." Rosario crouched before his son and lowered his voice menacingly. "An Indian legend says Diablo still runs over the hills when there's thunder and lightning."

Jules turned his head into his mother's neck.

"Oh stop," Justine said. "He'll have nightmares."

Rosario placed clean pants and a shirt on top of the other things in the duffle bag and pulled the strings tight. He laughed and looked at his son. "You won't have nightmares, will you, Jules?"

His son shook his head.

Rosario looked at Justine with a smile. "Besides, it's not a mare ... it's a stallion."

Justine's belly proceeded before her as she held André's hand and let his unsteady legs descend the porch steps to the horse and wagon. Jules suddenly burst out the screen door behind her, followed by a hysterical Pitou, and raced pell-mell towards the wagon. The horse threw up its head, rolled its eyes, and lunged forward in the traces. Justine grabbed Jules' arm just in time.

"You bad dog!" she scolded. "Keep away." Pitou ambled over to sit beside her. His burned fur had regrown, but stubs were all that remained of his delicate, tall ears. He bumped her hand with his wet nose, begging for forgiveness. Justine's irritation quickly changed to pity, and she scratched the sweet spot on his breastbone.

Rosario ran down the steps with his beige duffel bag and threw it under the seat. He shook his head and climbed on the wagon. "I'll only be gone overnight. I won't need half of what you insist on. Wish me luck in getting a fair price." He took the reins. "It might take all day. I'll spend the night in Saint-Boniface with Fernand and return with the team tomorrow. Are you sure you'll be all right?"

A fly buzzed around André's face. Justine brushed it away. "I'll be fine. The baby's still a month away. I can always go to your parents for help." She lifted her face for a kiss.

Rosario pecked her cheek then clicked his tongue. The horse pricked its ears and the wagon rolled forward.

Pitou and Jules raced after them. André tugged to get loose, but she held him by his hands under her belly.

At the gate, Rosario turned and waved.

"Pitou! Pitou!" Justine called. The dog raced back to his mistress, and Jules followed him as she knew the little boy would.

Justine walked to the road at nightfall the next day, hoping to see or hear the wagon. Perched on the tip of the tallest burnt tree, a grey owl pivoted its head and watched her with great unblinking eyes. She stared back, and it flew off with a slow sweep of wings, skimming over the fields, hunting for the grey mice that ran in the drills. A warm wind rustled through the high, dry grain. She felt heavy and full and placed her hands on her hips to relieve the ache in her lower back. A coyote howled from somewhere on the plain—a long, rising note followed by a series of short yips. "Something must be keeping him. He'll be home later, during the night," she said aloud to the wind as she turned back to the cabin.

She woke in the weak, grey light of morning. Her hand searched Rosario's side of the bed. It was cold and undisturbed. She heaved onto her side, placed her hand on the mattress, and pushed herself up. She tiptoed into the boys' room and peeked in. They were still asleep. If she was lucky, she'd have the chores done before they woke. She stopped for the pail of kitchen slops under the sink. Potato and cucumber peels and cornhusks spilled over from days of cooking. Rosario usually took the slops out to the pigs, but he had been pushed for time before setting out for the White Horse Plains. She grabbed the handle, lifted, and grunted at the weight. She stepped outside as the dawn shot through the strips of clouds in the east.

The sow slept in the far corner of the pig enclosure under a board cover that was makeshift and temporary until after harvest, when Rosario planned to rebuild the barn. Ten piglets slept, tucked against her. The sow caught wind of the slops and heaved herself up with a low rumble while the piglets squealed and scuttled out of her way. Long tits swung under her belly as she waddled heavily to the trough by the fence. Her piglets followed her, dancing behind on delicate feet. Justine climbed up on the first rail. The sow grunted greedily and lifted her snotty snout for a sniff. Her bigger piglets squeezed together at the trough, crowding out the runt that ran to and fro at their heels, trying to squeeze into a spot between the curly tails.

Justine lifted the pail over the top rail and twisted to tip out the contents. A wrenching pain tore through her belly. She gasped and the pail rattled down, spilling the slops onto the trampled dirt in the enclosure. The piglets rushed to the food. Their heavy mother lumbered over, unmindful of their squeals as she stepped on them to get to the slops. Justine clung desperately to the top rail waiting for the pain to let go. When it finally did, she took a deep breath and searching for the ground with a pointed toe, carefully stepped down.

With her hands gripping her belly, Justine walked towards the henhouse. She normally gathered eggs by putting her hand in the nests under the hens and searching for eggs under the feathers. Today she decided against it—she couldn't stand them pecking her hands this morning. She scooped up a pan of feed and left it outside on the ground in their wired enclosure.

She walked past the pigpen. The piglets were playing with the aluminum pail she had dropped, rolling it around with their snouts. She really should get it—they would play with it until it was all beaten up. She kept on to the house. Rosario could retrieve it when he got home.

A low pain persisted in her belly, and she frantically worried that she had hurt the baby. "Play inside today," she told the boys, letting them rattle her pots and pans while she rested in the rocker with her book on her abbreviated lap and read. She walked with Jules and André several times to the gate willing the team and Rosario to appear, but the road remained empty and deserted. She began to pray to Sainte Anne, the mother of Mary and the patroness of all mothers, to send her husband home.

Around midnight, an intense pain doubled her over. She groped her way to the rocker. She had to go to the Normands for help, but she couldn't take the boys. The surrounding fields were dry as tinder, and terror gripped her at the thought of leaving the boys alone in the cabin. She rocked and thought, gathering her strength for the next pain. The brown and red braided rug that covered the trapdoor to the cellar lay crooked, exposing the black iron ring nestled in the mounting plate flush to the floor. The next pain was faster. She took a deep breath then stood up. "I have to hurry."

Justine clicked the hook for the trap door into the ring on the wall to keep it open. She collected pillows and winter quilts and piled them beside the trap door, then she went to wake Jules and André. Justine put the sleepy boys down on the floor beside the black hole and ordered them not to move. She kicked the bedding down the cellar. Holding a lantern high, her foot sought the first step of the narrow wooden ladder, and she descended. Light reflected off neat rows of glass canning jars filled with green beans, yellow beans, peas, and fruit jars of crab-apple, blueberries, plums, Saskatoon berries, and rhubarb. The cellar was several degrees cooler and musty, and she shivered as she layered the quilts and pillows on the empty potato pallets.

Pain gripped her again. When it receded, she called, "André, *viens à maman.*" Sucking his thumb and clutching his blue baby blanket, André peered down at her then he stretched out his arms and fell into her hands. "Jules, come to the ladder," she said. She guided his bare feet to each rung as he moved down. Justine raised the lantern and showed them their bed. "*Maman a une surprise.* You're going to stay down here tonight. We'll have a picnic tomorrow," she continued, pulling the quilts over them snugly. Careful not to step on the hem of her dress, she climbed out of the cellar with the lantern. Safely in the kitchen, she held the lamp over the trap door and looked down. André's eyes were half-closed as he sucked his thumb. Jules frowned up at her. "*Sois un ange. Maman* will be back soon. I'll leave the trap door open a bit so you can see."

As Justine turned to find something to prop open the trapdoor, *Réglisse*, Jules' liquorice-coloured cat, sauntered in from the living room to see what was going on. Justine scooped her up and dropped her down the hole. She meowed indignantly, twisted, and landed with a thump on her paws. Garneau's book lay by the rocker. She grabbed it, undid the hook, and lowered the trapdoor, letting it come to rest on seven hundred pages of Canada's history.

It was a warm night, and Pitou lay stretched out on the ground near the cool foundation. He startled out of his dreams when she stepped out with the storm lantern and dragged himself up on his haunches. He tipped his head quizzically, and the heavy tail thumped the ground as she approached. Justine placed her palm firmly and straight up in front of his black nose. The tail stopped. "Stay! Guard the house and the boys."

She looked back several times as she walked away from the house in the dark. Pitou sat in the same spot with his head tipped as he watched her with interest.

Justine looked up at the Normand house standing white on the hill above the pasture. "It's not far. I can make it," she said aloud to herself, wrapping her long orange shawl tightly about her shoulders. The long rising note and short yips howled somewhere near in the woods. Justine squared her shoulders and set out resolutely across the pasture on the trampled short cut between the farms. The yipping sounded closer— by the barns. Her steps quickened. Halfway across the field, she fell to her knees.

Justine placed the lantern safely out of reach of her flailing hands, spread out the shawl, and lay down. Pictures of helpless, newborn calves and lambs taken by coyotes while the frantic mothers looked on rose before her. She drew her legs up as an intense pain ripped her belly. She closed her eyes. She had to push. She bore down unaware of the yellow eyes glistening in the lantern light.

Justine woke to the smell of dank fur. Something crept towards her. "*Sainte Marie*," she cried, pulling the shawl tight and rolling over to protect the baby in her arms.

A drop of something warm touched the back of her neck and rolled down onto her collar. The hairs on her neck rose, and she tucked her head down and tightened her grip. A wet, sloppy tongue tickled her ear. She peeked over her shoulder fearfully. "Pitou! *Idiot*." An earless head peered down at her. She threw an arm around the dog's neck, and pulled it down beside the baby. The sky was turning pink. She had done it. She had borne a child in the open just like *les premières blanches* and the *Sauvagesses*. But unlike the first white women like Marie-Anne Gaboury and Native women, she, Justine Bélanger-Normand, had done it alone. The corners of her mouth lifted, her eyes closed, and she fell into an exhausted sleep.

Rosario crouched over her with his rifle balanced on his knees. The sky above his head was turning from pink to magenta. "What are you doing out here? I was worried sick when you weren't in the cabin. The trapdoor to the cellar was propped open, so I went down and found the boys asleep. Then I saw your light in the pasture."

"The baby was coming. I had to go for help, but I was terrified to leave the boys in the house with the forest and grasses so dry. I thought they'd be safe in the cellar if there was a fire." The baby mewled and turned into Justine's dress. "What took you so long?"

"The haggling went on much longer than I expected. When I finally got on the road, the horses weren't used to one another. Those stupid horses tugged and balked until they broke the harness. I had to stop at a blacksmith." Rosario put the rifle down. "I'm so sorry."

Justine lifted an arm, and the shawl fell away to reveal the baby.

Rosario grinned. "Looks like you have the girl you wanted." He watched his wife undo her blouse. "After this, you've earned the right to name her. Have you thought of a name?"

Justine guided the baby's mouth to the nipple. Milk released at the first suck. She smiled at her daughter. "Hélène."

Rosario traced his daughter's snail-shaped outer ear. "*B'ehn*, Hélène. If you grow up to have courage like your mother, you'll be something."

CHAPTER 46

Fall 1888

Jules and André built a tower of blocks on the veranda and then knocked it down to a chorus of Pitou's playful barking. Justine swept up the breakfast crumbs. She paused by the stove to look down at the basket where her baby slept. Hélène's cheeks glowed rosy under a row of eyelashes so blonde as to be invisible. "*Mon miracle.*" She bent to kiss her, inhaling her warmth and the smell of sweet milk.

Pitou's barking became hysterical as he bounded off the porch. '*Sapré renard!*' she thought, crossing to the window. A red fox had skulked across the yard last week. It was thin with a mangy coat. Yesterday when she went to do her chores, she had found a mess of feathers, and her favourite hen was missing. 'Pitou must have it cornered at the henhouse.' Justine glanced at the two rifles propped in the corner and wished Rosario was at home. She traded her broom for one of the rifles and hurried out resolutely. She slowed in the middle of the yard. The hens quietly pecked the ground around the chicken coop. Pitou raced up and down the ditch, barking at a rider on the road.

With the sun behind, the face and body was in shadow, and the rider was indistinguishable. Whoever it was seemed to be in no hurry and rode the brown horse splashed with white comfortably. Without a saddle, feet dressed in moccasins brushed against the empty grass encroaching on the road and flopped loosely under the horse's belly. A thick, black rope of hair lay on the left shoulder over a reddish suede jacket the colour of a spring fawn. The way the leather moulded the chest, Justine guessed it was a woman, and she had something strapped to her back.

"Louise!" she exclaimed. She lay the rifle down carefully and ran across the yard. She pointed to the cradleboard on her friend's back, *"T'as l'air d'une sauvagesse."*

Louise grabbed the pony's mane, slipped her leg over its rump, and slid down. "You're a good one to talk. You're the one who dropped a baby on the prairie."

Justine's eyes twinkled. She smiled crookedly—embarrassed yet proud.

The cradleboard was designed for riding backward so that the baby could face out and see the world. A shade protected the child's face from the sun. Justine lifted the shade and peeked in. A round-faced baby with a fringe of straight black hair in a pink sweater with red rose buds embroidered on the shoulders gazed at her curiously. *"Quelle poupée,"* she exclaimed. "Blanche will be walking soon, and I've hardly seen her."

Louise took the reins. "I had to ride over to see Hélène before the weather turns cold. It can't stay warm like this forever."

"I've never seen this pony. Is he new? When did you get him?"

"Marcel won him at a card game last week. Real proud of it too and boasting to everyone—of course, he never tells me how much he loses."

Justine picked up the rifle. Dry, dead grass snapped and broke under their feet as they made their way across the yard to the water trough. With the harvest over, farmers told the sky it could rain, but it had remained stubbornly blue, withholding the cleansing, refreshing rains of autumn. The soil turned to dust under the persistent sun and warm winds.

"Where's Rosario?" Louise asked, removing the bridle and letting her horse drink.

"He's away today with the team, breaking sod on the far quarter. We can have a good visit."

The pony drank noisily and then dropped his head to crop the grass under the trough—the only green grass left in the yard. They left him and walked arm and arm to the house.

"What about the other children, Aurore, Étienne, Romain? Who's looking after them?"

"Marcel. He's between jobs. My parents are visiting, so I know the children will still be alive when I get home."

The infant on Louise's back was her fourth. The Lambert children rose like steps in a stair except for the vacant step, the year when Louise had miscarried.

"Jules, André," Justine called, entering the kitchen and returning the rifle to the corner. "*On a de la grande visite.* Come and see my friend's baby."

Louise slipped the straps off her shoulders and carried the cradle to the table. She loosened the crisscross of laces and opened the leather cover. She rubbed her nose against Blanche's and lifted the giggling baby out.

Jules and André hid behind their mother's skirt. "Look," Justine said, pushing them forward. "See how the papoose board is made." She opened the leather flaps and pushed aside a layer of soft, yellow-brown moss. Willow branches formed the outside frame and leather strips secured individual willow branches length-wise to the frame's edge. Wooden slats wove through. "When the cover is laced over the baby, the mother's hands are free to work. The baby is safe and comfortable and can watch what's going on."

"Why don't you have one, *Maman?*" Jules asked.

"Why indeed?" Justine said, closing the flaps and putting the cradleboard on the floor. "I'm not clever enough to make one, I suppose."

Louise's eyes sparkled. "I can show you how. We'll have it done before the next one arrives."

"Thank you ..." Justine said primly. "But there's no hurry." She lowered her voice and nodded towards Jules. "He repeats everything he hears these days." She mouthed, "We're going to take a break."

Louise snickered. "*Père* will notice. When Marie Pelletier stopped having babies, he mentioned it to her during her confession—there was a baby the next year."

Justine's nostrils flared. "We'll not be discussing this with *Père*." A cry not much stronger than a mewling kitten interrupted them. "Hélène's awake. Let me introduce you."

Justine went out to her garden for carrots and parsnips. Summer vegetables were long gone, but the root vegetables stretched in their rows, left to sweeten until after the first frost. Justine dug by the row of staked, bloomed out sweet peas. The seeds in the dry pods rattled in the freshening wind.

In the kitchen, Justine cubed the vegetables into an orange and yellow pile then threw the lot into a large soup pot of boiling stock. "It's so hot for October," she said, blowing frizzy, damp hair from her forehead. She joined Louise at the table with fresh cups of coffee.

Louise added two heaping teaspoons of sugar and stirred in thick, sweet cream. She lifted a spoonful of coffee, blew on the liquid, and let Blanche sip. "I heard Alexina took the veil this summer."

Justine smiled and sipped her coffee.

"Fat chance any of my sisters become nuns."

Blanche's mouth opened and closed like a bird for more.

"What was the ceremony like?"

"It was held at the *cathédrale*. Alexina wore a white gown. She stretched out on the floor at Bishop Taché's feet, laid her forehead on her folded hands, and professed her vows."

"*Sapristi!* It must have been cold on the boards."

"I was wondering about that too. There were five other women taking vows with her." Justine poured more coffee. "Thank goodness, we left the boys at Alice's. It took three hours."

"What's Alexina's first assignment? Is she coming here?"

"No. She's been posted to the school at St. Francois-Xavier parish. She'll be teaching there."

Louise tightened her lips. "I don't get it. What's so great about being a nun? All they do is work for the church night and day for no pay."

Justine glanced at Louise's thick, chapped hands. "We all work hard in our own way."

A short while later, Justine cut thick slices of fresh white bread, placed the bread by a bowl of glistening, salty butter, and dished up the soup.

André nodded to sleep in his high chair. Jules resisted going down for his afternoon nap until Justine offered him another molasses cookie, and by then, Hélène was hungry again. Wind dervishes whirled through in the yard, spinning out dust and dirt. "Let's feed the girls outside. We can get away from the wind behind the house by the garden. It's sheltered there."

Rosario had dragged a split log for her last spring out by the garden. In the summer, she shelled peas there while the boys collected orange-striped potato beetles in rusty tin cans. When the cans were full, they emptied them in the river and laughed as the beetles floated away like a flotilla of overturned umbrellas.

Justine brushed leaves off the log for them, and they sat to nurse their daughters.

The forest facing them still held traces of summer—stunted growth that refused to die—but blackened trees still stood against blue sky. Today's persistent wind picked up ash off the forest floor and whipped it up, imbuing the air with finished smoke.

"What a sad sight that forest is," Louise said, switching Blanche to her other arm. "What do you think is worse, flood or fire? For me, it's fire."

Justine gazed at the wood. The brush under the trees had burned, leaving a clear sight through the wood. "Fire's good for a forest. It cleans the wood of disease. I've found suckers growing near the river. *Pa* says that in a few years, we won't even know that a fire went through here."

"Still, it's sad," Louise said peevishly, turning her head towards the farmyard. Where the barn had stood, canvas stretched over a square of poles. Two big calves, one black with white patches and the other red with a white face, foraged in the shade beneath it. "When do you plan to rebuild the barn? That shelter's not enough for winter."

Justine laid Hélène in the indent between her legs and leaned back on her hands. "As soon as the ground freezes. Right now, Rosario wants to finish breaking the sod on the new quarter."

Pitou slept on his side in the shade of the log with his legs spread stiffly in front. Blanche too had fallen asleep in her mother's arms. Louise laid her in her cradleboard and folded the cover over. The horse nibbled at dry grass. He suddenly threw up its head, flared his nostrils to sniff, and whinnied. Louise rose to check. "What's he fussing about?" She sank back down. "He's just nervous in a new place. What about your new horse? The one from White Plain?"

"Stubborn and lazy. He hangs back in the traces and lets Jack do most of the work, but a few touches of the whip make him press his neck against the collar soon enough. That's why Rosario's out today. He wants to keep working them as a team as much as possible before winter."

Piles of burned boards and timbers lay in heaps around the yard. The charcoal-black glistened in the sun. "Rosario didn't stop all summer. He cleaned up as much as he could. And of course there was the crop to put in and then take off."

"When it's time to build the barn, Marcel will come over and help. God knows, he's got the time."

A gust of wind raced through the yard, and the pony whinnied again. Louise tightened the laces of the cradleboard. "I'd better get going." She pulled the right strap over her arm, swung Blanche securely on her back, and shrugged on the other strap.

As soon as they left the shelter of the house, Justine knew that something was wrong. The sharp line at the horizon in the west was grey and blurred. She shifted Hélène to her shoulder and pointed with her free arm. "Smoke!"

Louise saw it too. "The wind is away from us. You can't even smell it. You'll be safe this time."

"But Rosario's out there working with the team. Look!" She screamed. "I can see the flames."

Louise put her hand on her friend's shoulder. "*Calmes-toi, Justine.* He'll have seen it and got away."

"But …"

"You're worrying for nothing. He'll be fine."

Justine swallowed. "You're right. It's just a small grass fire, nothing more." Their buggy sat in the tall grass at the bottom of the yard. "Maybe someone in town would know." She shook her head. "Rosario's got the horses."

"I'll take you," Louise offered. "My pony can easily pull that buggy."

"But what about Jules and André?"

Louise turned her towards the house with a little shove. "We'll all go together. Wake the boys and get your stuff."

A dozen teams of wagons and buggies, parked every-which-way, stood in front of the church when they careened onto the main street. Justine frantically searched the horses for Rosario's team. Jack and the white horse weren't there. Justine's voice rose. *"Mon Dieu! Mon Dieu! C'est quelque chose de terrible. J'le sens."* Oh God! Something terrible had happened.

"Arrêtes!" Louise warned, glancing down at Jules' frightened face. "We don't know anything yet."

Froth dripped from the bit as the buggy arrived at the church. Louise jumped on the brake with both feet, and the buggy stopped in a cloud of choking dust. She swung Jules down and stepped off. She took Hélène in her arms as Justine climbed down with André.

With her sons in hand and Louise following a step behind with the girls, Justine approached the log church.

Monsieur Filmon, the man who owned the grocery and hardware store, hurried on the path between the church and the gravestones with a stained apron still tied around his waist. "The train set the fires. The brakes were on fire, but the engineer didn't notice and it burned for miles along the track. It's under control, but they say someone was caught out there. They've gone to look."

He stepped aside and opened the door for them.

Louise's mouth moved as if spoken underwater without sound. Justine couldn't understand.

At the front of the church in the semi-gloom, *Père* stretched to light the tall candlesticks on the right and left of the tabernacle. 'How odd,' Justine thought. 'He never lights those during the week.' Shouting men and the jangle of chains against the double-tree of a wagon came from the open church doors, and Justine turned towards the square of light.

Joseph set his reins aside, climbed down, and walked towards the back of his wagon. Marcel was there and Zéphirin, Hilaire, and David.

Louise pressed against her back.

Justine's ears hummed. Her brothers, grown tall and fit, clambered up the wooden wheels encased in iron and onto the wagon bed. At Joseph's nod, they bent as one and grabbed fistfuls of a grey blanket.

A dead weight slid across the boards into careful, waiting hands.

A bit of red and blue-striped cotton caught and tore on a nail as it slid along the wagon bed. The edges were singed and burned, but Justine knew it—remnants of it lay folded on her sewing machine.

CHAPTER 47

Spring 1889

Hughes caught sight of Adrien late one night in a curly-haired, North-West Mounted Police buffalo coat that Adrien had bought on the street. A company satchel sat on his hip, and he was delivering telegrams during one of Winnipeg's famous winter storms. The next day, Hughes tossed Adrien a ring with copper keys for the cabinets and a large key with a barrel shaft on a three-leaf clover. He told him to open and close the office. Adrien caught the keys with a laugh and surreptitiously rubbed the clover before slipping the ring in his pocket.

Adrien had to squeeze past telegraph stations in the busy office to get to his desk. More women than men now worked the keys; their quick hands were naturally inclined to the small repetitious action of the key, and they were meticulous. Adrien enjoyed training the new lady operators, but he couldn't abide anyone who was slow to learn the code or lazy, and he would let that woman or man go—with the exception, of course, of his manager's nephew, Allan Hughes.

Adrien put his red pen down, leaned back in his chair, and glanced over the empty workspace towards the corner office. The electric bulb over his old manager's head threw hints of gold in the washed-out sandy hair as his boss bent over a file on his desk. Adrien picked up the pile of telegrams that yelled STOP after every sentence. He tapped on the glass top-half of the door. "*Patron*, this is Allan's work." The telegrams he dropped on the manager's desk were marked and underlined with red.

Hughes looked the top one over quickly and then handed the pile back. "Perhaps you could oversee his work more closely."

"But sir," Adrien said indignantly.

Hughes waved to the door. "No more. And please close up. I'll be working late."

Several weeks later, Adrien slid the pennies across the counter to the last customer. The old woman recounted each one with her finger, and then slipped them into her change purse and snapped it shut. His boss, Hughes, followed her, opened the door for her to exit, and then turned the dangling OPEN sign to CLOSED and used his key to lock up. He placed his hands on the banister dividing the room and leaned on the wood. "Attention, please."

Hands moved off the keys, and the office grew quiet.

Hughes straightened, and his hands fell to his side. "As you know, the telegraph business is booming in Winnipeg. We are four times as busy as we were."

Adrien gazed around the cramped office. He knew everything about sending telegrams down to repairing the telegraph keys. The only thing he couldn't do was repair the strings strung from pole to pole transporting the live current. But even those poles could be climbed.

A broad smile spread over Hughes' face. "I'm pleased to announce that I will be opening another branch. It's time to expand."

Adrien rose to add his congratulations to his boss. The ring of keys felt warm in his pocket.

Adrien greeted the women operators as they removed their coats for the night shift. Then he crossed to Hughes' office and tapped softly on the open door. Hughes gestured towards the chair in front of his desk.

Adrien cupped one hand in the other between his knees and leaned forward. "Congratulations, *Patron*. The telegraph is the future. It takes a smart man to see it."

Hughes beamed.

Adrien took a deep breath. "I'd like a chance to run the new office. I practically run this one. You've said so yourself."

The smile on the manager's face shrank.

Adrien sat up. "I can run the new office. You know I can. I'd like the job of manager."

Hughes held up his hands. "It's already been decided. Allan will be managing the new office."

"Allan?" Adrien repeated stupidly.

Hughes voice rose. "Yes. My nephew—Allan."

Adrien blinked. "But he makes mistakes. No one takes him seriously."

Hughes lowered his chin. "His father is my partner. He's financing the new office, and Allan will manage it."

Adrien let his hands relax, splaying the fingers open on his legs. "I see."

The manager's eyes wandered to the window of his office. "You can still work here."

A ticker-tape machine suddenly came alive and started tapping wildly in the outer office. Narrow curls of paper wound to the floor. At ten cents a word, it was expensive. 'It must be from a government office in Ottawa,' Adrien thought as he walked by. He left it for Allan.

Adrien let Élisa choose the route away from Main Street. They crossed the bridge into Saint-Boniface. The smell of decaying, waterlogged wood and debris from the swollen, rushing Red River accompanied them.

As Adrien relived the scene in the office, Élisa's head bobbed up and down in a slow walk down the avenue of trees in front of the *cathédrale*.

In a fit of frustration, he suddenly cursed *"Maudit Crisse!"* and dug his heels into Élisa's flanks. She threw her head up, reared, and raced down the street. A black-robed man hurried along the walk with his head down. Without looking, he suddenly turned into the road. Adrien stood in the stirrups and pulled back on the reins with all his might, but Élisa was at a full gallop and her shoulder caught the man. The collision whirled the priest around, and he stumbled and fell on the road. His arms wrapped around his head, and his legs pulled up against the flying hooves.

Adrien jumped down. Élisa stood aside, stamping her feet. Her sides heaved as she watched warily from the side of the road.

"Père Drummond!" Adrien exclaimed, kneeling beside the fallen man. "Are you all right?"

Père's glasses lay crookedly on his face—one side had unhooked from his ear. He unfolded himself slowly, cautiously moving his right leg and then his left. He sighed with relief and held up a hand, *"Deo Gracias."*

Adrien pulled him up.

Dust and gravel covered the priest's *soutane*. "I wasn't watching the road. *Pardon*," Adrien said brushing at the skirt vigorously.

The priest knocked his hand away. "I wasn't either. There's no harm done." Drummond examined his glasses then tucked the gold wire ends back around his ears. He stared at Adrien. "Are you delivering a telegram? If it's for the Bishop, I can take it."

Élisa quietly nipped at the dead grass near the road. Adrien picked up her reins. "I quit today."

Drummond frowned. "Walk with me. I'm on my way to the livery stable." They walked in companionable silence along deserted streets, quiet except for the clop, clop of the horse. Drummond finally said, "It seemed to me that you were doing well at the telegraph. I assumed you were the assistant."

"I was. I practically ran the place …"

"And?" the priest asked impatiently.

"You saw how busy we were. There was always someone waiting. There had to be another office, and I assumed that I would run it … I ran this one."

The priest stopped. "I can guess."

"The nephew, Allan Hughes, is going to run it. The Hughes family is financing the expansion."

Drummond nodded. "It's always so—family connections, social connections, and access to capital. The wealthy are not about to make room for us."

They resumed walking.

"Didn't you own a house in Winnipeg? I seem to recall …"

As they approached the livery stable, the air carried the scent of urine and hay. Élisa raised her head, twitched her ears, and whinnied softly. An answering whinny was heard from up the street.

"It was lonely in that big house. I sold it and moved in with Alice and Fernand Bélanger. Their two daughters, Yvonne and Irène, got married and left the house. I rent their room. Alice says she can use the money."

The priest shook his head sadly. "I'm speaking at a town-hall meeting at Portage la Prairie. An MP from Ontario has also been invited to speak. Why don't you accompany me?" Drummond said. "I was on my way to arrange for a carriage. We can use your horse."

Adrien sucked in a corner of his mouth and nodded.

Adrien threw the harness across Élisa's shoulders, and she shuddered and shook her mane, but she backed straight in between the traces of the carriage. The sky was high and aqua-blue as they headed west out of Winnipeg. Adrien sat with his hands on his knees and the reins loose in his hands, his eyes fastened on the road, and his ears tuned to the easy whirr of the wheels beneath the carriage. "What's the speech about in Portage la Prairie?"

"The dual French and English schools in the province. D'Alton McCarthy, the Member of Parliament from Ontario, will also be speaking."

The sun was at its peak when Drummond pointed to an enclosure not far from the road. Strips of faded red and blue cloth trapped by the fence fluttered in the breeze. "Pull in there," he said. "It's an Indian cemetery." In the back row near the fence, a small wooden canopy protected a freshly dug grave. A fire burned at the foot, and food and tobacco had been left on the mounded soil. Drummond crossed himself. "This cemetery belongs to the Saulteaux, a branch of the Ontario Ojibway who were pushed west when the European trade opened up. This grave is recent and belongs to a Saulteaux man. His family will light this fire in the morning and at night for four days and offer food. They think it takes four days for the soul of the deceased to fly to heaven."

Adrien gazed at the wooden crosses in the graveyard. Many of the crosses leaned, and the cross-bars hung crookedly with age. First Nations names—Keechewees, Misvanyson, and Nawkamekup—had been burned into the wood.

Drummond walked around the grave whispering prayers and blessing the black soil. Adrien pinched tobacco from his pouch, crushed the leaves, and let them fall.

The priest in Portage la Prairie met them at the boarding house where he had rented them a room on the third floor overlooking the street. "I'm worried about McCarthy. From what I've read in the paper, he clearly wants to stir up trouble between Catholics and Protestants—trouble between the French and English populations. Trouble that hasn't existed before in the province."

Drummond laughed. "I can defend myself. I've met men like him before."

The priest's lips turned down. He picked up a valise and headed up the stairs. "He's come with the express purpose of attacking the use of French and the existence of Roman Catholic schools."

A shrill whistle made Adrien look up as they unpacked, and he went to the window. A Canadian Pacific Railway locomotive at the head of a dozen cars steamed to a stop at the station across the dirt-packed street. Further down, an ox pulled a Red River cart loaded high under a canvas tarp. The cart rolled on two wooden wheels taller than the driver who walked beside. Wheels screeching against wooden axles added to the cacophony of the railroad yard.

A persistent wind threw dirt in their faces and grit in their mouths as Adrien and Drummond walked towards the hall. A short man in a blue vest with buttons straining over his belly waited for them at the door. He waved them in and led them quickly through a dark corridor and up several steps to the stage where D'Alton McCarthy was already seated.

Adrien examined the hall. Double-doors in the back led to the street. At the ceiling, four sets of narrow, frosted windows hinged at the bottom were open and leaned into the room. Men and women in hats conversed with their neighbours in French, English, and languages that he didn't recognize. A current of excitement flowed through the room. Though there were a few empty chairs in the front row, men fresh from work in dark work clothes and caps crowded at the doors, eschewing the front. Adrien's hands tingled. He would have preferred to sit somewhere where he could keep an eye on the crowd, but he was forced to sit in the front row.

The moderator introduced the first speaker.

D'Alton McCarthy strode to the podium. He wore a charcoal-grey day coat, a white shirt, and light-grey pants. A white cravat was knotted wide under a high, winged, collar. A honey-blond moustache curled over his upper lip, complementing his handsome face. The blue eyes that looked out at the audience were intensely intelligent, and he spoke in a clear, unhurried voice—a voice honed in the Ottawa parliament. "The French today are more French than when General Wolfe conquered them on the Plains of Abraham. The British were the conquerors."

The smell of stale beer wafted from the man seated next to Adrien. He grumbled, "Damn right we were."

D'Alton continued. "Over a century has passed since that day, and have they assimilated?"

The priest who had met them sat further down in the front row. He cried out. "*Non et jamais!*"

Adrien's fists clenched. "*Non!*"

His neighbour scowled and turned his shoulder, twisting his knees away from him.

McCarthy continued. "The French population in Ontario at the time of the Conquest had their church and their schools and their culture. They were allowed to keep them. Thus they enjoyed the rights of the conqueror, not the conquered. They have resisted assimilation. The schools in French-speaking districts in Ontario must be made public and English-speaking."

Adrien recalled a lecture that Tessier had given. When New France passed into Britain's hands, the British acquired a population that was largely French. The English minority in Québec was given the rights to their schools, universities, churches, and associations, and the French minority in Ontario was guaranteed the same rights. The French rights in Ontario mirrored the English rights in Québec. Adrien exhaled in a rush. McCarthy wouldn't dare propose assimilation in his home province of Ontario, but he dared to do so in Manitoba.

The tingling in Adrien's hands increased during McCarthy's long speech. "French language and French ideas must go to the wall. Roman Catholic schools in Manitoba and the North-West Territories defend the linguistic and the religious rights of French Canadians, and they must be swept away. The attempt of French Canadians to preserve their nationality through their language and separate school rights is aggression and a blow at our hopes as one Canadian people."

He gathered his notes. "In a British country like Canada, we must have unity of language and race. As long as Frenchmen have their laws, their history, and their language, they will remain French in sentiment. In Manitoba and the North-West, the duality of language must be abolished." He tapped the pages on the lectern to align them neatly and then looked up. "Let them remain Catholic but not French."

"Of course!"

"French bastards …"

"One Canada, one Britain …"

The air in the room had become hot and tense as Drummond calmly approached the lectern. "Thank you, my distinguished friend. The first explorers of the West were *coureurs de bois*, who claimed the basin of land draining into Hudson Bay for the French King, Louis XIV. The first white men on the continent of North America to catch sight of the eastern spurs of the Rocky Mountains were the famous LaVérendrye family of explorers from Québec. And the first white woman was a girl from Maskinongé, Québec, Marie-Anne Gaboury. She and her husband had the first white child in Western Canada. She travelled with her fur-trader husband throughout Saskatchewan and Alberta. Her husband, Jean-Baptiste Lagimodière, saved the colonists caught in the fur-trade dispute at Red River by walking 1,800 miles to get help from Lord Selkirk in Montréal. Their daughter, Julie, was the mother of Louis Riel."

A long stream of brown tobacco hit the floor by Adrien's foot.

"We are not foreigners in Canada. We descend from the best explorers, the best trappers, and we have multiplied exceedingly with very little immigration." Drummond's voice grew firmer and louder. "French and English people in this province are equals. The Roman Catholics of Manitoba are largely concentrated in a few districts and impinge very slightly upon their Protestant neighbours. The dual system has existed for eighteen years without public complaint or criticism. There is no valid reason why this minority should not enjoy its school rights."

Adrien put his fingers in his mouth and whistled piercingly. Here and there around the room, French-Canadians came to their feet to clap.

McCarthy rose and walked to the edge of the stage. "This is a British country, and it's precisely this French nationalism that has to be checked. We must have unity of language and race in Canada."

Drummond turned and answered. "That would mean sweeping away the linguistic and religious rights of half the nation."

McCarthy jabbed his finger at the crowd. "The ballot box will decide this great question. And if that does not supply the remedy in this generation, bayonets will supply it in the next."

The priest from the rectory stood. "You tear at our rights. You come from Ontario to cause trouble in Manitoba where there is none."

The man beside Adrien stumbled to his feet. He attacked the priest. Large hands tore the buttons on the cleric's *soutane* and pulled apart the reversed white collar at his throat. Chairs over-turned as the men of his parish rushed to their priest's defense.

Adrien looked up. The man in the blue vest had his arm round Drummond to escort him off the stage. Adrien jumped on the pile of struggling men.

Whistles sounded. Adrien landed one more punch on the man he was straddling and then fled out the back door. He wiped his knuckles across his lips. The taste of rust flooded his mouth from his cut and bloody hands.

His throat burned from thirst as he made his way down the street. Light spilled from a square, two-storey building on the corner up ahead. Above the door, foot-high red letters painted on the wooden boards proclaimed Queen's Hotel.

He guzzled the first beer down in one draught and started on another. Five men, as dishevelled as he was, entered. Adrien folded his shoulders over his beer. In the mirror above the rows of bottles, a short man with a red neckerchief knotted at his throat nodded towards him with his chin. They passed behind him snickering and whispering to a table at the back.

Adrien knew that he should get going, but he was still too nerved up. A sliver of moon shone like a silver hoop earring in the black sky when he stumbled out.

They caught him just outside the circle of light cast by the street lamp. The man with the red neckerchief hit him in the gut and doubled him over. Hands grabbed his shoulders. The second fist caught his face. His head snapped back. Blood gushed from his nose. Two other men appeared. He had seen wolves kill calves like this. Adrien kicked with his feet. He fell into the dirt street. A boot caught him in the side. He felt his ribs crack. Another boot hit his head. The silver earring twinkled then receded.

Justine placed her bag beside her and took the forward-facing seat on the train ride to Saint-Boniface. She had left Jules and André to play for a few days with Benjamin and Hélène with her mother at the Bélanger farm. She opened her purse and took out a long list of things to discuss with her lawyer regarding Rosario's estate. As was her habit, she would stay with *Tante* Alice.

Adrien's eyes opened to a slit. He lay tucked under blankets on a narrow cot against a wall. A lace curtain with a brown stain on the right edge covered a skinny window on the opposite wall. Dirty glass let in yellow light. On a small table beside his head, a tumbler of water stood with a glass straw that was bent halfway up. The room seemed familiar, but his mind couldn't work to place it. A young, slender woman in a black dress entered quietly. Curly tendrils sprang around her face. She placed a fresh palm woven into the shape of a cross beside the glass.

The weight of something landing on his feet woke him in the night. A calico cat with an orange patch on its chest and a black patch over one eye posed on his feet and watched him curiously. They stared at one another until it grew bored and broke it off. The cat walked heavily over his legs and crept along the bed near the wall to sniff his face. Adrien tried to bat it away, but his arms had no strength and were trapped under the grey blanket. He twisted his face away but the curious animal persisted in sniffing. Finally, Adrien blew a puff of air up the cat's nose. The cat sneezed and moved off to knead mindlessly at the empty space between the pillow and the wall. It settled down. A loud purring throbbed from its throat.

Adrien moved his head. Justine slept in the red over-stuffed armchair from the living room. She had kicked off her shoes, and they lay on the floor. Her legs were pulled up and her feet were hidden under her skirt. She stirred, stretched, and put her feet on the floor.

The cat lifted its head.

Justine crossed to the bed, waving her hand above its head to frighten it off. The cat flattened its body and purred louder. Justine grabbed it by the scruff of its neck and lifted it up out of its hiding place. She dropped it on the floor. The cat took a few lazy steps then glanced back insolently. "Get going," Justine whispered sharply, toeing it into the hall with her foot. She followed it out with her shoes in her hand.

A warm wind lifted the lace curtain at the open window. It fluttered up, fell back, and lifted again.

CHAPTER 48

October 1889

In a few weeks, Adrien could sit up without the room spinning round, and it was a few more weeks before he took a few shaky steps. The raucous call of geese as they flew south woke him one morning. He dressed and was sitting on his bed when *Tante* Alice carried in his breakfast tray of toast, chokecherry jam, and coffee. He took the tray out of her hands. "*Merci*, I'll eat in the kitchen from now on."

The next week, she caught sight of him in the back yard as he strapped his duffle bag behind Élisa's saddle. "You're not strong enough to ride such a distance. Wait a while longer."

He winced and swung his leg over the saddle. "I'll be fine." The long, leather fringe on his sleeve quivered as he touched the brim of his slouch hat in a salute. "*Merci pour votre charité.*" He turned Élisa's head to the northwest, and they rode out of the city to the lumber camps in the Riding Mountains.

Élisa sensed that the man drooping over the horn in the saddle was unwell and kept her gait steady as they rode up the gently rising hills suffused in the sweet scent of sage. Every day the dark, green forest loomed nearer, and he grew stronger and sat up straighter in the saddle. One morning, Adrien crouched beside a creek to splash water on his face and laughed. The reflection showed a brown, healthy face under a black, scraggly beard.

The sun balanced above the treetops in the west as they forded a fast-flowing river to the main woods camp. Trees had been cut, and a large clearing spread at the foot of the encroaching hills. Two long, narrow bunkhouses flanked the cookhouse in the centre. They rode past a stable with an attached blacksmith shop. Through the open doors, a blacksmith in a blackened leather apron worked before a forge of glowing white coals, hammering a red-hot horseshoe on an anvil. At a bench on the sidewall, his helper used a flat hand file to sharpen the teeth of a buck saw, a wood-framed crosscut saw in the shape of a bow. Tethered to rings on the outside of the stable, three dirty white horses waited patiently while nibbling the grass.

A man stepped out of a small log building nestled in the trees. He lit a cigarette and stood by a hitching-rail of peeled, white spruce. "This the office?" Adrien asked riding towards him. A stream of smoke floated out of the man's nose and up his face. He nodded and turned towards the cookhouse. Adrien wound Élisa's rein over the rail and entered the office.

Sawdust imprinted with footprints sprinkled the floor. A man in an armchair, with arms straining to contain his enormous buttocks, worked at a desk with his back to the door.

Adrien cleared his throat. "I hear you're hiring."

The man's pen kept scratching along the lines of his ledger.

Adrien cleared his throat again.

The man finally looked up. "What do you know about clearing bush?"

"I've done clearing before at the home farm."

"Half the crew is clearing the logging roads and building the smaller camps in the timber berth. The other half will come later when the ground is good and frozen."

"I'm a hard worker, and I have a good horse."

The chair creaked as it relinquished the man. He lumbered over to the window near the door and peered out.

"I'll give her $1 dollar a day ... same as you. Report to the foreman when the crews come in for the night."

Exiting the office and entering the stable, Adrien saw stalls for a hundred horses stretched on either side. Stable boys with pails poured oats and kernels of dry corn into the feed trough at the head of each stall for the return of the workhorses. One of the boys pointed to the empty stall by the feed bunk. Élisa turned into it without coaxing. Her nostrils flared over the grain and her sensitive lips ruffled up, exposing an arcade of long, healthy teeth, and she ate until the trough was empty. Then her thick, pink tongue licked out every corner and the boards until they were wet and glistening. Adrien backed her out and led her to the paddock next to the stable.

The bunkhouse consisted of one long room without partitions, and its walls were made of rough lumber covered with tarpaper. Fifty bunk beds lined the walls, and clotheslines with gloves, socks, long johns, shirts, pants, and orange, red and brown striped sweaters crisscrossed the rafters. A space had been cleared around a large stove the size of an oil barrel in the middle of the building. Adrien walked to an unoccupied bed as close to the stove as possible, threw his duffle bag on the top bunk, and went out.

The sun had slipped behind the treetops, throwing the clearing immediately into deep shadow. Cuts had been made in the stand of surrounding trees, and the first of the wagons appeared in the openings pulled by two brown horses with white blazes on broad faces. A dozen men with caps or slouch hats pulled far down on their ears sat or reclined on the flat bed behind the driver. Axes and grub hoes had been jammed into the back rack, and their iron heads etched a jagged line against the graying sky.

Adrien joined the men streaming to the cookhouse.

A man caught up with him. "*Sapré, maudit!* Adrien Larence!" Another man joined them. "*Qu'est-ce-que tu fais dans le bois? Justine nous a dit qu'ils t'ont presque assasiné.*" The men were Justine's cousins, Edmond and Ovila. He remembered their fiddle playing at the *soirées* back home. They wondered why he was in the woods. Justine had told them he had almost been assassinated. Others called, "*Allô*." Adrien relaxed; these men were practically cousins.

The cookhouse was as large as the bunk houses. Long tables with chairs extended to the back of the room. Several men worked in the kitchen. One sat before a box of potatoes, slicing off slivers of peel, and tossing the round, white flesh into a kettle by his feet. At a sideboard, another man in an apron covered in flour painted butter on the tops of brown, crusted bread. A man with an apron stained with cooking oil and blood worked a knife at the butcher block in the middle of the kitchen. Roasts of beef as large as his head and generously spiced with pepper and salt sat in the pans on the block. With a practiced rocking motion on the chef knife, he quartered onions and threw them at the roasts.

Although it was morning, the sky was still dark when Adrien hitched Élisa beside one of the white horses that he had seen yesterday. Pink horn showed where the hooves had been trimmed and new iron shoes gleamed, protecting the soft under pads. He added his axe and grub hoe to the row of implements on the back rack and clambered up with the rest of the men. The wagon entered the slash in the trees. Torn up roots and stumps lay on either side of the rough, 30-foot-wide road. As far as he could see in the forest, trees had been slashed with white paint. He was told that a timber cruiser had passed through this area earlier and marked the largest trees. The smaller ones would stand for a later cutting. The horses halted before a wall of trees.

    The men worked in twos, and because it was his first day, Adrien was paired with the foreman. The foreman pointed to a 50-foot tree at the front. "We'll take that one."

    They attacked the tree with their axes, popping out chinks of wood until a large white wound appeared. The tree wobbled on its exposed core. It trembled and struggled to stand. Then with one last shudder, it lost its balance and crashed to the forest floor. Adrien and the foreman cut away its branches, throwing them on a slash pile for later burning.

The driver brought the horses and backed them to the fallen tree. Élisa threw her head back nervously to see what he was doing while he wrapped the heavy chains around the thick end of the log. When all was secure, the driver slapped the reins on the horses' backs. The muscles on their legs and shoulders bulged as their hooves dug into the soft mulch of the forest floor. They dragged the heavy butt end onto a sled and skidded it to a pile on the side of the road.

Adrien kept watching Élisa as he worked. She sweated and huffed, but her legs remained strong, and she never refused to back to a tree. He glanced over at the foreman and hoped that he too was noticing.

They cut deeper into the forest. Coming upon creeks, they skinned the trees and laid them across for bridges strong enough to hold a sled of 40 logs. Deep in the timber berth, the foreman called a stop and ordered them to clear the site for the smaller woods camp. The cookhouse, bunkhouse and stable that they built here were smaller, accommodating the six to eight men who walked out every day to the trees slashed with white paint.

Ice formed on puddles, and leathery leaves carpeted the forest floor when Adrien and Élisa moved to the camp in the bush. One night, as he finished his third piece of raisin pie, a stranger with a grey beard and bristles growing down his neck entered the cookhouse. Ovila greeted him. It was time to start the ice road. The new man would rut the road and layer it in ice eight to ten inches thick—thick enough to bear a wagon loaded with logs.

The first flakes of winter drifted gently down outside the window, and Adrien's thoughts wandered to the night of speeches in Portage. He admired men like Drummond, men of *sang-froid* who kept cool, calmly presenting facts and truth when confronted with injustice. He remembered how his hands tingled, how the hot blood rushed to his face, and how his heart raced when that pompous ass, the MP from Ontario, calmly suggested sweeping away French school rights and the obliteration of the French culture and race in the West. Justine had known he would face discrimination and hate on the English side of the river. The French were a minority now. She had tried to warn him.

The foreman found Adrien in the stable applying ointment to the wounds on Élisa's legs. "Looks like it's settling in for good," he said, brushing the snow off his shoulders. "The ice road is ready, and we can start hauling the sleighs down to the main camp." He leaned against the stall running his eyes over Élisa's body. Her legs were scabbed and scarred from working in the brush. He pushed away from the stall. "She's a pretty little thing, but she's getting wrecked working in the timber. The ice road needs maintaining especially on the south side of the mountain. That'll be her job—and yours."

Adrien screwed the lid on the can of ointment and stood up.

At the door, the foreman lifted the collar of his jacket up around his ears and said, "We can always use a good horse."

The foreman finally ordered Adrien to the ice road. Élisa was one of the four horses hitched to the water sleigh that followed the sleigh with logs down to base camp.

Adrien chopped a hole through the ice, carried buckets of water, and filled the water tank while men unloaded the sleigh and decked the logs near the river ready to be rolled into the water for the log drive to the sawmill in the spring.

The empty sleigh started back up the mountain and the water tanker followed, streaming water along the ruts all the way to the bush camp.

The men who lived close by went home at Christmas. The bush camp closed, and Adrien and the remaining men went down to base camp.

Adrien lay on his bunk bed, his hands under his head, and one ankle resting on the other and gazed at the half-empty clotheslines overhead. It was Christmas Eve, and he thought of home. His mother's meat pies would be ready and waiting on the stove. The altar boys would be lighting the candles on the altar for Midnight Mass. He thought about Justine. Would she be at Midnight Mass? Probably not. Not with her three young children. Would she have a tree without Rosario?

The door opened and Ovila stepped in, letting in a draft of cold air. "Cook wants us in the cookhouse."

Adrien swung his legs and jumped down. Other men joined them as they streamed out on snow that sparkled like sugar.

The cook met them with a jug of whiskey and tin cups. They were on their second fill when cook noticed Edmond's fiddle case under his chair. "Play us a tune."

Edmond drained his cup before lifting his fiddle out of its bed of red velvet. He fitted the fiddle under his chin. "I have a song that was written 250 years ago."

"Bah," snorted one of the men. "How do you know? It was so long ago."

Adrien knew the story of the *Noël Huron*. *Père* told it every Christmas in Saint-Cère.

Edmond drew the bow over the strings. "It was written by a Jesuit, Jean de Brébeuf." He nodded at Ovila.

"Brébeuf was a missionary with the Hurons. He wrote the hymn to teach the Hurons the Christmas story. In it, the Holy Family lives in a birch bark lodge, and the Babe is dressed in rabbit fur. The Three Wise Men are hunters bringing gifts of fox and beaver pelts." Ovila paused. "Father Brébeuf was tortured and burned at the stake by the Iroquois. He so impressed the Iroquois with his courage while he was dying that they tore out his heart and ate it while it was still beating."

Adrien looked around at the men. Admiration and disgust flooded their faces.

While Edmond played, Ovila sang:

> 'Twas in the moon of winter-time
> When all the birds had fled,
> That mighty Gitchi Manitou
> Sent angel choirs instead;
> Before their light the stars grew dim,
> And wandering hunters heard the hymn:
> "Jesus your King is born, Jesus is born,
> In excelsis gloria."
>
> Within a lodge of broken bark
> The tender Babe was found,
> A ragged robe of rabbit skin
> Enwrapp'd His beauty round;
> But as the hunter braves drew nigh,
> The angel song rang loud and high...
> "Jesus your King is born, Jesus is born,
> In excelsis gloria."
>
> O children of the forest free,
> O sons of Manitou,
> The Holy Child of earth and heaven
> Is born today for you.
> Come kneel before the radiant Boy
> Who brings you beauty, peace, and joy.
> "Jesus your King is born, Jesus is born,
> In excelsis gloria."

Adrien gazed out the window at the silvery woods. A grey shape walked through the white birches at the edge of the clearing. He looked again, but there was nothing except for a rising wind under the winter moon.

By March, the river was free of ice and most of the men had gone to their farms for spring planting. Adrien followed them out.

CHAPTER 49

Spring 1890

Patches of dirty, stubborn snow hung on in the shadows of the church. André and Jules splashed through puddles of greasy mud, chasing some older village boys through the churchyard. Justine warned them against getting dirty as she walked to the carriage with Hélène on her hip. Her sons raced on in the mêlée of boys, coats flapping open, without a backward glance.

Père picked his way around the puddles and joined her. He lifted the baby's frilly, cream-coloured bonnet and peeked at her face.

Hélène jerked away, almost tipping out of her mother's arms. Justine swung her to the other hip.

"She has your curls, but I think she resembles Rosario."

Hélène strained away from the priest, frightened by the black biretta and *soutane*. Justine put her shoulder between them.

Crocuses poked their furry, purple heads and yellow throats up through the patches of snow—the promise of summer. Jules stopped to show them to André.

"Have you given further thought about teaching in the village school?" *Père* asked. "The position is still open for the fall."

Justine shook her head.

André crouched over a clump of purple and uprooted a fistful of flowers.

At the doors of the church, Rosario's parents, Rose and Alphonse, chatted with a group of parishioners. Two little boys careened blindly into their legs. Without looking, Rose yelled "Jules! André!"

Justine sighed. She couldn't manage the farm on her own with three children. She had moved back in with her in-laws. It was worse without Rosario. Rose made the boys sit on the floor by the stove to eat.

Père had also seen the *contretemps*. "You need a place of your own. *La vieille* Lambert is moving. Her daughter says she's too old to live alone, and Madame Lambert is moving in with her. You could rent her house in the village."

A bird the size of a robin sailed by to perch on the tallest gravestone. A black band dropped from each shoulder to form a "V" on its chest. It threw up its head, puffed out its feathers, and opened a long beak. Flute-like notes cascaded in the clear, blue sky: "*Tee Too Tee La Leera Loo.*"

Père sang out, "*Ti-Jean a perdu ses culottes!*"

Justine burst out laughing. *Johnny has lost his pants.* Père had it note for note. "I'll use that to introduce my students to the meadowlark next spring."

Old Madame Lambert's white house was small and square, and because it was small and square, cheery windows on every side let light into the four interior rooms. Two bedrooms opened off the right of the living room at the front, and a narrow kitchen ran the width of the house at the back. The lane into the yard led to a small, weathered log barn, chinked with grey mortar. Joseph gave her his best black and white cow, and she brought a dozen of her brown hens. The cocky, glossy-feathered, red rooster came along to boss the yard.

"Rosalie could help," Louise suggested when she found out Justine was moving to town. "She can do your chores."

"But I've no room. Where will she sleep?"

"There's an attached porch at the back. She can sleep in there."

The widow had slept in the porch when her house grew unbearable in the sweltering heat of the Manitoba summer, as the glass in the windows could be changed out with screens. Someone had whitewashed the walls, but the paint had become transparent over time, and the walls were thin and not insulated. Justine floated the bottom sheet over the grey mattress on the iron bed. It would do Rosalie for now, but when the winter set in, she knew she would have company in her bed.

Justine tucked the hem of her brown skirt and petticoat into her waistband so as not to trip and carried the box of books up the steps and into the house. She entered her bedroom and slid the box as quietly as she could under the crib. Hélène slept in her usual position with her face on the mattress and her bum up in the air. Tendrils of damp, brown curls clung to her forehead.

Out of the window over the crib, Justine could see Pitou trying to scramble up a pile of firewood rising in a jumble to the barn roof. The terrified squeaks of a gopher could be heard from across the yard. Jules and André stood on the pile helping their dog by pulling at the logs.

She caught a flash of red out of the corner of her eye and she leaned forward to see what it was. Adrien! What was he doing here? She pulled back from the window. The last time she'd seen him he'd been unconscious at Tante Alice's. He must be home from the woods. She put her hands on the metal bars of the crib, leaned forward, and peeked again at the man walking across the yard towards her boys. He wore his hair longer than usual, long and into his collar. His clean-shaven face was tanned a healthy brown, and the red she had seen was a red flannel shirt that strained over a muscled back. Justine's hands went slowly to her belt and she let her skirt fall.

She met him at the wood pile. White sprinkled the black at his temples.

He turned from watching the dog. The corner of Adrien's mouth lifted as his eyes met hers. "*Ma'an* told me you'd moved to town and will be teaching in the village."

Justine nodded. "*Père* pestered me all winter. I have to do something."

The half-smile fled Adrien's face. "Yes, of course. I'm sorry about Rosario."

Justine fingered the gold ring on her left hand. She dreaded this voicing of sympathy. No matter how many times or who voiced it, she had no answer. What could be said? "Jules. André," she called instead. The boys looked curiously at Adrien and came to stand shyly at their mother's side. "Jules," she said putting her hand at his back and pushing him forward. "And André." She pushed her youngest son ahead with her other hand. They stuck their hands out as they had been taught, and Adrien bent forward, formally catching each small hand and giving it a shake with large fingers.

Pitou's digging grew increasingly frantic. "*Quel bête!*" Justine said. What a stupid beast he was. She shook her head. "I'd better stop him before he cuts the pads of his feet."

She grabbed Pitou's ruff and pulled him off. "Go," she said to the boys. "Play with him somewhere else." They ran to the house, cajoling and calling back to their dog. Pitou followed them with his tail low to the ground, but in a minute it was up again, the white tip waving like a flag as he raced to catch up.

Hélène called, banging the windows above her crib, and they went towards the house.

"I heard she was born on the prairie," Adrien said. "You must be proud."

A smile stretched across Justine's face as it always did when she thought of that night on the prairie with her baby and Pitou. "Yes, I am." The spicy scent of his aftershave came to her as they walked side by side. "And what of you? You seem perfectly recovered. I heard that you were in the lumber camps all winter. Are you home for a while?"

Adrien lifted his shoulders. "*Non.*" Élisa grazed near the gate at the front of the yard where he had dismounted. Her long neck curved down under her thick, black mane as she nibbled the spring's early grass. "It was too hard on Élisa. I'm going to the States. My Uncle Paul lives in Boston. He's making good money. He has a job for me."

Justine stopped to stare in disbelief. "You're going to leave? To be an American?"

Adrien laughed. "I'm not going to be an American. I'm just going down there to work."

From her collar, Justine felt the familiar heat rise. "Have you forgotten what that MP from Ontario said when you got beat up? We could be Catholic but not French in Manitoba and in the West. He spoke of bayonets."

Adrien stared back, then one shoulder lifted in a slight shrug.

Justine breathed faster. "Do you know that last February, the legislature abolished Article 23 of the Manitoba Act? French is no longer one of the official languages of the province."

"*Oui.*"

"And in March, the legislature voted to abolish French schools."

Adrien chewed the inside of his mouth. His eyes slid away to the wood pile.

She raised her hands. "The parish will have to support the school. My teacher's salary will be reduced. How can I support my family?" She began to pace back and forth in front of him. He was abandoning his people again. Just like he'd abandoned his child, Benjamin, on the steps of the orphanage. Running away from his responsibilities. She stopped and stared at him. "Arthur-Joseph has resigned his seat. He refuses to be with a government that violates its own laws."

Adrien raised his hands and opened palms full of work-stained calluses. "What can I do?"

"We need to fight for our rights. What if everyone gives up and leaves? How can we survive?"

Adrien shrugged. "Let Arthur-Joseph fight. He loves glory."

Justine blinked. Hot blood flooded her cheeks. *"Maudit sans coeur!"* she said. He was damned and heartless. She left him standing in the yard as she went in to Hélène.

The next day, Adrien boarded the train bound for Minneapolis and then down to Chicago and east around the Great Lakes to stay with his Uncle Paul in Massachusetts. He would be part of a diaspora of French leaving Canada for higher wages in the factories of the United States.

CHAPTER 50

Fall 1890

Jules and André waved forlornly out the window, and Hélène screamed in the kitchen. She would calm down as soon as Rosalie gave her toast. Justine turned onto the trampled track that served for a sidewalk at the end of the lane. She didn't look back.

"*Les Deuxièmes, montrez les petits comment on commence la journée,*" Justine said to her grade two students, asking them to model for the little ones how to start the day. The first graders in the tiny desks at the front looked around curiously and then they stood like their older brothers or sisters or cousins in the class.

Boys in baggy, patched pants and girls proudly wearing hand-me-down dresses that were new to them stared expectantly at Justine. Only a couple of children sported brand new clothes: A boy near the window wore new brown pants and a plaid cowboy shirt with pearl snap buttons, and his sister in the front row wore a yellow dress under a white sweater with embroidered blue and pink flowers down the front.

Justine looked up at the cross above the blackboard and touched her forehead. "*Au nom du Père …*" She glanced over her charges. Every child but one knew how to make the sign of the cross.

At the first peal of the noon Angelus from the bell in the church tower, Justine's pupils shoved their scribblers and books inside their desks and lined up quickly at the door. They had to hurry home to eat and hurry back in order to play. Going home was a luxury Justine couldn't afford; she ate lunch at her desk with a ham sandwich in one hand and a red marking pencil in the other. The tinny ding-dong of the school bell caught her at the board chalking in the afternoon's assignments. She rushed outside to find *Soeur Supérieur* straightening the lines of her grade one and two pupils. The nun waited for absolute silence from the children then signalled for the lines to move forward into the school.

A branch scratching at the window woke Justine. Her eyes opened a slit. It was still pitch-dark outside. She groaned, pulled the cover over her head, and burrowed deeper into her bed. The clock on the bedside table kept up its merciless tick-tock. Her hand shot out, pushed down the alarm button, and inched back.

Cocooned in feathers and wool in the fog between wakefulness and sleep, she began her round of morning prayers. First, she prayed for Jules, André, and Hélène. Then the circle expanded to include Thérèse and Joseph, her brothers, and Marie-Ange, with a special blessing for Alexina. Her mind's eye then flew above the town, praying for the sick and distressed. Finally, she lighted upon the grey stones around the church and Rosario. Her eyes startled open, and she slipped out of bed. It was the anniversary.

Their black and white wedding picture, flanked by two white candles in brass holders, occupied a narrow shelf above the wing-table in the living room. Justine's fingers searched the shelf. She found the metal box, extracted a match, and scratched it along the friction strip. It flared. The flame jumped to the dead wick, and light climbed up the wall and danced on the glass frame.

On their wedding day, they had posed in her mother's garden under the Mayday tree. Rosario looked down on her possessively, and her eyes twinkled under a confetti of white petals that sprinkled her hair. His face was half-tanned. She had warned him not to wear his hat that spring. "You'll have a forehead as white as a baby's bum." He had kissed her and promptly forgot.

Justine had been empty of tears since the funeral; crying only upset those who depended on her. She looked up at Rosario's face. A tear forced its way out and down her cheek.

A small hand touched her leg. "Why are you crying, *Maman?*" Jules asked.

Justine wiped her face with the sleeve of her nightgown. "*C'est l'anniversaire de Papa aujourd'hui.* He's been gone for two years."

"Is he in Heaven? *Tante* Alexina says that's where the angels live."

Justine heaved him onto her hip. "*Oui, mon ange.* That's where he is." She carried him back to his bed.

Louise drew her braid forward over her shoulder and patted it down before taking a sip of steaming, sweetened coffee. A different child slept in the papoose board by the stove, and Christmas cards in torn envelopes lay strewn at her elbow beside a plate of gingersnap cookies. She pulled the pile closer, drew out the first card, and read the hand-written message. She picked up a cookie, sniffed it, and took a bite. She chose another card. "You should stop wearing that gloomy black. It doesn't suit you. *Trop mélancholique.* It's been over two years."

Justine plucked the card out of Louise's hand and gathered up the others. "I'm not ready yet." She opened the dish cupboard and laid the cards and envelopes on the china plate rimmed in gold that she used when important people visited.

Louise scowled. "You could at least dress in brown for Christmas."

The boys came in from playing with their fort of blankets in the living room. They each took two cookies from the plate. They were reaching for a third, but Justine slid the plate out of reach and offered them a glass of milk instead. Jules gulped it down without breathing.

Louise bent to stare him in the eye. "*T'es comme un p'tit veau.*"

Justine smiled. Her friend was right—her boys drank milk like spring calves.

"What do you think?" Louise continued. "Should *Maman* wear something that's not black for Christmas ... perhaps dark green, like the Christmas trees?"

Jules looked curiously at his mother. "A tree? Can we have a tree this year? Please, *Maman*."

Justine wiped away the froth of milk on his upper lip with her thumb. "I have a small one in my classroom. Would you like that? We could bring it home after the concert."

Rosalie carried Hélène in and set her down on the floor.

Jules took his sister's hands and twirled her around. "We're going to have a tree. We're going to have a tree."

Flushed from her nap and unsteady on her feet, Hélène plopped down on her bum. She looked around indignantly then hollered. Justine lifted her up and blew kisses into her neck until the baby squirmed and giggled. She looked at Louise over the baby's head. "Did you say *gloomy?*"

Stars punctuated an inky sky as the audience climbed the long flight of exterior stairs to the dance hall above the dry goods store. Rows of chairs and benches lined the floor, transforming the hall into a theatre for the night. At one end of the room, sheets strung on wires curtained off an area for the stage.

Because they were the youngest, Justine's class sat on benches in the first row. *Soeur Supérieur* knew that innocence guarantees success and had assigned the grade one class the manger scene. Justine had practised and practised with them for weeks, but tonight, tears pooled in the eyes of yesterday's confident angel charged with the *Gloria in Excelsis Deo*, and the shy shepherd boy kept swallowing dry heaves. Justine tucked her feet together under the bench, gripped her program, and looked around for her parents.

Thérèse held Hélène, and Joseph, Marie-Ange, and Benjamin sat with Jules and André in the last row. A man with his head bent attentively towards a woman stood behind them. He wore a chequered black-and-tan jacket, and the blonde woman wore a tightly cinched suit over a promising bust. Justine's program fell open on her lap. Arthur-Joseph! What was he doing here? The lights dimmed, and she turned her attention to the stage.

Disconnected hands on the right and left pushed against the sheet wall and groped their way towards the middle of the stage. At the centre split, the hands grabbed and dragged the sheets along the wire to the side. *Soeur Supérieur* stood with her back to the audience in front of a young choir. The nun's arms went up, and girls in ringlets and ribbons sang out on time; the boys followed a half a beat later. *"Mon beau sapin, roi des forêts ..."* filled the room. To the oohs and aahs of the audience, schoolboys as big as men lit the candles on the small pine tree at the right side of the stage.

Much later, Justine handed out mittens, scarves, and tuques that had been lost in the excitement. *"Joyeux Noël et bonnes vacances,"* she called after her pupils as their parents led their exhausted children out. She heaved a tired sigh. André clomped over in his heavy boots and open jacket. A blue scarf striped with yellow dragged from a sleeve. She buttoned him up and wrapped the scarf around his neck. She did the same to Jules with his red scarf with blue stripes. She heard her name and looked up. Arthur-Joseph strolled towards her with a pretty young woman attached firmly to his arm.

"Allô! Quel plaisir," he said, lightly touching his lips to Justine's cheeks.

She pushed the boys in the direction of their grandparents. "What brings you to the village?"

Arthur-Joseph smiled at the blonde. "I'm visiting Camille. Don't you know her? I thought you knew everyone in the village."

Justine's brows pulled together then relaxed. "Of course, you're Edouard Gervais' daughter. I didn't recognize you now that you're all grown up."

Camille's chin went up a notch. She pulled her shoulders back and the ample bosom rose.

"The other purpose for my visit is monetary," he continued. "I'm collecting funds for the Riel monument. Friends of Louis in Montréal have raised funds for it, and his friends in Manitoba want to help."

"Where will they put it?"

"At his grave by the *cathédrale*."

Hélène ran headlong towards her mother. Her wrists showed at the sleeves of her pink coat, and the buttons strained over her chest. Justine thought of the store window on Main Street, which displayed a girl's lovely blue coat trimmed with white rabbit fur. Justine scooped her daughter up. "*Il fait tard.*" It was getting late.

The boys crawled under the benches. "Jules! André! Come." They ignored her and kept playing, so she sweetened her demand. "Let's take the tree home."

"Let me help," Arthur-Joseph said. He quickly carried the tree down the stairs, inserting the trunk into the curve of the waiting toboggan. Justine sat Hélène at the back, laying the tip of the tree on the little girl's shoulder. She made her daughter grab the thin rope above the slats and told her to hang on tight. Justine handed the pull rope to the boys. Alarm and excitement flooded Hélène's face as the sleigh jerked free of the ice and slid off on the hard-packed snow. At the corner, they swerved too sharply, almost tipping Hélène and the tree out. "*Pas trop vite!* Not so fast!" Justine called, racing after them.

Arthur-Joseph cupped his hands around his mouth and shouted at her back, "*Joyeux Noël, ma belle!*"

Camille watched unsmilingly from the top of the stairs then she went down.

Justine was surprised to see Arthur-Joseph take communion with Camille on New Year's Day. He caught up with her after the service as she buttoned Hélène's coat at the back of the church. Thérèse had let the sleeves down on the pink coat and moved the buttons over for one more year of wear.

"You're still here?" she asked.

"I decided to stay. I've nothing to do in the city now that I don't go to the legislature."

Justine popped the clasp of her purse, found her billfold, and took out a dollar bill. "Here's something for the monument."

He held his hands up and refused to touch it. "Thanks, but widows don't need to contribute to the fund."

"Take it. I can afford it."

The bill hung between them.

His hand moved forward reluctantly. "It appears I must give in."

Camille waited at the baptismal font with her friends, shooting looks of murder at Justine.

Arthur-Joseph lowered his voice. "Let's write. I can repeat what the gossips say in the city and report on the news."

Justine's eyes twinkled as she glanced at Camille. "Won't she mind?"

Arthur-Joseph wrapped his hand over Justine's. "She doesn't have to know."

Justine pulled her hand away. "*Si tu veux.*" If he wanted to …

CHAPTER 51

August 15, 1891

Justine handed her suitcase to *Père* and stepped down onto the small step placed by the conductor. The scene around the station was as she remembered it. Men driving wagons of lumber and grain yelled at their teams to go forward, to come round, to stop before the soot-covered sheds crowding the track. On Boulevard Provencher, pedestrians went in and out of the shops, keeping to the shade of the alternating green-and-white striped canvas canopies. Beyond, the *cathédrale* spire rose above the trees. Once when she stepped down from the train, she'd had a husband to carry her case. The setting was the same but different this time. It had something to do with the quality of light.

Père interrupted her gloomy thoughts. "There'll be standing room only at the assembly tomorrow. The Bishop has summoned representatives from all parishes." They chatted as they walked companionably to the Bishop's palace. Being with *Père* took no effort—he loved to be heard and could expound on any topic.

He hesitated in front of the *palais*. "Can I walk you to your aunt's?"

Justine shook her head. "It isn't far."

He turned. "As you wish. I'll see you tomorrow at the assembly."

Justine dried the dishes and wondered what her uncle had ever seen in the woman playing solitaire at the kitchen table. Alice had used an unwashed pot to cook the potatoes at supper, and the liver had been fried to leather. Burnt gravy with clots of uncooked flour had complemented the meal.

Alice dealt seven stacks of cards. "How was your winter in town?"

"The house was cold, but I can walk to school."

Alice placed the black seven of spades on the red eight, freeing a stack. "I heard that Adrien visited you."

Justine stopped wiping the cup she was holding.

Alice's thumb slid out three cards from the cards in her hand. She placed them face up on the table. "A widow has to be careful. Especially a teacher. People talk." The king of hearts sat on top of the three exposed cards. She placed it in the freed spot where the seven had been. "People talk."

Justine thunked the cup down and grabbed a wet plate out of her cousin's hands. "I can't worry about gossip. I have worse worries. I can hardly earn enough to support my family."

Alice slid out three more cards. The top one didn't fit anywhere in the row of cards, but a red ace of diamonds lay covered underneath that the rules forbade her to use. She sneaked it out. "*Bien sûr, chérie.* We all struggle with that."

Justine let the cream dress drop over her head and onto her shoulders. Tiny pink roses embroidered with silk covered the collar and the lapel was bordered with lace. The flared skirt swirled lightly around her legs; the linen felt deliciously cool compared to her black woollen dresses. She skipped down the stairs to the kitchen.

Alice eyed her over her coffee cup. "Ah, you're finished with mourning. I suppose it's different for young widows these days. My mother wore black until she died."

Justine stuck her purse under her arm and pulled on her gloves.

Her aunt pointed with her nose to the plate of toast lathered with congealed butter. "Aren't you having breakfast?"

Justine held up her hands. "I'm not hungry." She hurried out the kitchen. In the yard, she looked down self-consciously at her dress. Her joy had evaporated. Her aunt was right. It was too soon, but she didn't have time to change.

People summoned by the Bishop for the great assembly streamed onto the boulevard and the street paralleling the river. Two friends waved at her, and she hurried to join up with them.

Tall, open windows let in cool morning air, but the auditorium in which she had graduated was already hot. The soft fabric caressed her legs, and Justine couldn't stop her hips from swaying to set it swinging as she went down the centre aisle.

Père watched for her and waved her over, gesticulating to the empty chair beside him in the front row. The priest overflowed into her space. She folded her shoulders, tucked in her elbows, and squeezed into her seat.

Arthur-Joseph sat on the stage beside *Monseigneur* Taché. He was wearing the same chequered black- and-tan jacket he had worn at the Christmas concert. His head was down, and he stared at his notes. A foot twitching nervously dangled from his crossed leg.

The crowd hushed when the Bishop approached the podium in the full regalia of his office. Magenta piping trimmed the deep cuffs on his sleeves and the short cape at his shoulders. A row of red buttons extended from his throat to the hem of his black cassock, and a pectoral cross hung from a gold chain over a magenta sash. A silk zucchetto or skullcap in the same purplish-red covered the crown of his head. Blue eyes in the still-handsome face swept the auditorium. "*Demandons à Dieu de maintenir nos écoles.* Let us ask God to maintain our schools. Canada is a country where religious liberty is loudly proclaimed, but it has come to pass that fetters have been placed on this liberty. We were guaranteed minority rights to our schools. Now these rights have been violated by Premier Greenway and the very ones sworn to protect them."

Père's soft white hands curled into fists. "*Maudit menteur de* Greenway."

Justine had never heard Père curse, and to call the Premier a liar! She leaned away from her parish priest.

The Bishop continued. "We will defend our rights. We are poor in finances and small in numbers, but we are strong and united. Your Bishop and your priests will lead the fight. We will never surrender to injustice."

Père rose, followed by Justine and everyone in the auditorium. They clapped and shouted *"Non!"* and *"Jamais!"*

When the "nos" and "nevers" quieted and people settled in their chairs, Arthur-Joseph had taken the Bishop's place. He gripped the podium and stared down at his notes. The pause stretched on. People stirred nervously—some cleared their throats. Justine held her breath and stared at the blue curtains above his head.

He finally began. "*Chers Amis*, as you know, I have resigned my seat in the legislature. It was I who led the resistance against the new laws that abolished our schools and disallowed our language rights."

Justine leaned forward, her heart racing, and she clapped as hard as she could.

Arthur-Joseph smiled crookedly then he raised and lowered his hands for quiet. But instead of quieting, the sound of clapping rose, accompanied by cheers and "Bravo!" Justine hands ached form being banged together.

Arthur-Joseph turned towards the man sharing the stage with him, the leader of the Catholic community in Manitoba, the Archbishop of the North-West, and the representative of Rome. The zucchetto on Taché's head flashed as the Bishop lowered his chin and nodded his approval.

Arthur-Joseph faced the audience and raised his hands high.

An expectant hush fell as the room became quiet.

"It is time to make concrete plans. I propose that a committee be struck for the instruction of French in our parish schools. The committee will supervise the training of teachers and send out inspectors to the schools. We will hold annual exams to test to the highest standard of French. The committee will have the role of a 'phantom' department of education for the French in the province. Are we together in this?"

Hope leapt from the podium to the assembly. *Père* crushed Justine in a hug and then hugged the man next to him. Someone shook her hand. She pumped back vigorously.

Justine walked slowly back and forth before the doors at the top of the long stairs one last time. She gave up and had almost reached the bottom of the steps when the doors opened and Arthur-Joseph appeared with the Members of the French Bloc—his colleagues from the legislature. He stopped when he saw her, and a broad smile spread over his face. He ran down to kiss her cheeks. "I didn't know you were here." He stepped back. "You look lovely. Black is not a colour for a young woman."

Justine brushed her hand down her skirt. "*Tante* says it's too soon."

"I can assure you *Tante's* wrong." He put his arm through hers. "Do you have time for a walk to the river?"

The elm trees lining both sides of the quiet street shaded them as they strolled.

"You were inspiring today," Justine said.

He snorted. "They think they can force integration with legislation."

The soil-burdened river drifted slowly by, murky and brown.

"They wouldn't dare close the English schools in Québec," he continued. "There'd be an uproar heard all the way to London." He turned to look at her. "Can you live without the government's teacher salary? You have your own children to think about."

The wind lifted her collar and teased the hem of her skirt. "*Père's* promised that the parish will pay my wages. It's small compared to the salary the government used to pay, but I've some revenue from the farm, and Rosalie will babysit."

He touched her arm. "I could send you a stipend … each month."

"Ooh," Justine laughed and shook her head. "I couldn't possibly accept money from you. And what would Camille say about her *cavalier* sending money to another woman?"

"I'm not her boyfriend. She was a bit too young for my taste." He let out a long, exaggerated sigh. "At least let me buy you dinner. There's a restaurant I know of that is famous for its roast beef."

Her aunt's dinner table floated up in her mind's eye. A knife and a fork with dried food caught in the tines had been thrown carelessly on her clean dinner plate. "That would be delightful."

They walked across the bridge to a house on the river that served as a restaurant. A half dozen tables crowded what used to be the living and dining room, but white cloths covered the tables and the waiter knew Arthur-Joseph. Justine relaxed. How wonderful it was to have a quiet dinner with a charming man. Before she knew it, she was licking the sweet off her fingers from the sugar-dusted lemon squares and finishing a second cup of coffee. "It's been so long since I've been out without the children. I feel free … and guilty."

"You have a big responsibility."

Justine wiped the corners of her mouth with a white napkin. "I'm not the first woman to be in this situation." The sun dipped behind the trees. The clay-laden river turned from brown to slate. "It's getting late."

"I'll walk you home."

"It's best if you don't."

He fell silent, and then he rose and came around to pull out her chair.

Alice met her at the front door. "Where have you been? I held supper."

"Oh, I'm sorry," Justine said, setting her purse down on the hall table. "*Père* invited me to dine with the Bishop at the *palais*."

Alice's eyes widened. "Exalted company! What did the Bishop's housekeeper serve?"

Justine removed her gloves. "*Rôti de boeuf et tarte à citron.*"

CHAPTER 52

September, 1891

Justine threw the ball in a high arc at the bat hanging loosely in the boy's hands. A moment after the ball sailed by, the batter swung. Justine took a giant step closer to home base. "Keep your eye on the ball this time." The little boy squinted and dug his feet into the dust. The skinny muscles on his arms tensed. The ball arced in the air, the bat connected, and the ball rolled to third. "Run! Run!"

The boy looked around confused with the bat still in his hand. He dropped the bat and started to run after the ball. Justine met him mid-way between third and home and ran with him across the diamond while an older fielder heaved the ball to a girl on first base. She bent to catch it, but the ball rolled over her feet. Justine and the little boy hopped safely on the board acting as base. "*Excellent!*" she said, patting his shoulders. The bell rang, and the girls ran off to form their lines, but the boys had to be swept along.

The sting of the parish school's diminished status had burned hotter the first day back. *Mesdemoiselles* Simard and Pelletier had lost their jobs. *Père* had kept his word, and she had been spared, but she was short of supplies. She saved the newspaper ads that were printed on one side and cut the pages into small squares of useful scrap paper.

The autumn grasses lay pounded flat on top of dusty earth in the schoolyard as Justine pumped water for her pupils at the well after recess. She stretched over a perpetual puddle mucking the ground under the spout, careful not to wet her shoes or the hem of her skirt. The iron squealed and protested against the dry casing as she primed the pump, forcing the arm up and down, up and down. Water pulled up from the depths and splashed out, ice-cold and smelling strongly of rotten eggs. A rusty wire bolted to the well's wooden casing held a dipper. She unhooked it and filled it to overflowing. The first boy drank in great gulps. She pulled it away and gave it to another. "Don't drink too much! It'll give you a belly ache." A man's hand settled on the handle. Justine looked up. "Arthur-Joseph! We didn't expect you until the afternoon."

"Your school's first on my list. Here let me."

Arthur-Joseph pumped furiously. The water spurted out. Muck splashed on his shiny, black boots.

A little girl with brown braids wrapped around her head piped up primly, "You'll have to remove your shoes before you go in."

Justine smiled at him over the girl's head and turned her towards the school with a little push. "Thank you, Cécile."

"How do you like your job as school inspector?" she asked, picking up the bat and ball.

"Too soon to tell and it's 'visitor,' remember?"

"Ah, yes. The title of school inspector is reserved for the 'official' representative of the province. You are but a 'visitor' sent to verify the quality of education in parish schools."

Soeur Supérieur waited for them at the door with the school's timetable. Arthur-Joseph glanced at it. "The law prescribes that you schedule catechism instruction for the last half-hour. Write it so." A smile lifted the corner of his mouth. "But you needn't make your teachers adhere to it too closely."

He had saved Justine's classroom for the last. He knocked softly and tiptoed in. Paper oak and maple leaves coloured orange, yellow, and red floated across the panes on the tall classroom windows. Children crowded the floor at Justine's feet at the front of the room. On her lap, she held a large book with stained pages and worn edges. Black and white drawings depicted *Blanche Neige et les sept nains*. The heroine stood a foot above the seven men in caps. Her hair was black as coal.

Justine looked up and rose hurriedly, signalling her pupils to their desks.

Arthur-Joseph put up his hands. "*Non!* Your class should go play instead. What do you think boys and girls?"

"But—"

He lowered his head and whispered, "I've got something for you … in the carriage."

Twenty pairs of eyes turned to their teacher.

Justine sighed and nodded.

There was a rush and clamour as several arrived at the door at the same time. Following the crowd, Justine and Arthur-Joseph walked across the schoolyard to the carriage. A box wrapped in brown paper and tied twice round with thick string lay on the carriage floor.

Arthur-Joseph lifted it up and laid it on the seat. "Open it."

Justine kept her hands stiffly at her side.

"I'll do it for you then." He flicked open his pocket knife and cut the string. The paper fell away as he lifted the lid. Two brown sweaters with large crimson stripes across the chest and two pairs of khaki pants occupied half the box. A neatly folded yellow dress took up the other half. Thick, brown stockings were rolled and tucked beside.

Justine's left eyebrow rose.

Arthur-Joseph shrugged. "You wouldn't accept any help from me. These are for the children."

"But this is too much. I can't take this."

He pushed aside the yellow fabric. A book hid beneath. The cover had been uniformly orange once, but years of handling had dirtied the spine to brown.

Justine reached for it instinctively. She held it for a moment, gauging its weight, flipping it over and back. Her fingers ran over the black letters on the cover: *Life, Letters and Travels of Father Pierre-Jean de Smet*. She looked up. "Who was this man?"

"A Jesuit missionary. He worked among the Indians in the American West. He was instrumental in getting Sitting Bull and the Sioux to sign the peace treaties." Arthur-Joseph took the book and flipped open the cover to a translucent, onion-skin page engraved with a sepia-coloured lithograph. "I found it in a second-hand book store in Ottawa."

Justine leaned forward to view the illustration better. A bear and a bison hid in the base of two trees. A bow, hatchet, lance, and arrows hung above the bear's head, while a Bible, bell, trumpet, and a sword tipped with a feather hung above the bison's head. An Aboriginal man rose from the tangle of their roots, his muscled back straining to bear a Christian cross. A coyote, squirrel, rabbit, and beaver reposed on the ground beneath him. "You might as well come to dinner tonight," Justine said.

"*Maman*, look! A new dress," Hélène said, rushing at her. She had pulled the yellow dress over her old one. The buttons at the back were undone, and two long ties trailed down. Justine dropped her schoolbag and knelt to tie the tails into a bow. The boys' new clothes lay in a corner of the kitchen. The upside-down, empty box moved drunkenly across the floor. A pathetic meowing came from underneath. "*Soyez pas méchants*," Justine scolded, telling them not to be cruel. She lifted a corner of the box for *Réglisse* to escape its tormentors.

Justine hung her coat on the hook by the back door.

The cloth reserved for special occasions and embroidered with orange tiger lilies and purple crocuses covered the table. Arthur-Joseph stood with his arms folded and his hips resting against the sink as Rosalie took a ham out of the oven.

He murmured something, and her cousin giggled and blushed shyly as she set the pan down. Was it the heat from the oven or the slender man resting against the sink?

Justine nodded at him and picked up the de Smet book off the floor where it had landed in the rush of opening Arthur-Joseph's present. She sniffed the pages. Old and dusty. A small, contented smile lifted the corners of her mouth. She pointed at the dishes with her chin and said to him. "You can set the table."

The sliced tomatoes were still warm from the garden, and the cucumbers cold. Arthur-Joseph had two helpings of the fluffy mashed potatoes sprinkled with parsley.

Justine heard her children's bedtime prayers while he sat with Rosalie over a second cup of tea. "I have to check the barn," she said, returning to the kitchen.

Arthur-Joseph drained his cup. "I'll go with you."

The hens had settled for the night in their coop. She toed the flimsy chicken-wire door shut and turned the wooden peg to secure it.

The setting sun flooded the dark interior of the barn in orange. In the one stall, a black and white cow chewed her cud and swished her tail.

Arthur-Joseph stepped around the wet spot in the alley.

Justine laughed. "Don't worry. She's already been milked. Rosalie does it before supper." She entered the stall, ran her hand over the cow's soft flank, and pushed her aside. She slid the chain off that tied her to the manger. "Open the door at the end of the barn. I'll run her out to the yard that way."

The cow balked at the door, refusing to go out. Arthur-Joseph looked helplessly around. Justine slapped the cow's bony rump, and it took off to the grass.

It was semi-dark by the time they walked back to the house. A lantern in the porch spilled an elongated square of light onto the grass. Arthur-Joseph stopped at its edge. "I'm going to Ottawa."

Justine stopped too. "What?"

"As a Member of Parliament." He took her hands. "Dr. Christian Schultz is still around. He's the man who riled up the English against Riel during the Uprising. Now he's Manitoba's Lieutenant Governor. He signed the bill against our rights. Someone has to defend us in Ottawa against men like him."

The hands holding hers were smooth, without calluses. Warm. "But it's so far away."

He lifted her hand and kissed the smooth top part between the knuckles and wrist.

Rosalie's head appeared in the kitchen window, and Justine pulled her hand away.

CHAPTER 53

November 15, 1891

Snow kernels that bounced here and there like exploding popcorn accompanied Justine and Jules on their walk to school. By recess, snow covered the playground, and small, shadowy figures veiled in white ran and kicked ecstatically through the fluff. By Saturday morning, all that was visible in the garden were the green tops of the last neglected carrots poking forlornly up under the white.

She met Wilhémène Larence later that day while shopping with Thérèse in the dry goods store. Though Adrien's mother wasn't as plumped with pride as when she thought her son would be a priest, she now imagined Adrien as a rich American and was full of herself. "Half the population in Massachusetts is from Québec. The French quarter is known as *'petit Canada.'* They have their own doctors, lawyers, and grocers. A large part of his Uncle Paul's former parish have all emigrated there. Even the priest! Adrien feels quite at home."

"*Bonnes nouvelles,*" Thérèse said, throwing a glance at her daughter.

Justine's face remained blank. "Good news." She bowed and moved to the doll display where Hélène had her hands and nose pressed against the glass.

Justine wrapped the red angora scarf that Alexina had given her last Christmas around her neck and pulled the matching beret down tight over her curls. She stopped at the mirror in the hall and tugged it to a fashionable angle.

"Don't be late," her aunt called from her chair near the front window. "The dedication is early tomorrow."

"Of course, *ma tante*," she said stepping out quickly.

Arthur-Joseph had invited her to the ceremony at the new Riel monument, and she was attending as the special envoy from Saint-Cère. She turned right when she left the yard and walked towards the bridge to meet him for dinner.

He kissed her cold cheeks. "I've booked a table at a hotel in the city." He tucked her into his arm to shield her from the wind and led her over the bridge.

The dining room was on the second floor. He chose a table beside a set of triple windows overlooking Main Street.

Below, a young, blond man strolled along with a duffle bag on his shoulder. A woman in heeled boots, wearing a hat with black feathers pluming high, detached from the shadows beneath the window. She fell in step with the young man, pointing towards the hotels on the first block of Main Street. He asked her something, she nodded, and they walked off together towards the hotels.

Arthur-Joseph had seen them too. "Did you hear about the police chief, Sam Sherwood? He was found *flagrante delicto* at a whorehouse in the city."

Justine's eyebrows rose. "What do you mean?"

"He was caught in the act." Arthur-Joseph sat back, comfortable in his role as gossip and confident of her interest. "Sherwood had scheduled a raid on a madam's place—Belle's house on Colony Street not far from the legislature. But he forgot. He was with Belle when the entire constabulary of Winnipeg raided her establishment. She was dressed only in a shift when they put her and her girls in the patrol wagon."

Justine looked at something beyond Arthur-Joseph's shoulder. She knew this Belle. She had seen her when she and Adrien had spied on the prostitutes at the opera. She leaned forward. "What happened to her?"

Spoiled Heritage

"She had to pay a $40 fine. She's moving the business to Regina."

"And the police chief? The girls?"

"Of course, the chief had to be fired." A loaded wagon pulled by a team of four horses lumbered by beneath the window, and they looked down. "Her establishment closed. And the girls—they're back on the street."

Arthur-Joseph licked the last bit of *crème brûlée* off his spoon and smacked his lips. Outside the window, the world had turned white. The woman in the boots and the hat with tall, black feathers exited the hotel. She turned left towards the train station.

Arthur-Joseph eyes followed her. "Did you know Adrien helped build the bordello that the chief raided? His friend Adele and he were partners."

Justine hands fell on her lap. Adrien had built a bordello? What further depths had he fallen to? She blinked and shook her head. "But … but Marcel was Adrien's partner."

Arthur-Joseph snorted. "That *vaurien?* He's good for nothing. Marcel helped him build the hotel—he wasn't a partner. When the hotel became a bordello, Adrien quit and sold his interest in it to his friend Adele."

"Adele? Adele?" Justine kept shaking her head and trying to think clearly. "Who's Adele?"

Arthur-Joseph clearly enjoyed her shock. "A friend of his. Not only that, Adrien helped Adele with her baby when she got in trouble with a business man in the city."

Justine swallowed and looked down at her hands. The baby Adrien had left on the steps that Alexina had found was not Adrien's baby! Benjamin's mother was this woman's—this Adele. And by some unknown man in Winnipeg. Not Adrien! When she looked up, she felt lighter and a smile had spread across her face. "And what of this Adele? Has she gone to Regina too?"

Arthur-Joseph shook his head. "*Non.* She's staying on and running the hotel as a real hotel. She's a very good business woman." He sat back and crossed his legs, drumming his fingers on the table. "I should tell you about the painting I saw above the bar at the hotel's opening. There was a woman with long tresses …"

Flakes the size of down floated in the night, white and dazzling in the street lamp. Justine held her face up to the sky. Snow caught in her eyelashes and melted on her cheeks. Arthur-Joseph bent his head and kissed her, softly at first, but then when she didn't resist, he pressed harder, his lips moving over hers.

When he pulled away, Justine ran her tongue over her top lip. He had tasted sweet, like the vanilla in the *crème-brulée*.

He brushed the snowflakes from her face. "Come with me to Ottawa. The children will love the capital. There's music and theatre, and they'll be free to be French … and Catholic."

Justine looked up. "But what will happen to Manitoba if all the French leave?"

He rested his chin on her head. "We'll fight through the courts in Ottawa. We'll do our part."

His arm went around her shoulders, and she nestled her head against him as they walked towards the bridge and the lights of Saint-Boniface. Two sets of footprints meandered in the deepening snow, merging occasionally into one.

CHAPTER 54

November 16, 1891

The next morning, Justine threw off the blanket. 'Adrien is not Benjamin's father!' She washed and dressed quickly. Adrien was not Benjamin's father. She pulled her brush through her hair, and then checked the small oval mirror above the washbowl—it was still a tangled mess. She could hardly wait to tell Alexina. She firmly pulled on her red beret and put the thoughts aside.

The back pews were in empty darkness when she pulled open the heavy door to the *cathédrale*, but more and more people filled the pews as she tiptoed down the side aisle, searching for Arthur-Joseph. She slipped into a pew on the right. Julie Riel sat with her head bent forward. Though people surrounded her tightly, she seemed isolated and alone. Jean and his sister, Angélique, sat behind, with anxious brown eyes that observed intensely.

Bishop Taché entered from the sacristy, robed in a black chasuble, a seamless vestment heavily embroidered with silver thread, and accompanied by an altar boy. The Bishop stopped in front and bowed to the cross, but instead of climbing to the altar, he went to the shrivelled woman in the front pew and spoke to her quietly. He returned to the altar. When he touched his forehead to sign the cross, Justine's hand copied him mechanically. The mass had begun.

The back door creaked open, letting in a shaft of grey light and cold air. Swift footsteps echoed down the painted floor. Arthur-Joseph genuflected hurriedly and joined the Riels.

The mass ended, and Taché and the altar boy went back to the sacristy. He returned in a black winter cape and biretta. The altar server carried the aspersory of holy water and a wand for sprinkling. They exited through the side door, and Julie Riel followed supported by her two sons, Alexandre and Joseph. A daughter, Henriette, went behind with Jean and Angélique.

Justine slipped into the back of the queue of dignitaries, wives, relatives, and friends that came next. Arthur-Joseph had waited for her. He took her hand as they stepped into the snow.

The procession left the church and wound through the graves towards a monument in the northeast corner of the cemetery. A tall rectangle of polished, pink granite stood on stone pedestals rising from the fresh dirt. Four etched triangles capped the top. Someone had carefully engraved the name RIEL in large letters on the rose stone. Below, a rounded cross with arms of equal length separated the dates 1844 and 1885.

Arthur-Joseph pushed her through to the second row of dignitaries across from Riel's mother.

A black, silk apron over an ankle-length, black skirt showed under the hem of Julie Riel's coat. Her hair was divided in a severe centre part, pulled back over small ears, and braided in plaits on the back of her neck. High, aristocratic cheekbones rose over sunken cheeks. She wore no gloves, exposing long, elongated fingers. She paid no heed to the people surrounding her and kept her eyes on the grave.

The Bishop opened his black prayer book. *"Du fond de l'abîme, je crie vers vous, Seigneur."* Out of the depths I cried unto thee, O Lord.

The crowd of mourners and supporters responded automatically with the words learned as children. *"Pitié sur nous Seigneur."* Lord, have mercy.

Spoiled Heritage

The Bishop turned to the attendant and took the wand out of the aspersory. A cascade of droplets sprinkled the monument and the front row of mourners. The Bishop and server followed the contour of the mound, dipping and sprinkling, dipping and sprinkling, until the entire burial place had been blessed. Taché stopped before the monument, bent his head, and closed his eyes. His lips moved silently then he walked away. After a while, Julie's daughter, Henriette, put her arm around her mother's shoulders and led her and the children away.

A thin strip of light pinked the horizon in the east. Snow entered Justine's boots, and cold bit her ankles, but she lingered. Arthur-Joseph took her hand. "Let's go. You're shivering. I want to announce our engagement to my parents."

Justine hung back. "Let's not say anything—not yet."

"Why?"

The loneliness of the rose stone and the emptiness of the cemetery swept over Justine. She shook her head. "Riel had such dreams."

Arthur-Joseph pulled her into him and turned her away. "Let's not worry about this now. I'm going to Ottawa. You'll have time to think about my proposal over the winter. I'll be back in the spring. You can give me your answer then."

Relief flooded Justine. She sank against his warm body and turned up her face to receive his lips.

CHAPTER 55

May 21, 1892

Justine had slowly adjusted to teaching on a reduced salary. In her pantry, hams from the Bélanger herd swung on hooks under the rafters, and a large flour bin overflowed with the whitest flour milled from Joseph's wheat. Thérèse had filled the shelves with jars of strawberry and raspberry jam that shouldered against jars of crab-apple jelly so clear you wanted to drink it. A letter waited in her box every week from Arthur-Joseph. She tore it open, eager for his gossipy, interesting news. Sir John A. had suffered a stroke, and Arthur-Joseph had stood day and night with reporters under the dying man's window for news. The capital city had grown quiet as the bargemen on the Ottawa River silenced their whistles and horse-drawn carriages on Sussex Drive refrained from using their bells.

The sun began its trajectory to the south, and the fields of snow became patches of snow. The ice on the creek behind her property thinned, and it gurgled to life as water appeared at its edges. Justine threw up the windows to catch the fresh air, and she went to school with her hair swept by warm winds.

Joseph and Benjamin rode to town bareback one Saturday morning with a one-bottom plow rattling behind them. With the one plowshare turning the soil behind the wide haunches of the plow horse, the earth in her garden was soon turned and fat earth-worms wriggled and twisted away in the fresh, black soil. When he was done, Joseph treated the boys to a visit at Armand's forge, lifting them onto the horse's broad back, starting with André and stepping up to Jules and Benjamin. The clip-clop of the hooves echoed in the quiet morning as Joseph led it passively down the street.

Justine found the two grey sticks wrapped with garden string where she had left them in the barn. She tapped them together, and the string released a cloud of last year's dust. She pushed in one of the sticks and walking backward, unrolled the string to the far end of the garden.

A whinny made her look up. Élisa trotted into the yard with Adrien relaxed and smiling in the saddle. He dismounted, wrapping the reins around the saddle-horn, letting the ends drop on a brown, burlap bag.

She straightened slowly. She had misjudged him cruelly. He wasn't Benjamin's father. He hadn't abandoned his child. The stick with the string fell from her hand. "I thought you were never coming back."

"I got home yesterday."

Justine wiped her hands on her skirt and walked towards him. "You just missed Benjamin. *Pa* brought him into town." A Mayday tree in an explosion of fragrant, white clusters stood at her back. The air hummed and vibrated with bees busy in its crown. "Why didn't you say you weren't his father? You knew Alexina would tell me. We assumed he was your child."

Adrien shrugged. "You always assumed the worst of me."

Justine's eyes fell to the ground. "I'm sorry."

"How did you find out?"

"Arthur-Joseph told me about it last November when I was in the city for the dedication of the Riel monument."

Adrien folded under his upper lip and gazed down at her. The image of her had risen before him during the long evenings away and thoughts of her had followed him even into the factory in Massachusetts. What courage she had shown alone with her baby in that field. She would never run away. Thoughts of Riel had also risen before him. Louis had ridden bravely into the hail of bullets at Batoche with only his crucifix as his shield. Riel would not run away. He had thought of Taché and Père and the people who fought for their schools, their faith, their Frenchness. They were his people and he was one of them.

Justine looked up. "What brings you back?"

A corner of his mouth lifted in a crooked smile. "Arthur-Joseph."

Justine blinked. "I don't understand."

"He wrote to me saying that you might be joining him shortly in the capital." He stepped closer. "I figured I'd better come back."

Pink feathered Justine's cheeks. She shook her head. "He has visited but he was more intent on flirting with Camille and even Rosalie."

"*Ma'an*," a voice called from the house. "*Ma'an*," it repeated loudly, more demanding.

His hand rose to her hair. He touched the wispy tendrils, rubbing the strands between his thumb and forefinger. It was wiry, strong.

Hélène appeared on the porch, rubbing her eyes and carrying a cloth doll.

Élisa nipped Adrien's shoulder. He turned and pulled out a green bottle stoppered with a cork from the bag hanging from the saddle. "I brought this wine from the States."

Justine laughed. "*Bon*. Let's go in then."

BIBLIOGRAPHY

SPOILED HERITAGE—THE MANITOBANS

Barnholden, Michael. *Gabriel Dumont Speaks*. Vancouver, Talonbooks, 2009.

Blay, Jacqueline. *L'Article 23 Les péripéties législatives et juridiques du fait français au Manitoba 1870–1986*. Saint-Boniface, Les Éditions du Blé, 1987.

Brown, Chester. *Louis Riel: A Comic-Strip Biography*. Montreal, Drawn & Quarterly, 1999.

Bumstead, J.M. "Thomas Scott". *The Canadian Encyclopedia*. Edmonton, Hurtig Publishers Ltd., 1985.

Bumstead, J.M. *Louis Riel c.Canada: les années rebelles*. Saint-Boniface, Éditions des Plaines, 2005.

Charlebois, Peter. *The Life of Louis Riel*. Toronto, NC Press Ltd., 1975.

Chauveau, Pierre, J. Olivier. *Charles Guérin: Roman de Moeurs Canadiennes*. Montreal, La Cie de Publication de la Revue Candienne, 1900.

Coutu, Hector. *Lagimodière and Their Descendants.* Edmonton, Co-op Press Limited, 1980.

Dauphinais, Luc, *Histoire de Saint-Boniface,* Tome 1. Saint-Boniface, Éditions du Blé, 1991.

Flanagan, Thomas. *The Diaries of Louis Riel.* Edmonton, Hurtig Publishers, 1976.

Goulet, George R.D. *The Trial of LOUIS RIEL: Justice and Mercy Denied.* Victoria, Tellwell Publishing 1999.

Gray, James H. *Red Lights on the Prairie.* Toronto, Macmillan of Canada, 1971.

Gwyn, Richard. *John A: The Man Who Made Us: The Life and Times of John A. Macdonald.* Toronto, Random House, 2007.

Jolys, J.M. and Côté, J.H. *Pages de souvenirs et d'histoire.* Saint-Boniface, J.M. Jolys, 1974.

Jordan, Mary. *To Louis from your sister who loves you, Sara Riel.* Toronto, Griffin House, 1974.

Lovell, Clark. *The Manitoba School Question: Majority Rule or Minority Rights?* Toronto, Copp Clark Publishing Company, 1968.

Lovell Clark, "SCHULTZ, Sir JOHN CHRISTIAN," in *Dictionary of Canadian Biography*, vol. 12, University of Toronto/Université Laval, 2003–, accessed September 13, 2019, http://www.biographi.ca/en/bio/schultz_john_christian_12E.html.

Morice, A.G. *Histoire de l'Ouest Canadien.* Saint-Boniface, A.G. Morice, 1914.

Pfeiffer, Harold A. *The Catholic Picture Dictionary.* New York, Duell, Sloan and Pearce, 1948.

Rea, J.E. "SCOTT, THOMAS (d. 1870)," in *Dictionary of Canadian Biography*, vol. 9, University of Toronto/Université Laval, 2003–, accessed September 13, 2019, http://www.biographi.ca/en/bio/scott_thomas_1870_9E.html.

Saint-Pierre, Annette. *De fil en aiguille au Manitoba*. Saint-Boniface, Les Éditions des Plaines, 1995.

Saint-Pierre, Annette. *Jean Riel fils de Louis Riel: Sous une mauvaise étoile*. Saint-Boniface, Les Éditions du Blé, 2014.

Stanley, G.R.G. *Louis Riel: Patriot or Rebel?* Historical Booklet No. 2. The Canadian Historical Association: 1956.

Swan, Ruth and Reynolds, Janelle. "NAULT, ANDRÉ," in *Dictionary of Canadian Biography*, vol. 15, University of Toronto/Université Laval, 2003–, accessed September 13, 2019, http://www.biographi.ca/en/bio/nault_andre_15E.html.

Thomas, Lewis H., "RIEL, LOUIS (1844-85)," in *Dictionary of Canadian Biography*, vol. 11, University of Toronto/Université Laval, 2003–, accessed September 13, 2019, http://www.biographi.ca/en/bio/riel_louis_1844_85_11E.html.

Voyer, Eugene. *La famille Amable Nault*. Sainte-Anne-des-chênes, Margaret Letourneau, 1978.

Wade, Mason. *The French Canadians, 1760–1945*. Toronto, Macmillan and Company Limited, 1956.

Woodcock, George. *Gabriel Dumont: The Métis Chief and His Lost World*. Peterborough, Broadview Press Ltd., 2003.

Printed in Canada